When I started writing this, I edited myself, naturally.

I neglected to record some of my more objectionable remarks and barbarous actions, because I wanted you to like me. If you don't like me, you won't want to read my story, and I'll be wasting my time and a lot of forty-gulden-a-roll reed-fibre paper telling it, and the truth about the war (which actually matters) will never be known. It even crossed my mind to stick in a few not-strictly-true incidents designed to show me in a better light, because nobody would ever know, and then I'd be a lovable rogue instead of a total shit. Then I thought: stuff it. The truth, and nothing but the horrible, inconvenient truth. All those facts have got to go somewhere. You might as well have them, if they're any use to you. I certainly don't want them any more.

Praise for the Novels of K. J. Parker

"Full of invention and ingenuity....Great fun."
—*SFX* on *Sixteen Ways to Defend a Walled City*

"Readers will appreciate the infusion of humor and fun-loving characters into this vivid and sometimes grim fantasy world."
—*Publishers Weekly* on *Sixteen Ways to Defend a Walled City*

"Parker has created a world full of wit, ingenuity, unlikely tactics and reluctant heroes and there is nothing else quite like it."
—*Fantasy Hive* on *How to Rule an Empire and Get Away with It*

"With a steady pacing, solid, lean writing and variety of twists, the novel keeps on surprising the reader."
—*Fantasy Book Critic* on *Sixteen Ways to Defend a Walled City*

"Parker's acerbic wit and knowledge of human nature are a delight to read as he explores the way conflict is guided, in equal measure, by the brilliance and unerring foolishness of humanity....Thoroughly engaging."
—*RT Book Reviews* on *The Two of Swords: Volume One*

"A ripping good adventure yarn, laced with frequent barbed witticisms and ace sword fighting....Parker's settings and characterizations never miss a beat, and the intricate political interplay of intrigue is suspenseful almost to the last page."
—*Publishers Weekly* on *Sharps*

As K. J. Parker

THE FENCER TRILOGY
Colours in the Steel
The Belly of the Bow
The Proof House

THE SCAVENGER TRILOGY
Shadow
Pattern
Memory

THE ENGINEER TRILOGY
Devices and Desires
Evil for Evil
The Escapement

The Company
The Folding Knife
The Hammer
Sharps
The Two of Swords: Volume One
The Two of Swords: Volume Two
The Two of Swords: Volume Three

Sixteen Ways to Defend a Walled City
How to Rule an Empire and Get Away with It
A Practical Guide to Conquering the World

THE CORAX TRILOGY
Saevus Corax Deals With the Dead
Saevus Corax Captures the Castle
Saevus Corax Gets Away With Murder

As Tom Holt

Expecting Someone Taller
Who's Afraid of Beowulf?
Flying Dutch
Ye Gods!
Overtime
Here Comes the Sun
Grailblazers
Faust Among Equals
Odds and Gods
Djinn Rummy
My Hero
Paint Your Dragon
Open Sesame
Wish You Were Here
Only Human
Snow White and the Seven Samurai
Valhalla
Nothing But Blue Skies
Falling Sideways
Little People
The Portable Door

In Your Dreams
Earth, Air, Fire and Custard
You Don't Have to Be Evil to Work Here, But It Helps
Someone Like Me
Barking
The Better Mousetrap
May Contain Traces of Magic
Blonde Bombshell
Life, Liberty, and the Pursuit of Sausages
Doughnut
When It's A Jar
The Outsorcerer's Apprentice
The Good, the Bad and the Smug
The Management Style of the Supreme Beings
An Orc on the Wild Side

Dead Funny: Omnibus 1
Mightier Than the Sword: Omnibus 2
The Divine Comedies: Omnibus 3
For Two Nights Only: Omnibus 4
Tall Stories: Omnibus 5
Saints and Sinners: Omnibus 6
Fishy Wishes: Omnibus 7

The Walled Orchard
Alexander at the World's End
Olympiad
A Song for Nero
Meadowland

I, Margaret

Lucia in Wartime
Lucia Triumphant

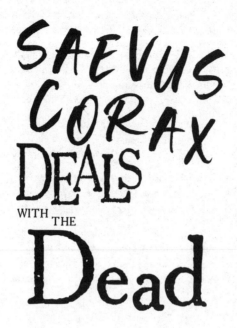

SAEVUS CORAX DEALS WITH THE Dead

The Corax Trilogy: Book 1

K. J. PARKER

orbitbooks.net

Copyright © 2023 by One Reluctant Lemming Company Ltd.
Excerpt from *Saevus Corax Captures the Castle* copyright © 2023 by One Reluctant Lemming Company Ltd.
Excerpt from *The Lost War* copyright © 2019 by King Lot Publishing Ltd.

Cover design by Lisa Marie Pompilio
Cover illustrations by Shutterstock
Cover copyright © 2023 by Hachette Book Group, Inc.

Orbit
Hachette Book Group
1290 Avenue of the Americas
New York, NY 10104
orbitbooks.net

First Edition: October 2023
Simultaneously published in Great Britain by Orbit

Orbit is an imprint of Hachette Book Group.
The Orbit name and logo are trademarks of Little, Brown Book Group Limited.

The publisher is not responsible for websites (or their content) that are not owned by the publisher.

The Hachette Speakers Bureau provides a wide range of authors for speaking events. To find out more, go to hachettespeakersbureau.com or email HachetteSpeakers@hbgusa.com.

Orbit books may be purchased in bulk for business, educational, or promotional use. For information, please contact your local bookseller or the Hachette Book Group Special Markets Department at special.markets@hbgusa.com.

Library of Congress Control Number: 2023937649

ISBNs: 9780316668903 (trade paperback), 9780316668880 (ebook)

Printed in the United States of America

LSC-C

Printing 1, 2023

For Bill Schafer,
Maecenas noster

1

Lying is like farming, or draining marshland, or terracing a hillside or planting a grove of peach trees. It's an attempt to control your environment and make it better. A convincing lie improves on bleak, bare fact, in the same way human beings improve a wilderness so they can bear to live there. In comparison, truth is a desert. You need to plant it with your imagination and water it with narrative skill until it blossoms and bears nourishing fruit. In the sand and gravel of what actually happened I grow truths of my own; not just different truths, better ones. Practically every time I open my mouth I improve the world, making it not how it is but how it should be.

In order to grow strong, healthy plants you also need plenty of manure, but that's not a problem. According to most of the people I do business with, I'm full of it. I accept the compliment gracefully, and move on.

Rest assured, however, that everything I tell you in the pages that follow is the truth, the whole truth and nothing but the truth. This is a true and accurate history of the Great Sirupat War, told by someone who was there.

A big mob of crows got up as we—

No, hang on a moment. I was going to leave it at that, but I did say I'd be honest with you, and now is as good a time as any.

People tend not to like me very much, and I can see why. They say I'm arrogant, callous, selfish and utterly devoid of any redeeming qualities; all, I'm sorry to say, perfectly true. I'm leaving out devious, because I happen to believe it's a virtue.

Arrogant, yes; I was born to it, like brown eyes or a weak chin, and the fact that I'm still alive after everything I've done, with luck not usually in my favour, suggests to me that I've got something to be arrogant about, even if it's only my devious-ness, see above. I'm callous because I'm selfish, not because I want to be, and I'm selfish because I like staying alive, though God only knows why. People say the world would be a better place without me and I think on balance they're right, but it's stuck with me for a little while, as are you if you want to hear the truly thrilling story. And you do, I promise you, but unfor-tunately I come with it, like your spouse's relatives.

When I started writing this, I edited myself, naturally. I neglected to record some of my more objectionable remarks and barbarous actions, because I wanted you to like me. If you don't like me, you won't want to read my story, and I'll be wasting my time and a lot of forty-gulden-a-roll reed-fibre paper telling it, and the truth about the war (which actually matters) will never be known. It even crossed my mind to stick in a few not-strictly-true incidents designed to show me in a better light, because nobody would ever know, and then

I'd be a lovable rogue instead of a total shit. Then I thought: stuff it. The truth, and nothing but the horrible, inconvenient truth. All those facts have got to go somewhere. You might as well have them, if they're any use to you. I certainly don't want them any more.

A big mob of crows got up as we walked down the hill onto the open ground where the main action had been. Crows hate me, and I don't blame them. They rose like smoke from a fire with no flames, screaming abuse at us as they swirled round in circles before reluctantly pulling out and going wherever it is that crows go. I got the impression that they had a good mind to lodge an official complaint, or sue me for restraint of trade. All my years in the business, and they still make me shudder. Probably they remind me of me.

You don't usually find crows in the desert; in fact, I think that particular colony is the only one. They used to live off the trash and dunghills of a large town, which was razed to the ground in some war or other thirty years ago. But the crows stayed. There are enough wars in those parts to afford them a moderate living without the need to prod and worry about in shitheaps, and for water they go to the smashed-up aqueduct, which still trickles away into the sand, now entirely for their benefit. I guess the crows figure the austerity of their lifestyle is worth it for the peace and quiet, which I'd just come along and spoiled.

I hadn't watched the battle but I could figure out what happened from the spacing and density of the bodies. Over there, a shield wall had held off the lancers but couldn't handle massed archers at close range; they'd broken and charged, and the hussars hidden in that patch of dead ground over there had darted in to take them in flank and rear. That was the end of them, but no big deal; they were just a diversion to bring the other lot's cavalry assets over to the left side of the action, nicely out of the way so that the dragoons could burst out of those trees over there and roll up the heavy infantry like a carpet. After that, it was simply a matter of the losers salvaging as much as they could from the mess; not much, by the look of it. The hell with it. All the more for me.

I glanced up at the sky, which was pure blue from one side to the other. I have strong views on hot, sunny weather. I'm against it. Nobody wants to work in driving rain, naturally, but I'd rather be drenched in rainwater than sweat any time. Heavy manual labour in searing heat isn't my idea of the good life, not to mention the flies, the seepage and the smell, and hauling dead bodies around when they've been cooking up in the heat isn't good for you. This was going to be a four-day job, quite possibly five unless we could face working double shifts by torchlight. We're used to that sort of thing, but even so. It was one of those times when I wished I'd stayed at home, or got into some other line of work.

Gombryas had been going round picking up arrows. He had a sad look on his face. "They were wearing Type Sixes," he said, showing me a half-dozen bodkin heads, their needle points blunted or bent U-shaped by impact on steel. Poor arrows; I felt sorry for them, in a way I find it hard to feel sorry for flesh and blood. Not their fault that they'd been wasted by an idiot in a futile attempt to pierce armour. Theirs not to reason why, and we'd see them right, so that was fine.

"It's only taxpayers' money," I said. He grinned. He grumbles, but he knows the score. It would be the job of his division to straighten out and repoint all those cruelly maimed arrowheads; then he'd winkle the broken shafts out of the sockets, fit new ones, replace the crushed and torn fletchings, all to the high standard our customers have come to expect from us. What Gombryas doesn't know about arrows isn't worth knowing. He swears blind he can recognise an arrowhead his boys have worked on when he pulls it out of some poor dead bugger in a place like this. Some of them, he says, are old friends, he's seen them and straightened them out so many times.

The Type Sixes that had annoyed Gombryas so much were mostly in a small dip, where the hussars had rounded them up and despatched them. Personally, I like the Type Six infantry cuirass. It's built from small, rectangular plates laced together, so all you have to do is cut the laces, fish out the damaged plates, replace them and sew the thing up again, and there you are, good as new. Buyers go mad for the stuff, though it's a shame the various governments can't get together and agree on a standard size for the plates. We have to carry a dozen different sizes, with variations in lace-hole placement, and occasionally you get really weird custom jobs where you have to fabricate the new plates from scratch.

Armour is Polycrates' department, and his boys were straight on to it as usual. They've had a lot of practice, and it's a treat to watch them when they get into the swing of it. One man rolls the body over onto its back, kneels down, gets his arms under the armpits and stands up, lifting the body so his mate can dive in underneath, undo the buckles and shuck the armour off in one nice easy movement, like opening shellfish except that the bit we want is the shell, not the meat. Then on to the next one, leaving the body for Olybrius' clothes pickers and Rutilian's boot boys. Rings, earrings, gold teeth and bracelets we leave for Carrhasio and his crew, the old timers who've been with the outfit for years but who can't manage the heavy lifting like they used to. Then all that remains is for me to come round with the meat wagons. By this point, of course, heat, wildlife and the passage of time have all started to work their subtle alchemy, which is why I handle the final stage of the process myself. I wouldn't feel right asking one of my friends to do a job like that. They may be tough, but they have feelings.

The Asvogel brothers – the competition; I don't like them very much – have recently taken to dunking the bodies in pits of quicklime, to burn off the flesh and leave the bones, which they cart home and grind up for bonemeal. I guess it's worth their while, though I can't see it myself. For a start, it takes time, which is proverbially money, not to mention the cost of the lime, and then you've got the extra transport, fodder for the horses there and back, drivers, all that, in return for a low-value bulk product. Waste not, want not, the Asvogel boys say. It's a point of view, but I'm in no hurry to get into the bonemeal business. I burn all ours, unless it's so damp you can't get a decent fire going. Chusro Asvogel thinks I'm stupid, pointing out the cost of the charcoal and brushwood. But we cut and burn it ourselves between jobs, so it doesn't actually cost us anything, and we take it there in the carts we use for the job, which would otherwise be empty. Burning gives you a clean, tidy battlefield, and the ash does wonders for the soil, or so they tell me. That's nice. I think it's our moral duty to give something back if we possibly can.

No rain in the night, but a heavy dew. The next day's the best time to handle them, in my opinion. The stiffness has mostly worn off, so you haven't got arms and legs sticking out at awkward angles, which makes them a pain to stack, and with any luck they haven't begun to swell. This point in the operation usually turns into a battle of bad tempers between me and Olybrius. I want to get the meat shifted and burned before it starts to get loathsome. Olybrius wants to do a thorough job with minimum damage to the stock in trade, which means carefully peeling off the clothes rather than yanking them about and cutting off buttons. Ideally, therefore, he doesn't want to start until the stiffness goes. He's quite right, of course. It's much easier to get a shirt off a dead man when he isn't stiff as a board, and sewing buttons back on costs a lot of money, which comes out of his share of the take. But he works for me, so he has to do what I tell him, or at least that's the theory. By now our tantrums are almost as ritualised as High Mass at the Golden Spire temple. We know we're getting fairly close to the end of the arguing process when he points out that in the long run rushing the job and ruining the clothes costs me money, not him, and I come back at him with something like, it's my money and I'd rather lose out on a few trachy than catch something nasty and die. When we reach this point we both know there's nothing more to be shouted; we then have a staring match lasting between two and five seconds, and one of us backs down. It would probably be easier and quicker if we flipped a coin instead, but I guess the yelling is more satisfying, emotionally and spiritually. Anyway, that's how we do it, and it seems to work all right.

On that particular occasion, I won the battle of the basilisk glares, so we got a move on and had the pyres burning nicely barely seventy-two hours after the last arrow was loosed. In the greater scheme of things, General Theudahad and the Aelian League had taken a real shellacking, losing 5,381 men and 3,107 horses to Prince Erysichthon's 1,207 men and 338 horses. It was a setback, but it didn't really make a difference. Theudahad's relief column was only thirty miles from Erysichthon's main supply depot, less than a day's brisk ride for the Aelian heavy dragoons, and without supplies for his men Erysichthon would be forced to risk everything on one big pitched battle somewhere between the river and the sea. He'd still be outnumbered three to one, his allies had had enough and wanted to go home, and he'd made Theudahad look a complete idiot, which meant the Great Man had a score to settle, so all the young prince had actually achieved with this technically brilliant victory was to get a superior opponent really angry. Another reason for us not to hang about. I'd paid a lot of money for the rights to this campaign, and the last thing I wanted was to turn up late for the grand finale and find the battlefield had already been picked over by the local freelancers.

"My money," Gombryas said to me as we stood back from the newly lit pyre, "is on the prince. He's smart."

"You're an incurable romantic, is what you are," I told him through the scarf over my face. "You always root for the little guy."

He glared at me. "Fine," he said. "I've got twelve tremisses says that Erysichthon'll squeeze past the allies and make it back to the city before Theudahad can close the box. Deal?"

The oil-soaked brushwood caught with a roar and the wave of heat hit me like a smack on the face. "In your dreams," I said. "I don't bet on outcomes, you know that. Besides," I added, a little bit spitefully, "surely you want Theudahad to win so you can make up the set."

Gombryas collects bits of famous military and political leaders – bones, scalps, fingers and toes and scraps of innards carefully preserved in vinegar or honey – and why not? After all, their previous owners don't need them any more, and it presumably gives him some sort of quiet satisfaction. He has quite possibly the best collection in the south-west, though Sapor Asvogel might dispute that, and one of his prize exhibits is the skull of Erysichthon's father, which he acquired six years earlier, when we cleaned up after the last war in those parts. He's also got Erysichthon's grandfather's ears and his uncle's dick – he swapped two royal livers and a minor Imperial shoulder blade for it with Ormaz Asvogel – and various other family bits and bobs, so it'd be only natural for him to want a piece of the prince, too. Given that Erysichthon had no children and all his male relatives had contributed freely to Gombryas' collection, it'd mean that getting the prince would complete the series (I think that's the technical term in collectors' circles) and a complete series is worth far more than just a dozen or so isolated pieces. Not that Gombryas would ever think of selling. He loves his collection like family.

Anyway, he decided to take offence at my tasteless remark and stomped off in a huff. I gave the pyres a last once-over to make sure they weren't going to collapse or fall sideways, then turned my back on the glorious battle of wherever-the-hell-it-was and trudged back to the column. One more thing to do and then I could give the order to move out. Fingers crossed.

Doctor Papinian was sewing someone up in the big tent. He hates being interrupted when he's got a needle in his hand. "We're about ready to go," I told him.

"Piss off," he said, without looking up.

Wounded soldiers abandoned on the battlefield are another bone of contention between me and the Asvogel boys. They don't bother with them. Knock them on the head or just leave them, they say; it's the combatants' responsibility to remove all viable assets from the field, and anything left behind is contractually deemed to be abandoned (*bona vacantia* in legalese), therefore legitimate salvage, therefore the property of the contractor, to deal with as he sees fit. And, yes, it does say that in the standard form of agreement, which is what we all use in the trade, so strictly speaking he's perfectly right. I, however, take a different view. I figure there's good money to be made out of collecting the wounded, patching them up and then selling them back to their respective regimes, and so far I haven't been proved wrong. Mostly that's thanks to Doctor Papinian, who has the most amazing knack of saving the merchandise, no matter how badly it's been chewed up. He was an Echmen army surgeon for thirty years before he got himself in a spot of bother and had to disappear, and he's got that Echmen fanaticism when it comes to saving and preserving life, bless him. Personally, I like the old savage, but he gets right up the noses of everybody else.

"What the hell are you doing to that man?" I asked.

"What does it look like?"

He had a bunch of what looked like weeds in his left hand, and he was stuffing them into a hole in the wounded man's belly with his right forefinger. I should've known better than to ask. "We're moving out now," I said.

"No, we're not."

There are some people you don't expect to win against. "Fine," I said. "How much longer are you going to be?"

"Depends on how long you're going to stand there annoying me."

He teased a wisp of green weed out between finger and thumb and poked it into the hole. Rumour had it his father was a butcher, noted for his exceptionally fine sausages.

"You could kill someone doing that," I said.

"Go away."

Gut wounds are certain death. Everybody knows that, apart from Doctor Papinian. If he ever finds out, a lot of wounded soldiers are going to be in deep trouble, so I make sure nobody tells him. "Get a move on," I said, as I walked away. "You're holding everybody up."

I was too far away to hear his reply, which was probably just as well. His orderlies were laying out the men Papinian had finished with in neat rows, like fish drying in the sun; the ones who'd made it on one side, the less fortunate on the other, as though there was a real possibility of getting them mixed up unless everything was done properly. About a dozen long-suffering assistants were going round seeing to the routine bandaging, bone-setting and arrow extractions. Nobody seemed to be in any particular hurry. That annoyed me. Time is money; by taking their time, they were taking my money, and I don't like people imposing on my good nature. Still, I knew better than to yell at them, since it was Papinian's fault, not theirs. I resolved to leave them to it and give the pyres a final once-over. A good reputation is everything in this game, and nothing says unprofessional like a stack of half-burned bodies.

Just as I was about to leave the big tent, a voice called out a name, one I hadn't heard in years. I spun round, maybe just a tad too fast.

He was in a hell of a mess, but I recognised him instantly. I gave him a cold stare; pretty good going, since my heart was pounding hard enough to break my ribs.

He said the name again; then, "It's me."

I knew that, of course. "My name is Saevus Corax," I told him. "Do I know you?"

I wasn't lying. I'd just left a word out: *nowadays* my name is Saevus Corax. "I'm sorry," he said. "I thought you were somebody else."

"That's all right," I said. "Get some rest," I added, because that's what doctors always say, and then I got out of the tent in a hurry.

I don't like being rattled. When something unexpected like that happens, I feel like I can't hear what my brain is telling me, so I have no idea what to say or do. In point of fact, some of my best decisions have been made on the hoof, with no opportunity for careful thought or due consideration of all relevant factors, but I don't like it, it bothers me, and I've spent a lot of time, money, effort and blood getting to a point where I don't have to put up with being bothered. I think maybe that's why I chose a line of work so closely concerned with dead people. When a man's dead, you can be pretty sure he'll still be dead tomorrow, and very likely the day after that. You know where you stand with dead people, whereas the living seem to delight in screwing me around.

Just as well I'd gone back for another look, because the main pyre was listing badly. My guess is they'd put the bodies we stripped first at the bottom, which is really bad practice, and if I've told them about it once I've told them a thousand times: a stripped body dries out faster, therefore burns more quickly, and then the weight of the unburned stuff on top makes the whole heap slip sideways. I got a dozen or so of the lads and some twelve-foot poles, and we poked and prodded about and succeeded in making things a whole lot worse. So then we did what we ought to have done in the first place; we got the long hooks, dragged the (relatively) fresh material off the top and stuffed it in at the side where the dry stuff had burned through. All a bit grim; you have to stoke the fire up pretty hot to burn people, so I had half a dozen men fetching and carrying jugs of water to keep us damped down while we worked; then, of course, the wind changed, and the pyre started shooting out jets of flame in our faces, like a dragon; and I don't think I'll ever be truly comfortable with that smell. The only good thing was that by the time we'd sorted it all out, Papinian had finished with his embroidery and was complaining about the holdup and why weren't we moving yet? So that was all right.

In this job you find yourself feeling grateful for all manner of weird stuff. For example, it was truly thoughtful and considerate of General Theudahad to choose a battlefield so close to a straight, fast, properly maintained road. It hadn't done him much good, because it allowed Erysichthon to bring up his reserve archers, who otherwise wouldn't have got there in time, but it made my life much easier. There's nothing worse than sixty heavily laden carts floundering about in sand or mud or on stony ground that breaks spokes and axles. A short trundle over the flat and we were straight on to proper metalled carriageway. Things like that make a big difference when you've just finished a job, and you're tired and fratchetty and you just want something to go right for a change. I sat back on the box of the lead cart, trying not to notice that I stank to high heaven of burned bones and smoke, and fell asleep.

I woke up starving hungry. It's a problem I have. While we're doing a job, I rarely eat. Partly, there just isn't time, but also there's something about my everyday workplace environment that takes the edge off my appetite, for some reason. Fortunately my friends know me by now. Someone had put a sack between my feet while I slept. In it I found a pound loaf of munitions bread, a fist-sized chunk of white cheese and an Aelian dried sausage. I like it when the Aelians lose, because they only make that particular type of dried sausage for the military; you can't buy them in a market, and the Aelian commissariat grimly refuses to share the recipe. There's one particularly hot, aromatic spice – it's only there to mask the dubious nature of the meat, but I love it. I hoped there was more where that had come from, because the Aelians don't lose all that often. Some people have no consideration for others.

It's just conceivably possible that bumping around in an unsprung cart on country roads for three days isn't your idea of a wonderful time. This goes to show how effete and dissipated you are, and how you've allowed your sybaritic lifestyle to sap your moral fibre. For us, cart time is down time. There's nothing you can do on a moving cart except sit with your mouth open (to stop your teeth smashing together when you go over a deep pothole). You can't mend armour or patch clothes or sew on buttons or write up the books. You can talk, if you don't mind shouting at the top of your voice so as to be heard over the rumble of the wheels and the clanking of the cargo, but that's about it. You sit. You do nothing. You rest. If death is like that – better, presumably, since you're lying rather than sitting, and you're perfectly still instead of being shaken about like a rat in a dog's mouth – I really don't see why people make such a fuss about it. Bring it on, I say.

When I used to write for the theatre – I promised you, didn't I? No secrets between you and me. Once upon a time, long ago and far away, I used to write plays for the theatre in Urbissima. I was good at it, and I'd have made a lot of money if I hadn't been cheated by unscrupulous people. But I didn't enjoy it very much, mostly because of a ridiculous convention they have in theatrical circles called the Principle of the Unities. The idea is, to be a proper play, it's got to be:

(a) about one thing,
(b) set in one place, and
(c) all in real time.

You can get round the first one easy as winking. The second one is understandable, because it's cheap; one set, no need to pay scene-shifters, and if you can't accommodate your narrative to fit, go write for somebody else. Fair enough. But the real time thing is pointless and infuriating and really made things difficult for me, because life isn't like that. Which is just as well – one damn thing after another, as the critics said about my *Leucas and Marses*; three hours of non-stop harrowing with pity and terror, if you had to live like that you'd die of exhaustion before you hit puberty. Take my life, for example: bursts of furious, exhausting, terrifying activity punctuated by long cart journeys. Nobody wants to watch five hundred men with their mouths open sitting on sixty carts bouncing along the Great Military Road for three days. Prose narrative is a relatively new venture for me and I'm not sure I know all the rules yet, but I don't suppose you want to read about it, either. So, with your permission, we'll skip all that. The theatre managers I used to work for would have a fit, but screw them. I'd be more inclined to truckle to their delicate sensibilities if they'd ever paid me any money.

We arrived, therefore, at Busta Sagittarum three days later, to find that the battle hadn't been fought yet. I hate it when that happens. It makes all sorts of difficulties. For one thing, you really don't want to get caught up in the action, and a battle is a bit like a moorland fire. You have no idea when the wind might suddenly change, and it can move so terribly quickly. I remember Ormus Asvogel telling me about one time when his lot got caught up in the action. He'd positioned his team on what he thought was the extreme western edge of the field, and suddenly he's got five thousand lancers racing towards him, with seven thousand horse archers on their tails shooting them out of the saddle. He had just enough time to get his carts in a circle and then they were on top of him. The lancers tried to break into the circle to shelter from the archers, but no dice; while they were standing about trying to squash their way in through the breaches the archers shot them all to hell; then, when there were no lancers left, the archers gave Ormus' boys half a dozen volleys just in case they were somehow involved, killing about three dozen of them. To make matters worse, it turned out that the lancers' side won, and their general repudiated the contract on the grounds that Ormus had indirectly assisted the enemy, so he forfeited the money he'd paid up front and had to go home with empty carts. His own silly fault for getting too close, except he hadn't; it was just bad luck and the fortunes of war. You can't predict these things. The Company of Jackals, an old and respected outfit that used to do good business out East when I was starting out in the trade, got slaughtered to the last man because they happened to be in the wrong place at the wrong time, and some peach-fuzz second lieutenant of hussars mistook them for the enemy supply train.

I, therefore, was taking no chances. We fell back a day's ride the way we'd just come, circled the carts and built a palisade of stakes round it, just to be on the safe side. Meanwhile, I sent a few scouts to keep an eye on the doings, and we filled in the time doing useful work on the stuff we'd collected from the previous battle. "There's a sick man down in the hospital tent reckons he knows you," Olybrius said, as we sat in the shade of a cart darning wound holes in Aelian issue tunics. I didn't look up. I pride myself on my darning. "Is that right?" I said.

"Only," Olybrius went on, "he reckons you're somebody else."

"Ah well," I said. "If he thinks he knows somebody else, he can't be talking about me. That's your actual logic."

I didn't look up, so I didn't see the look Olybrius almost certainly gave me. "Want me to deal with it?"

Olybrius doesn't know, of course, but he suspects. Mind you, that's just him. I think if he didn't have something to be suspicious about, he'd fade away and die. Olybrius isn't Olybrius' real name, it goes without saying. It's a name he saw painted on the shutter of a corn chandler's in Auxentia, in whose cellar Olybrius hid when he was running away from the man who'd just paid good money for him in a public auction. Olybrius' father was a tenant farmer in the Mesoge who got behind on the rent in a bad year and had to sell off two of his sons or get thrown out on his ear. Olybrius didn't fancy the thought of spending his life in a chain gang mining salt, so he bit off the nose of the overseer, scrambled out through a window, jumped fifteen feet into an alley and ran like a hare, ending up in the chandler's cellar. After ten years as a hired bruiser, he ended up with me; he feels he's come down in the world, but occasionally the people he'd been paid to hurt had hurt him back, and you reach a point in your life when that sort of thing loses its charm. He decided working with me might be better than having his ribs caved in by terrified debtors; shows how wrong you can be. "Deal with what?"

"You know." I imagine that at this point he made a

throat-slitting gesture. It's one of his favourites. I didn't answer, which annoyed him. "I can take care of him for you."

"You want to learn to be a nurse?"

I shouldn't tease him, I know. "Fine," Olybrius snapped. "Suit yourself. You should hear what he's saying about you, though. Interesting stuff."

I reached for another tunic off the pile and sighed. There was a darn on the back, just between the shoulder blades, surrounded by a faint brown stain. I don't know why things like that disappoint me, but they do. I showed it to Olybrius, who subjected the needlework to professional scrutiny. "Not ours," he said.

"I should hope not."

"Not the Asvogels, they don't bother. Must be the Resurrections."

You don't argue with Olybrius when it comes to darning techniques. "It's people like them," I said, "that give the trade a bad name."

Which is true, incidentally. It's an ancient scam, going right back to when men fought with bone clubs and flint spears. You're the purchasing officer for a regiment. You draw x gold nomismata to pay for new tunics. Then you buy only-one-careful-owner tunics from one of us for $1/4x$ and keep the change. The men don't like it – they get superstitious about wearing clothes people have died in – but they know better than to say anything, and I guess there's no harm done really. I sell to anyone who wants to buy, though I don't do cut-price deals with the purchasing officers like some people – the Resurrection Crew being a name that springs to mind in this context; they're so sharp, one of these days they'll cut themselves, and on that day my tears will trickle but not flow.

I darned half a dozen more shirts, then wandered down to the hospital tent. The man who'd recognised me was up and about, an amazing tribute to Doc Papinian. I found him playing chess with one of the orderlies. I gave the orderly the bad eye, and he made an excuse and went away.

The man who thought he knew me looked at me. "It is you, isn't it?"

I sat down opposite him and glanced at the chessboard. I could see why the orderly hadn't wanted to stick around: inevitable mate in three. I moved a piece at random, just for fun. "If it was me," I said, "and if I was here, instead of where I'm supposed to be, doing this instead of what I'm supposed to be doing—"

He moved his rook. I caught sight of something, just a vague possibility I couldn't rationalise. I acted on it, moving my one remaining knight. "What?" he said.

"Doesn't it occur to you that maybe I'd have a reason for all that?" I said. "And if so, maybe it's a good reason."

He lowered his eyes. "I'm sorry," he said. "I didn't think. It was just so amazing, seeing a friendly face in a place like this."

"Oh, it's not so bad," I said. "Compared with the alternative."

He laughed. "Yes, of course, I'm sorry."

"Your move."

He looked at the board. He was smart enough to see that everything had changed, but not quite smart enough to realise what was about to happen. He frowned, then carried on with his original plan. "I don't suppose anybody believed me," he said.

"Sick people say all sorts of weird stuff," I told him. "Forget about it." I moved my bishop. He saw me do it but evidently didn't ask himself why I'd done that. He moved his knight. "Check," he said.

I know it's childish, but I do like winning. At everything. I moved my rook. "Checkmate," I said. "Soon as this battle's over, we'll send you back to your people. Meanwhile, take it easy. Look after yourself, Posidonius."

"You too."

One thing I've learned in this trade is that nearly everything is useful, even weeds. There's one particular weed that comes in very handy sometimes, assuming you can be bothered to dig it up and boil its roots into a syrup, which you then distil slowly in an alembic. Two drops of the distillate in a cup of coarse red wine solves all manner of problems. I remembered that Posidonius always had a fondness for Medazi claret, and by coincidence there'd been a couple of bottles of the stuff in some dead officer's saddlebags. I sent one to Posidonius, with my compliments. If you've got to do something rotten, do it in the nicest possible way.

Doctor Papinian came to see me later that afternoon. "That man who claimed he knew you," he said. "He died."

"What, poor old Posidonius? What a shame. Still, I'm sure you did everything you could."

He looked at me. "You did know him, then?"

"What? Oh, yes, sort of. My father was a gardener, and Posidonius was the boss's son. He was all right, in his way."

"You said you didn't know him."

"Well, it's been twenty years. People change."

Papinian wasn't happy, I could see. The hell with that; Posidonius was my salvage after all, to do with as I liked. Thirty staurata in ransom money down the drain, if you wish to look at it that way, not to mention out-of-pocket expenses such as medicines, bandages and the doctor's time, but I wasn't the one kicking up a fuss. You have to be stoical in this business. Like my father (who isn't a gardener) always says: where there's livestock, sooner or later there's dead stock, and you just have to deal with it.

We sat there for two days while Theudahad and Erysichthon had a chess tournament of their own down in the valley. Actually, it wasn't as sophisticated as chess; more like the sort of game a dog likes to play, when he fetches the stick but dances around with it in his mouth when you try and take it back. Erysichthon was the dog, for what it's worth. Theudahad humoured him for a bit, then sat down with his legions and his field artillery, cutting the prince off from the only source of drinkable water for ten miles in any direction. The next morning, Erysichthon attacked.

A word in passing about battles. People should know better by now, they really should. There's loads of books on the subject, so there's no excuse. I have three rules of thumb. One: nine out of ten pitched battles are lost by the loser rather than won by the victor. Two: it's easier to win if you've got the smaller army. Three: the attacking side always loses, unless it's led by a tactical genius or opposed by an idiot. Erysichthon was smart, efficient and conscientious, but that was all. He had no call to go attacking someone like Theudahad, who'd been wiping out superior field armies when Erysichthon was still playing with toy chariots. He made a valiant attempt at a feigned-withdrawal-and-ambush on the left wing, but it all came unstuck when the feigned withdrawal turned into a real run-like-hell and Theudahad sent in his lancers to chop up the fugitives. Meanwhile, six regiments of Theudahad's crack heavy infantry descended on the prince's camp and baggage train and started helping themselves, assuming that it was all over. It turned out that it wasn't. By the time Theudahad's lancers got back from annihilating Erysichthon's left wing, there was nobody left alive on the battlefield proper who could talk Aelian. So they hopped it, reasonably enough, and Erysichthon very sensibly let them go. He'd won, or rather Theudahad had somehow managed to lose, and he wasn't inclined to push his luck. Two-thirds of his men were dead and he didn't have the strength to make good on his victory. He limped back into the city and shut the gates, having achieved nothing at all, and left the mess for us to clear up. Well, it's what we do.

About hot weather. I knew a man once. He was as fat as a pig, and on any day that was warm enough to melt ice he sweated. He could only wear linen, because of the way it slicks away moisture, and his hair was permanently plastered to his forehead. Whenever the sun came out, you'd say to him, What a lovely day, and he'd smile and say, Yes, it's glorious, isn't it? Then, after I'd known him for about five years, I met him in the street. It was scalpingly hot. "Glorious day," the fat man said.

"You think so?" I said. "I think it's ghastly. I hate hot weather."

"God, so do I," said the fat man, and he spent the next ten minutes telling me exactly what was wrong with heat and and bright sunshine. We were always great pals after that, which goes to show that, very occasionally, the truth can be a good thing.

Hot weather in my line of work is just plain misery. It's not just the smell and the flies and the bloating. Any perishable stores left in the baggage train are liable to go off, and anything made of metal gets so hot it takes the skin off your fingertips. The Aelians paint their armour, to stop it rusting and glinting in the sunlight; fine, except they paint it black, which absorbs the heat with maximum efficiency. This is such a stupid thing to do that I actually asked an Aelian supply clerk once, why black, for crying out loud? He gave me a sad smile. Black paint's cheap, he said. Of course, the colonel i/c procurement bills the Treasury for white paint, which reflects the sun and costs a third more, but somehow the troops get black, and you can track an Aelian column by the trail of bodies dead from heatstroke. We repaint Aelian stuff as a matter of course. If we didn't, nobody would buy it.

The day after the battle was a scorcher. Gombryas – you remember, the body parts enthusiast – comes from out East somewhere and feels obliged to wear wool next to the skin at any temperature lower than the melting point of copper, so he set off to work with a smile on his face and a song on his lips. The rest of us trudged after him, muttering. We scrambled up the steep slope and looked down at the battlefield. I noticed something and yelled out, "Hold it." Everyone stopped. I told them to wait, and went on ahead.

What I'd noticed was, no crows. That meant somebody had got there first. Nothing inherently sinister about that. People come looking for their friends, or something they dropped when they ran away. Strictly speaking, the man who drags his wounded comrade out from under a heap of corpses is robbing me blind, but as a rule I don't make a fuss about it. Ask me nicely, and I'll probably help you look. What I don't hold with is the taking of liberties.

"You again," I said.

She was kneeling over some dead man, and when she stood up there was a gold chain dangling from her hand. She made no effort to hide it. "Hello," she said, smiling sweetly.

It was early in the morning and already I felt tired. She has that effect on me. "This lot is ours," I said. "Go away."

"No."

Some people are so unreasonable it makes me want to cry. "It's my battlefield," I said. "I paid money for it. Piss off."

She gave me her angel look. "I forgive you," she said.

Sister Stauracia runs an operation called the League of Mercy. During the off season, she stands in the marketplace in some big city making speeches about the plight of wounded men left to die on battlefields, and because she's young and pretty, people think she's wonderful and give her money. She's got a gang of about fifty, all hard cases, dressed up like monks in habits and cowls. She never pays for salvage rights, and when you try and shoo her away she gets all soulful and says she's only doing God's work, which drives me spare. The Asvogel boys shoot arrows at her, which usually works, but I can't quite bring myself to do that. Instead, I lay formal complaints with the winning general, who tells me I'm some sort of monster for interfering with angels of mercy. By the time I've been through channels and made all my breach-of-contract noises, Sister Stauracia and her angels have stripped out all the cash money, personal effects and luxury items and faded quietly away, leaving us to do the heavy lifting. I know for a fact she's never bandaged so much as a cut finger in her life; she's a tax collector's daughter from Chosroene, and her grandfather was the last man in the province to be hanged for grave robbing.

"How would it be if I said please?"

She thought about that. "Better," she said.

"Piss off," I said. "Please."

"No."

I did that thing where you throw your arms up in the air and stomp off. It's supposed to make you feel better. It doesn't work. "It's her, isn't it?" Carrhasio said as I scrambled up the slope.

"Yup."

"Just say the word. Go on, just say it."

He's getting on a bit now, but Carrhasio was a real soldier once. Ninety-nine point nine per cent of real soldiers join up for the money; because they'd starve to death back home, or because they dream of the big score, sacking a city or looting a monastery, that'll set them up for life. Carrhasio was one of the point-one per cent who just likes to fight. If he goes more than six weeks without cutting into somebody he wilts and fades, like an unwatered flower. "No," I said.

"It's not right. You paid for that battlefield."

"My money," I said. "And there's plenty for everyone."

He glared at me, said, "Suit yourself," and limped away.

My attitude to violence is purely arithmetical. If the odds are six to one or better in my favour, I'm a lion. Otherwise I'm a man of peace. I did a quick headcount. Fifty-two, plus the good Sister. "Changed my mind," I called out. "Get them shifted."

It didn't take long. I can't say it was a pretty sight, men beating each other up against a background of dead bodies, but I could tell that the lads' patience was starting to wear a bit thin, and I always find that the essence of true leadership is to let people do what they want while giving the impression that you thought of it first. They rounded them up, all kneeling on the ground neatly trussed with rope, and asked me what I wanted done with them.

"Kill them," I said.

A bald man with his lip split open started to scream. Olybrius stared at me. Old Carrhasio took a long stride forward, then hesitated and stopped.

"Only kidding," I said. "Leave them where they are for now and let them go when we're done." I looked round. I couldn't see Sister Stauracia. "Where's that bloody woman? Anybody seen her?"

Nobody had. I didn't like that. Either she'd run off in a panic and was hiding somewhere – not a good idea in the desert, unless you've got plenty of water and a parasol; I had enough on my conscience as it was without Sister bloody Stauracia – or she was up to something. On the other hand, I had work to do and five hundred men standing about in the hot sun not doing it. "Tell me if she turns up," I said, and dismissed her from my mind.

It took us five days to clear the field, at the end of which everything was getting pretty ripe. But we got a lot of good, clean stuff – the Aelian Seventh Infantry broke and ran, discarding their shields and armour; a treasure trove of quality kit without the usual sharp-edged holes in it – and my back-of-my-hand initial calculations suggested that with any luck we'd cover our costs and show a modest profit. The pyres lit easily and burned well, Papinian had five days rather than the usual three so didn't need to swear at me too much for rushing him, and we were feeling relatively pleased with ourselves when someone spotted a dust cloud over in the general direction of the city. This proved to be a column of Prince Erysichthon's household cavalry, with the man himself at the head of it. Next to him, on a white palfrey and swathed in a pure white nun's habit, was Sister Stauracia.

Erysichthon's all right, for a young thug brought up from

infancy to believe he's the son of God. He was wearing scale armour made out of your actual pure gold – I tried not to calculate exactly how much Theudahad had cost me by not winning the battle, but I couldn't help it – and he was in a filthy temper. "You," he shouted, pointing at me with his riding whip. "I want a word with you."

I was filthy with pyre smoke and my back was killing me, but when the Son of God gives you an order, you don't hang about. "Your Majesty," I said. "Congratulations on a truly remarkable—"

"What's all this I hear about you molesting pilgrims?"

It took me a moment to figure out what the hell he was talking about. "With respect, your—"

"Holy men," he yelled in my face, "doing God's work, and you had them tied up and beaten. I ought to slaughter the lot of you."

It was one of those moment when you just don't know what to say. "Not beaten," I said. "We caught her men stealing from our battlefield, so we tied them up, but we didn't—"

Sister Stauracia breathed a patient sigh. The prince pointed his whip at me. "It's not *your* battlefield, you obnoxious bloody vulture. I gave the Sister permission to tend the sick, if it's any business of yours. Now let those men go before I lose my temper."

"With respect," I growled at him, "we paid good money—"

The prince was about to start roaring, but Stauracia put her hand on his arm and gave him a sweet look; forgive them, for they know not what they do. He calmed himself down with an effort and scowled at me. "I'll give you one last chance," he said. "Release the pilgrims, or my men will cut you down where you stand."

Stauracia's goons had finished their breakfast, so they were ready to go. They grinned at us and helped themselves to horses from the reserve stock. "It would be a nice gesture," the prince said, "if you donated your loot to Sister Stauracia's mission. Actually, I think it's the least you can do, in the circumstances."

"What a splendid idea," I said. "Why didn't I think of that?"

When I told the lads what I'd agreed with the prince, they were ready to lynch me. I told them to get a grip and let Stauracia's people help themselves to whatever they wanted. My attitude of true penitence wasn't wasted on the good Sister, because when I pointed out that if they took all our horses we'd die of thirst in the desert before we could get to water, she gave me a pretty smile and said that would never do and of course we could keep our horses. The prince beamed at her, and she made a nice little speech about how we can't expect to be forgiven for our own sins if we don't forgive other people for theirs. She's full of stuff like that, and it's worth a lot of money to her at fairs.

I was also allowed to keep my map, without which I'd get lost and wander hopelessly. The map told me that Stauracia would almost certainly take the southern post road as far as the oasis at Callinice, then leave the road and bear west across the relatively flat maquis, keeping the mountains on her right until she reached the sea: sixty miles, so three days at a comfortable pace for her heavily laden carts. I asked old Carrhasio, who knows about these things, how far you can see dust clouds.

He looked at me. "You what?"

"From what distance," I said, "is a dust cloud visible? Two miles? Ten? Fifty?"

"Oh, right." He thought for a moment. "Depends how big it is."

I sighed. "The sort of cloud," I said, "you'd expect to be kicked up by five hundred horsemen."

He shrugged. "Five miles," he said. "Something like that."

He wasn't being his usual assertive self, so I reckoned on eight, just to be safe. We'd have to get a move on, but it was doable. "What are you up to?" Olybrius said.

"You'll see," I said. I prefer to be noncommittal when planning strategy.

In the event it all worked out rather well. We set off across country roughly eight miles parallel to the road, then caught up with them as they crossed a dry riverbed (always an awkward thing to do when you've got heavy carts). I knew it'd take them the best part of half a day, and that by the time they'd finished it'd be getting dark, so they'd stop there for the night. No problem at all to sneak up on the carts and help ourselves to weapons before waking up Stauracia and her crew.

I do believe they were surprised to see us. "Just thought we'd stop by and pay our respects," I said.

Stauracia didn't reply, but that was probably because I had my foot on her neck. Her men had been no trouble at all – no deaths, just a few cuts and bruises. You can afford to be gentle when you're on the right end of odds of ten to one.

She was starting to make gurgling noises, so I lifted my foot. "Don't ever," I said, "do anything like that again, do you understand?"

She told me some things about myself which I already knew, though I prefer not to dwell on them. "Agreed," I said. "So what?"

"I'll tell the prince. He'll have you hanged."

"Unlikely," I said. "If you try walking back to the city from here, you'll die, trust me. Whereas if you head for the coast, you ought to make it, provided you don't dawdle. Besides, the prince will be dead in a month or so, the Aelians'll see to that. You really ought to take more of an interest in current affairs, if you want to stay in this business."

Someone was tugging at my sleeve. I was busy being wittily triumphant, so I didn't want to be interrupted. "Boss," Carrhasio said.

"Not now."

He tugged so hard he nearly tore the cloth. Stauracia giggled. My moment spoiled; oh well. "What?"

He dragged me off a few yards. "You're going to let them go."

"Yes," I said. "What about it?"

"Use your head, boss, just for fucking once. If they die out here, who the hell will ever know? And we'll be shot of them."

As I think I mentioned, Carausio isn't as young as he used to be. He's a bit deaf, and he assumes that if he's too far away to hear what someone's saying, they can't hear him either. "No," I said.

"Are you nuts or something? We can get rid of them and nobody will ever know it was us."

"Yes, I think you mentioned that. The answer's no."

"You'll regret it."

"Quite possibly. Unfortunately, killing them would be murder, and that's against the law."

"You killed your pal Posidonius."

To be fair, he'd been trying his best to whisper. But a man who's been a drill sergeant for twenty years is about as good at whispering as I am at scooping bits off the sun and spreading them on toast. "No," I said, "I didn't."

"I saw you."

"You can't have done, because I didn't do it," I lied.

Sister Stauracia is, as I think I mentioned, young. Young women have ears like bats. Also, at times I'm a bit slow on the uptake. I grabbed Carausio by the hair – he still has a bit, at the back of his head – and forced him to his knees.

"Smart," I hissed in his ear. "You blurt out my deadly secret so she can hear it, so I've got to kill her. Only I don't have a deadly secret, I didn't kill Posidonius and I'm not going to kill Stauracia and her goons. *Capisce?*"

He tried to nod, but I was holding his hair. "Got it," he said.

"Good man. Carry on."

Sister Stauracia was looking at me. I'm good at reading people but she was hard to figure out. "You still here?" I said.

"Who was Posidonius?"

Some people are naturally, well, let's say sticky. The more you're in contact with them, the more gummed up you get. "A man I knew once. He died of his wounds after the battle. Go away."

"That man said—"

"He says all sorts of things."

"Posidonius," she said, to commit the name to memory. "Interesting."

A curious fact. I can't remember ever getting myself in serious trouble through doing something bad. All the really catastrophic shit I've trodden in over the course of an eventful life has come from trying to do the right thing.

2

I think I could get to like this prose writing thing. If this was blank verse for the theatre, with that stupid Doctrine of Unities, I'd have to show you our sea journey from the Mesembrotene coast to the island of Ogyge, and that would do neither of us any good. Because of my rather rash promise to tell you nothing but the truth, I'd have to admit to being a truly pathetic sailor, and you'd have to endure three days of monotony with occasional revolting episodes of vomiting. But this way all I need to say is, *we took a boat to the island*, and we're both spared a lot of unpleasantness. Hooray for prose. Where have you been all my life?

We sailed over to Ogyge in three ships. It's a medium-sized island about three miles off the coast of Mesembrotia, and the nearest thing I have in the world to a home. It's not mine, of course. It belongs to the monks of the Glass Pillar monastery, and about a hundred years ago they founded a subsidiary house there – I think there's a technical term for it, daughter house or something like that; if they were merchants they'd call it a branch office. Nominally it's supposed to be a place of heightened contemplation, where men of true ascetic piety can commune with the Infinite with no distractions whatsoever. The fact is, the abbot of the Glass Pillar found himself lumbered with a prior he couldn't stand the sight of; after several years of trying everything he could think of to get rid of him, short of six drops of aconite in his breakfast porridge, he hit on the idea of building him a monastery of his very own, ever such a long way away. After the prior had joyfully agreed to this arrangement, the abbot told him precisely where his new dominion was going to be, and by then of course it was far too late.

Ogyge is about seven square miles, mostly mountains. There are bits where sheep can just about survive – old joke about Ogygian sheep having two long legs and two short ones on account of spending their entire lives standing on steep slopes – and a few places where the monks have painstakingly terraced the rock and dust enough to grow vines. There's about a hundred and fifty acres of your actual flat, fertile arable land down on the east coast at the point where the bigger of the two rivers drains away into mosquito-haunted swamp, and that's about it; a dump, somewhere you wouldn't send your worst enemy, the last place God made, that's Ogyge.

I love it. For a start, it's surrounded by bloodcurdling reefs and submerged rocks. That means there's only one place where you can land a ship (and you have to know precisely what you're doing and where the seamarks are) so the risk of being snuck up on is practically nil. The monastery may only be a hundred years or so old, but the buildings it occupies go way back. Nobody knows who built them, but whoever it was had more money than God and significantly better taste.

Needless to say the first thing the monks did when they got there was paint over the exquisite, immaculately preserved thousand-year-old frescoes and mosaics in the Great Hall, the chapel and the chapter house, but they ran out of enthusiasm and limewash before they could do the same for the crypt and the catacombs, an enormous underground space chiselled out of solid granite for which they have no use whatsoever. It so happens that the current abbot is an acquaintance of mine – meaning, each of us know things about the other that would make your hair curl – and about seven years ago we came to a mutually beneficial agreement. I use the underground rooms as a store and workshop, no questions asked, come and go as I please. In return, the abbot gets ten per cent of the gross, of which half goes into monastery funds. The other half I pay into an account with the Poor Sisters on the mainland. The account is in the name of someone who doesn't strictly speaking exist. None of my business.

Hooray, therefore, for Ogyge; hell on earth for everybody else, a slice of paradise for me. We arrived just as it was starting to get dark – an hour or so later and we'd have been in real trouble, because if you can't see the buoys and posts that mark the only safe channel, you're crabfood – and tied up at the pier which we built about five years ago, in the beautiful little natural harbour at the foot of the mountain, halfway up which perches the Silver Apple monastery.

The usual drill is, I go ahead and let them know we've arrived, they send down a couple of dozen mules. You can't get carts up the track, and they let me have two dozen mules because that's all the mules they've got. Accordingly, we decided that the stuff could stay in the ship till the morning. None of us fancied fooling around on that narrow track in the dark, especially with mules involved. For that reason, we all went up the hill together, just this once.

With hindsight (a wonderful thing but utterly useless) I should've started being nervous as soon as we landed, because there should have been a lookout in the delapidated little hut perched among the rocks on the end of the mole. There wasn't, but that didn't bother me, because quite often there isn't. It's a miserable job, involving sitting on a thin plank in a rickety shed; too dark to read, the breakers shoot foam up through the broken floorboards and soak you to the skin, and all so you can bear witness to a total absence of ships. So, although my agreement with the abbot specifies that the lookout should be manned at all times, as often as not it isn't, and somehow life goes on. Usually. Nine hundred and ninety-nine times out of a thousand.

For that reason, my hackles didn't start to stir until we got to the gatehouse, at the top of the narrow, winding track, and found nobody on duty and the gate wide open. Now that was unusual, like waking up and finding a crocodile on your chest.

Goes without saying, we'd left all the weapons in the ships. "Stay here," I said. "I'll go and take a look."

Absolutely nobody volunteered to go with me, which was fine and what I'd expected; even so, it would've been nice to be surprised, just for once. I walked up the so-familiar path to the porter's lodge, feeling like a mouse surrounded by invisible cats. Nobody in the lodge, alive or dead, and the door wide open. Through the archway into the front quadrangle.

My pal the abbot is serious about his lawns. There's not a lot of rain on Ogyge, but what little there is gets collected in massive lead gutters and conveyed to hulking great cisterns, from which a small army of lay brothers draw it off bowsers to sprinkle the emerald-green grass of the front and back quad-rangles. When they're not doing that, they're mowing with scalpel-sharp scythes or on their hands and knees trimming the borders and weeding out stray encroachments of moss like a general synod cracking down on heresy. My pal doesn't give a stuff about trees, shrubs or flowers, but he's fanatical about grass. I think it's the only thing he actually believes in, bless him.

It follows, therefore, that nobody walks on the lawns. But someone had been doing just that; a lot of someones, in heavy boots, carrying heavy weights. I darted under an arch and crouched listening, but not a sound to be heard, which in itself was completely wrong. No singing from the chapel (at that time of day they should've been a third of the way through vespers), no clatter of wooden-soled sandals on the flagstones, no click-clack of gardeners' shears, no bad-tempered high-pitched voices debating a *varia lectio* in the fifth book of Jubilees or bitching about the porridge at dinner. Instead, an empty quad-rangle with a beaten track diagonally across it.

I figured there was probably half an hour of daylight left and then we'd be floundering about in the dark; very bad idea. The sensible thing to do would be to go back down the mountain while we could still see where we were putting our big feet, get back on the ships, pole them away from the quay into the deep water in the south-east corner of the harbour and stay there till morning, when there'd be light to see by. Until then we'd be reasonably safe, and there was very little that could be done now that couldn't wait till then, except for just possibly saving the life of anybody who happened to be lying on a floor somewhere bleeding to death . . .

Hardly a significant factor in a sensible man's calculations, because how often do you stumble across someone bleeding out in the course of an ordinary day? Actually, in my job, quite often; but this wasn't a battlefield. Was it? No, far too tidy for that. Apart from the obscene footmarks on the sacred grass, nothing out of place anywhere. Which in itself was as odd as a five-legged pig. I've seen any number of looted towns, villages, cities, citadels, villas, not to mention monasteries and priories, and they tend to look like the aftermath of a cyclone or an earthquake; stuff everywhere, dead bodies, doors hanging off their hinges, and anything not worth taking tends to get smashed, as you'd expect from overexcited men in a hurry. That wasn't what I was looking at. The end of the world, maybe, but definitely not chaos. Therefore no loose ends, nothing overlooked, such as witnesses . . .

I compromised. "Go back to the ships," I told them. "Put out into the deep water and wait till morning."

Olybrius stared at me. "What about you?"

"I'll stay here and have a look round."

Nobody liked the sound of that, so I cut short the debate by walking away. Nobody came after me. There hadn't been time to nip back to the ship for armour or weapons, but what the hell. Now then, I thought, as I walked carefully on the sides of my feet across the no-longer-immaculate grass, if I was a terrified monk slowly bleeding to death – specifically my irreplaceable ally the abbot – where would I be?

Not lying in the middle of the lawn of the back quad where any unsuspecting passer-by could trip over me in the dark, that's for sure. I'd have more consideration. My foot caught in something and the next moment I was eating grass, while a voice wailed horribly nearby in the darkness. It was a voice I recognised. "Ekkehard?" I said. "Is that you?"

A long split second of dead silence, then a name that used to belong to me. "Yes," I said.

"Fuck," said my old friend Ekkehard. "What are you doing here?"

"Tripping over idiots. Are you all right?"

"No."

"What happened?"

"Pirates," Ekkehard said, "I think. Or soldiers pretending to be pirates, I don't bloody know, do I? I'm bleeding to death here, you arsehole. Do something."

"Keep your voice down, for God's sake."

"What? Oh, shit. Sorry."

"Can you move?"

"I've got a hole in me the size of a millwheel."

"Oh, for crying out loud."

Curious reaction, you're thinking, to the news that my old pal was seriously hurt; but Ekkehard and I have that sort of history. Instinctively I assume that anything he does is intended to screw me around, even when it's manifestly not his choice or his fault. "Hold still," I said. "I'll get you."

Footnote: Ekkehard is six foot four and built like a siege tower. The top of my head comes up to his armpit. Years of hauling dead bodies around have given me strength and dexterity, so I just about managed to get him on his feet, with his monstrous weight bearing on my shoulders and down through my spine into the long-suffering earth. "One thing," I said.

"What?"

"My name is Saevus Corax."

"No, it isn't."

"Yes," I said, "it is. Saevus Corax. Say it after me."

"Isn't that that grave robber?"

"Battlefield salvage contractor."

"That's you?"

"Yes. That other name you said—"

"Ah. Got you."

"That other person," I said, "is dead. We don't talk about him. Got it?"

"Yes, all right, I'm not stupid."

Which, broadly speaking, is probably true. Ekkehard isn't stupid; he's an actor. There's a difference, slight but real; as between lying and fiction, or appropriation and theft, or grave-robbing and battlefield salvage. Even so. "One chirp out of you about that other person and so help me—"

"Yes, all *right*."

"Fine," I said, and he trod on my foot.

Years of practice have given me a reasonable sense of where I am in the dark. "Mind your head," I said. "Archway."

"Fuck."

Like I said, he's taller than me. Now we were crossing the front quad, heading for the lodge. "Since when were you a monk?" I said.

"About six weeks."

"Bit of a change of direction, surely."

"I wanted some peace and quiet."

Poor Ekkehard. "You wouldn't happen to know what became of the rest of them?"

"Not a clue. All of a sudden the place was knee-deep in murdering bastards, so I hid, and then some bastard stabbed me. I got as far as where you found me and then I passed out."

"Archway," I said. "Right, hold on tight. One false step and we both end up on the rocks."

"Oh, crap."

Succinctly put. Somehow we made it down the track to the gatehouse. Nobody there.

I guess I must have radiated my concern. "Now what?" said Ekkehard.

"Nothing," I replied. "Right, this is the tricky bit."

"I hope you know what you're doing."

"Shut up."

"I'm just saying. You always were a clumsy sod."

Ekkehard is an outstandingly fine actor, which means he's very good indeed at being someone else. He's lousy at being himself, but you can't have everything. All in all, I was glad to get back to the quay, where Carrhasio jumped out at me and nearly stabbed me with a spear before he recognised my terrified voice. "Where the hell did you lot get to?" I asked.

"You were gone a long time. We thought something had happened to you."

So they went back to the ship. Figures. "Get the doctor," I said. "This man's badly hurt."

Olybrius had lit a lantern. "No, he isn't."

No, he wasn't. Even I could see it was just a flesh wound. "Get the fucking doctor," I said. "Now."

Gombryas shrugged and clambered up the ladder into the ship. "Who's he?" Carrhasio asked.

"Friend of mine," I snapped. "Don't just stand there. Water. Bandages."

Ekkehard was inspecting the damage. "God, that was close," he said. "An inch to the right, I'd have had it."

I didn't bother contradicting him. "Now, then," I said, "from the beginning. What happened?"

"I told you."

"Tell me again."

Getting anything like a coherent narrative out of him was like digging the meat out of a crab's claw, but we got there eventually. The bell had just gone for terce (so midday, broad daylight) and Ekkehard had gone back to the dormitory to fetch his missal. He heard yelling and screaming, looked out of the window and saw men in armour in the front quad. He wasn't entirely sure what they were doing, because he only glanced quickly before diving under the nearest bed, but if pressed he'd say the monks were being rounded up rather than cut down where they stood. The process went on for quite some time, and then everything went quiet. Ekkehard decided to give it another half-hour before venturing out of cover – he timed it by reciting the messenger speech from *The Witch's Tragedy* under his breath three times; but halfway through the third iteration he heard boots on the dormitory floor. He froze. Searching noises for a long time, then someone leaned down and grabbed his leg. He scooted out the other side, straight into an unpleasant individual in full armour, who stuck him with a spear.

Ekkehard is an actor. One of his best things is dying. He can die better than anybody else in the profession; what's more, he can stay dead, centre stage, for the rest of the act and even the nobs in the front row of the stalls can't see him breathe. So he died. He could hear the bad guys arguing about something, though he couldn't understand the language; then someone grabbed his heels and dragged him across the floor. Then some more arguing – tempers definitely beginning to fray, he said – and then two men picked him up by his wrists and ankles and pitched him down the night-soil chute.

Fortuitously – Ekkehard is one of the luckiest men I've ever met – they'd cleaned out the cesspit only that morning, so he went bump on the hard floor rather than splosh in eight feet of liquid unpleasantness. He carried on acting dead for a long time, then crawled to the sluice and out into the stable yard; at which point he felt desperately faint. He decided he must be very badly damaged (up to that point he hadn't really thought about it, his mind being on other things) but it was too dark to see; he managed to get on his feet and stagger about a bit, and then he fell over, and then some clumsy bastard trod on him—

"Describe them," I said.

"Murdering bastards in armour."

"What sort of armour?"

"Oh, come *on.*"

Fair enough. "Were they smart like soldiers or scruffy like bandits?"

He shrugged. "Sort of in between," he said, "I wasn't paying attention. It's not exactly my field of expertise."

At which point Papinian turned up and I held the lantern while he fussed about with swabs and a needle. "Just a scratch," he said, "he'll be fine. Any others?"

"We'll know in the morning," I said, which got me a foul look, which I ignored. "Right now, we're going to get these ships out of harm's way."

It wasn't a restful night, what with one thing and another. As soon as there was light enough to see by, we dolled ourselves up in Type Sixes, helmets and shields, poled the ships back to the quay and went exploring. We found two more monks, both dead and stiff as boards, pitched down a well; apart from them, nothing. The treasury, containing gold plate, jewelled reliquaries and a large lead coffer full of ready money, hadn't been touched, though the lock had been forced. The library, on the other hand, had been thoroughly gone over, and quite a few of the books were missing; likewise a moderate quantity of flour, butter, bacon and dried beans from the buttery, but they hadn't bothered with the beer, cider or brandy.

"That's crazy," Gombryas said. "Even if they were regular army, they should've nicked *something*."

Valid point, which I was at a loss to explain. Not pirates, not soldiers; all they'd taken were enough supplies to get them back home, some books and seventy-odd monks. "What about our stuff?" Olybrius said. "Has anybody looked to see?"

We went down to the cellars. Locks all forced. Everything gone. Our entire stock in trade, worth something in the region of seventeen thousand staurata. "Bastards," Carrhasio said.

"They wanted weapons," I said. "Well, now we're getting somewhere."

"All our fucking stuff," Gombryas moaned. "It's that bitch. She did it."

Tempting hypothesis, but unlikely. No way Sister Stauracia could have got there before we did. Also, what would she want with books, or monks? "The Asvogels," somebody else suggested. "They'd know we wouldn't be home."

"That's more like it," Rutilian said, with an edge to his voice I didn't fancy much. "In and out quick and on their way before anyone can do anything about it. That's their style all right."

I thought about that. Polycrates said, "Why would they take a load of old monks? Sure, they don't want witnesses. But—"

"The Asvogels aren't killers," Olybrius said. "But they could sell them out East. It'd be as good as killing them; nobody's going to be interested in anything they've got to say out in Echmen or Osroene. And monks can read and write, remember; people pay good money for clerks."

Another valid point. We seemed to be awash with them,

and all to no purpose. "Why would Ormus Asvogel steal two cartloads of books?" I asked.

They looked at each other. "People buy books," Gombryas said doubtfully.

"True," I said. "All right, then. Why would Ormus steal two cartloads of books and leave behind a hundred grand in gold plate and coin?"

A moment of dead silence, perhaps the deadest since the world began. "How much?" Carrhasio whispered.

"A hundred thousand staurata," I said. "At least."

"What, just sitting there?"

It shows how troubled I was in my own mind. I hadn't looked at it from that perspective, honestly. "And nobody would ever know—"

Quite. The pirates or whoever it was would take the blame, and we – Rainbow's end, the big score, the apotheosis of human desires. "They would," I said.

A moment while they considered that. "So fucking what?"

I shook my head. "I don't like it," I said.

"Who gives a stuff what you like and don't like?" Polycrates said, reasonably enough. "A hundred thousand staurata in gold—"

"Think," I told him. "The monastery gets ripped off, all the monks vanish, presumed dead, and ten minutes later, there's us with all that money. Don't you see? We're being set up."

"Doesn't matter," Polycrates said. "For that sort of money they can fit me up for anything they like. I'll be long gone and they'll never find me. The hell with it."

Polycrates is a cut above the rest of us, at least in his own estimation. He was a lawyer's clerk before the draft caught up with him and sent him to fight the Tessarines in one of Aelia's more remote northern protectorates. Because he could read and write they made him quartermaster-sergeant, a position of awesome dignity and power which he cheerfully abused, but not skilfully enough to get away with it. Five years in the stockade spent repairing holes in armour gave him a useful trade, and I reckoned he'd be an asset to the outfit; one of those good-ideas-at-the-time that haunt you ever afterwards, like venereal disease.

"I don't like it," I repeated. "Not one bit. Who's so rich they don't mind leaving a hundred thousand staurata lying about as bait?"

Money; that old thing. A hundred thousand divided by five hundred is two hundred each; the price of a seventy-acre farm in the Mesoge, or a dockside wine shop in Beloisa. Put it another way: salvation, rebirth, redemption, resurrection, for the sort of man who works for someone like me. The big score, and all your troubles will be over. But my father used to spend two hundred staurata on a saddle. "We need to think about this," I said firmly, while they were still even remotely disposed to listen to me. "Meanwhile, we put the money somewhere safe so it's not going anywhere."

"Such as?"

I grinned. "I know the perfect spot. And then," I said, "we're going to think this thing through carefully, before we get ourselves in shit over our heads."

Like I told you, the Silver Apple is an old building. It was old a thousand years before the monks arrived. My friend the abbot told me about the time when they were digging a new well and came up against solid rock. They went at it with picks and crowbars, and broke through into a vaulted chamber, which turned out to be either a dining hall or a storehouse, abandoned and then built over by the original occupants, several centuries before we Robur discovered writing. Being interested in such things, my friend was thrilled at the prospect of excavating a pristine site dating back maybe two thousand years. He told his men to cover over the breach while they got together the tools and equipment they'd need for a proper, careful job. A week later, they uncovered the breach, only to find the chamber had flooded. Presumably something they'd done had upset some delicate equilibrium, and the underground spring had changed course slightly, and that was that ... And at least they now had their well, not to mention a first-rate cistern, so that was all right.

Gold, I explained, doesn't rust, so it doesn't mind getting wet. We packed it up in oilskin bags made out of a spare sail and lowered it down on a chain. We'd need a big winch to get it back up again, but never mind about that. How many casual pickers-and-stealers go around with a big winch? Even if someone else found it, they'd have to go away and come back with the necessary gear, and I wasn't planning on leaving it for very long. It was a clever idea, though I do say so myself. Ultimately it was to cost me the life of the best friend I ever had, but it was still pretty darn clever.

Even so, all I'd managed to do was buy myself a very short space of thinking time, and as I may have mentioned already, I find it hard to think straight when people are moaning at me.

"You can't steal all that money," Ekkehard repeated, as we walked up from the quay towards the gatehouse. "You'll get us all killed."

"It's not stealing if you don't take it away," I replied. "Besides—"

"Yes, you said. But they'll know, the bastards who stabbed me. I bet you they only left it there because they were planning on coming back for it. And when they find it's gone, they'll know it was you and they'll come after you."

I wasn't really listening. I was thinking: since when did my old pal the abbot have that kind of money? Unlikely. The Silver Apple wasn't a real monastery, more like a jumped-up priory, which happened to live in an old shell several sizes too big for it. All that plate – gold, too, not silver. Also a relatively recent foundation, and it takes time to accumulate the good stuff on that sort of scale, not to mention wealthy benefactors living locally. Pious and grateful mermaids? Wealthy fish? On balance, probably not. Besides, if my pal had assets on that scale in his treasury, I'd have known about it. Quite probably I'd never have been allowed to hire his cellars if he hadn't been hard up and grateful for every trachy he could get. So—

"And when they find you," Ekkehard was whining, "it's not going to be fun for anyone who happens to be associated with you, even if they're completely innocent, like me. And I really don't want to find myself in harm's way because of your sticky fingers, thank you ever so much."

So if it wasn't the monks' money, whose was it? True, from time to time people deposit money with monasteries, where it's safe and the host can generally be trusted not to do a flit with it, but in this case that didn't seem likely. Rich merchants tend to use the big houses in the cities, where they can get at their money quickly and easily, and where the security is red hot. In which case, whose money was it, and what was it doing here; and, more to the point, *how long* had it been here—?

"What are we looking for, anyhow?"

I realised we'd reached the front quadrangle. "The library," I said.

"You want to borrow a book?"

Under other circumstances, yes, very much; the monks have a surprisingly good library for a small foundation, but they don't lend except to other houses. But they weren't here, so I could help myself and nobody would ever know. Except, of course, me. "I want to see what's missing," I told him. "That's why you're here."

"Me?" His normal reaction when anything's asked of him. "Don't look at me, I've only been here six weeks. I don't know what books they've got."

Ah well. "You know where the catalogue is. That'll do."

"You didn't need me for that."

Indeed. It's hard to imagine anybody genuinely needing Ekkehard, for any purpose under any circumstances. At his very best he's mildly decorative and moderately entertaining, and his very best comes along about as often as total eclipses of the sun. If you're patient he can be trained to perform simple tasks, and that's about it. "Over there," he said, pointing to a desk in the far corner of the library. "You look things up in the big book, and that gives you the shelf number."

It was a very big book indeed, and Ekkehard moaned like anything as he lugged it round after me. He wanted to go and see if he could find a wheelbarrow, but I wasn't listening. I needed to concentrate.

Needless to say, the catalogue listed the books by author, not by location on the shelves. What I needed to know was what had been taken. I could see the gaps, but I hadn't got a clue what had once filled them. The catalogue was, therefore, no use at all. "Tell you what," I said. "Here's a job for you. I want you to go round, starting at A and working down to Z. Look for each book on the list and see if it's still there."

"Are you nuts? There's hundreds of them."

I gave him a pleasant smile. "Was there something else you need to be doing, or are you at a loose end right now?"

He dropped the catalogue on the floor. "Get one of your monkeys to do it. I don't work for you."

"You can read," I pointed out. "And in return I'll give you a lift off the island. Or you can stay here on your own and wait and see if the bad guys come back. Your choice. And don't call them monkeys, it's not respectful."

He yapped a bit, like a small dog, and then I left him to it. I've put up with a lot from him over the years. Poor old Posidonius would've been only too glad to help out a pal.

Even so, I had a feeling – nothing stronger than that – that knowing which books had been lifted might well cast a glimmer or two of light on the mystery, and I needed all the help with it I could get. Why books, for crying out loud? And who could afford to spare a hundred thousand staurata just to bait a trap? All in all, it was the sort of intriguing, tantalising and highly dangerous enigma that I just love to run away from very fast, if circumstances allow me to do so. Sadly, I didn't have that option. Somebody had our seventeen grand's worth of merchandise, and we had somebody's hundred grand in gold and cash money. Therefore I was involved, and nobody was going to get me out of this mess. I'd have to do it myself.

Unbounded joy and happiness.

While Ekkehard was busy with his simple task I went round the rest of the monastery, every room, every corridor, even up into the roof spaces, which were crawling with big spiders, which I can't be doing with. So far as I could see, nothing had been taken, apart from the people (a substantial *apart from*, I'll grant you), certain books, a limited quantity of food and all our hard-earned stuff. Nor did I find anything in the way of bloodstains, spent arrows, holes in the plasterwork indicative of archery or javelin-throwing; no signs of a fight or a struggle. True, I had a witness. On the other hand, that witness was *Ekkehard*, for crying out loud; Ekkehard with very minor injuries . . .

I did find one thing that shouldn't have been there. Tell you about it sometime.

So I called a departmental heads' meeting on the quarterdeck of the ship. "Time to leave," I said.

Not the most popular statement I've ever made. "What about our stuff?" Carrhasio objected, and Olybrius said something about the hundred thousand staurata.

"Our stuff's gone," I pointed out, "and the abbot's money isn't going anywhere. But we should be. This isn't a good place to be right now, trust me."

"What, and leave all that money?"

"Think," I suggested. "Suppose we take it with us. What a good idea. It'd make it so much easier for anyone who wanted to take it off us. Come on, Olybrius, use your head. We can't defend something like that out in the open, on the road in carts. We'd have to stash it somewhere. Here is the best possible place, even you ought to be able to see that."

"Not if we divide it up and go our separate ways," Polycrates said quietly. "Maybe we should have a vote on that."

"Go ahead," I told him. "It'd be interesting to see how far you'd get, if I'm right and this is all a set-up. But tell me this. Who's going to watch your back and look out for you if you're on your own? At least while we're still together we've got a bit of a chance of looking after ourselves – five hundred, it's not an army but it's a damn sight better than being picked off one by one. Do you really think you can make yourself sufficiently hard to find, walking around with two hundred staurata in your pocket and no way to account for how you got it?"

It wasn't a very good argument, but for some reason my boys have got into the habit of thinking I'm smart, so they assume anything I say is pearls of wisdom until proved otherwise. Nobody said anything, and I took that for unanimous agreement. "There's something very funny going on," I said, "and if you ask me, some bastard is setting us up to take the fall for something nasty. Well? Anyone care to prove me wrong?"

More silence. It really is golden sometimes.

"Right now," I said, "we're a jump ahead of the game. We're the only ones who know where the stuff is. So, if the worst comes to the worst, they can't slaughter the lot of us, because if they do they'll never find it. Another bloody good reason to stick together, if you ask me."

They thought about that, slowly and painfully. Then Gombryas said, "So what do we do now?"

"Business as usual," I replied. "We go away and do our job. We wait and see what happens. Then, when we're absolutely sure it's safe, we come back, divvy up and spend the rest of our lives in comfort and peace. How does that sound, all of you?"

"Hang on," Polycrates said. He was beginning to get on my nerves. "They come back here and find the stuff isn't where they left it—"

"And they look around and see that we're quietly and peacefully carrying on with our daily round, which is exactly what we wouldn't be doing if we'd just made the big score." I paused and beamed at him, as though I'd just said something really clever. "Look, it's not ideal but we've got to play it safe, at least until we've got some glimmering of an idea what's going on. And if you ask me, the best way to give the impression that we haven't stolen their money is not to steal their money. And definitely the smart thing to do is stick together, not split up so they can pick us off one by one."

It bothers me sometimes that they have faith in me. I don't have faith in me, that's for sure. On the other hand, poor bastards, who else have they got?

Another problem: what to do with all the stuff on the ships? Bear in mind, we aren't seafarers. The trip out to the island is as far as we're prepared to go. If the island was now out of bounds, we needed somewhere to stash a large quantity of military equipment; and if good stashing sites were easy to come by, we'd never have bothered with the island in the first place. We also had something of a cashflow problem, since our modest reserve of actual coined money had been in the monastery cellars along with everything else. Food and drink weren't an immediate problem, not after we'd helped ourselves from the buttery, but there was a limit to how much we could cram on board our already overloaded ships, and we were reluctant to throw saleable arms, armour, clothing and camping gear into the sea to make way for jars of flour and barrels of salted herring worth only a fraction of their value, either by weight or by volume.

"Screw it," Gombryas proposed, "let's sail the ships down to Beloisa. We can sell the stuff there and be shot of it, and then we'll have some money."

"You really think we can do that?" I gave him a sad look.

"What's more likely is, we'll run the ships onto rocks and they'll sink and we'll drown. Also, we'll get fifty trachy in the stauraton at Beloisa if we're lucky. What we need is somewhere with big sheds or barns."

"Such as?"

I hate it when other people are right. There was no such as. "How far is Beloisa from here, anyhow?"

He shrugged. "Search me," he said. "All I know is, it's on the coast somewhere."

Among the things not stolen from the library was a map. "That's Beloisa there," I said, jabbing at it with my finger.

"That's not far."

Gombryas isn't good with maps. "It's a hundred miles," I said. "That's at least two days, assuming the wind's in the right direction."

"Is it?"

"Not a clue. Do we know anyone who knows about boats?"

He thought about it. "Actually," he said, "yes."

So back we went to the mainland. Strange how much difference direction makes. All of us had sailed from the mainland to the island loads of times; none of us had ever done it the other way round, because the monastery lay brothers always did the sailing for us on the return trip, in return for what we'd always felt was a rip-off fee. Turns out they'd earned their money. The currents and the winds and all that nonsense were completely different going the other way, and how we survived and actually got the ships safely to land I have no idea. At any rate, it served the useful purpose of persuading the lads that we weren't qualified to sail all the way to Beloisa without professional help, so it was a good thing really.

Gombryas, as it turned out, had a friend. I'm not sure why

I was so surprised, because even the unlikeliest people have friends. Gombryas' chum, a fellow body parts collector, had a cousin who caught sardines for a living. He (the cousin) wasn't prepared to help us, but he knew people who were, and after a couple of days kicking our heels on the dockside we found ourselves blessed with the company of a very old man, his two monosyllabic sons and two dozen ancillary staff who looked as though they'd been slung out of hell for antisocial behaviour: our crew, who'd sail us to Beloisa for a modest consideration, unless they decided to eat us instead.

Ekkehard was on deck as the crew slouched aboard. He was leaning on the rail looking moody, like the villain in a nautical melodrama. "Well," I said hopefully. "It was nice bumping into you again. Take care of yourself, and I hope things pan out all right for you."

Ekkehard gave me a look. "You what?"

"With whatever you decide to do next," I said. "Will you stick with the religion thing, do you think, or try something else?"

"Fuck that," said Ekkehard. "I'm coming with you."

"No," I said.

"Yes."

"Why in God's name would you want to do something like that?" I said. "It's a shit life doing what we do. You'd hate it."

"Oh sure. What about my share?"

"Your share of what?"

He gave me another look: the previous one, with interest. "Come off it," he said. "Anyway, you said we had to stick together." He assumed his cunning look. It's not very good. "You can't afford to leave me behind," he said. "I know where it's hidden."

For crying out loud. "No, you don't."

I'd given specific instructions to keep him out of the way, so he wouldn't know. "Fine," I said. "You can come if you like. You'll hate it."

"Don't be so sure. I can turn my hand to pretty much anything."

I managed not to laugh. "If you say so," I said. "Just remember. No whining and you do exactly as you're told. Got that?"

He actually looked hurt. "Of course," he said. "Goes without saying."

It wasn't two days to Beloisa; it was six. We got blown off course by an unexpected wind and were halfway to Blemya by the time our so-called expert crew managed to get the ships back under control. Then we had a whole day just sitting in the middle of the open sea, before some other wind condescended to blow and we were able to crawl back, zigzag fashion, to where we should have started off from in the first place.

The not-going-anywhere day was useful. I spent half of it slowly and painfully coming back to life after my marathon vomiting session, and the other half going over the list of stolen books, beautifully written out in Ekkehard's incredibly elegant handwriting.

It was one of those documents that conveys a vast amount of information and leaves you knowing far less than you did before you read it. According to Ekkehard, the thieves had taken forty-two books from a library of five hundred and sixteen volumes. They'd left behind six books which I know for a fact were worth a fortune: three missals, two breviaries and a psalter, wedding gifts from Sighvat III to his second wife, all profusely illuminated by the leading artists of the day, et cetera. How these outstandingly rare, beautiful, historic, valuable items ended up at a dump like the Silver Apple nobody seemed to know, not even my pal the abbot, but they were certified genuine with impeccable provenances, and I know for a fact he'd been offered a lot of money for them by other houses. If they'd been missing, that would be all the explanation you'd need for the assault and the wholesale slaughter of all witnesses. But they weren't missing. They hadn't been touched.

Instead, the raiders had selected a fairly wide range of secular technical literature: books on architecture, agriculture, agronomy, astronomy, mining and metallurgy, economic and monetary theory, forestry, shipbuilding, navigation and the art of war. About half the titles I recognised, mostly because they used to sit, lonely and unapproachable as a stylite on top of a column, on the upper shelves of my father's library when I was a kid. Not, therefore, especially rare or valuable. If you wanted a copy, you wouldn't have to sail to a remote island and sack a monastery; you could simply buy one, from any half-decent City copying house, and for considerably less than a hundred thousand staurata. The rest of the titles on the list I didn't know, but they sounded very much the same sort of thing; So-and-so on This and That, the True Mirror of Such-and-such, the Discovery of Whatever. No religious or literary titles, nothing devotional or fun. Tools, basically, like saws and chisels and files. Things you might need in order to do something.

"Well?" Ekkehard said.

"Thanks," I replied. "You did a good job."

He ignored all that. "What do you make of it?"

"I don't know. What do you think?"

He assumed his wise face. "Hard to say," he said. "I assume you noticed, they're all Western authors."

No, actually I hadn't. "You spotted that."

"Well, it's obvious. Sort of begs the question, doesn't it?"

Indeed. They write perfectly good technical manuals in the East, in Antecyrene, Sashan and Echmen, and nearly all of them have been translated into Robur, and the translations were still there on the Silver Apple shelves. "What do *you* make of it?"

He shrugged. "Why steal what you've already got? The bastards must be Easterners."

"You reckon."

"Stands to reason. Any fool can see that."

And he'd been doing so well. Never mind. Never rely on someone else to do your thinking for you, especially when it matters. I was saved from further pointless discussion by a sudden lurch of the planks under our feet. The wind got up and for the next few hours both of us were too busy suffering to bother ourselves about books, Easterners or anything not directly connected with navigation or misery.

Even so.

Beloisa: there's a name to conjure with. Bet you anything you like, the first picture that comes into your mind when you hear it is palm trees swaying in the wind, followed by bright light, blue skies, pavements so hot they burn your feet, then the smell of spices, foul water, shit and roses. It's the sort of place it's impossible to be lukewarm about. You love it, or you hate it, or both at the same time. Above all, though, whenenever someone mentions Beloisa you can't help listening, because anything that happens there is likely to be relevant. Important things happen there. It's a place that *matters*.

Personally, I can take it or leave it alone. Nothing good has ever happened to me there, but nothing catastrophically disastrous either. I can walk the streets in relative peace of mind because there are no active warrants for my arrest, but I can't relax for a moment, in case someone recognises me – scrub that; substitute, in case someone mistakes me for somebody else. You can make a lot of money there very quickly and easily, but it's even easier to lose every trachy you've got, and Beloisa is a horrible place to be poor, trust me.

Eight major governments have full-time purchasing agencies in Beloisa, so if you're in my line of work and you've got stuff to sell and there's no big fair on, Beloisa's where you've got to go. I really don't like that, because it means the buyers set the prices. Also, instead of cash money you get given a piece of paper with a fancy seal at the bottom, which you then have to take along to an embassy or high commission, where you spend a day hanging about in porticos or on steps leading to a magnificent closed gate until someone's useless nephew condescends to come out and talk to you; at which point, if you're lucky, you exchange one piece of sealed paper for another, which you take to a different part of the building, where's there's invariably a queue winding round the block. In the fullness of time you get given a draft on an actual bank, the Knights or the Poor Sisters, which you can then turn relatively easily into clinking money. The hell with that. You get better prices at the fairs, and the customer pays you cash on the spot. Trouble is, there are only eight fairs each year and the next one wasn't for nine weeks.

Another thing I don't like about Beloisa, though this time it's just me being unreasonable: doing business there is no fun. At a fair, you sit behind a stall under a canopy with a drink in one hand and a bowl of candied figs or stuffed olives in front of you, and people you know come up and pass the time of day, tell you the latest hot news, who's died, who's been arrested, who's made the big score, all that. Buyers bargain, haggle, try it on, you cheat them and they cheat you, and for eight days in every year we all feel like we're part of one big happy battlefield-scavenger family. You can kid yourself into thinking you feel good about what you do in an environment like that. You can even pretend that people like Ormus Asvogel or Valentine Philopoemen are your friends and you're pleased to see them. They buy you a drink, you buy them a drink, you spend a pleasant half-hour together saying harsh things about various generals and Sister Stauracia, and then you go back to your stall and sell a load of old junk to some fool for silly money. That's how it is at fairs. There's a buzz. I quite like them.

In Beloisa, by contrast, the punters don't come to you; you go to them. You show an inventory to a clerk, who makes you an offer; take it or leave it. You leave it and go next door and an identical clerk makes you an identical offer. No excitement, no crack; no humanity.

Still, needs must. I unloaded our entire haul from the last campaign on a bored-looking clerk with tufts of white hair growing out of his ears, sealed the paperwork, got up to leave and literally bumped into Chusro Asvogel, who grinned at me.

"Hello," he said. "In a hurry?"

"In Beloisa?"

He laughed. "Hold on while I see the man, and I'll buy you a beer."

We aren't friends exactly. "Sure," I said, and went and sat on a bench in a corridor. A few minutes later, Chusro came back, holding his bit of paper. "I've been hearing things about you," he said.

"Have you really?"

"All sorts of interesting things. You can tell me if they're true or not."

Next door was the Faith Justified, which used to be the old Curtain Theatre before it burned down. People have drunk the beer in the Faith and lived to tell the tale, but why push your luck? Chusro was buying so I asked for a small peach brandy.

"So what's all this," he said, "about you ripping off the tax ship from Calza?"

I stared at him. "You what?"

He studied me, as though trying to figure out where the piece left over was supposed to go. "I thought it wasn't your style when I heard about it."

"Too bloody right. What are they saying?"

He shrugged. "You and your men in five galleys robbed the revenue ship somewhere off Cape Ousa. Apparently you scuttled it with all hands and got away with a hundred thousand in gold and valuable works of art."

"Where in God's name did you hear that?"

"Oh, here and there." He looked at me some more. "I thought it couldn't be right, because everybody knows about you and boats. On the other hand, for a hundred thousand staurata—"

"Hang on," I said. "Did it actually happen? I mean, did someone really rob the taxes?"

"Oh, yes," Chusro said. "And sank the ship and drowned all the crew. The Vesani authorities are making ever such a fuss about it." He sipped his beer. "That's another thing that didn't sound right to me, slaughtering the crew. You're far too goody-goody for that."

"And people are saying—"

He nodded. "I was surprised to see you here," he said, "in public, in the open. You want to keep your head down for a bit, until it's all sorted out. I mean, you're probably all right in Beloisa, but even so. There's bound to be a reward, and you know what people are like."

Indeed. I'd never heard that the Asvogel boys went in for bounty hunting, but even so. I glanced round quickly, just to make absolutely sure I knew where the doors and windows were. "When was this supposed to have happened?"

"Now you're asking. Let me think." He did the full pantomime, pulling faces, stroking his chin. "They were talking about it in the customs house at Lonazep, but I don't think anybody mentioned it at Borlasc fair. Ten days ago, maybe less than that. Why, where were you?"

Ten days ago? I counted on my fingers. Wonderful. I had an alibi, but my witness was Sister Stauracia.

"Ah," Chusro said, when I told him. "That's awkward. She doesn't like you."

"No, but even so." I thought about it. "More to the point, I've got Prince Erysichthon. There's no way anybody could've got from the middle of the desert to the coast and then out to sea in that time."

"Hadn't you heard? Erysichthon won't be vouching for anybody, not any more."

Oh. Ah well. I felt a pang for Gombryas, missing out on the complete set. "Well," I said, "the stuff speaks for itself, doesn't it? If we were there clearing that battlefield, we couldn't have been out in the middle of the ocean ripping off revenue ships."

"The stuff you've just sold and delivered, and therefore haven't got any more."

My head was starting to hurt. "Oh, come on," I said. "You know me. I don't do that sort of stuff."

He held up both hands. "I believe you," he said. "So does everyone who knows you. The thing is, though, there's an awful lot of people out there who don't. I'd watch your step for a bit if I were you. You might want to make yourself hard to find till it's all blown over."

"I might just do that," I said. "Thanks for the drink."

I went straight back to the ships. "We're leaving," I said.

Gombryas looked at me. "You got the money."

"Sort of."

Which was true. A sealed government requisition is as good as cash money anywhere, if you aren't fussed about a two-thirds discount. But what did that matter? We had a hundred thousand staurata; we could afford to be generous. We rounded up the expensive crew, paid them silly money and set off for the south coast of Antecyrene, where I'd bought the rights to a rather promising little war in the western highlands.

We almost missed the war. That's how it goes in Antecyrene. They have wars there the way they have rain in the mountains: simple geography. For some reason the Invincible Sun thought it'd be a good idea to cram a tiny country mostly composed of barren hillsides in between the three biggest, richest, most aggressive nations on earth. Then, just to make it unequivocally clear that He's got a sense of humour, He sent the Antecyrenaeans to live there. Result: little wars, three hundred and sixty days every year (the other five are religious festivals; the Antecyrenaeans are red hot on religion).

Little wars, quickly over. This one was a minor spat between two nephews of the elderly, childless Grand Duke. We love

Antecyrenaean wars, because all the equipment they use is provided free of charge by the neighbouring superpowers by way of military aid to the various factions – nothing but the very best, the latest pattern, all brand-new, and Antecyrenaean tribal warriors are past masters at living to fight another day. They dump all that heavy kit and scoot as soon as the going gets rough, leaving their Blemyan and Sashan officers yelling blue murder at them from distant hilltops.

We met a couple of them – you're supposed to call them military advisers – on our way to the battlefield: Sashan, a couple of colonels and a captain. They had that dazed look that you come to expect from highly trained career soldiers who've had dealings with the Antecyrenaeans. "Which way did they go?" I asked.

"Everywhere," a colonel replied, waving his arms vaguely. "One minute they were lined up in a textbook porcupine formation, the next there we were, feeling lonely. Bastards," he added with feeling. "God knows why we bother."

I nodded. "Who won?"

"No idea. Good hunting."

"Thank you," I said and they went on their way, magnificent on their thoroughbred milk-white stallions. We backtracked their hoofprints in the sand until we came to a sort of dip, where we found the best part of a thousand Type Nine scale cuirasses, ditto Type Four helmets, ditto Sashan standard issue figure-of-eight heavy infantry shields, pristine condition, most of them with their waxed leather covers still on. You'd have thought the victorious enemy might have condescended to pick up some of this valuable materiel, but why bother? Nice men from Blemya or the Vesani Republic would be along any day now to give them stuff just as good, and they deliver.

Once we'd found that, no great rush to search out the actual scene of conflict. A glance at the sky – they have kites instead of crows in Antecyrene; same principle – told us where the bodies were, a hundred or so, mostly spear wounds in the back, foot soldiers ridden down by cavalry while running away. Even a Type Nine (far and away the best mass-production body armour ever issued) won't stand up to the momentum of one ton of galloping horse, concentrated into a needle-sharp lance head; but no problem, you just snip out the ruptured scale and sew in a replacement and there you are, good as new and no harm done. Carrhasio and his crew had a thin time of it, because the dead men inside the luxury shells were just peasant levies, no gold earrings or sapphire good luck charms, just a few religious texts scratched onto bits of broken pot and worn next to the skin. No boots: the military advisers issue them, but the Antecyrenaeans are used to going barefoot, so they throw them away.

Their religion is incredibly fussy about dead bodies, of all the silly things to get worked up about. They believe in a Day of Judgement, on which all the dead will arise incorruptible; cremation is, therefore, a very bad thing, because who wants to spend their eternal hereafter as a handful of powdery grey ash? Their first time in the country, the Asvogel boys couldn't be doing with local superstition and burned the bodies anyway, which is why they no longer get any work in Antecyrene. Instead, you have to bury them, no less than six feet four inches deep, wrapped in linen, facing towards the Holy City, and the proper mass for the dead has to be recited before you can start filling in. To make sure we did it properly, half a dozen priests came out from the city and stood over us, watching like hawks, even though properly speaking the dead men were the enemy.

They charged us seven staurata for reading the mass, then went away again.

For some reason I hadn't yet told the others about what we were supposed to have done to the tax ship. I guess I didn't want to worry them unnecessarily, not until we were in the middle of a desert, where they'd think twice about running away. It's all right for the locals, who know where the wells are, but foreigners in Antecyrene need to stick together.

"That's crazy," Olybrius said, after I'd broken the news. "We didn't do it. We were miles away at the time."

"Yes," I said, "we were. Anybody care to suggest how we can prove it?"

Awkward silence; no reply. "You think we're being set up," Carrhasio said.

"It does look that way," I said.

"Why? Why the hell bother?" Gombryas put in. "If somebody's big and nasty enough to do all this cunning shit, he could just cut our throats on the road somewhere and have done with it. Nobody's going to make a fuss about us. Everybody thinks we're dogshit."

"Yes," I said. "So, what does that tell you?"

Gombryas isn't interested in scientific analysis. "They're not setting us up just to get rid of us," Polycrates said. "We're supposed to take the blame for somebody else."

I snapped my finger and thumb together and pointed to him. "Give the man a jar of olives, yes. Something big and complicated is going on, and we've been picked on to carry the can. Now, does anybody have any views about that?"

Polycrates was scowling at me. "You waited till we're all in the middle of the desert to tell us."

"Yes."

"Swell." He looked round at the others, didn't like what he saw. "I told you, we should've shared out the money before we left the island. Now we're really screwed."

I agreed with him on both points. "Don't be stupid," I said. "We're still way ahead of the game. One, only we know where the money is. Two, we're in Antecyrene."

"Yes, I noticed that. What about it?"

"Diplomatically sensitive Antecyrene," I said, "where the Vesani daren't make a grab for us, for fear of pissing off the locals."

Polycrates laughed. "Bullshit," he said. "Yes, there's no extradition. Doesn't mean they can't jump out on us from behind a sand dune and whisk us away to a waiting ship."

"Of course not," I said. "But there's five hundred of us, so they'd need a small army. You can't bring armies into Antecyrene without risking a world war. It's the arsehole of Creation, but it's safe. As safe as anywhere can be, under the circumstances."

"So that's the plan, is it?" Rutilian said. "We stay holed up in fucking Antecyrene."

"I didn't say it was a nice plan," I said. "Just better than the alternatives."

"We'll starve," someone else put in. "We're nearly out of cash money, and nobody's going to buy this shit in Antecyrene; we'd have to take it somewhere else before we could sell it. So there's no—"

"Quite right," I said. "Which is why I brought *him*."

I pointed, somewhat melodramatically, at Ekkehard. He's smart enough in his way, but I swear he hadn't seen it coming. He stared at me, just as everybody else started yelling.

"He's not one of us," I explained, as soon as I could make

myself heard. "Nobody knows he's with us. He'll go and sell the stuff and bring us the money, and everything will be fine."

"Now just a—" Ekkehard started to say, but got no further because I gave him a clip round the ear. I had a stone in the palm of my hand at the time. He went nice and quiet, which was what I wanted.

"Yes," I said, "I know. But we can trust him, because he's a friend of mine, I've known him for a long time, and he knows what I'll do to him if he pisses off with our stuff. Also," I added, "I'll go with him, just to make sure."

They didn't like that one bit. In fact, as far as I could see, I was the only person present who didn't absolutely hate the idea. That made eight against and one in favour, so I exercised my casting vote and the motion was carried. I call it nuanced democracy. Just like the traditional version, only better.

3

"You're out of your mind," Ekkehard told me.

I was inclined to agree with him. "No I'm not," I said. "I know exactly what I'm doing."

"Bullshit. You haven't got a clue what's going on, so you're just blundering about in the dark, and you're going to get us both—"

"Shut up."

One good thing about Antecyrene is, you can get practically anywhere from there. Don't fancy either of the two major ports? No problem. There are fishing villages all along the coast where you can buy a ride on a boat as far as Scona, which is only four hours away, in good weather. From Scona you can go where the hell you like and nobody will able to keep up with you, for the same reason it's impossible to keep track of a single bee in a swarm. True, the boat you hire in Antecyrene will be a smuggler, and the penalty for being caught smuggling is death. But the Antecyrenaean royal navy consists of two elderly sloops, one of which has a mast, the other of which has a sail.

Antecyrene gets a large proportion of its desperately needed foreign exchange from smuggling. Not a problem.

"I don't know why you make such a fuss about sailing," Ekkehard said, as the coastline faded behind us. "I've been on ships hundreds of times and I've never once felt ill."

"Is that a fact?"

He nodded cheerfully. A fresh breeze began to blow. I tightened my grip on the rail. "Yes," he said, "it is. It's not something I boast about, because it's not exactly a virtue or an accomplishment. I didn't spend ten years studying day and night how not to chuck my guts up on boats; it's just the way I am. It doesn't bother me. Never has."

"Good for you."

He took a deep breath, threw his arms wide; picture of vigorous health. "I know what you're up to," he said. "It's obvious."

Hint for you. If you've got to do two things that are sure to make you profoundly unhappy, do them both at the same time. Spending time with Ekkehard; being on a boat. There's a level at which the misery maxes out and the surplus just runs away, like water from an overflowing barrel. "So what am I up to?"

"Oh, come on. You're going to double back to the island and steal the treasure." He grinned, and the sun flashed on his perfect teeth. "You probably made up all that crap about tax boats and the Vesani. I'm amazed those idiots believed you."

One kick in exactly the right place and he'd be over the side and in the water. Unfortunately he can swim. "No," I said, "I didn't make that up."

"Not sure I believe you. Doesn't matter. We hire a winch on Scona, then off we go. Just for once, I think you may have got something right. I'm amazed you were able to sucker those clowns into letting you go, but—"

The ship lurched. I hate sea travel.

"No," I said, "you've got that all wrong. No winch."

He shot me a look of pure hatred. "You know what," he said, "I've had about enough of you. I know exactly what you're up to, and trying to kid me is just insulting. And don't you dare try and cheat me out of my half, because if you do, so help me—"

One kick, one splash, a massive weight off my shoulders. Sure he could swim, but we were a long way from the shore and it takes ages to stop a ship the size of the one we were on and turn it around, even assuming anybody heard his cries for help – if I timed it just right, when everybody was up the other end of the deck, no problem at all. And I didn't really need him for anything. The idea was, he'd be useful cover, something to hide behind as I went about my business. I guess it's something to do with his profession, but when you're with Ekkehard people don't tend to notice you. Instead they're looking at him, this enormous human being with the loud, carrying voice and the expressive gestures. If you want to sneak past a guard or slip something quietly into your pocket while everyone's looking the other way, Ekkehard makes it all so easy. And if you want not to be noticed, you can practically guarantee it if you've got him standing next to you. So: useful, yes, but essential, no. I've got a lifetime's experience in slipping quietly along, like oil seeping into a rusty hinge. In fairytales they make a big deal out of cloaks and hats that make you invisible, but don't bother getting me one for my birthday; I'd rather have socks. I don't need anything like that. It's one of my very few talents.

Even so. If being incredibly annoying was a capital offence, we'd have queues for the gallows ten miles long and nobody left to do any work. I granted Ekkehard a last-minute reprieve, for which he wasn't the slightest bit grateful. "It's not like that,"

I said patiently. "I'm not going to steal the money, because I think it was put there for me to steal and I'm not stupid. And if you try anything, I promise you, I'll cut your throat. Got that?"

He gave me a startled look. Deep down he's a bit scared of me, God only knows why. "Yes, all right, there's no need to be like that about it. So what's the big idea? You must be out of your mind going out and about, if you really think—"

"I think," I said, "that somebody's playing funny games with me, and I don't like it. Fine if they want to play games, but I want to know the rules first."

Startled turned to disaste. "So why bring me into it? Sorry to be personal, but you don't care who you drag into the shit with you."

"Because you aren't one of my known associates, and nobody's looking for you. Are they?"

"Me? God, no." A bitter recollection troubled him. "Nobody wants *me*, you can hardly give me away. That's what comes of working with Andronica. You know what that bloody woman said to me? I was upstaging her. Me, of all people. All I had to do in Act Two was just stand there and listen, so that's precisely what I did. I didn't move a muscle, I didn't *breathe*. And she says—"

She had my sympathy. "Fine," I said. "So you joined a monastery."

"I've had it with the profession," he said. "It's ever since women started getting into management. You get some doll-faced halfwit, she spends her life being told how wonderful she is, next thing she decides she knows how to run a theatre. What do you expect?"

Female actor-managers run two-thirds of the theatres in the Vesani Republic; the ones, oddly enough, who actually make money. Ekkehard has a positive genius for missing the point. "Nobody's looking for you," I said. "That's good."

"You want me to do something, don't you?"

I smiled at him. "Nothing dreadful," I said. "Just hang around in bars listening, maybe ask a few artless questions."

"About what?"

"The tax ship, for one thing. I want to know if it really did get ripped off, or whether Chusro Asvogel's playing merry japes on me."

He gave me his wise look. "Would you say he's a friend?"

A good question, deserving a considered answer. "On balance," I said, "yes. But that doesn't mean anything. I'd probably say you were a friend, too."

That got me a ferocious scowl. "Would he deliberately deceive you so as to put you in harm's way?"

"Soon as look at me. But that doesn't necessarily mean he just did. He could just as easily have been telling the truth. So, we have to find out for ourselves."

"*I* have to find out."

"Yes."

For which purpose, we'd come to the right place. If you want information, go to Scona. If you want to find out about the big things – does God exist, is homicide ever justifiable, how do you solve quadratic equations, what were the underlying causes of the Third Social War, what's the position on conflict of jurisdictions in Echmen civil law – you go up the hill to the university, where they keep the sum of human knowledge cooped up in a converted castle, with guards on every door so it can't escape. If you want to know what's going on in the real world, there are sixty-seven drinking establishments on the seafront where you'll eventually find someone who knows the answer to your question, if you don't get your throat cut first.

Being an actor, Ekkehard spends a large proportion of his life in bars. He's at home there, like a shark in water. Doesn't matter whether he's leaning on the counter or sitting at a table in a corner, people come up and talk to him. He's a good listener, another side benefit of his trade. People tell him things without even realising they're doing it. For some reason I always put strangers' backs up, but Ekkehard is just a friendly bottomless pit into which information falls and is swallowed up. He smiles and nods and listens, and from time to time they buy him drinks. Just goes to prove what I always say: everybody's good at something.

"Yes," he told me later, "the ship bringing the tax money from Calza back to the Republic was attacked somewhere in the open sea between Auris and the Nine Fingers; they don't know precisely where. Whoever attacked it scuttled it with all hands. Presumably they took the money, but since there are no witnesses—"

"Hang on," I said. "If there're no witnesses, how the hell do they know?"

He shrugged. "That point wasn't addressed," he said. "One of the pirates confessed, or a prophet saw it all in a dream. I don't bloody well know, do I? Nobody I talked to was interested in any of that; they just stated it as an accepted fact, all right?"

"So who do they—?"

"You," he said, with a faint grin. "Specifically by name, Saevus Corax. And there's a price on your head. Three thousand staurata. And, yes," he added, "it did cross my mind. But I thought, no, he's my friend, even though he doesn't act like it a lot of the time. I said I'd never heard of you, so they told me all about you."

"Right. So?"

He shook his head. "You don't want to know what people are saying about you. Maybe it's true, I don't know. The bottom line is, you're not popular."

"Why? What did I ever do?"

"Plenty." He was enjoying himself. "Did you know that you regularly kill wounded soldiers on the battlefield just so you can render their bodies down for tallow? That's weird. For one thing, I don't see how it's cost effective. I mean, there's charcoal, plus all the specialised equipment, great big coppers and ladles and God knows what, and then there's transport—"

"What else?"

"Let's see. Oh yes. You start wars just so you can get the salvage. People don't like that one bit."

"Fine. How do I do that exactly?"

He grinned. "I was wondering about that. I mean, you're nobody. How can you manipulate international diplomacy? But apparently you do. You must be smarter than you look." He yawned ostentatiously; enough fun for one day. "You know what I think?"

"Go on."

"I think," he said, in his beautiful voice, "that someone's been going round telling people all this shit. It's not the sort of stuff they'd have made up for themselves; they haven't got the imagination. Embroidered a bit, naturally, but someone deliberately put the speck of grit in the oyster. Also, how come so many people have suddenly heard of you? Yes, you robbed the tax ship, but you're still nobody. But everybody knows everything you've been doing for years. Therefore," he concluded magnificently, "someone told them."

"All right," I said. "Who?"

"Ah." He smiled. "There you have me. Try as I might, I can't figure it out. Why would anybody go to such inordinate lengths and such eye-watering expense just to victimise *you?*"

Who indeed?

I confess, I haven't been entirely straight with you. Everything I've told you so far is true, but maybe not quite the whole truth. The fact is, I haven't always been in the salvage business. I come from a good family, well-respected—

Which is just like the melodramas I used to write for the Rose, a few years ago. They're always the same – audiences know what they like south of the river, and if they don't get it they throw things – and one of the essential ingredients is the honest, fearless working lad (farmboy, mill-hand, Jolly Jack Tar) who loves a lass above his station, but that's fine because right at the end of Act Five, when the shit's hit the fan and our hero's standing there with the noose round his neck, it turns out that he's really the long-lost heir of the Duke of Somewhere Else, whereupon all is forgiven and everything ends happily, curtain falls, delighted public drifts away to eat sausages and get drunk. It always bothered me slightly that the audience, made up of farmboys, mill-hands and Jolly Jack Tars, so desperately needs the hero to be a toff in disguise, as opposed to a genuine nobody like themselves, but I guess it makes sense, in their terms. You don't go to a show to question the accepted order, because all that would achieve would be to send you home disaffected and grumpy. The point of a show is to reassure you that the accepted order is all right really, because, after all, the hero did get the girl in the end, and, who knows, this time tomorrow you too might turn out to be the heir to a million acres of prime arable land. That's a happy thought, and well worth the price of admission.

The thing of it is, in my case it's true. Write what you know, they always tell you, so I did, up to a point. I wrote stirring tales of honest, fearless working lads who turn out to be young noblemen who made one silly little mistake and had to leave home in a hurry; the difference being, at the Rose in Act Five the hero's father shows up at the last minute and forgives him. The last time I heard about my father was when he doubled the price he'd put on my head, from twenty to forty thousand staurata. No wonder the critics used to say my endings were always the weakest part of the play. I had real trouble imagining a forgiving father, and I guess it showed.

But you don't want to hear about all that. Suffice it to say, I have enemies in high places. Not just people who don't like me very much; your actual eat-my-flesh-and-drink-my-blood enemies. Nothing but the best for yours truly.

"It's like God," I told him, as we sat in the shade of a lime tree outside the Garden of Innocence on Cripplegate.

He looked at me over the rim of his glass. "God?"

"Yup," I said. "Step one: ascertain whether God exists. Step two: figure out who He is. Because it's no good spending your life devoutly worshipping the Invincible Sun if God turns out to be the Eternal Flame. That's not just useless, that's counterproductive. You'd be better off staying atheist, because then at least you could plead ignorance."

"I have no idea what you're talking about."

Ekkehard is not the sharpest knife in the drawer. "The

people who are out to get me," I said. "How I go about avoiding them depends on who they are. Until I know that, I can't decide on a course of action."

"You mean, you don't know where to run to."

"Partly." A priest walked past, chin on chest, muttering. I turned my head away. "If running away is the best way to proceed. Or maybe it's exactly what they want me to do."

"It's what I'd do in your shoes."

"I'm not you."

"Granted." I was boring him. "So, do what they least expect."

"Assuming they know me well enough to have expectations."

He yawned. "Admit it," he said, "you haven't got a clue." He finished his drink. "The way I see it, you can sit there agonising about it till someone recognises you and turns you in, or you can get on the first ship to Mesvatan. Though," he added cheerfully, "they're probably watching all the ports."

"You wouldn't like it in Mesvatan."

"I have no intention—"

"Where I go, you go."

"You must be kidding."

I shook my head. "Sorry," I said. "Your own silly fault. You shouldn't have been so nosy when we were hiding the money."

"That's stupid. That's like saying you don't trust me. I resent that."

"Of course I trust you. I trust you to behave in a certain way. It's my job to see that you aren't tempted beyond your capacity to resist."

"Arsehole."

I smiled. "Your job," I said, "is to find out more information, so we can make an informed decision."

"Really. Is that all?"

I nodded. "Piece of cake," I said.

There was a problem with this approach – several, actually, but the most pressing difficulty was lack of funds. If Ekkehard was going to weasel out information by buying people drinks, he needed money, and I was running low.

The idea had been to sell the stuff we'd collected in Antecyrene – find a dealer, show him an inventory, arrange for him to collect in return for a substantial discount, he hands over a bill of exchange on the Knights or the Poor Sisters, we have funds, safe, easy, happens every day of the week. But if I was right, we couldn't do that. We might as well hire a brass band and march through the streets under a banner saying *Hey, It's Us.* Therefore, if we had to have money, I needed to get it another way.

Brought up in the lap of indolent luxury and profusely educated by the finest itinerant scholars money could buy, I only know three ways of earning a living: writing plays, scavenging battlefields, and the other way. There aren't any theatres on Scona and, anyhow, I didn't have time. Ekkehard asked me, why in hell didn't you bring along a few small items of value from what you picked up in Antecyrene – rings, earrings, gold-handled daggers, all that shit? Because, as I think I mentioned, the dead bodies were all peasants and didn't have anything like that. Also, I didn't think.

The other way, therefore. Fortuitously, I'm good at it.

The easiest way of doing it the other way is to jump out on someone in a dark alley and stick a knife next to or into his neck, but that's a bit too tactile for me, and it gets you noticed. I prefer stealing from God. He's good for the money, He's promised to forgive me provided I repent afterwards, and He leaves His valuable possessions lying about with deplorably lax security. Furthermore, He's got so much stuff that His servants and ministers have trouble keeping track of it all, so there's a reasonable chance that you'll be out of the jurisdiction before they even realise it's gone. Blessed be the name of the Lord.

Take, for example, the Needle Eye Temple in Scona. For six hundred years pious men and women have gone there to pray; for peace of mind, recovery from sickness, success in business ventures, forgiveness of egregious sins, you name it. One reliable way of getting His attention is to dedicate an object (it's got to be precious metal or it doesn't work) that symbolises your request – a silver leg for gout, a gold model of a ship for mercantile prosperity, so on and so forth. They're called votives, though strictly speaking that means a gratitude offering after your prayer's been granted. But on Scona everyone wants cash up front, even God.

Everybody does it. Four hundred and sixty-something years ago, one of my illustrious ancestors came to Scona and dedicated an icon, painted by the immortal Theudibert before he was famous, in the nave of the Needle Eye. My ancestor wanted God to bless his plan to invade an island off the Olbian coast, loot the moveable property, enslave the population and set up a plantation growing citrus fruits for the City trade; and God, much to everyone's surprise, duly smiled on the venture and our family got seriously rich.

When I first visited Scona, many years ago, the first thing I did was go to the Needle Eye to see if our icon was still there. It was, but I had a hell of a job finding it. Eventually, with the help of a couple of elderly vergers, I tracked it down. It was hard to find because two hundred years after my ancestor donated it, someone hung up a suit of golden armour right next to it, and our icon, which is only eight inches by six, was completely obscured by the wing of a solid gold couter.

Well, then. Hardly stealing at all. God reneged on the bargain three hundred years later by inciting the slaves to rebel, so we didn't have the plantation any more; and besides, I happen to think monuments that glorify slavery and oppression are repugnant and ought to be removed.

They lock the doors at night, but the lock's five hundred years old. I made a pick and a wrench out of a couple of brooch pins, took me three minutes; less than that to finagle the lock itself, and I was inside.

They keep lamps burning all night in the nave, because God is Light and never goes out. They're not big lamps, but all that shiny metal reflects His presence magnificently, making my job that much easier. Our icon was eight feet off the ground, but there was a massive ivory lectern in the form of a spread-winged eagle, just the right height to stand on. I lifted the couter out of the way, popped the icon in my pocket, job done. I hadn't even disturbed the dust. I locked up carefully as I left, because there are dishonest people on Scona.

No chance of selling the icon itself, because any fool could recognise the work of the immortal Theudibert, and that would beg the question of how I'd come by it. But the frame was twenty-four carat, with twelve small rubies and six sapphires, which came out quite easily.

"You robbed a temple," Ekkehard said. "How could you do that?"

"There's a knack to it," I said.

With his massive forefinger he stirred the little heap of

gold cubes I'd painstakingly hacked the frame into. Nobody could possibly figure out what it used to be. "Vandalism," said Ekkehard. "An irreplaceable cultural artefact, four centuries old, and you—"

"Bling," I told him. "Showy and vulgar, just what you'd expect from my family. Also a blatant attempt to bribe God, which is unethical." I peered at the heap. Was it my imagination, or was it slightly smaller than it had been? "That's all right," I said. "Keep it."

"Keep what?"

To dispose of a scrap gold on Scona, you go to the Aqueduct. Under the third arch from the left (coming up Haymarket from the Bridewell end) you'll find a bunch of expensively dressed men huddled in the damp gloom sitting on packing cases, loomed over by serious muscle. They've been there as long as I can remember and they have no competitors. I have no idea what nationality they are or what language they speak; words aren't necessary. You put the stuff down on a packing case. They pick out a random chunk and drop it in a small glass bowl full of spirits of nitre. Assuming it passes the test, they weigh the rest with a pair of exquisite brass scales and put a selection of coins down in front of you; take it or leave it. You take it and go, and nobody gets hurt.

Twenty staurata for a gold frame easily worth thirty-five. Twenty staurata, on the other hand, is a seriously large sum of money, which meant I could keep the gemstones in reserve and not have to brave the jewellers' quarter, where the locals have suspicious minds and a good eye for faces. The icon itself – well, I got rid of it in what I hoped was a suitable way. No need to clutter up this stage of my narrative with superfluous detail.

I gave Ekkehard five of the twenty staurata. "Don't you trust me?" he said.

"You keep saying that."

He whined some more, then left. He was going to try the bars in Fourways and the Linen Yard – a long shot, because that's where you go to hire a very specific sort of industrial contractor, and I had my doubts about whether Ekkehard could play that kind of part successfully. He's the right size and build, but there's no escaping the fact that he made his reputation in light comedy, not transpontine melodrama. Still he said he could do it; a case of the clown who yearns to play Valens if you ask me, but I was limited in my options.

Once he was safely out of the way, I set about my own agenda. I know people on Scona. Trouble is, by the same token, they know me.

To break into the Poor Sisters, you go to the junction of Lattengate and Cornhill, take the third alley on the left as you go down the hill – nobody's ever bothered giving it a name – at the end of which there's a tannery, long since abandoned and locked up. You pick the lock of the wicket gate and then you find yourself in what used to be the main yard of the tannery. To your left you'll see a brick wall, twelve feet high, give or take a bit. You climb that, and on the other side there's a small paved area, twenty feet by fifteen or thereabouts. Interesting place; it has high walls on all four sides and no doors or windows. I think it represents the thickness of a red line on countless generations of plans attached to title deeds; each time a plot of land gets sold and the deed gets copied, the thickness of the line increases just a tiny bit, until a small parcel of real estate simply ceases to exist. Nobody owns it, so nobody goes there.

The neighbours rebuild with tall, positive walls, and what's on the other side of them is none of their concern.

This small nonexistent yard is paved with good-quality sandstone slabs, about three feet square. Counting from the left as you come in from the tannery, fifth row, seventh slab: lever it up and you'll find a manhole, timber-lined and with a ladder going down. My guess is, it used to be access to the sewers, which the Knights built about six hundred years ago when they ran Scona. They flooded them two hundred years later and they haven't been used since, and I gather that large sections have collapsed. Not that I'm particularly interested.

Down the manhole you go to the bottom, where you get down on your hands and knees and scuttle along for precisely a hundred and twelve yards, which is very difficult indeed to judge when you're crawling in the dark. (Don't bother taking a lantern, by the way – you'll be bound to knock it over and spill it and cover yourself with burning oil, which is nobody's friend; happened to me once, no fun.) If you don't get the distance exactly right, you're screwed. The tunnel goes on a long way and it's too tight to turn round, so you have to backtrack, which is a real pain, especially if you're not at your happiest in confined spaces, like me. If you get it right, you wriggle over onto your back and grope about for a steel ring about a handspan wide. Push on this – it's hellish stiff – and you lift a heavy oak trapdoor. You feed yourself through this – I don't think it's anatomically possible, but you manage it somehow – and flail around until your hand alights on the bottom rung of a ladder. Be a bit careful, because the rungs aren't as sound as they used to be. Everything's still dark as a bag, by the way; life doesn't improve on that front for quite some time. Anyhow, you climb seventy-nine rungs. It's quite important to keep count, because at rung seventy-nine you reach out to your right and your fingertips should brush against a wooden rail. Make sure you get a good grip on it, because in a minute you're going to step off the ladder and haul yourself onto the platform behind and below the rail. Doing this isn't nearly as easy as it sounds, believe me.

I have no idea what the platform is, because I've never seen it, but it's about ten feet wide, and then there's a wooden partition with a door in it – call it a door, it's more like a hatch, about two foot six square – and here's where it gets awkward. There's a bolt on the other side of that hatch, and sometimes it's bolted and sometimes it's not. There's presumably a pattern to it, but I have no idea what it is. If it's bolted, all you can do is go back the way you came, taking care not to fall to your death groping for the pesky ladder. If it's unbolted, you give it a good sharp nudge and you're through.

What you're through into is another nonexistent space. I think it came about when one of the previous owners of the building – it's quite old, and the Sisters have only been there four hundred years or so – decided to raise the ceiling of the room below, encroaching on a redundant hayloft. What you're through into is the top half of the loft, if that makes any sense, and I reckon the hatch itself was put in to fill the gap left by a disused skylight when what used to be the roof got extended sideways and upwards. Like it matters. You crawl about thirty yards – you can't see the spiders, but you know they're there because you get the webs in your face; I don't like spiders – and you come to a corresponding hatch, which is also bolted but the bolt's on your side. It's stiff. Bet you anything you like you cut yourself thumping it with the heel of your hand to get it loose.

The hatch opens into stunning, dazzling sunlight, and you need to be a bit careful, because it's a sheer drop directly below, twenty-odd feet into a stable yard. But now you can see what you're doing, so you poke your head through the hatch and look up and you'll see an old iron derrick (I think that's the word; the sticking-out arm a rope goes through, for hauling hay up and down from the loft to the yard), from which there should be dangling a length of rusty chain. If you stand on tiptoe and make a grab for it, you can get hold of the chain before you plummet to the stone flags beneath; you'll then hear the reassuring clicking of a ratchet as the chain feeds through some sort of mechanism, lowering you to within eight feet of the ground. That's as much help as you're going to get, so you let go and drop the rest of the way. Do try not to break a leg if you can help it.

And there you are, right in the middle of the Poor Sisters, the most secure and heavily guarded building on Scona. I won't tell you how I came to find out about this wonderful secret, because that would mean betraying a confidence, but the fact that it's still there implies that very few people are aware of it, so for crying out loud don't tell anybody.

Needless to say, the stable yard hasn't been a stable yard for centuries. These days, it's a series of storerooms for documents – mortgages, indentures, loan agreements, at a rough guess I'd say about a third of the value of the known world is caught up in those bits of paper, rolled up tight, stuffed into little brass tubes and stacked like logs in plain cedar cupboards in those converted stables. Everything's numbered within an inch of its life, goes without saying, so you can be sure that the chief archivist knows exactly where to lay her hand on any one of those tens of thousands of documents, the same way you can instantaneously call up a memory. But – perish the thought – what if there was a fire?

Assuming your tinderbox hasn't dropped out of your pocket

while you've been hurling yourself around, light a small fire using a dozen or so of the crisp, dry documents so thoughtfully provided by the management, then duck down somewhere out of the way. The Sisters' watchmen have dogs specially trained to recognise the smell of burning parchment. As soon as a dog barks, the captain of the watch rings the alarm bell and the whole of the security staff mobilises. There are cisterns with stacks of buckets at stategically placed intervals, and everybody knows exactly what they're supposed to do. It's a treat to watch them in action, but you mustn't, because you've got other things to do.

As soon as you hear the bell, you walk quickly across the yard and stand on the right side of the main door, which opens inwards. If you're lucky, you won't get squashed by the door as it's thrown open. Stand perfectly still until the clatter of running boots has passed you by, then nip smartly out and through the doorway, then up the narrow spiral staircase you see directly on your left. You needn't worry about meeting anybody, because they're all on the level below, rushing about doing what they've been meticulously trained for. You only get that degree of efficiency in a really high-class outfit like the Sisters, and without it the place would be impregnable.

Then all you have to do is saunter at your leisure up the stairs till you reach the fifth landing, and there you are. You can go on further if you like; on the sixth floor they keep the reserves of cash money, rumoured to be in the millions, and on the seventh are all the heirlooms and fabulously valuable treasures and objets d'art lodged by kings and emperors as security for various loans, but I've never been up there because that sort of thing doesn't interest me. The fifth floor is where most of the offices are, and that's what I've come for.

*

A gentleman would've knocked, but I haven't been one of those for years. She was sitting on the window seat, with a view out over Foregate, reading some document or other.

"Oh, for God's sake," she said.

We go way back. I won't tell you her name because I don't want to make trouble for anyone, not even her, but once upon a time she was a very young parlourmaid in my father's house in the City, until she got dismissed for stealing. She's two years older than me, but you'd never think it to look at her.

I opened the blade of my folding knife, the good one I paid a lot of money for. It locks with a very dramatic click. "Hello," I said.

"I should've known, soon as I heard the bloody bell," she said. "You arsehole."

I sat down, exactly halfway between her and the only door. "Sorry about that," I said. "But what'd you have done if I'd shown up at the porter's lodge and asked to see you?"

"Have you arrested, of course."

"Well, then."

She sighed. "Hundreds of stauratas' worth of damage—"

"Thousands, probably."

"Shithead." She stood up. "Wine or brandy?"

She keeps three decanters on a small table beside her desk. Two of them are laced with enough poppy extract to put an elephant to sleep. "Not for me, thanks."

"What is it this time? Money?"

"Actually, no," I said.

"Not money?"

"Would you believe I just wanted to talk to you?"

Obviously not. She's done well for herself, I have to say. The Poor Sisters almost invariably recruit from the surplus daughters of the nobility, the ones not needed for marriage alliances. For someone with her antecedents (she'd have lied about them, naturally, but the Sisters know the truth about everything) to rise to the position she's reached takes genuine talent combined with a special sort of personality. I can vouch for both, but for some reason she's never asked me to write her a reference.

"Put that stupid knife away before you cut yourself with it."

She has a bit of a thing about knives, understandably enough. Long story. "In a minute," I said, brushing the edge with my thumb, which made her shudder. "I need to ask you something."

"Get on with it, then."

"Thanks," I said. "Right then. Who robbed the Vesani tax ship, and why are they trying to blame it on me?"

She looked at me. "Easy one," she said. "You did, and they aren't."

The other route to success for talented women of low birth is, of course, the stage, and she'd have made a great actress. All the years I've known her and I can never quite make out when she's lying. "No," I said, "I didn't do it."

"You didn't?"

"As you know perfectly well," I said, waggling the knife just a tiny bit, to make sure it had her attention. "Because you know who really did it, and why."

"No, you're wrong there." She was trying to maintain eye contact, but every time the blade moved she couldn't help looking at it. "I really thought it was you. It sounded so plausible."

"Oh, come on," I said. "You know me."

"Exactly."

I shook my head. "Two things you need in order to be a pirate. You need to be as brave as a lion—"

"Good point," she said gravely. "You're vicious, but you're chickenshit."

"And a good sailor, not constantly puking your guts out every time the wind blows. Does that really sound like me?"

She frowned. "Put it like that, I don't know," she said. "Maybe you hired some real pirates to do it for you."

"Why, for crying out loud?"

"For the money."

I could feel a sort of web starting to cling to me. "Let's skip all this," I said, wiggling the knife and nearly slicing a chunk out of my own thumb with it. "You know I didn't do it. You know who really did. Any minute now, someone'll come through that door and I'll have to leave. Accordingly—"

I stood up and took a long stride towards her, at which point old instincts and bad memories came into play. She had the window open before she remembered she was on the fifth floor. "All right," she said, in a different tone of voice. "Put it away and I'll tell you."

"The other way round," I said. "You tell me, I put it away. Now you can't say fairer than that."

Funny how some people are. I've been stuck at least a dozen times over the years, but knives per se don't really bother me. Spiders, on the other hand –

"Fine," she said. "The Sisters know who you are."

"Of course they do. Presumably you told them."

"Yes. So do the Knights."

You know when you're walking single file in the woods and a branch suddenly whips back and smacks you right in the face. A bit like that. "Do they really?"

She nodded. "Don't look at me," she said, "I don't go around telling on people; it's not my way, you know that."

"Certainly not out of mere spite," I conceded. "So you're saying—"

"No," she said. "I'm not saying anything. I really and truly thought you did it."

"Really and truly?"

"Yes. I thought, if the Knights are after you, you'd try and make one last big score before you had to vanish completely for ever. That's why I was so absolutely certain you wouldn't be walking in through that door ever again that I left it unbolted. Silly me."

"Yes, but piracy, for crying out loud—"

She sighed. "Exactly what you'd do," she said, "because everybody knows you can't stand boats. Therefore—"

I made a vague gesture with my free hand. "Yes, I get the idea. It's logic like that that leads to half the trouble in this world." I hesitated. Footsteps somewhere outside. Naturally they'd report to her about the outcome of the fire alarm. "The Knights? Really?"

She shrugged. "Don't ask me," she said. "As far as I'm concerned, you're guilty till proven innocent, always. But *if* you didn't do it, then that's where I'd suggest you start looking."

I was looking round, assessing the objects in the room. Nothing much of any use. In the end, I opted for a small Late Mannerist statuette of a shepherdess, mostly because it was made of bronze. "Thanks," I said. "Oh, and on the off chance that you might just possibly give me a straight answer, what do you know about the Silver Apple monastery on Ogyge?"

"The what on where?"

I looked at her, but it's like I just said: high finance's gain was the stage's palpable loss. "Nothing," I said. "Forget I spoke." The footsteps were close, and coming that way. "Next time, you might consider telling the guards to let me in. Cheaper, for one thing, and much less hassle for me."

"In your dreams, you lunatic."

I flattened myself against the wall next to the door. I had the knife where she could see it. There was a knock. I looked straight at her. "Come in," she said.

The door opened. A man came in. I hit him with the statuette and he fell over. He turned out to be a little old bald man. Scalp wounds always look much worse than they really are. I dragged him inside by one foot. "Sorry about that," I said, and closed the door behind me on my way out.

Nothing like having something on your mind to take the terror out of doing something horrible. I was so preoccupied with what she'd told me that I scarcely noticed the return journey, although it's so much worse going out than coming in. Before I knew it I was back in the no man's land yard next to the tannery, carefully replacing the paving stone over the manhole.

The Knights, for crying out loud. The last thing you want to hear when you know the Invincible Sun is out to get you is that the Eternal Flame has just put a price on your head. I've been in trouble so long I could quite reasonably claim it as my domicile for tax purposes, but there's trouble and trouble. The Knights, for God's sake.

Oh, come on, you're saying. Who's afraid of a bank? Or two banks, even?

Yes, but there's a difference. The Sisters are a bank, but only as a means to an end; making a ridiculous amount of money by any means necessary in order to finance their vast programme of charitable work in the Mesoge. The Knights, on the other hand, are a bank the way a cavalry sabre is a knife, a specialised sort of bank designed for a specific purpose, also very big and deadly sharp.

Not many people know this, so keep it to yourself, but the Knights aren't the ivory-tower, sweetness-and-light outfit they purport to be. Once, maybe. Originally, as you know, they were set up to protect the Great Library of Perimadeia from the threat of Sashan invaders. When Perimadeia fell, the Knights rescued all the books and built a castle in the Conessus Mountains to keep them safe for ever. So far, so laudable. Mostly they got into banking by accident – they were known to be men of unimpeachible integrity in a naughty world, so you could trust them with your money even further than you could spit them; they made a modest profit to pay for the upkeep of the library, but they were about scholarship and the future of civilisation, not the bottom line. And, for the next few hundred years, the world got steadily worse and they stayed roughly the same, until you had to be crazy to think of entrusting your money to anybody else.

But during that time, all the wise scholars and profound thinkers who ran the place fell to brooding on the nature of human society, and came to the conclusion that, left to itself, it didn't work terribly well. And why? Because, they argued, plausibly enough, it tends to be run by idiots; kings (ruled by their own base desires and hopelessly interbred) or dictators (anyone who seizes power by that very act disqualifies himself from being trusted with it) or oligarchies (irredeemably self-serving and corrupt) or, God help us, democracies (in the republic of the stupid, the half-witted man is prime minister) – there had to be a better way, and to the wisest men in the known world, it was painfully obvious what it was. If a job needs doing, do it ourselves.

The Knights have an army: twenty thousand men, superbly trained and equipped, but not nearly enough to conquer the world by force. Besides, people resent being invaded. But if you control all the money, you don't need an army. So, said the Knights to themselves, let's do that.

They'd have done it, too, if it wasn't for the Poor Sisters. I don't suppose any of the wise men could have foreseen their spectacular rise – women, for God's sake; nuns, for crying out loud – but it screwed the Knights' plans good and proper. Controlling two-thirds of the money is no earthly use if your implacable rival controls the other third. Time and again the Knights have tried to buy the Sisters out, but they refuse to listen. The outcome is, of course, the worst of all possible worlds. In order to crush the competition, each side tries to out-trade the other. Their business is providing loans to kings and governments. Kings and governments only borrow money in order to wage war, the most expensive field sport ever devised. Accordingly, it's never been easier or cheaper to finance an unprovoked invasion or settle diplomatic disputes by other means – great news for me and the Asvogel brothers, not so sweet for everybody else. Someone recently calculated that, thanks to all the wars, the population of the known world has fallen by sixteen per cent over the last twenty years. I have no idea how someone could possibly know that, but judging by what I see and hear in the course of my business, it sounds about right.

It may strike you as curious that two institutions devoted to the noblest of all possible ideals – education and feeding the poor – should between them be responsible for the deaths of millions. If so, I suggest you get out more and keep your eyes and ears open. It doesn't surprise me at all, not one little bit.

But never mind about all that. What bothered me was the thought of having the Knights on my case, given my history and their agenda. Were they capable of robbing a tax ship and planting the proceeds in a monastery just to manipulate poor little me? Answer: yes.

Swell.

4

When I got back, he was drunk. In the line of duty, he protested, you can't buy drinks for people without having one yourself: it makes them suspicious. I told him he was a disgrace to his species, which is true even when he's sober, and left him to sleep it off.

Fine. I was glad not to have to talk to him, or anyone. When you've just heard something that changes everything, the last thing you need is someone jabbering away in your ear. I needed to think. So I did.

Time, I thought, to go and be someone else, a long way away. I had twelve small rubies, six sapphires and fifteen staurata cash money. The fifteen staurata would get me to far-distant Echmen, riding in coaches and wine with my dinner, and the jewels were a far better start in life than I'd had the last time I was reborn from the ashes, let alone the time before that. It's hotter than hell in Echmen and I despise the heat, but Echmen isn't the end of the world; far from it, by all accounts. To the east of it there's somewhere called Lukka, and beyond that there's somewhere called Paschan, where apparently they have snow-capped mountains and ancient, wealthy monasteries, quite possibly with defective security arrangements. It's a big old world full of gullible people, crammed with opportunities for a man with twelve small rubies and an easily concealed knife, and only a fool dies of a shortage of geography.

On the other hand, running away would mean running out on my friends, people who relied on me, who needed me to survive. If I disappeared, who'd take over the business? Well, there'd be a short, intense civil war and then either Olybrius or Polycrates would be the new chairman of the board. Olybrius would pick a fight with the Asvogels before six months were out, and the entire company would be out of business or dead and buried in a dunghill shortly afterwards. Polycrates would run the business into the ground trying to strike hard bargains, and everyone would soon get sick of him and drift away, and what would they all do then, poor things? Carrhasio was far too old to get a proper job, and Gombryas is one of the sweetest men I know but he's far too stupid to be let out on his own. They needed me, all of them. Casting them adrift to fend for themselves would be little better than murder. They needed me, all of them.

Pull yourself together, I commanded myself. If you stick around you'll be dead or worse, and no use to your friends or anybody. The world just changed, irrecoverably and out of all recognition. If ten people fall off a cliff and one of them manages to grab hold of a dangling branch, he's not going to make things better for himself by letting go so he can rush to help his friends. Besides, in the great scheme of things, we all have our duties and responsibilities; mine is keeping me alive, a job which nobody else would touch with a ten-foot pole, for obvious reasons. Like the man who sweeps the litter off the temple steps every morning only to see them covered in garbage the next day, I sometimes wonder what possible good could ever come of my efforts. Mine, however, not to reason why. It's my duty, and I do it.

Right, then. Ships leaving Scona heading east, preferably for either Sashan or the Olbian delta.

I had a dozen to choose from, Scona being that sort of place. I decided on a lemon boat. There's good money to be made out of lemons, so the ships are well built and properly maintained, and time is money so they don't hang about. Nor do they take passengers, unless the passenger happens to be offering silly money; two staurata for a ten-day ride, who could possibly resist?

Shortly before the ship was due to set sail, I wandered down to the dock. Nobody was following me, as far as I could tell. That clown Ekkehard was still fast asleep. I stopped at a market stall to buy a jar of figs in honey for the journey, then strolled across to the quay, where they were loading the last few crates of cargo.

A man barged into me, not looking where he was going. He apologised. Don't worry about it, I assured him. Then he grabbed my arm, looked round quickly, and hissed, "Over there, now."

The last thing I needed was anything that'd make me conspicuous, so I let him lead me across the road to a sort of colonnade thing, with nice dark shadows under the arches. "If you don't let go of me," I said nicely, "I'll cut your heart out."

He shushed me, took another glance over his shoulder. "Listen," he said. "You don't know me."

"True."

"*Quiet*. Sorry," he added, "but there's no time. You can't go aboard that ship. They know who you are."

That godawful feeling in the pit of your stomach. I know it so well. "What are you talking about?"

"Two years ago," he said, "I was a soldier in a battle, in the Mesoge. I got cut up and left for dead. You found me and your doctor saved my life and patched me up."

Now he came to mention it – I remembered. He had an arrow right through his neck. I told Papinian, forget it, he's a goner, but the old fool wouldn't listen. "Maybe. So what?"

"And now," he went on, "I work for the Knights."

"Ah."

"I'm supposed to be looking out for *him*." He showed me a small picture, egg tempera on limewood, about the size of the palm of your hand. A very good likeness of me. "But you're not him, are you? You're Saevus Corax."

I nodded.

"There's at least two dozen of us," he said, "watching all the ships, and we've all got copies of the picture. You wouldn't believe the money they're offering, but I couldn't. I'd be dead if it wasn't for you. I just couldn't."

I'd got two staurata forty-five for him from his government, I didn't tell him; thirty-five per cent profit. "Thank you," I said.

"That's all right. Now get out of here before anyone sees us."

Scona is, of course, an island. It's one of the first things you notice about it when you go there.

How do you get off an island when you daren't go near a ship? Answer: you don't.

"I bought you some figs," I said. "Good for hangovers."

He groaned and opened his eyes. "You what?"

"Figs," I said. "In honey."

He blinked. "Thank you," he said. "That's a really kind thought."

"I'm very considerate," I said. "It's why everybody likes me."

It was a while before he was capable of coherent speech. Then he told me what he'd found out.

The official story, which everyone believed because they had no reason to doubt it, was that I'd hired a fast clipper, crewed it with a selection of my very best desperadoes, intercepted the revenue ship, looted and scuttled it and hidden the proceeds, amounting to just over a hundred thousand staurata. Everybody had heard it from some reliable source, who'd heard it from someone equally reliable. When questioned, nobody could explain how exactly it was established that I was the man who'd done it. It had been reported as a simple fact, like today's date.

Except that one man mentioned the name of a ship: the *Squirrel*, four hundred tons, out of Dui Chirra, a clipper built for the spice trade. The well-informed source was comprehensively stewed by the time Ekkehard managed to get the name out of him, slurring his words and falling asleep in the middle of sentences, so his testimony was somewhat tainted; nevertheless, he was adamant that the *Squirrel* was the ship I'd hired to do the dirty deed, because a cousin of his had done the hiring out – long, involved story about various business dealings; properly speaking the cousin shouldn't have hired out the ship because it was mortgaged to the drunk as security for contingent liability on a loan; the drunk, therefore, had a moral lien on the hiring fee, and wasn't it just as well he'd taken pity on his cousin and not pressed the point, because if he had and his cousin had given him the money, then the Vesani authorities would've arrested him for aiding and abetting, not his cousin . . . Yes, definitely the *Squirrel*, because they'd taken his cousin away in fucking *chains*, and there but for the grace of the Invincible fucking Sun –

"Hold on," I said. "The *Squirrel* out of where?"

"Dui Chirra, I already told you that."

"Are you sure?"

Exasperated sigh. "No, of course not. All I know is what he told me, and it was hard to make out anything he was saying, and he kept falling asleep. I think he said Dui Chirra, but I can't swear to it. Look, does it matter? The point is, I did some more asking around, and guess who owns that ship?"

"The drunk's cousin, you just said."

He shook his head, which made him wince. "No, he just leased it. Three guesses who he leased it from. Go on."

I raised my hand and made a fist. He scowled.

"Fine," he said. "He leases it from the Poor Sisters. It's their ship."

You know what it's like when you're trying to write a letter or add up a column of figures, and next door's dog keeps on barking so you can't think. "You what?"

"Straight up. That ship belongs to the *Sisters*. The one that was used to rob the—"

"Yes, all right." Too much all at once. "Doesn't mean anything," I went on. "The Sisters own hundreds of ships; so do the Knights."

"What've they got to do with anything?"

"Eat your nice figs."

*

All, I told myself, beside the point. The point was that the Knights were after me and I was trapped on an island. That was everything I needed to know for the time being.

It must have cost them an absolute fortune to get all those portraits painted. More to the point, in order to get such a good likeness they must have found someone who knew me really well and made him sit with an artist for hours on end – no, the nose is a bit too long; make the eyes a bit closer together; no, now the mouth doesn't look right. True, lots of people knew Saevus Corax, but I had an idea that Saevus wasn't who the Knights were after. The Sisters, on the other hand—

Indeed. I was thinking about ships and Knights and Sisters because that was the mystery I wanted to solve, because, ulti- mately, it didn't matter; the answer wouldn't scare me to death when I found it. The thing I should be thinking about was Dui Chirra, but I didn't want to look there, for fear of what I might find.

So I told myself: coincidence. It's a trading port, ships are built and registered there, it doesn't mean anything; just like the way you tell yourself the persistent cough is just a cold and the pain in your chest is almost certainly a pulled muscle. Dui Chirra, for crying out loud. Now there's somewhere I haven't thought about for a very long time.

"Here's three staurata," I said to him. "Book yourself on a grain freighter to Auxentia City, and buy yourself a big trunk."

He narrowed his eyes. He learned to do it for a play once. "It won't work," he said.

"Yes, it will."

"No, it won't. You'll suffocate and die."

"We drill holes in the bottom of the trunk. Soon as we're

at sea, I come out, we give the captain a lot of money, no bother at all."

"It's the sort of thing they do in those stupid plays you used to write. It won't work in real life. We'll get caught. Besides, I really don't want to go to Auxentia."

"Why not?"

"It's the arsehole of the universe."

True. "Bullshit," I said. "You'll like it once you get there."

A man with my unfortunate problems with sea travel, locked in a trunk for a very long time. Let's not go there.

Instead, let's go to Auxentia City. Actually, it's not as bad as all that. Ekkehard hates it because it's murderously hot and ridiculously overcrowded with people who shit in the street and club you to death if you look at them the wrong way. I like to think I'm rather less parochial in my outlook. It's a dump, and only desperate losers end up there, but it's a long way from Scona. Also, since nobody in his right mind would go there and everyone knows I'm perfectly sane, they wouldn't be looking for me there, now would they?

Auxentia City was built for the grain trade. Hundreds of thousands of tons of barley come up the river from central Blemya on barges, to supply the slave plantations of the Sashan empire with the cheapest food available anywhere in the world. Since Blemya and the Sashan have been at war since the beginning of time, all that grain has to pass through an intermediary, and that's how Auxentia came to exist. Its sole purpose is to make it possible for the world's oldest and most implacable enemies to trade with each other – without that trade they'd both of them be bankrupt in no time flat – so, if you wanted one word to describe the place, it'd have to be *businesslike.* Everything in Auxentia is pared down to the absolute minimum, with the exception of the population, but since human life is the only thing that's cheap in Auxentia, that doesn't really matter. I like to think of it as the distilled essence of human nature, like attar of roses only not quite so sweetly fragrant.

I know people in Auxentia City. "My God," he said, as they pulled the hood off my head. "Look what the cat dragged in."

"Hello," I said. "Was that absolutely necessary?"

My pal nodded, and his colleagues untied my hands and placed me in a chair. "You know the score," he said. "You're lucky they didn't cut your throat. What were you thinking of, saying that name in a public place?"

"Got your attention, didn't it?"

My pal – excuse me if I don't tell you his name, see above – is a bit like me, or a butterfly; once he was a caterpillar, with a different name. There are warrants out for the caterpillar in all popular jurisdictions. I've known him on and off for many years; I've put his life in mortal danger several times, and because of me he's made a great deal of money. I guess that means we're friends. Remind me, and I'll tell you some more about him some other time. "It's all right," he told his colleagues, "he's harmless. I'll shout if I want anything."

Alone together, we eyed each other like two dogs in an alley. He'd put on weight, and the beard suited him. "Well?" he said.

"Actually, I'm just passing through," I said. "So I thought I'd drop by and pay my respects."

He nodded, and placed on the table in front of him the thing he'd been gripping in his hand. A small screw of parchment, containing twelve small rubies and six sapphires. "Can I have it back, please?" I said.

"In a minute. What are you doing in Auxentia?"

"I told you. Passing through."

He picked out a ruby and put it on one side. "Sorry," he said. "Didn't quite catch that."

"Running away," I said. "I was on Scona. Nasty men were looking for me."

He chose an emerald, held it up to the light, put it back and chose another one. "That's an old cut," he said. "They haven't done it like that for centuries. Have you been robbing churches again?"

"Family heirlooms," I said, "straight up." I paused to pull myself together. "I need a favour."

"Course you do." He covered another ruby with the tip of his little finger. "Still writing plays?"

"Not for ages. I'm in scrap metal these days."

He smiled. "It's a pity you stopped," he said. "I like your stuff; it's quite well written. Of course, the early ones were the best."

That's what Ekkehard always says, when he's trying to annoy me, and it always works. He'd be wondering where the hell I'd got to. Oh well. Once I was out of the picture, he'd be safe. "So people tell me," I said. "Look, I need to get to Echmen without anybody recognising me."

"Why would anybody recognise you?"

I told him about the little pictures. I think he was impressed. "They must really want you for something," he said.

"Apparently," I said. "And, yes, quite probably they'd pay a lot of money, so I can only trust my very oldest and dearest friends, men of unimpeachable loyalty and integrity, like you."

He thought about it. I could see his train of thought in his eyes, like columns of mathematical calculations, ending up with *therefore x =.* "It'd be a piece of piss," he said eventually, "if it wasn't for you being such a lousy sailor. Nobody's going to take you for a Jolly Jack Tar when you're forever chucking your guts over the side."

"I can cope," I said. "I came here in a—"

"Trunk, I know." That threw me. He grinned. "I was going to have you picked up anyway, before you started shooting your mouth off. For your own good, naturally. I heard you were in town long before you showed up in the Prince of Peace."

I nodded, to acknowledge that I'd underestimated him. He accepted it gracefully, with a tiny smile. "Fact is," he said, "you're *it*. People want you."

For some reason my mouth went dry. "That's awkward," I said.

"I didn't know about the little pictures," he went on. "That's just plain sneaky, if you ask me. It makes it very hard indeed, if they've got men watching all the ships."

He'd know about that sort of thing. "Have they?"

He nodded. "Luckily for you, in Auxentia they subcontract. Guess who to. They didn't issue us with little pictures, though." Something occurred to him, and he laughed. "Sorry," he said, "who did you say was looking for you?"

"The Knights."

"Ah, right. Talking at cross purposes there for a moment. I was hired to find you by the Sisters."

Oh, for crying out loud. "Them, too."

"It must be nice to be popular." He looked at me, as though trying to decide whether to have me for breakfast or dinner. "Why Echmen?"

"It's a very long way away."

He shook his head. "Wouldn't if I were you," he said.

"There's only a limited number of ways of getting to Echmen overland, so you'd be easy to spot. What you want to do is go north."

"North."

"Olbia," he said. "The Schlecht basin, the Hexapolis, Sirupat, somewhere like there. Nobody's going to be looking for someone like you in a logging camp."

"Maybe you're right," I said. "You know about that stuff."

Well, he ought to. He's the third biggest gangmaster in Auxentia. "You could tag along with one of the teams I send up to the diggings in the Schlecht country," he said. "I ship 'em out by the hundred; even the Knights couldn't check out each individual coolie. And once you're there, you could—"

"Die of typhoid."

"Find something to occupy your mind with," he said mildly. "Cost of living up there's next to nothing, by all accounts. With one of these little beauties, you could be a grand duke."

"Just one?"

He gave me a sympathetic look. "I've got a living to earn," he said. "And, like they say, no pockets in shrouds. I'm sure your ancestors would be thrilled to bits, thinking their heirlooms have saved your neck."

I considered for a moment. "That one."

"Really? I particularly like that one. Oh, go on, since it's you." He propelled a ruby across the table with his forefinger. "And I'll throw in a nice warm coat and some woolly socks. You'll need them."

I like to think I can get along with most people, but my fellow workers were no fun at all. It wasn't the language barrier as such, though most of them were tribesmen from the desert south of Blemya, forced abroad to work by six years of drought. It so happens I can get by in Blemyan, which is a fairly easy spoken language but a real bitch to write. What depressed me was their attitude. They'd got it into their heads that a heartless and uncaring gangmaster was packing them off to be worked to death in chain gangs in a godforsaken wilderness where the sun never shines and it snows all year round. Not true, I told them. My pal doesn't chain his workers, because it slows them down, and the rain only freezes in Olbia nine months of the year. They just looked at me. Screw them. I have no sympathy with defeatists.

The economics of the mass-labour business are hard for the uninitiated to understand. It would've taken three weeks to get us to Olbia by ship, as opposed to three months on foot; time is money, especially in civil engineering (we were off to build a road), so naturally it'd make sense to send us by sea. Wrong answer. The terms of the contract were that my pal would be paid so much per capita per day for each worker from the time he left Auxentia until the time he got back or died, and method of transit wasn't specified. My pal interpreted that as meaning that the road consortium was happy to pay good money to have us walk all the way up the coast and back, six months extra hire charge for each man and a substantially increased chance of us dropping dead en route, from disease, starvation and exhaustion. I ought to mention that there's a reparations clause in the standard contract, a fixed sum in compensation for every worker who dies on the job. Quite possibly for that reason, we'd be taking the east road, through the fever-ridden marshes around Lyssa Bay. Well, you can't blame a man for wanting to make a modest profit.

I had no intention of going to Lyssa Bay. Long before we

got there we'd be passing through Antecyrene. I know a lot of people in Antecyrene. It'd be a bitter disappointment to the Sisters (or the Knights) who'd have been told to expect me in Olbia, but I've been letting people down all my life, so what the hell. By the time they realised I wasn't coming, I'd be safe in Echmen, where they appreciate really fine antique gemstones.

Even so. Three weeks' trudge in badly fitting shoes – my pal buys bulk footwear from the Asvogel brothers – in the company of a lot of miserable people. My pal had promised me he'd have a word with the guards – sorry, security escort – with a view to them making life marginally less horrible for me along the way, but I guess it slipped his mind. Fair enough. It'd probably have slipped mine if I'd been in his shoes.

Which, of course I was, and the seams split on day four. Walk a mile in a man's shoes and you'll understand him: quite. He's a cheapskate. I already knew that. I padded the loathsome things out with dry leaves and grass but it didn't help much. Luckily on the third day after that, while I was asleep, one of my fellow sufferers stole my shoes and left his in their place. They were a much better fit and the seams were intact. Three cheers for dishonesty.

Twelve days of weary marching, and we stopped for the night in the ruins of an old military way station, somewhere on the long uphill stretch between Dendra and Colombel. The lance-corporal of the platoon who looked after the party I was with had shot a goat that morning, and out of sheer good nature the guards let us have the bits they couldn't or wouldn't eat, minced up fine in our daily ration of barley porridge. Nearly two weeks of deprivation makes elderly billygoat taste like heaven.

We slept well that night, even the idiot who would insist on having screaming fits in the wee small hours; even me. I was fast asleep and deeply into my extensive repertoire of recurring nightmares when not being able to breathe woke me up. There was a hand over my face. Odd, I remember thinking. How did that get there?

Someone hissed *quiet* in Aelian in my ear, and I was just tensing myself for the sideways roll followed by the grasshopper jump-upright when I felt a sharp point against my throat, just under the jawline. Bother, I thought, or words to that effect.

The hand left my face and got a good, effective grip on my hair, while the point pressed just hard enough to break the skin. I got up, following my hair. It was as dark as a bag, even for me with my exceptional night vision; I got the impression there were at least three of them, but I wouldn't want to swear to that in a court of law. Too many was all that mattered. They walked me carefully out of the tangle of sleeping bodies, then hit me on the head. Back to dreamland.

The bag over my head was a barley sack. Barley dust is one of my least favourite things. It makes you sneeze uncontrollably, which ruins your back, and the tiny, tiny specks are hard and sharp; they get in your eyes and lodge in the grooves round your nostrils and the little crease under your nose and itch like crazy.

I don't know how long it was before they took it off, because I was lying all cramped up in the bed of a cart, expertly trussed up with thick, tarred rope, probably naval issue, and time works differently under those conditions. Then I was hauled about a bit and carried shoulders and feet up a long, winding staircase, and finally poured out onto a straight-backed chair.

My face was covered in snot from the incessant sneezing, and my eyeballs felt like they'd been scoured with sand. When the bag eventually did come off, the light was so painful I squealed like a pig.

"Oh, for heaven's sake," said a voice I knew.

I blinked, and my eyelids scraped embedded grains of barley grit over my irises, like a glasscutter's diamond. "He's a disgrace," the voice said. "Couldn't you have cleaned him up a bit?"

I didn't catch the reply, which came from behind me. Through the damp red mist I was looking at a woman, maybe sixty-five, elegant as a falcon, plainly but immaculately dressed in white linen, with very fine old lace at wrists and neck. She was sitting bolt upright on an ornately carved oak chair, six hundred years old if it was a day; I guessed it was a family piece she'd insisted on bringing from home. Behind her was a wall covered floor to ceiling with books; not rolls in brass tubes but the really expensive lots-of-pages-sewn-together-between-covers type (the proper word is *codices*) you only see in rich men's libraries or monasteries. No prizes, therefore, for guessing where I was, or whose guest.

The woman looked at me and sighed. "You're pathetic," she said.

"Hello, Aunt," I said.

No kidding. The senior deacon of the Poor Sisters is my aunt Feralia. That doesn't make things better. Quite the reverse.

She's my mother's kid sister and the resemblance is definitely there, in the nose and chin, though Aunt Feralia is dark and my mother's skin was pale, almost a sort of beige. One thing Aunt Feralia and I have in common. Our family is very grand but we've got what's charmingly known as a touch of the lime brush, which means most of us come out no better than a kind of pale terracotta. But Auntie and I are throwbacks to the deep, pure Imperial Robur brown. She's absurdly proud of it; I'm not bothered. I'm more concerned about what's inside my skin, and how to keep people from making holes in it.

Still, my aunt Feralia's a real piece of work, no doubt about it. You don't get to be fourth in the hierarchy of the Sisters unless you're very smart and savage as a wolf. Auntie's both.

"Sit up straight, for heaven's sake," said my aunt. "Let's see, how long has it been?"

"Eighteen years."

"You haven't changed a bit."

She didn't mean it as a compliment. "Neither have you," I said. I meant it as a compliment, though I didn't mean it. You can see that Auntie was a raving beauty in her youth, but the sort of beauty that desiccates. I was, of course, wasting my time.

"You're still stupid, vicious, undisciplined, thoughtless, irresponsible and utterly self-centred," she went on. "You were the death of my mother and my poor sister. I trust you realise that."

"Yes."

She nodded. A guard punched me in the face. Straight from the shoulder and plenty of follow-through.

She gave me a moment to pull myself together. Then she said, "The king is dying."

That hit me harder than the guard's fist. She was watching me like a hawk. "Is that right?"

"Yes."

"Don't see it's any business of mine."

This time I was expecting it, but the guard knew his job and

1

hit me from the other side. I felt my brain bounce off the wall of my skull, a thing I particularly dislike.

"They give him three months at the very most," my aunt went on. I could only just hear her. "Obviously that gives us very little time." She paused to scowl at me. Your fault, her scowl said.

"I won't go," I said.

She can't have heard me. "Fortunately, I've already made all the necessary arrangements for getting you there. The time of year complicates matters rather, because of the change in the prevailing winds. You'll have to go straight across via the islands rather than following the coast. That will waste precious time, but it can't be helped."

The fact that you've known for years that something is probably inevitable ought to help you to cope when eventually it happens, but it doesn't. I could feel this tide of panic starting to rise in the pit of my stomach. I don't do well with panic. It's like being drunk. Suddenly you find you can't rely on the various bits of you to do as they're told, especially the brain. When I start feeling that way it panics me even more, and I can feel myself unravelling like a piece of knitting. Also my head was splitting because of the two punches, and I can't think worth spit when I've got a headache. "I won't do it," I said. "I'll kill myself. I'll stop eating and starve myself to death."

The look she gave me was nearly all disgust, with only a faint trace of amusement. "You're welcome to try," she said. "I've assigned you to one of our very best managers, so I'm not the least bit worried about any lack of cooperation on your part. I'm only sorry I can't come and manage you myself, but regrettably I'm needed here. It would've been entertaining to watch you trying to hurt yourself."

I looked at her. She was nice to me when I was a kid. People change. "I swear to you," I said, "I won't do it. I'll screw it all up. Just to spite you."

She sighed. The guard hit me again. Afterwards I could still hear what she was saying but I really wasn't up to making any contribution to the conversation.

"Listen to me," she said. "You will do exactly what you're told, and you'll do it diligently and well, because if you don't, I shall hand you over to your father and brother." She paused for a moment. "Do we understand each other?"

I felt as heavy as lead. "Yes," I said.

"Splendid. You always were a cowardly little brute. I'm pleased to see that hasn't changed."

I suppose I ought to tell you a little bit about my family.

My mother and father had eight children. Four of them died in infancy. They were the lucky ones.

The other four were, in reverse order: my brother Scaphio, my sister Phantis, my brother Scynthius and me, the eldest. Scaphio was very much an afterthought and Phantis – well, these things happen. It didn't matter particularly, because there was always Scynthius. Whenever skies were grey or I or my sister were being particularly tiresome, all my parents had to do was think of him and, no matter what, they couldn't help smiling. He was perfect. You only had to look at him to see that all of human history had led up to him. He justified everything. It had all been worth it, because he was the result.

Does that make it sound like I resented my brother? You bet I did. I hated everything about him, especially the fact that he was so much better at everything than I was. That made it awkward, because half of me desperately wanted to be like him, and the other half reckoned that anything he was good at couldn't be worth shit; unfortunately he was good at everything. To put the tin lid on it, he was devoted to me, in spite of everything I said and did to him. He forgave me, instantly and without hesitation. Could you have handled that? I couldn't, that's for sure. He was two years younger than me, and by the time he was fourteen he was a foot taller than I was, stronger, faster, smarter, better looking. I used to fantasise about freak accidents; me lying on the edge of a cliff, him dangling while I held him by one wrist; the fear in his eyes, conquered by love and trust, because he knew I'd save him, because we were brothers. And then I'd slowly let go.

He was good at everything, but he was an outstanding fencer. When he was fifteen, our sergeant-at-arms went to my father and said he couldn't teach him any more; he really ought to go to one of the high-class salles in the city and study under one of the Vesani or Perimadeian masters. My father started making the arrangements; he'd go up to town two days a week, staying with my aunt Falcata, and attend classes with the great Pleionax, the royal warrant-holder. Meanwhile, to keep his hand in, Scynthius sparred with me. The sergeant knew a good trick to encourage young prodigies and keep them from getting sloppy. The boy genius would use a foil, same as always, but his sparring partner would be given a sharp, with the point unbated. My mother wasn't happy about it, but my father and the sergeant both assured her that his defence was so perfect that there was no risk whatever, and it would get Scynthius used to facing sharps, which were all that were used in master Pleionax's establishment. You had to graduate to sharps once you passed a certain point in your development as a fencer. It was a rite of passage, like girls putting up their hair. He'd done it when he was the boy's age, my father told her, and he hadn't been a patch on young Scynthius.

Two days before he was due to start at master Pleionax's, he came and asked me to spar with him. I was in the orchard behind the house, lying in the shade, reading a dirty book I'd sneaked out of my father's private library. "Would you mind sparring for a bit?" he said. "There's a couple of forms in defence I want to work on before I go up to town."

"You don't need to practise any more," I told him. "You're perfect enough as it is."

He peered down at what I was reading, before I had a chance to snap the book shut. He didn't comment and his face didn't change. "Oh, go on," he said. "Please."

I did the usual risk assessment. Would he tell my father I'd pinched one of his naughty books? No, probably not. "I think I pulled a muscle in my shoulder," I said.

"A bit of exercise will do it good. Look, I really want to run over these forms, especially the riverso in fourth. I don't want to show up at Pleionax's and look like a cabbage farmer."

"Get the sergeant. It's what he's paid for."

"He's sprained his ankle. It's the footwork I really need to concentrate on. Please."

So we went indoors and sparred. My father had given him the first-floor gallery to practise in. It's long enough for tracing and wide enough for traversing, and it's still got the original oak floorboads (or it had when I last saw it; don't suppose anything's changed since), which is the perfect surface for fencing on, or so they tell me. We fenced for an hour or so, until I was sodden with sweat and gasping for breath and bruised all over from being prodded with that damned foil.

"Go again," he said.

"No." I dropped the sword on the floor. "That's enough."

"One more time. Please."

Sweat was dripping into my eyes and down my nose. "I said no," I told him. "You don't need any more practice. You're the ultimate fucking killing machine. I'm going to have a bath."

He gazed at me out of those deep hazel eyes. "I'm still having problems with the disengage from third," he said. "I need to coordinate the hand and foot movements, and they're always slightly out of time. It leaves me open to a passado."

I yawned. "Then cover with your elbow."

"Yes, but that's sloppy. My form's got to be perfect or I might as well not bother."

"I'm tired, Scyn. My back hurts."

"Interesting looking book you were reading."

I looked at him. He was bluffing, of course. "Fine," I said. "One more time and then that's it."

"Thanks." He beamed at me. "You're the best, you know that."

So we fenced, one more time. I'd decided that the only way to get him off my back was to help. If he could sort out his stupid hand/foot coordination, he'd be happy and let me go and I'd finally get my life back. So I upped the pace a bit, trying to pressure him on his defences, not caring about getting hit myself. I was doing the right thing. "That's it," he kept calling out as he whacked me across the shoulder or prodded me in the guts, excellent, yes, thank you. He was deliberately leaving openings, places where I could attack him so he'd be forced to defend; his natural style was fluent aggression and he was good at it, the perfect closed attack that allows no counter. He had to make a special effort to be vulnerable. I was dog-tired by now, with that deep burning in the chest that limits your breathing to short gasps, and the sweat in my eyes made everything blurry. "That's great," he sang out. "I think I'm finally getting it, thank you," and then he stuck me in the ribs with his foil.

"Sorry," he said, "did that hurt?" I was too blown to reply. He was still fresh as a daisy.

"Can we just run through that one more time?" he said. I nodded. I was too tired to resist.

We fenced. He offered an opening. I went for it, and got the foil on the point of my chin, which made him laugh. He offered another. This time he got me on the knee. Another opening. I went for it. He made the obvious parry. His mind was already on the riposte, how he was going to draw me out of line so as to open me up for a counterthrust to the groin. He was smiling. He fluffed the parry, ever so slightly. The point of my sword skidded off the flat of his, lifted and hit him in the eye. He was still smiling, and he died.

I was automatically tracing and traversing, a long step backwards and to the left, anticipating his counter. I pulled the sword out of him. He tipped forward onto his face, the way something falls when you've accidentally barged into it. I looked at him.

For a split second all I could register was, *I beat him. I won.* Then it all hit me like a ton of bricks.

It was an accident. It was his fault, for making me fence when I was tired. The reason you fence with sharps is to keep you sharp; he'd set himself a test, and failed it. My father knew all about that. Would it make any difference? The hell it would.

It was one of those moments when the world changes; like in the theatre, what they call the transformation scene. It's everybody's favourite bit. The drama reaches a point where the mess is so intense it can't possibly be sorted out, so the good fairy waves her wand and suddenly a gauze comes down, the scene-shifters whisk the old set away and wheel on Fairyland. Pretty girls in floaty dresses are lowered on wires and hang there in midair. The music starts. The lights go red, then pink, like sunrise. All the characters disappear and reappear in different costumes, representing the stock characters of the pantomime – the Lovers, the Clown, Mischief, the Grumpy Old Man, the Guards. Then Clown calls out, "Here we are again," and everybody starts clapping.

But nobody clapped. I looked at the pool of blood on the oak floor. I saw it through my father's eyes, and considered what he was about to see. His beloved son, with whom he was well pleased, only fifteen years old, dead. His unsatisfactory son, standing over him with a sword in his hand. Now he's thinking, what happened? He doesn't need me to tell him. No secret that the brothers never got on. One of them so perfect, the other: how did I ever come to have a son like that, so different, so badly wrong? Accident? Don't make me laugh. Scynthius' defence was perfect, he could never be killed in a fair fight with an inferior opponent; so the other one, the treacherous little shit must have waited till his brother was off guard and then deliberately murdered him, hoping to pass it off as a horrible misadventure, so he'd inherit—

(Because, a few weeks earlier, my father had disinherited me and announced that Scynthius would be the heir, even though he was technically younger. Didn't I mention that? Sorry.)

The transformation scene. I used to write really good transformation scenes, back when I was in the business. I think I know why. It's like all writing: you have to feel it.

Mind you, I always loved the theatre, ever since I was small. I always wanted to be the Lover. But we don't always get what we want, and it looked like I'd turned out to be Mischief. Well, you play the part that's given to you, and be grateful you're in the cast at all.

I was about to drop the sword but I thought, no, I might be needing that, so I held onto it tight, like a rope in a shipwreck. I was on the first floor. Two staircases leading down, and a fair chance of meeting someone on both of them. The windows looked out over the rose garden, beyond that the lawn, beyond that the river. My father had very fine hounds, capable of following a scent almost anywhere, but a river defeats even the best noses money can buy. I looked round for small objects of value, but everything like that was cleared out when they set it up as a fencing salle. The hell with it, I thought. Mischief is always an acrobat. I opened the window and jumped.

I won't bore you with my subsequent adventures. I had a good start, best part of an hour before I heard the hounds baying in the distance; by then I was out of the grounds and deep in the woods. I knew the country like the back of my hand, but so did my pursuers, and, of course, everybody for miles around knew what I looked like. But I knew the tenants' houses, which of them had rickety old doors and broken shutters; I had no trouble getting food and clothes, and I didn't have to fight or kill anybody. I kept close to the river, and one night I met a bargeman who was happy to take a fine gentleman's rapier in exchange for a ride on his barge as far as Rumaine Hisar. Barges go slowly, and I wanted to stay out of sight, so I made a sort of nest for myself among the woolsacks and tried to figure out what I was going to do next. I remember waking up out of a dream, in which I'd been Mischief and all the people I'd ever known were the Lovers, the Clown, the Guards, the Grumpy Old Man; and I thought, why not? There was nothing to write on in the barge so I had to remember it, but by the time I got off at Osebridge (the bargeman had been giving me odd looks, so I thought I'd better leave early) I had three-quarters of a rattling good show safe inside my head. Theatre's all about escaping from reality, which is probably why I'm so very good at it.

In Rumaine I learned that my father was offering twenty thousand staurata for me, dead or alive. I knew why he'd hit on that precise figure; it was all the ready money he could raise without selling or mortgaging anything, which takes time. I figured Rumaine was probably a bit too close to home, so I burgled a temple and bought myself passage on a ship to the Vesani Republic. God's always been good to me that way, letting me have money when I really need it.

I was seventeen years old, God help me. It's an awkward age at the best of times. I feel like a bone that was broken and never properly set, but which healed up eventually, some bloody fashion. You can walk on it but it's never right, and a lot of the time it hurts. Never mind. I'm still here, and there's a lot of people worse off than me.

Anyway, you can see why *I shall hand you over to your father and brother* scared me far more than simple, straightforward old death ever could. She'd do it, too, the old witch, like a shot, if she couldn't find any use for me.

They put me in a room at the very top of the Old Tower, no window, only way in or out a spiral staircase, massively guarded by men of violence. It was clean and dry and completely empty, not so much as a footstool or a towel. I pointed out that without a chamber pot I'd be compelled to make messes on the floor. That's all right, they told me. It's stone;

it'll wash off. I shared it with three guards, who watched me every second of every minute. If I tried talking to them, they hit me. You've got to admire attention to detail.

I was sitting there, thinking how it couldn't possibly get any worse when the door opened and someone I knew came in. Shows how wrong you can be. "Oh, come *on*," I said. She smiled at me.

"Has he been behaving himself?" she asked the guards. One of them nodded. I hadn't moved for several hours.

"You," I said.

"Me. I'm your new keeper."

Curious the way circumstances alter one's perceptions. Under other circumstances, a man might welcome the prospect of a long journey in close company with a very attractive young woman, and, no doubt about it, Sister Stauracia was that all right. She wasn't drop-dead gorgeous or anything like that. Looked at objectively, she was about an eighth of an inch away from being plain; there was rather too much distance between her nose and her upper lip. But it was one of those defects that somehow adds to rather than detracts from the allure, making you remember the face long after you've forgotten all the perfect beauties. She'd have made an absolute fortune on the stage with a face like that.

"You're kidding," I said.

She looked at me down her perfect nose. "They sent for me specially," she said. "Because I know all about you."

"Like hell you do."

Behind her was a man in full armour carrying a stool. He put it down and she sat on it. "The original plan," she said, "was to break your arms and legs. That way you wouldn't be able to run away or make any trouble, and by the time you got to Sirupat you'd be nearly healed, so no harm done. But you got me instead."

"Do I get a choice?"

"No." She frowned. "That's not very nice," she said, "but I forgive you. I told them, there's no need for all that, I can manage him. I finally talked them round, but they made a point of saying, I do have that option if I think it's called for. So it's up to you, really."

"Since when did you work for the Sisters?"

"I don't. I just told you, they sent for me."

Exactly the sort of thing my aunt would do. "I don't believe you. I think you've been working for them all along. In fact, I bet you're a Sister yourself."

"I wish." She nodded to one of the guards, who kicked me in the stomach so hard I thought my head would burst. "All this chatter," she said, as I lay gasping on the floor, "isn't good for you, I can tell. You need to rest and get your strength up. Big day tomorrow."

I really, really, really, *really* didn't want to go to Sirupat. On the other hand, it didn't seem like I had a choice.

Not even death. For example, I tried provoking the guards, to see just how far they'd go. There's a certain sort of man – my pal Carrhasio is a prime example – who gets into the violence business not because of poverty or greed or dreams of the big score, but because he likes hurting people. Quite often you'll find them working security, in one capacity or another. Ordinary soldiering doesn't really do it for them – too much counter-marching and latrine digging and strategic withdrawing and not enough bone crunching – so they gravitate towards law enforcement and prisoner control, where there's plenty of action and the odds are generally very much in your favour.

Someone like that, skilfully aggravated by someone with a gift for words, can often be goaded into going too far, even when he's under strict orders not to kill *anybody*.

No such luck. They knew how to hurt without causing lasting damage, and I wasted a whole playful of good cutting remarks on them before I finally figured out that they didn't speak Robur. Come the next morning I was one huge bruise but still very much alive, and then it was time to go.

I had no way of telling the passage of time, so it could have been the middle of the night, but I'm guessing it was shortly before dawn when the blacksmith turned up. He had two men to carry his portable anvil up the horrible winding stairs, two more to lug up his toolbag and another man brought the chains, draped round his neck like garlands. They fitted me out with a chain rather less than a yard long, ankle to ankle, and another one rivetted to an iron collar which joined up with the ankle chain, just long enough to let me stand nearly upright but all I could see was my own feet. A pair of manacles completed the ensemble, also connected to the neck-to-feet chain, the whole lot weighing something in the order of sixty pounds. It took well over an hour to do all the rivetting, and cutting rivets off takes much longer than setting them. Trust me, I know about these things. Forget about cutting a few strands of rope and leaving me to run for it under my own steam. Anyone stupid enough to try and rescue me would need a wagon, or at the very least a heavy-duty handcart, and plenty of porters.

Not that anybody was likely to do any such thing. My friends – a hopelessly inappropriate word to describe Gombryas, Olybrius, Polycrates, Carrhasio and Doctor Papinian – had absolutely no way of knowing where I was, and because I'd always taken exquisite pains to keep them from finding out anything about me, even less way of knowing where I was likely to be taken to. Rescue was, therefore, out of the question. Abduction was another matter entirely. First the Knights; then bounty hunters working for my father and my brother Scaphio; then more bounty hunters working for my sister and brother-in-law; and other interested parties as well, several of them, but let's not complicate things unnecessarily. Long story short: someone trying to snatch me en route was a very real possibility, but given the choice I'd probably opt to stick with the Sisters. What a horrible thing to have to admit, but there you go.

"You missed one," I told the blacksmith.

"You what?"

"There should be three rivets on the left ankle. You've only done two."

He scowled at me. "Everyone's a fucking boss," he said.

Starving myself to death proved to be a non-starter. As soon as I announced that I wasn't going to eat or drink, Stauracia produced a dear little carrying case covered in green velvet, from which she took a beautifully crafted set of tubes, either ivory or walrus tusk. She explained how they worked. The hell with that, I thought, and let them feed me with a spoon.

I was back on a ship; lucky, lucky me. This ship was a galley; fifty oars, just in case the wind dropped unexpectedly. No danger that we'd be stopping for anything, and I could tell just by looking at it that it could outrun anything misguided enough to try and catch it. As well as the fifty oarsmen there were twenty marines and a large, highly polished brass object the size of a large capstan, which I recognised as a Peguilhan siphon. You don't see them around much, because only the

Mezentines have them and the way they work and the fuel they use are deadly secret; they squirt a highly inflammable liquid, with a range of over thirty yards. Just the sight of one would be enough to make any sane captain put about and run for his life, and if I could get my hands on one I know a dozen buyers who'd pay so much I could afford to collect elephants as a hobby. Now there's irony.

Galleys don't have holds, for obvious reasons, so they sat me on deck, strapped in a chair. If you're like me and you think sailing is bad, being rowed is worse. I was pretty sure I was in with a chance of dying after all, but Stauracia didn't seem to think so. She's a born sailor, never so much as a queasy moment, and thought the whole thing was hilarious; she didn't have to clean me up, so fair enough. Every time the man in the lookout saw a sail, the marines rushed to battle stations and the two specialists assigned to the siphon started pumping their bellows like mad, but all the alarms turned out to be false: traders or fishermen, a couple of big grain freighters, one squadron of Blemyan frigates who sailed on by without seeming to notice us.

I'm no navigator, but I've been up and down that coast often enough to know more or less where I am, just by counting promentaries. At Hesychia Point we headed west, out into the open sea. No more coastline to look at, just a stupid amount of water, presumably full of fish, but fishing's cruelly hard work, and apart from that no use to anybody whatsoever. Three days of that and we sighted the first of the String Islands.

Not anything to get excited about. There's nine of them, and all the great admirals in history have probably been able to see them with their eyes shut. God put them there to be fought over, another proof of His malicious sense of humour;

beyond that, they're pretty useless, being mostly mountain and dense forest. The Asvogel boys tried to get into naval salvage a few years back and built a small fleet of ships to go round the islands scavenging in the wake of sea battles, but they made a serious loss and sold the ships off cheap to one of the big herring consortiums. Take it from me, naval warfare is a complete waste, no good to man nor beast. Anything worth having goes straight to the bottom, and not even Sashan divers can hold their breath that long. The String Islands, therefore, don't interest me, apart from the morbid fact that if you want to get to Sirupat and it's too late in the year to hug the coast, that's the way you've got to go.

We put in for water at Cyon but I didn't go ashore, needless to say. The legs of my chair were nailed to the deck, so there was no point spraining my imagination. There used to be pirates in the narrow channel between Cyon and Aechmalota but some busybody had them all wiped out, so no hope there. On to Aechmalota, then round the Cape of Tears and out again into the open sea, next stop Olbia. I was running out of time, something I didn't like one bit.

Not long after we'd rounded the Cape, which we did with distressing ease – lots of ships hit the submerged rocks and sink, but our fool of a skipper contrived to miss them all – I heard people behind me talking in worried voices. I couldn't turn my head to see, but I could just about hear them, and I understand Sherden, which Sister Stauracia evidently doesn't know. I gathered that we were being followed. No, said another voice, it's a coincidence, this is the main channel, they just happen to be going the same way. Coincidence be fucked, said the first voice; turn out the guard.

So they did that, and I got another chance to see the

Peguilhan siphon operators running through their pre-battle drills; useful, since by watching them I had a slim chance of figuring out how the wonderful machine actually worked. Sister Stauracia came down from the foredeck with an anxious look on her face and conferred with the captain, though I couldn't catch what they were saying. From the look on his face, my guess is that she was telling him that if there was any serious risk of us being boarded, he was to scuttle the ship. I told myself not to get my hopes up. The impression I'd got from the Sherden-speakers behind me was that there was only the one ship chasing us, and barring a miracle the Peguilhan siphon would sort him out in a matter of seconds if he ever managed to catch up with us. Shortly after that, it all became academic anyway. The wind dropped; we powered ahead with our oars, leaving our pursuer swearing at his empty canvas. Ah well.

A long night, freezing cold, someone draped a blanket over me but it blew away when the wind got up again; dawn broke over the Olbian peninsula. Under other circumstances it's an imposing sight, mountains soaring up into the clouds, all that. I found it infinitely depressing.

Oh, come on. You don't seriously expect me to believe you've never been to Olbia. Really? Fine. The first thing you see is those silly mountains. They used to be volcanoes, the way my cousin Gainas used to be an alcoholic, but some idiot thought it'd be a good idea to build a city right under them, because they were reformed characters and had promised never to do it again.

The next thing you notice is the beach, which is black as soot, and then the gently sloping hillside on which the city stands, which is also black, and very soon after that the city itself, which is white. There's a reason for that. Faced with building out of the local materials – black rock, black sand – the founders opted to buy in their stone from the quarries fifty miles or so down the coast, where they have the finest vein of pure white marble in the world. Olbia shines so hard it hurts your eyes, especially on a bright sunny day. Blue sea, black beach, white city, black mountains capped with white snow. You certainly have no excuse for not knowing where you are.

Get a bit closer and the next thing you see is are the domes – the Salvation, the Divine Mercy, the Redeemer and the Perfect Love, all gilded, blazing so bright you'd swear they're on fire – and the Bell Tower, which I gather is still the tallest man-made structure in the known world. The tower was built so the Olbians could keep an eye out for pirates, and they do say that the tower can see you before you see it – something to do with the way the horizon curves, though I don't believe a word of it.

The next thing you see is almost certainly an Olbian customs sloop, coming straight at you like an arrow. They're red hot on harbour dues and tariffs in Olbia, understandably enough for a society whose only asset is their location. The drill is, they search your ship from top to bottom and calculate how much you've got to pay, and only then are you allowed to land. This gave me a bright idea about yelling my head off and telling the customs men that Stauracia and her boys were pirates, holding me for ransom. Saying the P word gets you listened to in Olbia, and at the very least I hoped the customs men would arrest us all and take us ashore to let the magistrates sort it all out, in which case I stood a much better chance of escaping from an Olbian jail than from Stauracia's nailed-down chair; or else Stauracia would make a fight of it and kill the customs men, in which case the Olbians would chase us with warships and either capture us (see above) or ram us, sending me to the bottom still strapped to my chair. Well, you never know your luck.

But Stauracia told the skipper to hoist a flag, one I'd never seen before, and nobody came near us, not even a fishing boat or the people who try and sell you baskets. That really depressed me, because the Olbians, though vicious as rats, are fiercely independent and don't take orders from anyone. Anyhow, we didn't land at Olbia. A tender came out to meet us, bringing food and water, and then we were off again, north-west, following the coast.

I'd never been further than Olbia before. A few years back we were booked to do a war in the southern highlands but some fool made peace and it all fell through; I wasn't sorry, because even Batou, which is where we'd have started off from, is far too close for comfort to where I was now headed. Silly really, because it goes without saying, nobody in Sirupat had the faintest idea what I looked like. That, however, was all about to change, unless I got very lucky very soon.

Define lucky. The wind had changed at Olbia, and now that horrible galley was skimming along like a bird, on a sea so calm and flat that even I didn't feel too bad at all. Mid-morning, blue sky, warm sun. We shot past the mouth of an estuary like an arrow, and noticed three ships moving out to intercept us.

Battle stations, naturally. We crammed on every last square inch of sail, but soon it was obvious that they were faster, so Stauracia told the skipper to stop and get the oars out; if we couldn't outrun them, we'd just have to sink them with our Peguilhan siphon. Fine: I'd always wanted to see one of those things in action, and there was always a chance we might lose. We turned round to face the enemy and I saw them for the first time. Nuts, I thought.

Footnote. The Knights are first and foremost a bank, but they have an important sideline in shipping and trade. Nobody likes getting robbed, so a few years ago the Knights built a small fleet of escorts, without doubt the most sophisticated and advanced warships anywhere west of Echmen. The technical name is galleass; all the best features of a galley and a sailing ship with none of the disadvantages of either. They can cross open sea like a brigantine, outrun a clipper and manoeuvre in a dead calm like a quinquireme, and they carry long-range torsion artillery – catapults and scorpions – front and aft, with an effective range of over a hundred yards. No government has anything that can match them, simply because in order to build them they'd need a massive loan from the Knights, and if you're smart you don't lend your neighbour sixpence so he can buy a knife to stab you with. Ever since they deployed these monsters to escort their convoys, nobody's robbed a single one of their ships, which is marvellous for business, and the last I heard they were building another five, bringing the total up to eleven—

Indeed. Three of them, all in one place at the same time. Rather flattering, I suppose.

Stauracia was standing next to me. I hadn't seen her approach, too busy gawking at the ships. "Well now," she said.

"Yes," I told her, "they're what you think they are. You're going to be in so much trouble," I added happily.

"*We're* going to be in so much trouble," she amended.

"No skin off my nose," I said. "I'm no better or worse off whichever of you gets me. I guess on balance, if I have to express a preference, I hope they win, because then they'll kill you and feed you to the crabs, but I'm not really fussed either way."

She couldn't be bothered to hit me. "You're smart," she said. "You're an evil little shit, but you're smart and you know about war and battles—"

"Not sea battles. Entirely different discipline."

"You know more than I do," she said, "and the captain's a complete idiot. What do we do?"

"Surrender," I said. "You haven't got a hope. Really."

"We've got the fire siphon."

"Effective range thirty yards. They can stand off three times that and sink you with their catapults."

"They won't do that. They want you alive."

I shrugged, as best I could with my wrists chained. "That would be their first choice," I said. "Second best would be making sure your horrible Sisters don't have me. One well-aimed stone and they can all go home." I grinned. "And then I won't have to go to Sirupat. Ideal."

"You said surrender."

"I was trying to be helpful. Sure, they'll kill you and all your crew, because they don't want witnesses, but you'll get to live half an hour longer, and life is something to be cherished, even tiny little bits of it."

"Fuck you," she said, and I could see she was terrified. "Tell me how to fight them, or we're all going to die. You don't want that."

"Don't I?"

"You're just bullshitting. What do we do?"

The thought of her trusting me, in a situation like that, was so funny I couldn't keep myself from laughing. That had a deplorable effect on her. She burst into tears.

"Oh, come on," I said. "Try and be plausible."

"Fuck you."

Well, I thought. There really wasn't all that much in it, and death was genuinely better than either the Sisters or the Knights, but if I absolutely had to choose I decided I'd rather have the Sisters, simply because Aunt Feralia is family, and bringing me to Sirupat would earn her prestige within the Order; I have no close relatives among the Knights, so screw them. Also, I do enjoy a good fight, provided I don't have to take an active part in it. "This won't work," I told her, "but what you could do is—"

Actually, I'm quite proud of my battle plan, although it was a silly idea and it really shouldn't have worked. A moving target is far harder to hit with artillery than a stationary one, so ramming speed straight at the right-hand galleass, then at the last moment steer right a bit, at the same time quickly shipping oars on the left side; our momentum carries us up their right side, in so close that the beak of our ship crunches up all their right-side oars, leaving them dead in the water, unable to move; at the same time, hose them down with burning oil from the siphon. Then all oars in the water and back up like mad, to keep their burning hulk between us and the other two ships. That way, if the other two want to get at us they've got to come round the burning hulk; if they try and draw back, to keep out of the way of the siphon and throw stones at us, that gives us time to dodge round behind the hulk, always keeping it between us and them; as a plan, doomed to failure because there's two of them, so one of them keeps us busy playing hide and seek, while the other goes out and comes in again on a better line and drives us onto the hulk so we can't dodge about and sinks us with a catapult shot from a safe distance. Technically a flawed plan, but ideal for my agenda; I get to see a really good scrap and the siphon in action, and then I die and don't have to go to Sirupat. Brilliant.

Didn't work, though. The oar-cutting manoeuvre went off exactly right, and the moment when the siphon suddenly blossomed into flame and the enemy ship went up with a roar like a gala-night audience cheering and so much heat I felt my eyebrows frizzle – not something you get to see every day, and almost worth the price of admission. But then it all started to unravel. Instead of one ship chasing us round and round the castle while the other pulled out and came back, the stupid idiots tried to pen us in against the hulk so they could board us, which meant both of them ended up coming in range of the siphon. It's just like in the theatre. Do it once and the audience love you. Do it three times in a row and it just gets old. The ship-engulfed-in-flames thing was fun the first time, but when the second and then the third one went up it was just depressing. Three magnificent warships, the state of the art, worth an absolute fortune, reduced to sizzling embers in no time flat. Who'd pay to watch that?

When it was all over, and we'd conscientiously run down the last cluster of survivors clinging to floating wreckage – being a witness is so often a really bad idea, I wonder why people bother with it – I called her over. "Well?" I said.

"Not bad," she said. "I knew you'd think of something."

"You owe me."

She shook her head. "Not really."

"The hell with that," I said. "I saved your life."

"No, you saved yours. I just happened to be along for the ride. There's a difference."

"You mean to say you aren't the least bit grateful?"

She smiled at me. "Fundamental rule of business," she said. "You can't expect to get paid after you've delivered the goods. If you don't get cash in advance, basically you're giving someone a present."

"That's not very nice."

She shrugged. "Besides," she said, "what do you expect me to do, let you go? They'd flay me alive."

"I got washed overboard during the battle. You spent hours searching for me, but the weight of the chains sent me straight to the bottom. Not your fault. They can't blame you for that."

"Can't they just? Anyhow, if I deliver you safe and sound I get a bonus. What do I get if I let you go?"

"A clean conscience. Sleep at night."

"Nothing," she paraphrased. "Not even the credit for being the first person to sink a galleass, because everybody knows girls don't do sea battles, so they'll all assume it was that shit-for-brains captain. It's so unfair, it really makes me mad sometimes."

"You didn't sink anything. It was my idea."

"Really? Where's your witnesses?"

I let my eyes wander over the flat blue sea. During the battle I'd been too caught up in the action to feel sick, but my stomach was starting to clench in the old familiar way, even though the wind had dropped away to practically nothing. "Good point," I said. "Not that it matters worth a damn. I'll be dead soon, and you'll have to find someone else to pick on. Your life won't be the same without me, admit it."

"You're nothing special," she said, and walked away. A man tied to a chair rarely gets the last word.

Nothing special; as a human being, absolutely. I'm not smart or pretty. I can do a full day's work, but I'm no strongman. God knows, I'm not brave, loyal or reliable, and as I think I may have mentioned at some point, I'm a fairly indifferent sailor. If you're looking to me for exceptional qualities, things that might make me special, I'm sorry to say they're all negative ones – exceptionally dishonest, exceptionally cowardly and (to use my dear sister's charming phrase) as self-centred as a spinning-top. It's external factors rather than innate qualities that make me special – special enough to be worth a hundred thousand staurata to my father, dead or alive; rather more to my sister, preferably dead (I'm not absolutely certain about the current amount; all I know is that she and my father have this sort of bidding war going, and she's got more money); special enough for the Sisters to go to such lengths to get hold of me, and for the Knights to risk, and lose, three of their glorious new warships. Actually, that's not the half of it; but I don't like talking about all that stuff. Maybe later.

A long, cold night in the chair; I fell asleep just before dawn and woke up with my hair full of dew. Shortly after dawn, more warships.

This time, however, they were in front of us, not behind. I could see nine sails: red and white vertical stripes. Only one fleet uses that particular livery. So that's that, then, I thought.

"Nice of them to come out to meet us," she said, standing behind me so I couldn't see her. She was happy; job done, success, her bonus secured. In twenty minutes I'd be someone else's responsibility.

"You're in trouble," I said.

"Bullshit."

"It's exactly what I'd do if I were the Knights," I said. "Or pirates, or bounty hunters. Doesn't take long to paint red stripes on a white sail."

It was a cheap shot, but often they work the best. She swore under her breath and called for battle stations. I grinned. All that trouble for nothing, and she'd be made to look like an idiot in front of the Sirupati commodore. Unless something went seriously wrong and she panicked and started squirting her siphon at the Sirupatis, it was all pretty pointless and silly. But fun.

I knew something wasn't right when the line split into three: four ships on the left, two in the centre, three on the right. An escort wouldn't do that. But given the lack of wind, if you only had sailing ships and you wanted to surround us, you'd want to deploy so that your four ships against the wind were the net, the three with the wind behind them were the hounds, leaving two as the huntsmen, to close in and make the actual kill. "It's all right," I called out to her, "I was only kidding. It's the Sirupatis all right."

"Shut the fuck up," she shouted back. Well: she's no fool, and maybe she'd read a book about naval warfare before she came on the mission. Or maybe not. "All right, admiral," she said, standing over me and yelling angrily in my face, like it was all my fault. "Now what do we do?"

She'd been eating something with garlic in it. "Don't ask me. You're the one who sank three galleasses."

She hit me. She's not particularly strong, but she had a horseshoe in her hand; that's an old Auxentia City custom, though I guess she could've picked it up anywhere. "What do we *do*?"

It's not easy to think brilliantly when your head feels like an anvil. "Outrun them," I said. "You've got oars; they haven't."

"You know that for a fact, do you?"

Someone pushed past us, running. "Not many people have galleys," I said. "They're expensive and no good for freight."

"I hope you're right," she snarled at me, and went away to yell at the captain: put about, oars, full speed. Me and my big mouth.

That was when the wind chose to get up. I was too busy

being very ill to pay close attention for a while, and besides, the enemy were behind me now and I couldn't turn round to look at them. I didn't need to see to figure out that our advantage had just gone down the drain. A moment later, I heard the captain yelling, ship oars, put on all sail. A tiny spurt of hope, like heartburn, shot up inside my head – we were now heading away from Sirupat, at top speed. It didn't last long. Assuming the nine ships weren't Knights, they were almost certainly privateers, strongly motivated by my father's money. Or my brother-in-law's. Same difference.

In which case, I decided, I wanted to do something to help. Hard to know what. Nine to one is poor odds, even with the Peguilhan siphon, so the only thing I could think of was to keep out of their way till the wind dropped again, and that could be a matter of minutes or days.

She was back. "Well?"

"You want to dodge around a bit," I said. "They'll try and box you in. Don't let them."

"You're no fucking use."

"Fine," I said. "Presumably your orders are to kill me rather than let anyone else get me."

"Yes."

I smiled. "That's all right, then. Carry on."

She thought about it for maybe thirty seconds, a very long time in context. Then she yelled for someone to cut the ropes. Two marines marched me up the deck. The weight of the chains made keeping my balance on the moving deck a constant challenge, and if there'd been anything left in my stomach I'd have hurled it harder and further than the Peguilhan siphon; hardly ideal conditions for my first serious naval command. Still, I like to think I'm fairly adaptable.

"Gap," I said, pointing. Luckily the helmsman had a brain and didn't need everything spelling out. We darted forward into the gap, which was promptly closed by an enemy ship. But that was fine, because I'd chosen that heading so as to draw that particular ship away from where I really wanted to go; and so on and so forth, for quite some time. I found out that the galley wasn't nearly as manoeuvrable as I'd assumed it would be. It was a bitch to slow down and stop and it didn't like being turned sharply. But the enemy ships were even more cumbersome, and they didn't have artillery, and they'd seen the Peguilhan siphon and knew roughly what it was capable of, and we taught them its effective range the hard way. That brought the odds down from nine to six, which was still far too many. Then I made a couple of wrong guesses, and suddenly there were four of them closing in on us at once; we could burn one of them, but not all four, and then we'd have been boarded and it'd all be over. So I pointed at the ship dead ahead of us, which was moving across our bow to hem us in. "Oars out," I said. A flood of corrosive fluid filled my mouth and took all the skin off my throat: rotten timing. I swallowed it. "Ram them."

Ramming a ship, even when it's side on and you hit it just right, like we did, is no fun at all. It's not that much different from hitting a rock. The shock comes up through the soles of your feet and makes your brain rattle about in your skull, and the noise is unbelievable, like God's bones breaking, but somehow long drawn out, like it's going to go on for ever. I landed awkwardly on my elbow. One of the marines was thrown sideways and ended up in the water, where he discovered that heavy armour can be a mixed blessing. She landed on the other one, knocking all the wind out of him and nearly braining herself on the rim of his helmet, a Type Three kettle-hat. I had my chance. A few tottering steps, then over the rail and into the sea—

I hate being on boats. Some fool always leaves bits of rope lying around. I caught my foot in one and went down on my nose, and by then it was too late. They hauled me to my feet and dragged me back to the helm. She was up, gripping like mad onto what was left of the rail, bleeding like a stuck pig from a scalp wound. I yelled at the captain to back up; our ram was stuck in the side of the enemy ship, which was sinking fast. Even if we got untangled, the wake could easily drag us down if we didn't get far enough away before she sank. You'd have thought the skipper would've known that, but apparently not.

"Try that again and I'll have your legs broken," she howled in my ear. I had just enough freedom of movement to elbow her in the ribs, which gave me enormous satisfaction.

We backed up just in time. The enemy ship went over on its side, its mastheads hitting the water only a few yards short of the tip of our ram and drenching us like a summer shower. The sea was full of men bobbing up and down, screaming, thrashing about like kids playing in a fountain. Some of them were swimming toward us, but we backed up faster than they could swim, just about. When we had the right distance, we held left and squirted ourselves through the narrow gap between the wreck and the next enemy ship. It was a good line to take: right angles to the wind, so that finally our oars gave us the advantage in speed, and all five surviving bad guys were out of position. We passed so close to one ship that I could see the stunned look on the sailors' faces, just before the siphon gave them something else to think about. And then we were free and clear, with the enemy getting smaller and smaller behind us.

We carried on rowing long after they were out of sight,

just to be on the safe side, steering a dog-leg course so they couldn't simply follow our line. Then the oarsmen gave up; they'd been rowing flat out for best part of an hour, and they were completely blown. We'd lost one mast and cracked our spine ramming the bad guy, and the marines were bailing water using their helmets. No matter; the wind had died away completely. We were safe. Well, my shipmates were, all thanks to me. I was in more trouble than a Rogation Day goose, but that's what you get for trying to help people.

5

I'd never been to Sirupat before, for obvious reasons. It wasn't at all like I'd expected.

On the map – I'm thinking of the one in my father's library, engraved on a big brass sheet with all the names inlaid with silver – it's a long, narrow island lying parallel to the Friendly Sea coast about fifteen miles out and ninety miles west of Olbia. It's got a central spine of tall mountains, and the rest is fairly flat – premium arable land, watered by fat, good-natured rivers. It's these rivers that make all the trouble, because as well as water and nourishing silt, they wash down something else from the mountain slopes: gold dust.

Now you can see the difficulty. Nobody would give a stuff about Sirupat if it wasn't for the gold, and its people would be left in peace. Their king would be a stolid little man, double-chinned, smart but not clever, knowing very little about poetry and art but a lot about hounds and falcons; a sound judge of horses and human nature, loved by all his people who'd never met him, underestimated by his enemies, treated by his wife with affectionate contempt. He'd have considerably less money than my father, and his favourite food would probably be mutton with carrots and pearl barley.

Gold, unfortunately, changes everything. Two-fifths of the gold in the West comes from Sirupat, and Permia, the next biggest producer, will soon be completely worked out. But all the major governments are steadily shifting away from silver and into gold, partly because there's so much bad silver about that nobody trusts it, partly because so much more money gets spent these days, what with all the wars supercharging the leading economies, making prices rise like ducks off a pond. So Sirupat has what everybody wants, and the only reason it hasn't been invaded by the Vesani Republic is because if they tried it, they'd find themselves at war with the Aelians and Perimadeia and the Mezentines and probably the Sashan as well, because none of them would dare let all that gold fall into the hands of an enemy. Everybody needs the stuff, all the noble, sophisticated nations with manifest destinies, and the people who've got it are a bunch of backwater primitives who've only recently discovered the benefits of not pissing in wells. You'd laugh yourself sick if it wasn't so deadly serious.

This makes life awkward for the king of Sirupat. Gold floods out of his rivers like God's diarrhoea, filling his treasury, but then the trouble starts. He's surrounded by mighty neighbours, all desperate to get their hands on the stuff, all determined that nobody else will. He can't simply refuse to sell, because that would cut off the supply of specie and bring about economic collapse throughout the West. Then someone would be forced to invade Sirupat, to get the flow going again, and then there'd have to be a war, and by the time it was over there'd be nothing left alive this side of the Sashan border except insects.

(Footnote. You think I'm exaggerating. I'm not. I didn't make up the name Saevus Corax. It used to belong to a man who made it big in my line of work six hundred years ago, during the last serious war, when the Third Empire collapsed. By the time it was all over, the population of the West had declined by two-thirds. Only a few million died in actual fighting. The rest were the women and kids and old men who starved because there was nobody to get in the harvest or sow next year's corn, or died of plague cooped up in besieged cities. Six centuries later and we still haven't really recovered; there's still tens of thousands of acres of briars and withies that used to be farms, and forests that used to be cities. I chose the name to remind me what another war like that would do to idiotic humanity, not that I need reminding. A war over Sirupat would make the original Saevus' war look like a scuffle at the race track. Think about it. I do, often.)

There's nothing the king particularly wants. His island is self-sufficient, his population is small – just about enough able-bodied men to make up one regiment of the Vesani army; they've got forty-six. There's a limit to how many priceless works of art a man can find houseroom for, and anything in the way of welfare reforms or social engineering would bring the religious authorities down on him like a thunderbolt (tell you about them later). The perfect paradox: all the money in the world; can't spend a penny of it.

So he doesn't spend it. He puts it in the bank. Actually, two banks. Guess which ones.

It works, just about. All the Sirupati gold ends up in the vaults of the Knights and the Sisters, who lend it to the major governments, who spend it on fighting each other, with a view to tilting the balance of power in their favour so much that one day they'll be able to invade Sirupat and get away with it. Meanwhile, the king of Sirupat steadily builds up a credit balance with both banks that could never ever be repaid; if he withdrew even a tenth of it, the banks would fail, and if the banks went under, all the kingdoms of the earth would be dragged down with them.

The king of Sirupat is an elderly man in poor health. Nobody seems quite certain what's wrong with him, but I'd be prepared to bet it's something stress-related. Anyway, that's quite enough about that for the time being.

I suppose I'd been expecting something a bit like Olbia – magnificence, show, melodrama, vulgarity. Instead, I saw a long, flat blur on the skyline that could just as easily have been low cloud until we got up close enough to see treetops. There was no shining city on a headland, and I remembered that there's only one big settlement on Sirupat, and it's four miles inland, up an estuary, the mouth of which we were rapidly approaching. A mile or so out from the coast we passed two islands, pillars of rock with nowhere to land a boat, covered with screaming gulls so densely packed together that all you could see was white. I got the impression that not many ships passed that way. Well, why should they?

The mouth of the estuary, where we turned in, was heavily wooded so there was nothing to see for a mile or so, when the woods ended and we were rowing up a broad river with flat country on either side, all the pale green of half-grown barley. In the distance you could just about make out the mountains, where all the trouble came from, but they looked misleadingly far away. I spotted maybe half a dozen houses – big, substantial farms with barns and sheds and clusters of cottages for the hired men – and that was all. For the most important place on earth, it was all pretty dull.

She was worried, I guess because nobody had come out to meet us, though of course she didn't confide in me. The Sirupatis do have a fleet (twenty-five fairly modern warships, a present from the Mezentines, though I think His Majesty would rather have had socks) but I could see the point in not sending them. An escort would only draw attention to us, and quite possibly slow us up. I called out to her a couple of times but she pretended she hadn't heard me. I'd been put back in my chair after the battle was safely over. I couldn't help thinking I'd missed my chance there. My own silly fault, like practically everything bad that's ever happened in the history of the world.

Just when I was starting to think that we must have turned into the wrong river, the watchman on the masthead started yelling, and a minute or so later we could all see for ourselves. Nothing particularly exciting: a spire and a tower, and then a long, grey city wall. Welcome to Dui Chirra, capital city of the Principality of Sirupat.

The blacksmith was kneeling at my feet, pulling the nails out of the chair legs with a claw hammer. I felt like I ought to give him a blessing or make him an earl.

"Watch him like a hawk," I heard her saying, but to be honest with you I hadn't even bothered with the usual strategic analysis – gaps in the cordon, weakest point in the perimeter, possible lines of escape, all that rigmarole. There's a point where you just shrug and give up, and I'd reached it. I guess I'd always known that one day I'd end up in Sirupat, no matter what I did or how hard I tried. When there's nothing you can do, do nothing.

They carried me off the ship, one marine to each leg of the chair, shoulder-high like an emperor. There was a moment when we were on the gangplank; I tried shifting my weight so I'd topple sideways, with the principle of leverage to help me, but it didn't work. After that we were on dry land, with no opportunities whatsoever. They carried me to the city gate and put me down. The gate opened, and half a dozen men came out. Three soldiers, in shiny gilded scale armour; two priests; an old man in a plain grey gown. I wouldn't have fancied wearing heavy wool in that heat, but I guess it's about what you're used to.

She came round me from behind and started to speak. The old man lifted his hand, meaning shut up. He looked at me, then knelt down. So did the priests. None of them looked at me.

The old man held out his hands, palms upwards. "Your Majesty," he said.

Didn't I mention that? Sorry. Careless of me.

I'm pretty sure I told you about the king of Sirupat; old man, not well. My great-uncle.

A long time ago, before they discovered all that nasty gold, one of my maternal grandmother's many, many sisters married the king of Sirupat. It was regarded as an unfortunate match by my family, who'd hoped for so much more, but minor provincial royalty's better than nothing, and by all accounts she was a remarkably plain girl, though she played the harp quite well.

The years rolled by. Gold was discovered. For the first time in history, king of Sirupat was something people wanted to be, rather than an inconvenience you accepted with a resigned shrug. Knives and poison took over from pneumonia as the main cause of death among the Sirupati royal family. Once the dust had settled and the blood had soaked away into it, the surviving contenders tried throwing their weight around with the various kings, heads of state and bank directors; not surprisingly, most of them came to bad ends. The upshot was that the present king, Badulia III, was left secure on his throne with no rival claimants and a secure succession in the form of his son and heir, Gobazes. It was the outcome everybody wanted, even the priests, and it went to prove the ancient doctrine that family trees grow best when rigorously pruned.

Then Gobazes fell off his horse and broke his neck. Stupid thing to happen; he was taking part in the annual grand review of the army, and all he had to do was sit still and look royal, but a pigeon suddenly got up a few yards away, Gobazes' horse shied and reared and Gobazes hit the cobblestones head first. It all happened faster than you could sneeze, and it was one of those moments (see above) when the world changes irreparably, and nothing will ever be the same again.

Fine, but what's all this got to do with me? Answer: because one tiny sucker of the royal tree went unpruned, because my family was far away and had excellent security. With Gobazes dead, the only possible heir to the throne of Sirupat was my mother's eldest son. Me.

Which was why (I don't know if you were paying attention when I mentioned it earlier) my father disinherited me on my seventeenth birthday. I couldn't succeed him as the fifteenth duke, because I was destined to be king of Sirupat when old Badulia died. Sirupati law is understandably very clear on this point: the king can't hold any other honours or titles, because of the danger of a conflict of interests.

Big deal, I hear you say. There's still the one brother you didn't murder, whatsisname, Scaphio. He can be king. Why drag you into it?

Because, I deeply regret to say, it doesn't work like that. As well as being the rightful sovereign of a small island, the king of Sirupat is a religious figure. According to some people, *the* religious figure. It goes something like this.

There are, as you know, two major religions in this world: the Invincible Sun and the Eternal Flame. You also probably know that the fire-worshippers are split into two distinct groups, the Left Hand and the Right Hand, who hate each other like poison. About a quarter of the total number of believers are Left Hand, and they accept as a fundamental tenet of their faith that the Redeemer has already arrived on earth and lives among them in the person of the king of Sirupat; that's the bit that annoys the Right Hand so much, because to them it's unforgivable heresy. Furthermore, they believe that there is only one Redeemer, reincarnated every time the king dies and is replaced. This leads to a certain degree of doctrinal complexity, because how can the holy essence be reincarnated into someone who's already alive? The only way it could work would be if the new king were born a split second after the old one dies, but that would be a real problem, since every reign would start with a seventeen-year regency, and everybody knows that's a recipe for disaster. Accordingly the priests came up with a doctrine that states that when the true heir is born, half of the holy essence leaves the ruling king and lodges inside the heir; when the old king dies, his half of the essence leaves him and reunites with the other half during the coronation ceremony. There's a special hymn, apparently, and someone lights a candle, and they ring a special bell.

This doctrine had a pretty rough ride during the Troubles, when heirs apparent were going down like flies under the assassin's knife, but they explained it away by saying the murdered princelings couldn't have been real heirs after all, only pretenders. They said the same thing when Gobazes died; he couldn't have been the real heir, or he'd never have been permitted to fall off his horse in the first place. In fact, the priests pointed out, it only went to show that the doctrine was right after all, because all these wicked, deceitful pretenders had come to very bad ends, which is what you get for trying to usurp the Chosen One.

Long story short: so long as I'm alive, I'm it. I can't resign, abdicate or be stripped of my title on account of exceptional depravity. Like it or not, I'm the spiritual leader of several million Left Hand fire worshippers, most of whom live in countries I've never even heard of, whereas any Right Hander will earn eternal bliss in Paradise if he kills me on sight. Meanwhile, in my dual capacity as the Redeemer reborn and the richest king in the world, everything that happens to everybody everywhere is incontrovertibly my fault.

Lucky, lucky me.

When the thing you've been dreading all your life eventually happens, among the various reactions is a sense of something resembling calm. I speak from experience, so pay attention. I figure that the bad stuff, whatever it is, will only represent a third of the total misery, in itself, as a thing. The other two-thirds are the terror, stress, anxiety and tortured anticipation, and they come from the possibility of options – I'm probably going to get caught but I may just possibly escape; they're bound to kill me in the end but it's just possible that they won't. When the hammer hits the nail and drives it through your skin and gristle and bone, fixing you to the very bad thing so there's no possibility of escape or reprieve, two-thirds of the pain of being alive falls away, leaving you feeling light and easy and almost young again. Of course the remaining third is very bad indeed, and make the most of the light and airy feeling, because it's likely to last for the rest of your life, which is no time at all. Even so.

The blacksmith came and cut off all the rivets – I'd hate his job, because no matter how well I'd peened each rivet-head, I'd know that sooner or later it'd be up to me to cut them off again; no permanence, no sense of achievement – and I felt the weight fall off me; see above, but this time literally. There was a moment when I thought about it, but you've got to be realistic. I'd been sitting in the chair for days on end, I was cramped like you wouldn't believe; couldn't fight and run to save my life, you might say. A stroke of luck for the blacksmith and the guards and the old man, one or more of whom would probably have been badly hurt if I'd tried anything. I felt like I'd just exercised clemency, and it gave me a warm fuzzy feeling.

Actually, I was so crocked up I had to lean on one of the guards, just to hobble the few yards through the gate into the lodge, where there was a carriage waiting to take us to the palace. It was one of those closed carriages, and I rather enjoyed the look on the priests' faces as they struggled to cope with the fact that the Redeemer Made Flesh didn't smell very nice. Nobody said anything, and it suddenly occurred to me to wonder what language they spoke in Sirupat. You assume everybody speaks either Robur or Aelian, and in civilised places that's a reasonably safe assumpion, but we were in the armpit of the universe, so God only knew what sort of noises they made when they wanted to communicate with each other. I considered saying something, just to find out whether anybody understood me, but in the end I couldn't be bothered.

The palace was a serious disappointment. Would you

believe it, the richest man in the world lived in a wooden building, practically a barn. True, a very old barn, and I guess tradition is very important to these people, but even so. Imagine a very big shed, like the ones they keep the warships in at Boc Bohec. It's really just a frame with planks nailed to it – very thick planks, two inches or more, oak and grey with age. The main gate looked like it hadn't been opened for centuries; people went in and out through a little wicket. I had to stoop to get through it, and I'm on the short side of average. I thought of my great-aunt, coming here from our family's grand town house in the City, vainly trying to keep the hem of her dress out of the mud.

"Why are you here?" I asked her, as we waited to file through the wicket. "You've done your job. You can go home now."

"I want to see the look on your face when I hand you over."

"Did it occur to you," I said, ducking my head under the lintel, "that I'm the crown prince around here? I could have you killed."

"Bullshit," she said. "You're a prisoner. Nobody's going to listen to you."

"We'll see. Bet you sixty trachy."

Inside the palace. Dark, illuminated by firelight from a big hearth and a few narrow windows. Rushes on the floor; fresh rushes lying on a bed of black, crumbly compost. The smell was recently roasted meat, woodsmoke, mould and rats' piss. We were in a long hall, with a broad table running up it three-quarters of its length, flanked by oak benches polished shiny by the back ends of generations of the Sirupati elite. There was a fine coating of dust over everything, like an autumn dew, and the far end of the table was sprinkled with what I at first assumed were olive pits, until I remembered that olives don't

grow this far north. The other thing that looks like that is rat
turds, from very big rats.

I got the impression from her reaction that she's not overly
fond of rats. "This place could do with a woman's touch," I said.

"Piss off," she replied.

That told me something. She's far too politic to swear out
loud if she thinks people could understand her; therefore, in
Sirupat they don't talk Robur. I stopped dead in my track and
turned to one of the priests. "Say something," I said in Euxine.

"Your Highness?"

Right first time; nice to have something actually work, for a
change. "Who am I?"

"Highness?"

"Answer the question."

I learned Euxine some years ago, when I spent six months
in jail in Boustrophedon. I was innocent, needless to say, but
they wouldn't listen. Only goes to show, nothing's ever wasted.
"You are the Redeemer, Highness."

"You mean half of him, surely."

I could see I was torturing the poor man. "In a sense,
Highness. Strictly speaking, until the moment of transcend-
ence during the coronation ceremony—"

"Yes, I know all that. Sorry." I smiled at him, which made
him nervous. I don't suppose he'd ever talked to the back legs
of God before. "Apart from that, though."

"Majesty?"

"Am I the crown prince and heir presumptive to the throne?"

"Yes, Highness. I mean Majesty."

"Fine," I said. "Arrest that woman."

The guards had been listening. Two of them grabbed her:
hands on shoulders, toecap on the inside of the knee, head

pulled back by the hair, sword blade under chin. For country boys, they were really very good. "Lock her up," I said. "I'll deal with her later."

They dragged her up by her hair and frogmarched her out the way we'd just come. She tried to scream something at me but got a hand over her mouth before she could find her first word. "You owe me sixty trachy," I called out after her in Robur. Something for her to think about in her cell, with the rats.

That made me feel a little bit better. I turned to the priest and gave him a happy grin. "Now I suppose I ought to see my great-uncle. What's your name, by the way?"

"Artabas, Highness."

"Artabas. And what do you do around here?"

He looked at me as though I was winding his guts round a stick. "I'm the precentor of the College of Priests and deputy chairman of Your Majesty's privy council."

"That must be an interesting job."

"Yes, Highness."

"Oh, one more thing. If I wanted to leave the island and go back to Scona, would you stop me?"

"Yes, Highness."

"Ah. Oh well. Lead on."

For reasons that I'll explain later, I never got to see more than a few hundred square yards of the majestic island of Sirupat, so I know virtually nothing about it at first hand; but I read a book about it, by a very distinguished scholar who'd never been there but had read about it in very old, therefore authoritative, books. This combination of erudition and birthright makes me uniquely qualified to tell you about the place, far more so than if I'd actually traipsed all round it making notes.

Sirupat is basically the shape of a man's hand, with the wrist opposite the mainland and the fingers stretching out into the sea; there are six of them rather than five, but it's probably too late to do anything about that now. What you might call the palm and heel of the hand are mountains, gashed by rivers that eventually reach the sea between the roots of the fingers – I'm beginning to wish I hadn't started this hand analogy, except that it's singularly apt. The river valleys are the only worthwhile land for farming, and that's where all the gold is, too, having been washed down in the mud from the mountains. It's beastly hot in summer and beastly cold in winter; there's a brief spring and an autumn so short you miss it if you blink. Plenty of fish off the wrist-side coast, but nothing worth having off the fingers, because during the spawning season the rivers are poisoned with iron ore and lead, flushed out of the lower mountain slopes when the rivers are in spate and the levels are high enough to bite into those particular strata. There are enormous forests (mostly pine) up in the mountains but all the trees in the lowlands were felled long ago, apart from a spindly variety of thorn, which grows everywhere and bears a small, bitter black fruit that the locals crush and mix with honey to make a sort of semi-sweet butter.

The Sirupatis say they came from Olbia, driven out by the Robur when they founded their colony there. I don't think so; they're shorter and stockier than the indigenous Olbians, they're Left Hand rather than Right and they don't speak the same language. I think they're probably descended from Hus or Dejauzi prisoners of war relocated to Olbia by the Sashan when they ruled the peninsula a very long time ago. At some point they broke away and made it as far as Sirupat, where it wasn't worth anyone's while trying to get them back. That would account for their being Left Hand, which as far as I can tell was the original orthodox form of the fake religion concocted by the legendary and probably fictitious conqueror Felix the Great, to pacify his vast empire. The trouble with that hypothesis is that Felix is supposed to have been around about a thousand years later than the time the Sirupatis would have settled Sirupat, but since he's purely mythical I don't suppose it greatly matters. I like my theory and it fits more of the established facts than any other, so let's make it the truth.

The Sirupatis are much like country people anywhere. They're very good at what they do, and have no interest in anything else. It's easy to mistake this lack of interest for boorishness and stupidity, but the Sirupatis are neither. It's easy to talk about closed minds and narrow horizons, but a Sirupati left to himself and not pushed around is probably happier than most people in this world, and does very little harm. Not many people starve or die violently on Sirupat; the four main causes of death on the island in the normal course of things are old age, pneumonia, logging accidents and falling into flooded ditches when drunk. They marry later than most people, have fewer children and fewer deaths in infancy, and property is divided between all the surviving male and female heirs rather than passing to the eldest son. They're forever taking days off for some religious festival or other, and you gain prestige with your neighbours by holding extravagant parties, with a pig roast and wheat bread and honeycakes and all the coarse white wine you can drink. There's probably a body of written law somewhere in the palace archives, but I don't suppose anyone knows where it is. Most people seem capable of striking a balance between doing what's right and what they can get away with, and nobody wants to involve the authorities, because when did that ever make anything better?

All in all, there are worse places to live, if you're a farmer with a small flock in the mountains and fifteen or so lowland acres, like most Sirupatis. Nobody's going to conscript you into an army or empty your barn to pay taxes to pay soldiers, and you know the difficult and dangerous trade of staying alive on a chunk of bare rock surrounded by sea because your ancestors figured it all out centuries ago. You'd probably think they were dumb yokels but it's a life I envy till it hurts compared with mine, unharmed and harmless, and whatever they may have done at various times, they most definitely didn't deserve to be saddled with me. Still, as I keep saying, I didn't start it.

Through the hall to a door. Knock three times on the door and two soldiers open it. They step back to let you pass, and you go up a wooden staircase, call it a staircase, more like a ladder. That brings you into the hayloft, sorry, royal bedchamber. In which there's a bed, and in the bed there's a man.

We'll get to him in a moment. Standing beside the bed are six priests, four soldiers in shiny gold scale armour and a man who looks like a farrier but, this being Sirupat, is presumably a doctor. They're standing because there's nothing in the room to sit on except the bed, and that wouldn't be respectful. The priests are clearly priests because they're dressed in long, plain red gowns, which is what the Keepers of the Flame all wear; I guessed they were the rest of the privy council, correctly as it turned out. The room smells of tallow and pee – human, not rodent – with a few grace notes of cardamom and cloves. There's no window; the light comes from four candles, thick as your arm, spiked on a tall iron stand. My poor, poor great-aunt, I thought. No wonder she died young.

I looked down at the man in the bed. "Hello," I said. "I'm your cousin Florian met'Oc, from Choris. Pleased to meet you."

He looked at me. A few years back, I was in Blemya with some time to kill, so I went to have a gawp at the Great Necropolis, like you do. That's where they keep seven thousand years' worth of kings, all perfectly preserved, in a huge vault under a mountain. When a king dies, they gut him, embalm him and put him out in the sun to desiccate. Then they do something rather clever, though I'm not sure I see the point of it. There's this tree that grows in the jungles of the far south. If you stick a knife in it, it bleeds sap, which eventually sets hard, like amber. So the Blemyans import this sap in huge jars – takes something like a thousand trees to fill one jar – and they pour it over their sun-dried kings, and it goes off as hard as rock, transparent apart from a deep golden haze, and there you are, the immortality of the flesh. For seventy trachy Vesani you can take a tour of the inner hall of the mausoleum and look into the milk-white eyes of two hundred and eighty-seven Blemyan god-kings, all looking fresh as the day they were stabbed, lynched, poisoned, strangled, beheaded (they stitch it back on) or shrivelled down to the bone by disease or old age. Seventy trachy I'll never see again and if I had my time over again I'd rather spend it on a nice steak with onions, but not something you'd easily forget. Anyhow, the king of Sirupat looked a bit like that.

The old man opened his eyes and looked at me. When he spoke – just my name, repeated – it sounded like the scuttling of mice up in the roofspace; or maybe I only thought that because rodents were so much on my mind at the time.

"He's very tired," said one of the priests. "You should leave now."

No argument from me on that score. The smell was starting to get to me and sick people are depressing. I'd noticed something else, but I wasn't quite sure what it was. My new friend Artabas led me back down to the hall and I sat down on a bench without being asked or told.

"What's the matter with him?" I asked.

"I'm not a doctor, Highness. We pray for him."

I didn't doubt that for a moment. "There is a doctor on the case, isn't there?"

"Yes, Majesty, the royal physician. You saw him just now."

"Yes," I said. "But a second opinion wouldn't hurt, I don't suppose. Preferably an Echmen. They're miles ahead of the West in medicine."

I'd said the wrong thing. The Echmen are Right Hand. "That might not be appropriate."

No Highness this time. "Maybe not," I said. "Still, we do want him to get better, don't we?"

More thinking aloud than a question, but it was one he'd rather not have been asked. "Of course, Highness. But God's will be done. We can hope, but we must be realistic."

The way he said it made my neck itch, even though the rope burns healed up years ago. Like the look in the eyes of the kings of Blemya, not something you forget in a hurry. "This place," I said, "is a mess. Any chance of getting it cleaned up a bit?"

"Of course, Majesty. Would you like me to show you to your apartments?"

"Not particularly."

Maybe he hadn't heard me. "If you'd care to follow me."

I'll say this for them, they'd made an effort. Apartments,

plural; I had a nice big bedroom, a sitting room and a dressing room with an actual polished-steel mirror. No windows, on account of being a long way underground, with only one narrow stair for access, but the walls were panelled in a nice cheerful light oak, floorboards rather than stone slabs or beaten clay, nice sheepskin rugs and in the bedroom an actual carpet, four feet square, Sashan work, probably a gift from a diplomat. One wall of the bedroom covered in bookshelves filled with books, though they all turned out to be commentaries on the scriptures. Beeswax candles, not tallow. A cedarwood chest as big as a coffin, containing linen shirts and a few floor-length priest's gowns. The guards on the door were there for my protection, no doubt.

There was a small round table supporting a silver jug of wine, a silver-gilt beaker and a bowl of pomegranates. What I really wanted was a bath, but there didn't seem to be one of those.

They kept me safe for a very long time, during which I managed to get some sleep. I was woken up by a tall red-haired man in a white gown, escorted by two soldiers. He was carrying a brass tray, on which were a wooden bowl and a knife. Various thoughts flashed through my mind – was the bowl for catching the Divine blood, lest a single drop fall on the ground and be defiled? – and then the man said he was there to shave me.

"Why?"

"Your Majesty would wish to be clean-shaven."

Fair point. I had a week's stubble, and it itched. I told him to go ahead. "Any chance of a bath?" I added.

He looked at me as though I'd just told him to take off his

clothes and bend over, but he agreed to see what could be done. "It might take some time to arrange," he said.

"That's fine. Don't worry, I'll take full responsibility."

I got the impression we weren't going to be friends. "Majesty," he said, and left. I made a mental note not to tease people, especially if there was a risk that they might turn out to be the Minister of the Interior, and went back to reading a treatise on the Eucharist.

She was my next visitor. "I suppose you think that was really clever," she said.

She hadn't brought my sixty trachy. "No," I said. "Really clever and they'd have hanged you. How did you get out?"

"I banged on the door till someone came, and then I told them who I am."

"Were there rats?"

She had bits of cobweb in her hair. "They got me an interpreter and I spoke to the president of the privy council."

"Artabas. Nice chap."

"He apologised."

"I bet he did. What did you threaten him with?"

She sat down on a chair, of which I had two. I lay on the bed with my hands behind my head. "I pointed out that I was a duly accredited representative of the Poor Sisters. I think he got the message."

"Drink?"

"No, thank you. It's time we had a talk."

After she'd spoken to Artabas. Plenty of time for a cosy chat when we were on the ship, but she'd ignored me when she wasn't begging me for help. "Sure. What's your favourite colour? What sort of music do you like?"

She couldn't hit me any more, I noted. If she'd been allowed to, she would have. "You aren't stupid," she said. "You know why the Sisters had you brought here."

"What are they poisoning the old man with?"

"I have no idea what you're talking about."

"I'm guessing calaber beans," I said, "on account of the dribble at the side of the mouth and the stink of pee. Presumably now I'm here you'll finish the job."

"We need to talk about capitalising your investments."

I knew what that meant. Instead of the king being owed vast sums of money, he'd own a share of the bank. Not that it would do him any good, because the Sisters would still hold all the voting shares. But he wouldn't be able to withdraw all his money in one go and bring the bank to its knees. "Are the priests in on the murder thing?" I asked. "When I saw him lying there I assumed yes, but now I'm not so sure. I can't really see what would be in it for them. Or is it just one or two of them, and the rest of them think he's just naturally poorly?"

"In exchange for the release of the balances currently standing in the king's name," she said, "we're prepared to offer forty-one per cent of the equity. Now that's a really good offer."

I nodded. "You kill the king," I said, "and I sign away your debt to me, and then you make me foreclose on the Knights, wiping them off the face of the earth. That leads to the biggest war in history. With you so far. It's what happens after that where I'm still a bit confused."

She glowered at me. "Bullshit," she said. "It's not like that at all."

"The question is," I said, "who have you got? You're acting like you've got the whole privy council, but I have my doubts about that. I bet the Knights've got at least half, which is why

I'm locked up in here, you're in such a tearing hurry, and the king's still alive. There's nine of them, right? I counted nine, in the royal bedchamber."

She stood up. "You're delusional," she said. "I'll come back when you're feeling better."

"Sit down." She didn't. "You're really in a fix, aren't you?" I said. "You got here thinking the Sisters have the whole thing sewn up, but then you had your chat with Artabas and he told you it's not like that. He told you the Knights have half the council, so unless you get my seal on the contract right now, you're dog food. Then why didn't you make me seal the contract on the ship – no, wait, the royal seal's here and you couldn't get your paws on it. Oh, that's hilarious."

"I don't have to listen to this. You're just trying to be annoying."

The most fun I'd had in ages. "Let me guess. The Knights' man hasn't arrived yet, so you've got this slender window of opportunity, because once he gets here—"

"Fuck you," she said, and left.

And informative, too. Basically I'd been making it up as I went along, trying to see what made her wince. Much to my surprise, she'd confirmed nearly all of it. Well, it's nice when you finally have some idea what's going on.

She'd told me Artabas was one of hers. I'd already guessed that, though I'd wondered a bit when he let the guards arrest her. That raised some interesting possibilities, involving separation of powers and the chain of military command. If the military didn't take orders direct from the privy council, I might be in with a chance.

You know how it is when your brain's been racing away,

like a millwheel in a flood and some fool's neglected to disengage the gears, and then you want to stop and calm down, but you can't. I decided to let the wheel keep turning. If I stopped it, I'd be left with the ghastly reality of my situation – a prisoner, caught, confined; I think I mentioned I have this thing about confined spaces. It's not just physical spaces, cells and small rooms and tunnels, and just thinking about it makes my skin crawl. It's confinement in the wider sense. Believe me, I'd rather die (as witness my actions on the ship) than lose control. Over myself, naturally. I don't yearn to rule the world; I'd be very bad at it and I'd hate it, and I can't see why anybody would want to. But I need, on a very fundamental level, to be master of my fate and captain of my soul. If someone's the boss of me, I feel like a worm stuck through with a pin. I'd rather die and get it over with than spend the rest of my life as somebody's puppet, whether the confinement takes place in a jail cell or a throne room. You know those hair shirt things that really serious monks wear next to the skin, to mortify the flesh? That's how I feel when somebody's got control over me. I can't rest; I can't get comfortable; I itch all over. All I can think about is jumping out of a window, and if it happens to be twelve storeys up, that's still better than the alternative.

So, rather than dwell on depressing realities, I reckoned I'd be much happier letting my mind race free over the green, flat pastures of other people's horrible problems: the Sisters, the Knights, the Fire priests, the kingdoms of the earth. For instance, suppose that between them the Sisters and the Knights have the whole privy council sewn up, but not the military. Easy mistake to make, if you're used to dealing with the grown-up governments down south. You could easily overlook the possibility than in a one-horse regime like Sirupat, things are done differently. Take away the religious complication, and Sirupat's just a modest-sized island, no bigger than the country estate of your typical nobleman, someone like my father. Estates don't have governments. They have bureaucracies, yes, but that's not the same thing. My father doesn't have a Chancellor of the Exchequer; he has a steward. He doesn't need a Minister of Labour; he's got Guron, our half-blind, brain-dead old bailiff. And he doesn't have a Minister of War or Commander-in-Chief; if he wants to mobilise armed force, he sends for Courill, the head keeper, and tells him to hand out bows and arrows to the farm labourers.

Sirupat, I figured, probably worked the same way, apart from all the God stuff. So, if my father was running Sirupat, what would he do?

Yes, but you can't just put the God stuff on one side like it doesn't exist. Presumably His Majesty my cousin had spent his entire life being jerked around by priests, with their constant thou-shalt-noting in his ear every time he wanted to do something that isn't in the Catechism. You can't run a farm like that (and an estate is just a farm, and Sirupat is just an estate). So at some point he'd have built invisible walls – these are the things the priests can interfere with; these aren't – and the fact that he'd survived so long suggested that one of these invisible walls partitioned off the monopoly of force. In other words, the priests are within their rights to nag him to death about everything, but the soldiers answer to him alone. Which was why, as soon as I said the word, the two copperjackets forced Stauracia to her knees and put a blade under her chin, not waiting for an order from Artabas the priest.

A tiny snippet of data to build a huge hypothesis on; even so.

Worth a shot. I got up off the bed, went to the door and tried the latch. The door opened, which was encouraging. Two very large men in armour turned their heads and looked at me.

"Got a minute?" I said.

They stared at me as though they'd been eating breakfast and God had swooped down and stolen the filling from out of their pasties. "Majesty," one of them said.

"Because if you're not too busy I'd like a word. In here. Now."

There's a form of execution where they tie your arms to one team of horses and your legs to another, and then you're pulled apart. In this case, presumably, the sergeant was one lot of horses and I was the other. "Majesty, our orders."

"You can guard me just as well this side of the door. Shift."

They shifted. I closed the door behind them. "Sit down," I said. "That's an order."

There were two chairs. They sat on them. I perched on the end of the bed. It's not easy to sit in a small, straight-backed chair while holding a seven-foot spear and a full-length shield, and I know from experience that when seated, scale armour bites your bum and the small of your back.

"Couple of quick questions," I said. "Who do you take your orders from?"

They looked at each other. "Duty sergeant, Majesty."

"Splendid. And he answers to?"

"Officer of the Watch, Majesty."

"Who reports to?"

Why is he asking this? Is it some sort of test? Are we in trouble? "The king, Majesty."

"Yes, but the king's sick. Who does he report to?"

"Captain Datis, Majesty."

I nodded, trying not to let them see my hands shaking.

"I'm a bit out of touch. Does Datis report to anyone or is he the top man?"

"Yes, Majesty."

Idiots. "He's the top man?"

"Yes, Majesty."

I nodded again. My chest was so tight I could scarcely breathe. "In that case, I think I'd like to talk to him, right now." Panic filled their eyes. "You," I said, "fetch him. You stay here and guard me. Got that?"

"Majesty—"

One of those moments when the world might change for ever, or it might not. The weight of a hair in one pan or the other would sway the balance. Trouble is, there's never a hair around when you need one.

I had to use just the right tone of voice. Calm. In control. "I gave you an order, soldier."

"Sarge said we weren't to leave our posts, Majesty. Not for anything."

I could almost see the two pans hovering. What I needed, therefore, was a third pan. "Ring the bell," I said.

I hadn't seen one, but it stood to reason, there'd be an alarm bell close nearby. How else could you summon reinforcements? They looked at each other, then one got up and went away. A moment or so later there was this horrible, ear-splitting noise. Not just a bell but a *really good* bell.

The soldier came back and sat down. We waited. I counted under my breath. On seventeen, the door flew open and five soldiers burst in, stopped dead and stared at me.

"As you were," I said. "Right, you—" I pointed at random. "Fetch Captain Datis and bring him here. The rest of you, back to your posts."

I counted three hundred and forty six, and then Captain Datis came in. Since he was potentially my fourth pan, I took a moment to size him up. A tired man. He was wearing his issue padded jerkin over a frayed red tunic, issue leggings, shoes rather than boots. A man who doesn't put his armour on unless he has to, and his feet give him trouble. A bald man who doesn't brush the last stray lock of his front hair sideways. A what-is-it-now look on his face, rather than anger or blind terror at being summoned into the presence of his Redeemer. "You sent for me."

"Yes, thanks," I said. "Quick word in private."

He nodded; the soldiers cleared off. He shut the door and sat down without being asked. "I'm Florian."

"Yes, Majesty."

I smiled. "I'm new around here," I said, "so I thought it's about time I found out how things work."

I'd said the right thing. A tired man doesn't want some new face barging in, not knowing the ropes, getting everything in a tangle. "Of course, Majesty. What do you want to know?"

Good question. "Let's start with the chain of command."

"Pretty straightforward," said Captain Datis. "Ninety soldiers assigned full time to the palace, reporting to five sergeants, reporting to one of three watch officers in rotation, reporting to me."

"And you report to?"

He had to stop and think. "Well, you, presumably. Majesty."

And the trumpets sounded for me on the other side. "While the king's sick."

"That's right."

I nodded, as though he'd just confirmed what I already knew. "Now you've got two men assigned to me."

"Yes, Majesty. If two's not enough, I can give you more."

It was as though the man pointing the arrow at my heart had just turned out to be a salesman trying to sell me a bow. "Make it five," I said. "What have you been told?"

He paused to phrase his answer. "We know that there's assassins," he said, "but we don't know how many or whether they're outsiders or locals, so I was told not to take any chances. I figured two men ought to be enough, with five more handy."

"Good response time," I said. "I checked, as you'll have gathered. Still, you know the old saying: when seconds count, the watch is only minutes away. If one of those two had been the assassin—"

He looked bothered. "Yes, Majesty."

"So I think we'll make it five," I said, "and tell them they're answerable to me only, just in case one of the sergeants is in on it, too. I'm sorry," I added quickly, "I'm telling you how to do your job, I know. But this is all pretty personal for me, so please, indulge me."

"Of course, Majesty."

"Also," I went on, "this room. It won't do at all. I know, it's defensible, only one way in. It's also a deathtrap. If I'm stuck in here and one of your men proves to be the rogue, I'm a sitting duck. I'd rather take my chances somewhere I can get out of in a hurry, preferably with a choice of exits. Is that a problem?"

He was thinking what a mess he'd made of everything; this man, this *civilian*, having to explain the basics of protective strategy. "No problem at all. There's the steward's lodgings. We could give it a dust over and a lick of paint, and—"

"Later, maybe, I'm not fussed about that."

And so on. I vaguely remember sounding plausible and Captain Datis nodding sage agreement, and then he went away, promising to try harder in future. When he'd gone, I collapsed. Luckily I was on the bed at the time, or I could've hurt myself.

They'd made a mistake – or, more likely, there'd been a foul-up in communications somewhere along the line between the Sisters and their men on the ground in Sirupat. As a result, Stauracia had brought me here before the Sisters had ousted the Knights' men in the privy council (and the other way round, of course); in the confusion, it hadn't occurred to either the Sisters or the Knights that the military didn't take orders from the council. They'd assumed it worked that way, because in properly run countries it does, but not in silly little principalities like this one. Maybe they'd been blindsided by the religious aspect and jumped to the conclusion that everyone in Sirupat did as the priests told them. Maybe not a bad conclusion, at that; whether or not Datis would dare to defy an order from a priest I didn't know and was in no hurry to find out. Sufficient unto the day, and all that. Meanwhile, what I did now know for a fact was that under ordinary circumstances Datis was prepared to accept an order from me – and that was like giving me a thunderbolt and a Get-out-of-Death-free card all rolled into one. More to the point, I had a shrewd idea that Stauracia didn't know or hadn't considered any of this. She'd assumed that when the soldiers took me away and put me in a small underground room, it was to keep me in, not to keep unspecified bad people out. Huge difference.

The assassins-on-the-loose story I was prepared to discount, although there was an outside chance that it was true and referred to someone hired by my father or my sister; entirely possible but let's not go there for fear of getting paralysed by anxiety all over again. Instead, let's say for the sake of argument that there are no assassins, and protecting me against them was friend Artabas' excuse for keeping me in close confinement; well, it's what I'd have done, in his sandals. My guess was, Artabas was banking on me *thinking* I was under close arrest (which is, of course, exactly what I'd done, until the trachy dropped and nearly stove my head in) just because there were soldiers outside my door . . . It would all be different, of course, once the Knights' men were safely dealt with, and it was only logical to suppose that he had a plan for that and it was all under way. I couldn't help feeling, though, that he was waiting for someone. I'd intuited (is that a word?) as much earlier – the Knights' man, Stauracia's opposite number, had got held up and hadn't arrived yet, and the coup couldn't happen till he got here. Accordingly, Stauracia trying to get me to sign her loathsome contract, before she had anything solid to threaten me with. She was far too smart to do that unless she had no choice.

In which case – my head was whirling. Euphoria can do that to you, when you haven't been expecting it. I wanted time to get all these fascinating things straight in my mind, preferably with the help of paper and several different colours of ink, but in practice I had as long as it was going to take to get the steward's lodgings ready, and to choose five good men to be my personal bodyguard. As soon as I made a move, Stauracia would realise I'd broken free and was on the loose, and then she'd have to do something about it.

Decisions, decisions. In moments of crisis I find it hard to think for myself; so much easier to get inside other people's heads and figure out what's going on in there. Also helpful, because it gives you the data you need to make an informed decision.

I realised what I had to do. Obvious, really.

*

I wrote the letter in Dejauzi, with a few introductory lines in Robur asking a certain specified person to read the rest of it to another specified person, who spoke Dejauzi but couldn't read. Hell of a complicated way of doing things, but better safe than sorry. Then I called in the sergeant who'd been assigned to my personal guard. He was a big man, a bruiser. "I need a letter sent."

"Majesty."

"The thing is," I went on, "it's a bit sensitive. Affairs of state. Vital trade negotiations. Probably not a good idea for it to go through the usual channels."

He looked at me. I'd chosen him carefully. If I'd read him right, he was the sort of sergeant you went to when there were holes in your boots, and he'd tell you boots were difficult right now because of some snafu at Supply, official requisitions were taking up to three months, but he might be able to sort something out quicker than that, only it'd cost you. He had a gold ring the size of a walnut on his left hand, and I don't think he'd inherited it from a favourite uncle.

"I got a cousin who's a fisherman," he said. "Got his own boat."

"Is that a fact? Two other things. I haven't got any money."

"Majesty."

"But I will be needing a chief of domestic security. Someone I can trust."

He grinned, respectfully of course. "Reckon I could do that," he said. "Majesty," he added.

I handed him the letter. It was sealed with the royal seal. I'd noticed it lying on a small table next to the bed when I went to pay my respects to my royal cousin, shortly after I arrived. Somehow, when nobody was looking, it found its way into the palm of my hand, and then into my pocket. Presumably the privy council were tearing the place apart looking for it, since nothing could be done officially without it. I hadn't told anyone I'd got it, because nobody had asked.

The sergeant (his name was Pharnaspes) had seen and recognised the seal on the letter. I got the impression he knew the seal matrix was missing. "Something wrong?" I asked.

"No, Majesty. I'll get on it right away."

"Splendid. Oh, and if you see Captain Datis, tell him I'd like a word with him."

He went out. One of the sharper knives in the drawer, I decided, and if you play with sharp objects you can hurt yourself. Or other people. Also, I wasn't playing any more.

Datis came a short while after that. My new apartments were ready, he said, and the things I'd asked for had been put there. "That's grand," I told him. "Lead the way."

Up those stairs, which I'd seriously doubted I'd ever climb again. I was pretty sure I wasn't supposed to, but if the enemy couldn't get their act together, was that my fault? "Did you mention me moving quarters to the privy councillors?"

"No, Majesty. Should I tell them?"

"Not for now."

A clerk was watching us. For a split second I considered having him killed, just so he wouldn't tell anyone he'd seen me walking across a courtyard. What the hell. So long as I got to my new room before the councillors knew I was out, it didn't matter. Timing is everything.

"It's a bit cramped," Datis said, as he opened the door for me. He wasn't kidding. As I think I may have intimated, I'm not crazy about small spaces. But this one was bearable, just about.

"It's fine," I said. Furniture: bed, one chair, a chest in the corner of the room. It was made of oak reinforced with iron bands, and it had three padlocks, with the keys sticking out of them. A few good men with axes could get into it in about ten minutes, but like I just said, time is of the essence. You judge it just right, and all sorts of problems simply slither away into irrelevance.

"The guards are in place," he said, handing me a key. I managed to keep my hand steady, taking it from him. "They know where to find me if you need me."

"I should be fine," I said. "Oh, one thing. That woman who brought me here."

"Majesty."

"I have my doubts about her. Lock her up."

He nodded. Simple as that. I say, lock her up, and it gets done.

"Preferably," I remembered to add, "not in the cells. Put her somewhere nobody would usually think of looking. None of your men speak Robur, do they?"

"No, but there are a couple of Robur speakers in the Excise division. I can have one brought up here if you like."

"No, don't do that. One of your men will do just fine."

Timing, I thought, turning my key in my lock after Datis had gone. They'd find her eventually, it wasn't a big palace, but when she was most needed, with any luck she wouldn't be there. And I'd be here, safe, for as long as I needed to be. Sure, Datis' guards wouldn't hold up a superior force indefinitely, but indefinitely is for gods, not mere mortals on a schedule. The other thing that only gods can be trusted with is omniscience. When you're dealing with human beings, it's good to make sure that everybody doesn't know everything.

Having done all that, I'd done everything that I could do. Now I had to wait, and I'm not naturally a patient man. I turned the three padlock keys, lifted them off and opened the chest. In it, besides other things, was a book: nine books, to be precise, together forming the holy scripture of the Eternal Flame. It was handed down to my remote ancestor on a mountaintop by a fiery angel – that's an article of faith and I can't be bothered to doubt it – but I'd never actually read the wretched thing, not cover to cover. On balance I'd have preferred something with more jokes and a bit less shouting, but needs must.

It starts off, "In the beginning . . . ", and I really I wish I could write a book that started that way. In the beginning, in the valley of the River Oc, there lived a man and a woman who loved each other very much, and in due course they had a son, and his name was Valentinian, and when he was old enough he went to the big city, and because he came from the Oc valley they called him Valentinian met'Oc – and so on, through sixteen generations of enterprise, courage and selfless devotion to public service, to me.

Instead of that, what do I give you? I give you Saevus Corax, a creation of my own, like the old legend of the sculptor who made a wonderful statue that came to life, or the other one about the wise philosopher who built a man out of corpses, who subsequently killed him.

Big question: who am I? Saevus or Florian? Not a question I'm qualified to answer, I'm afraid. Give me ten minutes clear thinking time when I'm not being chased by masked assassins or running away one jump ahead of the law or cowering in a confined space (I hate those) hoping my past won't catch me up, and I might be able to give you a considered response. As it is, I make myself up as I go along, on the fly, adapting myself to circumstances.

Saevus or Florian, two hovering pans striving eternally for balance. If you insist on me choosing, I opt for the third pan (or *a* third pan; there may or may not be others). Torn between the man I was born as and the man I built for myself to live and hide in, I choose the third man – won't tell you his name quite yet, because I might be able to get to the end of this story without needing to disclose it, and once you get to know me you'll realise I never give away information if I can possibly help it; not even to you, my reader, my conscience and my only true friend in all the world.

The third man wrote plays for a while, and some of them were really rather good, even though he does say so himself. Florian originated him but he wasn't like Florian, not one bit; he was very popular, everybody's pal, made good money and got through it very quickly buying drinks for people, helping out pals who were down on their luck; no matter, because there was always more where that came from. All he had to do was invent people – heroes, villains, lovers, martyrs, henchmen, true friends, false friends and the inevitable feisty kickass female lead with attitude who's so difficult to make credible, for some reason. Inventing people came so naturally to him that he hardly had to think about it. Like a randy young man with a handsome face and no principles, he went around pop-ulating the world with his by-products, and people actually paid him money for his activities. It was a good life, and he wasn't called on to hurt or kill anyone (apart from fictional characters, who he tortured and killed by the score in the name of entertainment) and he wouldn't have minded it going on and on for ever, but there was an actor called Ekkehard who inadvertently let something slip to someone who came around asking questions, and that was that; and meanwhile, far away, Saevus Corax was born—

(Stop and consider that, if you can be bothered. The Left Hand believe that the Redeemer is half-born in a series of partial reincarnations, and that I'm the Redeemer. Feel free to laugh like a drain at the latter proposition, but I put it to you: who do we know with a proven track record of partial reincarnation, off with the old skin, on with the new, like a slow worm in a great hurry, not even prepared to wait till the old body's dead before diving into the new one?

Bodies, incarnations, characterisations, personae – trouble with them is, they're all confined spaces. I like to be able to stretch out without skinning my knuckles on the roof.)

6

I'd got as far as the Sermon beside the Chasm when I heard a noise I recognised.

I've come to know it best as something I hear in the distance, and to me it means get ready, tomorrow's going to be a very long, smelly day. In the distance is fine by me. If it starts getting closer, I move away. On this occasion I got up, went to the window and unbarred the shutters, though I didn't open them, not yet. The sound was that special metallic peck-peck of weapons hitting each other. I can't say it's a favourite of mine, and on balance I prefer light opera.

In too much of a hurry, as usual, I went to the chest in the corner, unlocked it, opened the lid. Inside it I found (among other things) a short-sleeved scale cuirass – no maker's mark, probably locally produced but good quality – which I quickly struggled into, nearly cutting my nose on a burred edge. It was almost a good fit, excellent guesswork on someone's part, a little bit too big, but so much better than a little bit too small, which can prove fatal. I put my shirt back on over it, because I hate to disclose information unless I have to. Also in the trunk I found a sword, Type XII heavy-duty cutter, not a favourite of mine, but since it was really only for show, never mind. I slipped a couple of other things into my pockets, closed the lid and locked it, and then the door flew open and in came Sergeant Pharnaspes.

He was in a pretty bad way: one stab wound in the thigh and a cut across his forehead that probably looked worse than it actually was, but even so. "Did you send the letter?" I yelled at him.

He gave me a hurt look. "Yes," he said. "You've got to get out. We can't hold them back much longer."

He'd also lost the little finger of his right hand; I hadn't noticed that. "Who are they?"

"Dunno. They just came at us out of nowhere. Real bastards."

"Can you get your men out?"

It wasn't a question he'd anticipated being asked. "You what?"

"Get your men out. Get them safe."

He thought about it. "Yes, some of them. But they're coming for you. You got to go while we hold them off."

I shook my head. "I suggest you use this window," I said. "Datis stationed some men in the courtyard. I don't know if they're still alive, but if they are, you'll be safe."

"But what about—?"

He actually gave a damn. Duty, I suppose, and the thought of a goldmine slipping through his remaining fingers. "I'm staying," I said. "It's fine. I know what I'm doing. Come back for me if you can."

He rolled his eyes, then went back out again. He returned

shepherding half a dozen men, badly cut up but still mobile. That meant four hadn't made it, or were still out there covering their mates; amounted to the same thing. They scrambled through the window and left me alone. I took a deep breath, then adjusted my clothing somewhat. Not comfortable, but necessary.

The door was still open. Through it came one of the privy councillors, not my pal Artabas, escorted by three men, weapons but no armour.

"Thank God," he said. "You're safe."

I gave him a filthy look. "No thanks to you," I said.

Something I've noticed over the years concerning people. They do two things: they talk, and they listen. A key thing to be able to do, if you want to manage people, is to stop them doing one and make them do the other. A lot of the time, for example, I need to make people talk to me, in order to extract from them information that I need. This was the other sort of moment. The councillor wanted to talk to me. I needed him to listen.

"What the hell were you thinking of," I therefore said, "letting them take me like that?"

You get people to listen by making them believe that you have pertinent data which they lack. In this case, the data I was offering, like a fisherman offering a fish the free gift of a worm, was: I'm in on this, too, and you nearly screwed it up for everybody. "I'm sorry," he said, plainly shocked. "We thought you were on their side. We thought—"

"Oh, for crying out loud." I gave him my disappointed look. "You thought I was in with the *Sisters*? When they brought me here in chains?"

Guilty look. "Yes, but then you were talking to Artabas like you knew him or something, and we know he's on their side, so we assumed—"

"You clown," I said. Quite likely he'd never been called a clown before, not to his face. I fancy the experience was good for him. "You nearly got me killed. When our man gets here, I might have something to say about that."

Well, I'd definitely got his attention. "We thought," he said, "when you were moved, and we didn't know where to find you—"

"You thought I'd done a deal with Artabas and the Sisters and cut you out, so you came here to get me before I could sign anything. Well?"

He wilted. I'd like to think it was the force of my personality, but I don't suppose that had much to do with it. More the terrifying thought of what the Knights' man would think, when he got here. Apparently I was right about the Knights having a man who hadn't arrived yet. Nice to have it confirmed, since I'd based my entire strategy around it.

"Never mind about all that," I said, before he had a chance to spot any of the obvious inconsistencies. "You're here now. Where's that bloody woman got to?"

More guilt. "We don't know; we can't find her."

I nodded. "Ten to one she's gone for help. If she gets it and comes back here with superior force before your man arrives, we're screwed. You do appreciate that, don't you?"

Words failed him. He nodded.

"And the Great Seal. Did you find it?"

"No."

I sighed. "Bet you anything you like she's taken it with her. She knows we can't do anything without it."

"We'll find her."

Shake of the head. "Don't bother looking," I told him. "She's miles away by now, I can guarantee it. I expect if you make enquiries you'll find there's been a fishing boat or something gone out and not come back. She'll be on the mainland by now. We need to get ready."

"We thought—" he was ashamed to confess, but he felt he had to. "We thought you'd got the seal."

"Me?"

Nod. "We reckoned you must have stolen it, when you went to see the king."

"Really?" I said, flooding myself with red-hot righteous indignation. "Well, let's see." I turned out my pockets and laid the contents on the top of the chest. "Well? Is it there?"

"No. No, of course not. I'm sorry. We got the wrong end of the stick entirely. We didn't know."

I started putting the things back. "No, of course you didn't. Not your fault, nobody told you, so how were you supposed to know? That's something else I'll be discussing with the man, when he gets here. You should have been informed, but somehow or other—" I made a vague gesture of absolution, for which he was very grateful. "What's your name, by the way?"

"Vonones. Minister of Justice."

"We need that seal," I said. "And since it's probably halfway to Olbia by now, I suggest we get a new one. Just like the old one, if you get what I'm driving at."

"But, Highness—"

"Don't Highness me, it makes my head ache. You do know how to fake a seal, don't you?"

Apparently he didn't, so I told him. You get a genuine impression of the seal and press it in really fine-grained clay.

Then you bake the clay. Hey presto, a seal matrix, very nearly as good as the real thing. I'd have thought everybody knew that, but apparently not.

"But surely," he said, "people can tell the difference."

"Of course they can," I said, "given time and peace and quiet and bright light and trained experts. But in the heat of the moment, a fake's just as good, for the time being. Timing's everything. Now, do you think you can handle it or do you want me to come and do it for you?"

"No, I—" He stopped and thought. Did he have anyone who he could trust to make a fake seal? Yes, apparently, one man, and he was talking to him. "Could you?"

In my mind's ear, those trumpets again. "Yes, why not?" I said. "If a thing's worth doing, do it yourself."

So they escorted me through the palace to the Great Hall. On the way we saw a number of badly wounded men, and four dead men in armour. I felt bad about them, but what the hell; I didn't start it. While we were waiting for the clay to arrive from the potters' quarter, I asked to be excused. "I really need to have a shit," I said. "If that's all right."

Not the sort of thing the Redeemer usually says to his clergy. "Yes, of course," they assured me.

"Where?"

People don't think straight when they're embarrassed half to death. "We usually go out into the back yard," someone said. "Through that door there."

"Thank you," I said, and hobbled quickly and convincingly in the direction indicated. Convincingly because I'd just spent a quarter of an hour with the Great Seal of Sirupat shoved up my arse, in case anyone saw fit to search me for it. I removed it, slipped it in my pocket and went back into the hall.

Not long afterwards there were two Great Seals, one in my pocket, the other one lying on a table in front of me, cooling down after being baked in the hearth. "Now," I said, "we're getting somewhere. Have you got the papers, or is he bringing them?"

He was bringing them. My opinion of the efficiency of the Knights dropped another couple of notches, thank God. "Did you find out about boats leaving the harbour?"

Yes, they'd done that. A fishing boat, belonging to a cousin of one of the guard sergeants, had gone off some time earlier and wasn't to be seen bobbing about in its usual fishing grounds. "Thought so," I said. "She'll be on the mainland by now."

That was supposed to scare them, and it did. "But we've got Artabas and the other three," someone said. "We've got them locked up in the cells, under guard."

"That's one good thing," I said. "Don't hurt them, whatever you do; we may need them."

They looked a bit dubious about that and for a moment I was worried I'd gone a step too far. The important thing when you've made an error of judgement like that is to move on, quick as you can. "So how many men have we got?" I asked. "That we can count on, I mean."

Awkward silence. Then Vonones said, "Fifteen of our people, monks from the Vestry, and nine of the guards."

Words to gladden my heart, but I acted appalled. "That's all?"

"We weren't ready," someone else said, and Vonones looked daggers at him. "The reinforcements are supposed to be arriving with the special envoy. We thought—"

"Never mind," I said firmly. "Twenty-four plus you four, and me too, I suppose: we should be able to manage. Is the outer gate secure? Then secure it, for fuck's sake. And do try and take this seriously. It's *important*."

What a lot of trouble I make for people by insisting on staying alive. Simply by being who I am – there's some goddess in some religion down south who leaves a trail of roses growing wherever her feet touch. Me too, only not roses.

The obvious thing would be to get rid of me, but even I couldn't manage that, on the ship to Sirupat. I'm one of those stubborn stains you can't shift unless you scrub the weave so hard you fray the cloth. Many times over many years I've tried to come up with some sort of justification for my existence, but no dice. Nevertheless, in my efforts to stay alive, I cause havoc, like a frightened pig strayed into a flower garden: the more you try and shoo me away, the more harm I do.

I read a book once by a lunatic who claimed that the world wasn't made by some god; it started off empty and stuff just gradually grew, like lichen on a rock. To begin with there was just moss, and then the moss turned into plants, the plants turned into fish and birds, the fish and birds turned into lizards, the lizards turned into monkeys and the monkeys turned into people. All this happened, the nutcase said, because in each generation there'd be smarter moss, more ruthless plants, more self-centred and arrogant fish, birds, lizards and monkeys who outperformed their wretched fellows and aspired to change. They were the ones who got the girls, so their progeny survived while the losers perished. Arrogance, selfishness and a total disregard for others is, therefore, what turned moss into men.

Wouldn't it be nice if that were true; if the ability to survive (which I've got, in spades) justified doing it, even made it a virtue. It would mean there's a reason for why I'm a total shit sometimes; in a thousand years, my descendants will be supermen, riding on clouds and controlling the weather with a single uplifted finger. But it's just bullshit, obviously. I keep going because the alternative is death, the thought of which terrifies me.

When I started writing this, I promised to be honest with you. I'm going to find that quite hard, from now on. So easy to tweak the facts, to make them better, to make you feel sorry for me. That poor man, I could make you think. It wasn't his fault, and he did his best to be good.

Death still scares me, almost as much as what I'm prepared to do to avoid it. Let's just stick to what actually happened, what I really said and did, what I really thought. That way, I get at least some of the poison out of my system, and you hear the truth about the Great Sirupati War. You may not like it, but you sure as hell won't hear it from anyone else.

I've read up on this, and apparently it's true; there's no verified case on record of a playwright or dramatist exercising high military command or ruling an empire. The only instance I've come across is a part-time playwright (really he was an actor) who kidded people into thinking he was the emperor, but I did say "verified" just now, and his account is widely regarded as a pack of lies, so forget about it. But it's weird, when you come to think of it. Most of the stuff you need to do those jobs you can learn from books, but the innate and inherent qualities you need, the things that you can't learn and have to be born with – an intuitive knowledge of character and human nature, that's one, and an ability to use words to convey and direct motivation, that's definitely another. Any dramatist above the rank of assistant pantomime writer has these assets at his fingertips, so you'd have thought the annals would be stuffed full of us making our mark on history and taking over the world. But apparently not. Odd, that.

I went back to the steward's lodgings, this time accompanied by the five privy councillors and a trio of their armed monks, and we sat around for a long time, not really achieving anything. Nominally we were negotiating the minor details of the already-agreed deal whereby the king and the Knights became partners in a venture capital association (lending money to governments so they could fight wars), with the king providing the capital and the Knights providing contacts, administrative expertise and goodwill; the capital in question being all the king's investments in the Knights' bank, past and future. The bit we needed to thrash out was exactly how we were going to foreclose on the Sisters and put them out of business for good without starting a war nobody could win. I had a few ideas about that, but I got the impression they weren't interested in anything creative.

The fact of the matter, as I quickly came to realise just by keeping my ears open, was that it wasn't up to me, or us, to decide terms. The deal would be what the Knights wanted it to be, because they had more ships closer to the island than the Sisters did, and when they got here any resistance we could put up wouldn't slow them down for more than two minutes. That would be fine and there wouldn't need to be any resistance if it wasn't for the wretched Sisters; they were further away with fewer ships, but that wouldn't matter if news of what just happened reached them before it reached the Knights. If the Sisters' forces got to the island first and had time to dig themselves in, the Knights didn't have anything like the manpower or resources to dig them out again. They'd need to get help from one or other of the governments who owed them money; and if government A sent troops to help them, governments B, C and D would immediately come in on the other side, and we'd have that war we were talking about just now, except that we (meaning the Knights) wouldn't have the money from the Sirupati gold to pay for it.

Timing, I didn't say to them; told you so, I didn't point out. The Knights' forces were closer, but the Sisters had got their agent to the island in good time, while the Knights' man still hadn't arrived yet. Timing makes superior resources irrelevant.

Funny old stuff, time. A few seconds in the right place can make all the difference, and yet here we were, five principals in the drama, sitting around with basically nothing to do. I'd told sergeant Pharnespes to come back for me if he could, and though for his sake I sincerely hoped he wouldn't, there was always the chance that he might – in which case, there'd be a fight and presumably several of the armed monks would die, thereby whittling down their sides' resources and upsetting the balance. I wondered about having all the privy councillors killed – Stauracia's and, for want of a better word, mine – which would supposedly give me a free hand in Sirupat, for a little while. But the councillors were simply the tip of the pyramid, namely the church hierarchy in Sirupat, and though I might be able to hand-pick their successors or have some say in who they were (no idea if that was the case or not), it wouldn't really matter. Sooner or later the Knights and the Sisters were coming, and if they had to do that, I wanted them to come in nice easy-to-deal-with instalments, not all at once like a tidal wave. Accordingly I reprieved the councillors, though they didn't seem the least bit grateful. My guiding principle was that, for the time being at least, all human life was precious. That's a bit like an elderly cousin of mine who never threw anything away and lived surrounded by towering piles of broken old junk, because, he said, you never know when something might come in handy. Or, by the same token, someone.

Vonones had stationed a monk down at the harbour. He came running in – I got the impression that, for him, running was a novelty, like candied sea urchins, and similarly not to his taste – and told us there was a sail on the horizon; a red and white striped sail. Sail singular, not sails plural.

"About bloody time," I said loudly, as my stomach clenched into a knot. "Right, let's get down there."

Slight delay while the pinhead monk they'd got as head of security sent men ahead to make sure the coast was clear, then arranged his pitiful forces to cover us from possible attack. I was thinking: if I was Sergeant Pharnaspes, still alive and still taking an interest in current affairs, what would I be doing? I got my answer as we came out of the city gate.

Usually in human life you have at least some idea of which side you're on, but not always. Pharnaspes and five battered but enthusiastic guardsmen in armour jumped up from behind a stack of barrels and laid into Vonones' twenty-odd unarmoured monks with a level of enthusiasm that surprised me. What the hell did they think they were fighting *for*, I wondered, as a thrown spear passed three inches from my head and I hurled myself behind a cartwheel; for the Sisters? Not likely. For the liberty of Sirupat, secular government and the promise of free and fair elections at some unspecified future date? For *me*? Presumably not. Maybe they fought so fiercely because they were soldiers and they didn't like monks. Made no odds in the end. Simple arithmetic. Six into twenty doesn't go, though it can make an awful mess trying.

It all lasted a couple of minutes, and then it was over; but not before Sergeant Pharnaspes got close enough to me to grab me by the arm and pull me out from my hiding place. "Come on," he yelled, fully expecting me to cooperate in my own rescue. He was stronger than me and hauled me to my feet. Then Vonones, who'd been hiding under the other end of the cart, darted out. He had a knife in his hand. He looked me straight in the eye, and stabbed me in the guts.

Complete waste of time: goes without saying. You'll recall that I was wearing that nice scale armour Captain Datis had got for me, and the knife glanced off; it wasn't much of a thrust anyway, as you'd expect from an amateur. I saw the look of stunned surprise on his face and then Pharnaspes swung at him; he ducked and somehow got out of the way, and then Pharnaspes started dragging me along by the arm, swearing with amazing fluency – I guess he thought I'd been hurt – and we went a full ten yards or so before Pharnaspes got hit on the head by a well-flung stone. He stopped dead, his eyes rolled and he measured his length on the ground, pulling me down with him. A monk came up and stood over him, lifting a spear.

"Leave it," I snapped. The monk looked at me. "I said leave it." I couldn't think of a justification. Fortunately the monk didn't seem to require one. He held out his hand and pulled me to my feet.

Vonones was staring at me. "I'm sorry," he said. Stupid thing to say.

I breathed out slowly. "I understand," I said. "Couldn't let me fall into enemy hands, all that." Then I thought of Pharnaspes, the look in his eyes as he expected me to cooperate, and I thought, why not? So I made a fist and punched Vonones in the mouth, as hard as I possibly could.

He went down. I helped him up. "Don't ever," I said, "stab me again, got it? If you do, I'll be seriously annoyed."

It occurred to me that he still didn't know about the scale armour under my shirt. As far as he was concerned, a miracle – screw him, I thought, let him believe if he absolutely has to. "Are we safe?" I said.

Coming from a man with an unpierceable skin, it probably sounded like an odd question to ask. "I think so," he said, and then looked round to see if he'd been telling the truth. "I think so," he repeated. "Where's Brother Candaulis?"

I had no idea who he was talking about, but Vonones answered his own question by gazing unhappily at a dead body with half its head sliced off. Ah, I thought; the pinhead monk in charge of security. Also among the dead were Pharnaspes' guardsmen. Very, very dead. We were in grave risk of running out of people on Sirupat.

"Doesn't matter," I said, trying to sound like I meant it. Like I said a moment ago, I wasn't at all sure I knew which side I was on, who was us and who was them. I decided I must be in the third pan, on nobody's side but my own. A bit lonely, but probably for the best. Meanwhile, fortunately, Vonones thought I was on his side, and his pathetic forces had just won the battle. "We'd better get down to the harbour," I reminded him. "That ship—"

He'd forgotten about the ship. Being in his first fight since he was a boy will do that to a person. "We need reinforcements," he said. "There may be more of them. If the guards—"

Captain Datis. I'd forgotten about him. Last time I looked he was on my side, but that could easily be an entirely conditional alignment. "They're not here," I pointed out. "We need to get to the ship. Come on."

We scuttled down to the harbour. The ship was still some way out, tacking or gybing or whatever it is they do. It occurred to me that, standing on the dock with the sea on one side of us, we were in a catastrophically bad tactical position if there was anyone out there who wanted a fight. Stauracia? The councillors in the pay of the Sisters? Datis, just possibly. I was starting to have trouble keeping it all clear in my head. Fortunately, nobody came, and eventually the ship drifted up and dropped anchor. It was well supplied with armed men, on our side, presumably—

I looked up and saw someone I recognised. He saw me. This could be awkward.

They put out a gangplank and he walked down it, looking at the faces turned towards him. He was used to doing that. Then he looked at me.

I looked at him. "You took your own sweet time in getting here," I said, and hoped like crazy.

He'd opened his mouth to speak, but stopped abruptly. Praise be, he'd recognised the line. I was afraid he wouldn't. For choice, I'd have spoken it stressing the accented syllables – you TOOK your OWN sweet TIME, et cetera – to make it obvious it was a quotation, but that would've sounded strange, and it's a nondescript little line, quite close to the rhythms of ordinary speech, which is what you want when writing rhyming couplets for burlesque. Always one of my strengths, though you don't tend to get praise for it from the critics.

Anyway, it had the desired effect of stopping him in his tracks and making him think. "We were held up," he said. "Contrary winds off start point."

He was looking at me, trying to read the message. I wasn't trying to convey one. Too risky, with all those people watching. "You're here now," I said. "Did you bring it?"

"Sorry, what?"

"The contract."

The penny hadn't dropped; it was floating, like a feather in the breeze, trying to decide whether or not to land. "Yes, I've got it here," he said.

"No time like the present," I said. "Come on."

No chance of a quiet tête-à-tête on the way back to the city; Vonones was hovering a bit too close. The essential thing – one of the essential things – was to avoid names, at least till we'd had a chance to talk and get our stories straight. Until then, he didn't know I was Florian and I didn't know he was Ekkehard. I just hoped he'd figured that out for himself.

The line, by the way, was from the second act of a burlesque I wrote (can't remember what it was called) for the Gallery of Illustration, the year Ekkehard joined the company. The rest of the speech has slipped my mind, and I only remember that line because the heavy spondee in the third foot (sweet time) always bugged me but I couldn't figure out how to fix it. The context was a man in disguise trying to get across to an old pal he's just met that they're not supposed to know each other. Not quite on all fours with the current situation, but close enough for government work, and not bad for the absolute spur of the moment.

"I figured it out, of course," I said. "Right from the start."

"Liar," Ekkehard said.

"From the moment I saw you lying there in the grass on Ogyge," I told him. "I knew you were working for the Knights.

That's why I trusted you not to run off with all that money the moment my back was turned. Because it was their money."

He frowned. "Really?"

I smiled. "You're a fine actor," I said. "But only in comedy."

"Shit."

"Don't beat yourself up about it," I said. "Have another drink."

We were back in the steward's lodgings. It had taken all my resources of tact and cunning to get rid of Vonones, who quite understandably wanted to be in on the negotiations. Fortunately a direct suggestion from Ekkehard (go away, he'd said) had done the trick. I'd closed and barred the shutters and we were keeping our voices down. I wasn't entirely sure why. Mind you, there were an awful lot of things I wasn't entirely sure about.

"Fine," he said. "So, yes. They ran me down after I got in a spot of trouble over some money, if you must know. Help them out or go to jail."

"Betray your oldest, best friend or go to jail for a bit. Yes, I can see, you had no choice. Do go on."

He scowled at me. "They told me no harm would come to you," he said. "They told me they were going to make you a fucking *king*."

"Quite true."

"Well, then."

"Only I'd rather die first."

"How was I supposed to know? You never told me."

"No, I didn't. Anyhow, it's not important. So, all that time, you were leading me to them."

"Hardly." Another harsh look, which I don't think I deserved. "My job was to keep an eye on you and report to my control. It was only when you got snatched that they gave me this job." His frown turned thoughtful. "Talking of which," he added, "I'm not really sure I know what I'm supposed to be doing."

I sighed. "You're bringing the papers for me to sign."

"Yes, got that. But afterwards. Am I supposed to be like a sort of governor here till the troops arrive from the mainland, or are you in charge now, or what?"

"Good question," I told him. "Basically, it's like this. The Knights and the Sisters both want this island, and because I'm the heir apparent they want me."

"With you so far."

"Neither side is in control," I went on. "The ruling council's split between Knights and Sisters. I managed to find out that the military, such as it is, answers directly to the king, not the council."

"Interesting."

"Probably not as helpful as you think. Anyhow, I've sort of convinced the Knights' people that I'm on their side."

"Are you?"

"Very good question."

He gave me a sort of beseeching look. "It'd make my life much easier," he said.

"I bet it would. Oddly enough, that's not my number one priority. Meanwhile," I went on, "earlier on the Knights' lot made a grab for me, when they thought the Sisters' lot had got me, and the soldiers beat them off. The soldiers now think I'm the Knights' prisoner. Whether they'll do anything about that remains to be seen," I went on, "particularly now you're here with your marines."

"Eighteen of them."

"That's a lot in context," I said. "There's about seventy surviving soldiers in the royal guard, plus the council's got a few so-called fighting monks, though they're about as much use as a cheese helmet. Eighteen marines plus the sailors off your ship tilts the balance of power no end."

"Yes, I suppose it does. Look," he said, "whose side are you really on?"

"Mine. What about you?"

"Only if you're in with the Sisters you ought to tell me. This is all way over my head. People could get hurt."

I gave him my grave look. "I'm not in with the Sisters," I said.

"No shit?"

"No shit. Well, hardly any. Not the Sisters, and not the Knights if I can possibly help it."

"Oh." He looked disappointed. "That's awkward."

"Sorry."

"You sure? I mean, what do you care? If they want the stupid island, let them have it."

"They want me, too. Otherwise I couldn't give a damn. But I'm stuck here. Don't you see? My cover's blown. Now everybody's going to know that Saevus Corax is Florian met'Oc. I can't possibly ever leave. If I do, I'm dead, soon as I step off the boat."

"Really?"

"Really. Being Florian met'Oc is very, very bad. It carries the death sentence in nearly all jurisdictions."

"Oh."

"So," I went on, "this little nest of vipers is my home for the foreseeable future. Accordingly, I take an interest in who runs it. And who runs me. I'm damned well sure it's not going to be the Sisters."

"They're worse than my lot?"

"Their representative and I don't get along," I said. "You, on the other hand, are no worse than a bad dose of malaria."

"You say the sweetest things."

"That one comes from the heart. But if I let you have your wicked way with me, what'll happen? The Knights take over; the Sisters start a war; everybody's in deep trouble. I'd rather avoid that if I possibly can."

"Since when were you interested in politics?"

"Since politics got interested in me," I said, and it was a good line, though probably misleading.

He thought for a moment. "You really knew all along?"

I nodded. "You were the obvious choice," I said. "Someone who's known for ages who I really am, but who's always kept it to himself. And who's still alive. Someone, therefore, I trust. You're who I'd choose, in their position."

He gazed at me. "But you didn't trust me, did you?"

"Of course not. I'd have to be crazy to do that. All that means is, they don't know you as well as I do. I know you really well. You can vouch for that."

He nodded. "So you're really smart; big deal. Do you think you're smart enough to get out of this in one piece if you don't do what the Knights want you to?"

"No."

"Well, then." He sighed, briefly and softly. "Naturally I'd like to help you but my hands are tied. You've got us both involved with some seriously unpleasant people."

Fair comment. If it hadn't been for me – yes, but I didn't start it, did I? "The hell with that," I said. "Once you start trying to figure out whose fault things are, you might as well give up and eat foxgloves. When do the rest of the soldiers get here?"

"Soon."

"How soon is soon?"

"I didn't get copied in on that. Days rather than weeks, probably. I was supposed to be getting the marines off three galleasses, which is three hundred men, but they got diverted to another job at the last minute and when I left to come here, nobody seemed to know where they'd got to. I think the man who organises that side of things must be someone's brother-in-law, because he's not very good at it."

"Three galleasses."

"I just said so, didn't I? I wish you wouldn't repeat what I say in that stupid tone of voice; it's a very annoying habit."

Timing. The Knights have thousands of armed men at their disposal, but the ones earmarked for this particular job are crabfood on the seabed, because I (nauseous and terrified naval tactical genius) put them there; therefore, until someone's brother-in-law finds out that this is the case and organises replacements, the Knights' men aren't coming. In which case, the military resources available to the Knights on Sirupat consist of the eighteen marines that Ekkehard brought with him, a few sailors and a bunch of nervous monks. Suddenly all the pans were wobbling again. How many men would Datis have left? Seventy?

I went to the door. Nobody there. Nobody at all to guard us from our enemies, for crying out loud. I yelled, and eventually a monk showed up. "Get me a map," I said.

"Highness. A map of what?"

"Everything. The world. And get some guards on this door, for pity's sake."

The monk went away. Ekkehard was looking at me. "What?"

"No guards," he said.

"I know. Someone's going to get it in the neck because of that, you mark my—"

"No guards," he repeated. "Don't you get it?"

Then I got it. "What," I said, "you mean, run away?"

"Well, of course I mean that, stupid. I've seen you in action. You could be out of this castle and into those forests I saw as I came in, and nobody would find you."

"I don't know," I said.

"Oh, come on. It's not like they've got endless manpower for a search. You could hide up somewhere, and long before they track you down all hell will have broken loose and they'll have other things on their minds besides looking for you."

"I'm not sure it's as simple—"

"Look," he said. "Sneak out of the castle. Hide in the woods. Sandbag one of the gold-panners for a little spending money. Steal or hire a fishing boat. Next thing you know you're on the mainland, with money in your pocket. Then you vanish. You melt away like mist on a summer morning and you're never heard of again. What's wrong with you, for crying out loud?"

"I could do that," I said.

"What are you still doing here? I'm not going to stop you."

I considered him, the way a fish might consider an unexplained floating worm. I'd neglected to mention to him that his three hundred marines weren't coming, so his statement that there wouldn't be enough men to search the island and find me was possibly disingenuous. That didn't alter the fact that it was, albeit unintentionally, true.

"No," I said. "I'm staying."

"You what?"

"I'm staying," I said.

"You're nuts."

I breathed out slowly. Where my last statement had come from I had no idea, but when I heard myself say it I realised I'd meant it. "I think I can win this," I said.

"You fucking lunatic."

"I can win this," I said. "And then I won't have to run away any more. I can stay here and be king of godforsaken bloody Sirupat."

"You maniac," he said. "Think about it, for God's sake. If you run for it, you'll get clean away, and then they won't have any use for me any more. I can go back to the Republic and get on with my life. If you stay, there's going to be a shitstorm like the world's never seen before, and I'm going to be stuck here right in the epicentre."

Ah, I thought. But somehow I got the impression he was saying that to cover a different agenda. Maybe, maybe not. "Tough," I said. "Of course, there's nothing to stop *you* running away."

"You what?"

"No guards on the door," I said. "You leave the city – it's not a castle, by the way, it's a city. You leave the city, you bushwhack a gold-panner, you hire a fishing boat—"

"Fuck you, you selfish bastard. I'm not like you. I've got a life. A *career*." He was genuinely angry with me now. "If and when I get can ever get out of the cesspool you've dragged me into, I'm going back to the Republic and I'm going to get on with the life you and your loathsome friends tore me away from, thank you ever so fucking much. I'm not disposable. I'm me."

Coming from an actor, that was quite something. I believed the anger, but not the content. "Fine," I said. "Stick around. Oh, by the way. Whose side are you on?"

He'd have hit me, except he knows I'm a hundred times

faster. "Arsehole," he said. "It's so unfair. I've got genuine natural talent, everybody says so, and I worked really, really hard to get ahead in the profession, and it was all just starting to happen for me, and then you came along. And now look at me."

"You didn't answer the—"

"How dare you?" He was right about one thing. In the right part, he was quite good.

"Now then," I said. "Calm down. Breathe. I take it you're trying to say you're on my side."

"Shithead."

"Because," I went on, "if I find a way out of this mess, I'm honour-bound to take you out of it with me. Well?"

"Turd," he said. "You wouldn't know honour if it crawled up your arse and ate your brain."

An unlikely thing for honour to want to do, I'd have thought. "Honour-bound," I repeated. "All right?"

"One of these days I'm going to get you for all this."

"All right?"

He nodded.

"And besides," I said, "you weren't getting anywhere until I happened to see you in that ghastly show at the Phoenix, and then I wrote *Pistacchio* for you, and *that's* when you had your breakthrough moment, so if it wasn't for me—"

"Shut up. You made your point. Why is it you always must insist on having the last fucking word?"

Mind you, he was a wonderful Pistacchio. It's a real old-fashioned clown part. Typecasting.

Time, I decided, to do something. "We need to find Stauracia," I said.

"Who the hell is Stauracia?"

Ah. "Friend of mine," I said. "You'll like her."

First, of course, we had to find Captain Datis. I opened the door. It was being guarded by two monks.

"I need Captain Datis," I said.

"I'm sorry, Highness, but we were told we aren't supposed to leave our posts."

"Move. And bring me that map."

They moved. Sometimes it's good to be the Redeemer.

Captain Datis arrived quickly, with a troubled look on his face but no map. "Majesty," he said, "you're all right. I was worried."

I looked at him down my nose. My nose is too short to look down properly but I did my best. "I'd have you put under arrest," I said, "only there's nobody to arrest you. How could you have been so stupid?"

If he'd been a dog his ears would've gone back. "Majesty."

"Ten good men died because you didn't do your job."

"I know. But nobody told me—"

"You shouldn't need to be told."

He looked very sad, and I didn't blame him. He had no idea whose side he was on, let alone which side was going to win. For a soldier, worse than being struck blind. "Fortuitously," I said (it's a great word for squashing people with), "we've got a breathing space, and we might just be able to sort this thing out without everybody getting killed. But that will very much depend on you doing exactly what you're told. Do you understand?"

Like hell he did. "Yes, Majesty."

"Well, that's something. That woman, Stauracia. You've got her locked up, like I told you."

"Yes, Majesty."

"Fetch her."

He gazed at me as though lava was just starting to dribble down my slopes. "Does this mean you're—?"

"None of your business."

When he'd gone I lay on the bed and tried to breathe. I'm fine while stressful situations are actually happening, but as soon as they're over, all I want to do is curl up in a little ball and hide till spring.

"Out of interest," said Ekkehard, "who is this woman and why do we need her?"

"She's the agent for the Sisters."

"So you're going to kill her, right? Or is she going to be our hostage?"

I smiled at him. "Everybody thinks she's on the mainland, raising an army," I said.

"That's not answering my question."

"No," I said, "it isn't."

That didn't go down well. He grabbed my arm. "You have got a plan, haven't you?"

"Sort of."

Maybe I should explain about Ekkehard and me. We go way back.

I'd been writing for the theatre for about two years, and I'd started to make a name for myself. Nothing special; people in the street had no idea who I was, but actors and managers were beginning to know me as someone who could turn out three acts of reasonable quality rhyming couplets, with jokes and rhymes that actually rhymed, and which actors could actually speak, on time, at short notice, reliably. That, rather than sheer quivering genius, is what you need if you're trying to run a theatre. Sheer quivering genius may fill the house for a hundred consecutive performances, standing room only, but it may equally well close after a week, depending on whether or not the public is smart enough to get it. But my sort of tripe runs for forty nights to three-quarters capacity and then I write another one, and you can rely on that; me, the dawn, the seasons, the coming in and the going out of the tide, immutably fixed points in a terrifyingly uncertain world. Also, I didn't ask for silly money.

I first saw Ekkehard toiling away in a supporting role in a rubbish melodrama in one of those gloomy, barn-like places on the wrong side of the river. He was playing a heavy villain. He was hilarious. It wasn't a comedy. A cog clicked into place inside my mind.

Pistacchio made him a star, and the play didn't do me any harm either. It ran eighty-two nights, in midsummer when the theatres are usually deserted, and suddenly everybody all over town wanted burlesques of heavy melodrama. I had another one ready, of course, but so did that bitch Ostrys at the Rose. She poached Ekkehard from me by offering him more money, and I had to find someone else in a hurry to play the Archduke Cochineal in the new piece; not that it mattered a damn, because I found someone even better, and my play did all right whereas Ostrys' cheap ripoff bombed, and a week later Ekkehard was back in the taverns looking for work. I decided to forgive him. I'm like that.

So we got along quite amicably for a year or so, me writing parts exactly crafted to draw out his strengths, him whining and asking for more money, until things suddenly went wrong. I'd finished a new piece and wanted to start rehearsals. He was fifty nights into the last one, still drawing good houses. He vanished.

That sort of thing happens in the theatre. Someone goes missing, and suddenly you're scratching around for under-studies and replacements, until the missing star turns up with two black eyes and a murderous hangover and everybody can breathe again. But Ekkehard stayed missing.

We asked around, all the bars and brothels and jails and gambling joints, but nobody had seen him. Invisibility isn't a trait you associate with established actors. We found out where he'd originally come from and sent someone to see if he'd been called home at short notice, somebody dying, something like that. But, no, they hadn't seen or heard from him in ages and good riddance. The manager decided that he must've got drunk and fallen in the river, in which case his body would be floating somewhere out to sea by that point, and no sense crying over spilt milk. I wasn't so sure, but there was nothing more I could do, and I had a show to get ready. The hell with Ekkehard, I thought, and got on with my life.

At that time I was sleeping in a sort of store cupboard out the back of the theatre; it was convenient and didn't cost me anything, and my life didn't really call for a home at that point in my career. When I say sleeping, I mean it. Getting a three-act burlesque ready in a cheapskate theatre is hard work, like coal-mining. By the time I called it a night, I was ready to drop.

So there I was, early hours of the morning, fast asleep on a bed of coils of rope, and something woke me up. I opened my eyes and fumbled beside me for my knife. I had a good one in those days, a folder you could open one-handed, giving you a certain element of surprise (because timing is everything). I heard someone trip over something and swear.

"Ekkehard?" I said.

It was Ekkehard. "Light the lamp," he hissed. He didn't sound drunk.

"Where the hell have you been?"

"Light the fucking lamp." He looked awful. One side of his face was swollen up, a mass of bruises, purple and black like a cardinal's robes. His clothes were in shreds and caked with black mud, and what was left of his shirt had this big brown stain. He was leaning against the wall, and his left arm drooped like an empty sleeve, the way broken arms do. "You arsehole," he said. "You complete shit."

"What happened to you?"

"You did," he snarled, and the effort was too much for him; he started coughing, and ended up on his knees, doubled over.

"Ekkehard, for crying out loud," I said. "What did I do?"

"They're on to you," he said.

"You what?"

"Florian." He spat the name out like a tooth. "Florian fucking met'Oc."

"Oh."

"They grabbed me," he went on, "as I was coming out of the Two Dogs. They wanted to know all about you. I told them, but they kept hitting me."

That cold feeling, tensing your guts and relaxing your bowels. "What did you—?"

He held up his hand. "I said you couldn't possibly be this met'Oc character, because I'd known you for years. We were boys together, I said, back on the farm in the old country. They didn't believe me. They hit me with an axe handle. I think it's two, maybe three busted ribs. They wanted to know where to find you. I said you'd gone out of town. I told them a place I know, so I'd be able to describe it convincingly. I said, you always go out of town when you're writing, for the peace and quiet, and you've got a woman there. I gave them a name, so she's in for a surprise. Serves her bloody well right if they smack her around a bit, the cow. Anyhow, they bought that, I think, because then they tied a stone block to my ankle and threw me in the river."

He stopped and looked at me, blaming me for everything. "How did you—?"

"I got lucky. Their goons aren't very good at knots. Just as I was about to drown, the rope must've slipped off the stone, and I got up to the surface and crawled out onto the riverbank. I lay there three days. I couldn't move. I thought I was paralysed. I really thought, that's it, that's me done for, I'm going to die, all because of that *arsehole*—"

"But you didn't."

"No fucking thanks to you." He was so angry he was hurting himself. "Soon as I could, I came here, to warn you."

"Thank you," I said.

"Go fuck yourself."

I hesitated for a moment. "They didn't happen to mention—"

"What?"

"Who they were."

He glared at me. "No, they didn't. They're people who don't like you very much, and I can't say I blame them. What a bloody stupid question to ask. Don't you know who wants to kill you?"

"It could be one of several."

"Dear God." He rolled his one moveable eye. "No, they didn't specify. What the fuck did you do, anyhow? Murder somebody?"

I didn't answer.

"Anyway," he said, after a thoughtful second or so, "you piss off out of it, if you know what's good for you. It'd really annoy me if I thought I'd been through all this and they got you anyhow." He stopped. He'd exhausted himself. I stood up. He looked at me. "You got any money?" he said.

"Yes. How much do you need?"

"Idiot. I meant, do you need any, in which case I was going to give you my poor miserable savings. But you don't need them, so fuck it."

"Did they follow you here?"

"Oh, for God's sake. I don't know, do I?"

It's a silly habit of mine; I always have what I like to think of as my running-away bag, preferably within reach at all times. Money, spare pair of shoes, a few other things. I hung it round my neck. "Thanks," I said. "I won't forget this."

"Stick it up your arse."

"I will," I said, "first chance I get. It's the least I can do, considering."

"Funny man. Now go away, please."

I was at the door. There were four ways out of the theatre, not counting the roof. I decided on the roof. "The new play," I said. "It's not ready. I'm sorry."

"Shit."

"The manuscript's just there, by the window. You can get Lysaor to finish it. Really good part for you in it: you'll love it."

"Lysaor's a wanker. He couldn't scan a line to save his life."

"He's all right." I opened the window. A bit of a scramble and I'd be out on the leads, and I was fairly sure I could manage the jump from the theatre roof to the warehouse next door. "You're a true friend, Ekkehard."

"Piss off."

So I did; and about nine months later, some upstart nobody had ever heard of called Saevus Corax started up in the battlefield salvage business, a thousand miles away on the Sashan border. I found out later that Ekkehard was the one who let slip whatever it was that put them on to me in the first place, which was why they pulled him in and beat him to a pulp, but never mind about that. Anyhow, that's all there is to know about me and Ekkehard. Well, nearly all.

7

They finally brought me the map. I was engrossed in it when Stauracia arrived.

She wasn't looking her best. I'm guessing that at some point she'd tried to make a run for it. Running for it, like surgery and writing plays, is something best left to experts, like me. She was covered in dust, her hands were filthy and she had a red mark on her cheek. The guards put her in a chair and, at my direction, tied her to it. Then they withdrew. I carried on looking at my map, while Ekkehard ate cashew nuts from a small jar he'd picked up somewhere.

"Who's he?" she said.

I looked up. "Sorry?"

"Who's he?"

I smiled. "Ekkehard, this is Stauracia. Stauracia, Ekkehard. Ekkehard represents the Knights."

That put the fear of God into her. "Why's he here?"

"Same reason you are. So you can't be somewhere else."

Ekkehard shot me a glance, which I ignored. She hadn't

noticed. "What the hell do you think you're playing at? Get these ropes off me, right now."

"Absolutely not. Come on," I added gently. "Strapping somebody to a chair is no big deal. It can't be, or you'd never have done it to me."

Ekkehard was thinking. You can tell by the look on his face, not to mention the slight smell of burning. "She's a hostage, right?"

"Among other things."

In which case, what did that make him? Well, he shouldn't have asked if he didn't want to hear the answer. "What are you up to?"

"I'm trying to make sense of this map." Which was true. It was all right as far as it went, but I got the impression that the scale was all wrong. It made Sirupat look very big, and everywhere else very far away. I looked at her. "How fast does that ship of yours go?"

"Seven knots. Why?"

"What's seven knots in real money?"

She shrugged. "Search me. The captain said seven knots and I believe him."

"Fine," I said, desperately trying to remember stuff I hadn't given a thought to for years. One knot is one and a bit miles every hour; really helpful, that. "Thank you."

"If you're thinking of stealing my ship, forget it. The crew take orders from me."

"I don't want your rotten ship, thanks all the same. The last thing I need right now is another sea journey." I put the map down. Now at least I had some idea of what I had to do. Whether I'd be able to do it was another matter entirely.

*

I sent for Captain Datis.

"These two," I said, "are the accredited representatives of the Poor Sisters and the Knights of Equity."

He looked at them. "Why's she tied to a chair?"

"She bites. As you know, the Sisters and the Knights want to take over the island. Between them they've suborned the entire privy council, and I have reason to believe they're killing the king by slow poison." I paused and looked at him. "I'd be interested to hear your views on that."

"He's lying," she said. He looked at her, then at me. "I know about the council," he said. "At least, I suspected."

"And the poisoning?"

"I've been trying not to think about that."

"Then you're an idiot," I said, and he took it meekly enough. "Well?" I said. "I'm asking you whose side you're on."

He took a moment. The sight of the Sisters' emissary tied to a chair probably wasn't lost on him. "Are you considering making a treaty with the Knights?" he asked.

"How many chairs are there in this room?"

"One."

"That's why he's not tied to a chair," I said. "Also, he doesn't bite. No, I'm not considering a treaty with the Knights, or the Sisters. Now, whose side are you on?"

He looked like a little boy told to kiss his aunt in the presence of a lot of people. "The king," he said. "Naturally."

"Glad we've got that straightened out, because we've got a lot to get through. Now, I'd like to run through the balance of power on this island, if that's all right with you. You've got, what, seventy men?"

"Seventy-eight, Majesty."

"Please don't call me that. When people start with all the

Majesty stuff, I can't think straight. She," I pointed, "has eighteen marines and sixty-odd sailors, but as far as I know they're still down at the harbour. He's got about twenty monks. You're a soldier; what do you reckon?"

He thought about it. "The monks we can handle," he said. "We've had a look at the marines: they could be a problem. Recommend we lure them into a trap and neutralise them."

"What does neutralise mean?"

He didn't like the question. "We aren't really set up for containing prisoners. We haven't got the manpower."

"He means kill them," Ekkehard put in. "Sounds good to me."

"Shut up," I said. "He's only acting tough because he's scared," I explained. "Really he's soft as butter. If he treads on a snail, he throws up. I think it'd be much better if the Sister here sends the ship to the mainland with a message. That'll get the sailors out of our hair, and then we can lock up the marines."

She glared at me. "What message?"

"Oh, I'll think of something." I turned to Datis. "Can any of your men shoot a bow accurately?"

"Yes, one. Me."

I smiled. "When I'm king I'm going to institute a grand national archery competition, with valuable prizes. Right, get the captain of that ship up here. She wants to see him."

It was a brief interview. Enter captain, sees Stauracia sitting in the chair, facing one of those ornamental screens. Ekkehard and I discovered them standing by the window, talking to each other about something else. Stauracia: I want you to take the ship and go to Boustrophedon. Know where that is? Captain: yes. Stauracia: go to such and such a bar, find a man called

Something-or-other, give him this letter. Wait for a reply, it may take a while so give the men some shore leave. Captain (happily): yes. Stauracia: you may run into trouble getting there, so take the marines, just in case. The letter must get there, understood? Understood, said the captain; exit stage right. Datis emerges from behind screen, in agony from the pain in his knuckles from holding a seventy-pound bow at full draw all through this conversation, the arrow aimed directly at Stauracia's heart, or where it would be if she had one. It's easy to get people to do what you want, if you know how.

I wrote the letter in Gordouli, a language practically unknown in the West and almost never written down. Tell you about that later.

Stauracia wasn't the least bit grateful for being untied from the chair. Ekkehard offered to give her a game of checkers but she just sat there fuming at me and sulking while I discussed tactics with Captain Datis. Food arrived at some point but she just picked at a couple of slices of bread and some dried figs. Then some priests came to see me.

I hadn't seen any of them before. Could they talk to me, they said, without the unbelievers present? I explained that the unbelievers were hostages and I didn't dare turn my back on them for a split second, but neither of them could understand a word we were saying so it really didn't matter. The priests looked unhappy. The presence of unbelievers, they said, gave them a pain, like kidney stones only worse, and even discussing religion in front of infidels was a mortal sin. You should know that, they didn't say but strongly implied. That's fine, I said, not explicitly pointing out that as the Redeemer I made the rules. What did you want to talk about? It's like this, they said.

Apparently, while I'd been busy with other things, the hierarchy of the Left Hand had held a brief impromptu general synod, during which all nine members of the privy council were anathematised *in absentia* for conspiring with unbelievers – the Knights and the Sisters – and condemned to death; this sentence had now been carried out, and if I wanted to see the heads, I could look out of the window—

I looked out of the window. In the courtyard was a short row of stakes, as though someone had been planting standard roses. On top of the stakes, eight heads.

The synod had elected new leaders, namely the five gentlemen now talking to me, and charged them with securing an audience with the Redeemer and finding out from him exactly what was going on. Naturally anything the Redeemer saw fit to do was beyond their remit to question, but even so—

"Names," I said.

In one ear and out the other; I'm not very good with names, though I'm red hot on faces. I gathered that the man I was talking to, who seemed to be the leader, was called Riobarzanes. I reckoned that'd have to do.

"The fact is," I told him, "things are very bad. The unbeliever banks who hold all our money are trying to kill the king and take over the country. I assume you know that already, or you wouldn't have killed the traitors."

He nodded eagerly. I think he was prepared to like me.

"That man and that woman," I said, "represent the two banks. That's why they're hostages. I've sent for help, people we can trust, but until they get here, I need you to make sure that any other supporters and sympathisers they may have hidden among the clergy and the people are rooted out and dealt with, right away. Do you think you can do that?"

"Oh, yes. Highness," he added.

"Good man. Now," I went on, "it's almost certain that when the banks find out that their attempt to take us over by stealth has failed, they'll mount a full-scale invasion. Clearly we can't hold out against several thousand trained soldiers."

"We can die trying."

"Let's not," I said. "Instead, we need to play one side off against the other. We don't care how many unbelievers slaughter each other, so long as they do it somewhere else."

"Of course." He liked that bit, very much.

"On the other hand," I went on, "we need the unbelievers, because they're all that stands between us and the Right Hand, who as you know would sweep in here and slaughter us all if it wasn't for the protection we enjoy from the Poor Sisters and the Knights of Equity." I paused. "You did know that, didn't you?"

He looked at me as though the handyman's assistant had just turned out to be his father. "No," he said. "I didn't. We assumed—"

"That the Redeemer kept the Right Hand at bay by sheer force of divine will. And, yes, he does, but he needs a mortal instrument to do it with. That instrument is the banks." I paused for breath, and to let it all sink in. "You can appreciate the delicacy of our situation. We need to keep the two pans of the scale perfectly balanced. Presumably my great-uncle had his reasons for not explaining all this to you, but the situation has changed. I need you on my side."

"Of course," he said. "You can count on us. Our lives—"

"Yes, thank you. So what we need to do," I went on, "is stall for time. Once the forces I've sent for get here, we'll be strong enough to hold out against a straightforward assault. Probably," I added. "If He wills it."

"Highness."

"But a siege is another thing entirely. We can't stop either the Sisters or the Knights occupying the countryside and cooping us up inside the city. So I need you to make arrangements. I want as many of the country people inside the city as possible, as much food as you can lay your hands on, lumber and bricks and stone for fortifications, tools, that sort of thing. Also, I want you to make sure that no ships of any sort leave the island until I say so. Apart," I added quickly, "from the one I arrived on. Is that clear?"

"Highness."

"Do you agree with what I'm proposing?"

"Oh, yes, Highness."

"Splendid. Go away and see to it, then come back and tell me how you're getting on."

The priests bowed low and left. Ekkehard looked at me. "What the hell was all that about?" he said.

"I've given the priests something to do," I said. "With luck it'll keep them busy and out of our hair." I was starting to shake again, but I didn't want him or Stauracia to see. "Datis, who are those people?"

He gave me potted biographies. I listened, not taking very much of it in. "Politicians," I said.

He was about to contradict me, then hesitated. "Yes, I suppose so," he said. "They have a pretty good idea of what people are saying, in the city."

"That's good," I said. "Now I want you to send three men to guard the king. The best you've got."

"But I've already got—"

"Different ones," I said. "Just in case. And arrest that doctor and bring me his medical bag."

He nodded. "What you said just now. Is there really going to be a siege?"

"Count on it."

He took it well, all things considering. "But that's all right," I told him. "By then, everything will be under control. I know exactly what I'm doing, and everything will be just fine."

I think he believed me. For some reason, I found that mildly depressing.

It's always better when people have plenty to do. It passes the time and makes them feel like they're helping, and it gets them out from under your feet when you're trying to think.

I had a lot to think about. For one thing, I knew next to nothing about siege warfare, understandably enough. There's never anything worth having in the aftermath of a successful siege. The Company of Vultures tried to make a go of it a few years back. They raked through the ashes of Capite Censi after the Aelians burned it to the ground, but all they got were a few barrels of carpenters' nails, which had to be painstakingly straightened before they could sell them. They tried marketing the ash as a soil improver, but it cost too much to collect and transport, so they gave it up. No, the unanimous verdict of the trade is that sieges are bad news and we don't hold with them.

Unfortunately, however, they work. In sixty per cent of cases where a relief army fails to turn up, sooner or later the city surrenders on terms. In another twenty per cent, the siege ends in a successful assault. The twenty per cent where the city actually survives tend to be where the besieger runs out of time or money, or he gets an outbreak of plague in his camp which he isn't able to pass on to the people inside the walls. Not good odds if you're on the wrong side of the wall. Bad business.

To make matters worse, I had her to keep me company. True, she couldn't talk the language, but a disturbingly high proportion of the people who mattered in Sirupat turned out to know either Robur or Sashan, and I really didn't want to leave her anywhere she could start talking to people if I wasn't there to hear what she was saying. Therefore she had to go around with me.

"I wasn't always like this, you know," she said, as we stood on a battlement watching them strengthen the main gate.

"Like what?"

"A liar," she said. "Treacherous, duplicitous, manipulative. That's not really me at all."

I was chilled to the bone by the wind, having given her my cloak. "Of course not," I said. "You're a victim of circumstances."

"Yes, actually, I am. You think you know me, but you don't really."

"Can we really honestly say we know anyone? Sometimes I doubt it."

"I had wonderful dreams when I was a kid," she ground on. "There was this great big wonderful world out there, just calling to me. Here I am, it said, ready and waiting, and you can be anything you want to be, so long as you truly follow your heart. If you genuinely want to find your dream and make a difference, there's no power on earth that can stop you."

I nodded. "Seems perfectly reasonable to me," I said.

"Didn't turn out like that," she persevered. "I wanted to go to the university, did you know that? They wouldn't let me, because I'm a woman. But I couldn't accept that; it just wasn't right. So I fought them. I kept on and on—"

"I bet."

"Talking to them, arguing, pleading, and finally they gave

in and let me go as a deaconess, so I wasn't a real student but at least I could sit in on lectures and read books in the library. That was so wonderful, like a whole different world. Poetry and science and philosophy and mathematics. After all those years stuck in that stupid little provincial town, I felt like I was really alive." She did something with her sleeve to the corner of her eye. "It didn't matter that nobody wanted to talk to me and they wouldn't let me join in with anything. For the first time in my life, I was being the real me." Pause: count to three. "And then they threw me out."

"For stealing."

"I didn't do it. They set me up, to get rid of me. They couldn't bear the thought that a woman could be as good a scholar as a man, or maybe even better. So they planted those goblets in my room."

"I hate it when that happens. Do go on."

"And then do you know what they did to me?"

"No," I lied. "Tell me all about it."

"They put me on trial," she said, "and they wouldn't let me defend myself, because women aren't allowed to be advocates in a court of law, so they made me have this old fool to defend me, and he didn't want to offend the college authorities, so naturally I was found guilty. And then they sentenced me to five years indentured service, which is practically slavery. They sold me to a fat old merchant, as a housemaid." She sighed. The cold was making my teeth hurt. "But I wasn't going to give up. The old man just laughed at me, but his wife recognised I was worth more than just dusting and sweeping floors. She made him give me a chance, helping with book-keeping and writing up the accounts. I was really good at that. In the end, even he had to admit—"

"Didn't he die suddenly?"

"Heart attack. Then his wife took over the business, and she and I made a real go of it, and she made me a partner. Two women, running a successful chandlery—"

"She died, too, didn't she?"

"That was an accident: the coroner said so himself. And then I was left all alone, fighting to keep my dream alive, with every man's hand against me. They all wanted me to fail, of course, but I wasn't going to give them the satisfaction. I was only twenty-one, but I knew, if only I stayed true to my dream—"

"And then you heard the call."

She went all solemn. "That's right," she said. "The greatest moment of my life. We were on our way to Gemmagene with a cartload of premium worsteds, and I looked up and I saw a light in the sky—"

"You might care to lower your voice," I said. "People are looking at you."

"Stauracia, it said, Stauracia, why are you ignoring me? It hurts you to kick against the goad. And then I knew, that instant, that my life would never be the same again. It was one of those moments."

"Yup," I said. "I get them, too."

"So I founded my mission, feeding the poor and helping the sick, and men dying on battlefields. They didn't want to listen to me, but I made them. Whenever the going got tough and I felt like giving up, I thought about my vision, that voice on the road to Gemmagene, and I just knew that I couldn't let all those poor people down, when they were relying on me. And so, when the Sisters heard about my work, and what I'd managed to achieve, all on my own with every man's hand—"

"They made you an offer you couldn't refuse."

"Arsehole," she said. "You're just like them. You think, just because I'm a—"

I'm a patient man, but not as patient as all that. "Give it a rest," I said. "Please. Actually, you've made your point extremely well. We ought to be able to understand each other because we're alike, in so many ways."

Aha, she thought. "Easy for you to say."

"We are, though," I said. "The only real difference is that when I got caught thieving I did hard time in a jail, but because you're a girl they let you off with indentures. And they never could prove you killed the old man and his wife, but I never made any bones about killing my brother."

She looked at me. "You really did that."

"Oh yes."

"Self-defence?"

"Not really, no."

"Really, I honestly assumed you didn't do it. Because what did you possibly have to gain?"

"You had to have been there."

She shrugged. "I didn't kill the old man," she said. "It was a heart attack."

"Convenient."

"Sometimes convenient things happen."

"God's will?"

"I wouldn't be at all surprised," she said. "He was a real bastard. He used to hit his wife, all the time. Actually, I think she may have killed him. If she did, he asked for it."

"And her?"

"She was horrible. She tried to cheat me. She'd have run that business into the ground if I hadn't been there to keep it going."

"So sort of self-defence."

"She'd have cut my throat in a split second, only she knew she needed me."

"Pre-emptive self-defence," I said. "I'm all right with that."

"I know you are," she said. "What was that man's name? Posidonius?"

I sighed. "That was just bad timing," I said. "If I ran into him now he'd be safe as houses, because I no longer have anything to hide. Timing's everything."

"Pre-emptive self-defence. The idea that your life is worth more than someone else's, which justifies taking extreme action."

"*Justifies* is a bit strong," I said. "I'd be happier with *explains*."

"Justifies," she repeated firmly. "And you believe it. You believe you're justified. Because if you believed it was wrong, you wouldn't do it."

I thought for a moment. "That's you, not me," I said. "I do all sorts of really bad stuff, all the time. You face a lot of challenging choices. That's where we're different."

She turned and looked at me, all dewy-eyed and beautiful. "But at least we understand each other a bit better now," she said. "Don't we?"

I smiled at her. "You really seriously believe you can salvage something out of this, don't you? You really think you can still grab the reins and turn a profit." I studied her. No sign. "I can see why the Sisters chose you," I said. "You just don't give up."

"I feel sorry for you," she said. "You gave up so long ago."

I make it a rule to let other people have the last word, when I'm interested in what they have to say. I like to think of it as always having the last listen.

*

Several days. Also several nights, when I couldn't get a wink of sleep for fear of what they might get up to if I did. It wasn't so much Ekkehard, who deep down is a simple soul, but she needed watching. Which meant she could sleep when she was tired, but I couldn't. I don't do well when I can't get my regular six hours. Clearly she knew that, bless her. I realised long ago that the only thing I have going for me is my knowledge of human nature. It's usually enough, but not always.

Several productive days, however, if you measure value by things getting done. The priests herded about five thousand of the country people into the city and saw to it that the granary was filled. They had the sense to realise that the first thing a besieger would do would be to cut off the water supply, which came in under the wall beside the east gate, so they had the two wells dredged and relined; we'd have just enough water to get by, if we weren't too pernicketty about washing. Datis organised the fortifications, strengthening the gates where they'd got a bit delapidated and clearing birds' nests out of the loopholes. Whoever built Dui Chirra all those years ago – it wasn't the people who lived there now – they made a pretty good job of it. Obviously we couldn't hold out indefinitely, but of course I had no intention of trying. Just long enough, that's all. Timing. That, and how things look from the road, as my father used to say.

There's an old play, can't remember who it's by, based on an even older story. It's called *The Palace of Truth*. The idea is that there's a building somewhere, and inside it you can't tell lies. If you try, what comes out of your mouth isn't what you wanted to say. Instead, you tell the truth. The king on whose land this horrible building stands tolerates it because he's got a magic whatsit that allows him to tell lies even inside the palace; everybody else is forced to be completely honest, but he can still lie. The play's a comedy with a happy ending, so presumably the palace gets demolished and the ruins sown with salt. Even so. The moral, I think, is that the world only works when everybody's got to live by the same rules *except you*. Under those conditions, happiness is at least theoretically possible. Otherwise, forget it.

I was on the wrong side of the city, sorting out some stupid misunderstanding about carrots being stockpiled in the wrong sort of sand, which meant they'd go off instead of storing properly. I'd let Ekkehard off the lead for a bit, because he was really starting to annoy me. I was stuck with her, of course, so she was there, giving unhelpful advice and interfering generally. One of Datis' sergeants – we'd promoted him a few days earlier – came trotting up. "You said you wanted to be told if a ship—"

I was on my feet and running like a hare before he could finish what he was saying. As I ran, I agonised over what he'd said. A ship, singular. A single ship was either irrelevant or it meant we were irreparably screwed. Maybe I should've stopped and let him finish.

When I got to the tower that looks out over the harbour, though, it was ships, not ship: seven of them, with plain dirty-white sails. People say a lot of unkind things about God, but just occasionally He comes across and does what you want Him to, and I think that makes up for all the other times.

"You arsehole," Gombryas said, as he stepped off the gangplank. "Why didn't you tell us?"

I was so pleased to see him I could scarcely breathe.

"Because you'd have turned me in for the reward," I said, and he had the grace not to argue. "You got my message, then."

Carrhasio and Polycrates came down to join us. "Is it true?" Polycrates said. "You're a fucking *king*?"

I was even glad to see Polycrates, at least for a short while. "I didn't think you'd come," I told them.

"Nearly didn't," Gombryas said. "But we were out of money and you know how much stuff costs in Antecyrene. Did you really murder your own brother?"

Five hundred men, fifteen hundred sets of good-quality used armour, and the hold of one of the ships was completely filled with bows and arrows. "No, of course not," I said, "it's a lie put about by my enemies. You really think I'm capable of something like that?"

"Sorry," Gombryas said. "Had to ask, but no, of course not. I never believed it for a second. Are you really the ki—?"

"Yes." I hadn't meant to shout. "And if we get out of this in one piece, I'll make you all dukes and earls and marquises and barons, and you can live in palaces and ride about in coaches."

"Sorry," said Gombryas. "Get out of what?"

The message I'd sent, care of Sergeant Pharnaspes' cousin with the fishing boat, had been quite short and simple: I'm on Sirupat; come here as fast as you can; bring the stock. The truth, but not the whole truth. Careless of me.

They'd heard the other stuff – me being king – when they stopped for water in Coele, where apparently the Knights had sent their remaining galleasses, stuffed full of marines. There they'd bumped into Sapor Asvogel and a few of his boys, who just happened, likely story, to be passing through; here, did you know that idiot boss of yours is king of Sirupat? Sapor had heard it from associates of the Sisters, who'd heard it from agents of the Knights, and by then it was all over the place: my genealogy and biography, most of it, and the unfortunate circumstances surrounding my leaving home. On hearing all this, naturally my dear friends and colleagues assumed that now I'd come into my inheritance I was anxious to share my good fortune with those closest to me, my true family, all that. They made it up the coast to Olbia in record time, slight delay because of contrary winds on the last leg of the journey but here at last they were, ready and eager to embrace a life of sophisticated ease.

They looked at me. "You bastard," Polycrates said, "you complete arsehole. You got us here to fight a *war?*"

We were sitting on the palace verandah, overlooking the city's old quarter as the sun began to set. It sounds much nicer than it was. I'd just told the assembled heads of department what I'd neglected to mention in my letter. "It may come to that," I admitted. "I don't think it will, but there's an outside chance, yes."

"Us against the Knights," Olybrius said.

"Possibly."

"And the Sisters."

"Them, too. But it's far more likely that once they see we've got the city adequately garrisoned, they'll do the maths and realise they can't take it by storm, and then we snuggle down for a nice relaxing siege. So the risk of any actual fighting is pretty remote."

The pans of the scale were swaying. In one pan, fighting and death; in the other, the inconceivable wealth of Sirupat, there for the snatching. "Have another drink," I said.

"I don't know about all this," Olybrius said gravely. "It's a great opportunity, obviously. It's the big score. But fighting—"

Carrhasio called him an uncouth name. But even Carrhasio had been unusually quiet. "It's a risk we run every day," I said. "People try and rip off our stuff, or we get mistaken for somebody's army. And like he just said, it's the big score. The real thing. The biggest score there is."

"Look, Saevus—" Polycrates stopped. "That's another thing. Do we still call you Saevus or is it Florian now?"

"Saevus. Definitely."

"That's all right, then. Florian is a poof's name."

"I quite like it, actually," I said, "but it's not me."

"Saevus," Polycrates said. "Let's get one thing straight. We work for you. You're the boss and you pay us money for doing stuff. We aren't your fucking subjects. If you want to fight a stupid war, make your peasants do it. We're free men. We do what we choose."

I nodded. "Absolutely right," I said.

Polycrates peered at me, his piercing look. It doesn't work, but nobody's ever told him. "So if we decide to get back on the ships and piss off out of here, you're not going to try and stop us."

"I wouldn't try and stop you," I said, "if you still had ships. But while we've been having this chat, your ships have been towed out into the bay and scuttled. Sorry about that. It's not that I don't trust you or anything."

Dead silence, then everybody talking at once in raised voices. I held up my hand. They stopped talking.

"There's other ships, obviously," I said. "But anything big enough to take you lot back to the mainland has been rounded up and sent away round the top of the island. You can go and look for them if you like, but I don't suppose you'll find them before the Knights get here, and then you'll be caught out in the open, not safe behind the city wall. You could always explain to the Knights that you've decided to be neutral. They might accept that, you never know."

"You shit," Olybrius said. "I thought we were friends."

"I thought so, too. Which is why it never occurred to me you might want those ships for running away. Look, are you in or aren't you?"

In the split second it took for them to answer, it occurred to me that I hadn't seen Stauracia since I left her at the carrot depot. Presumably someone had had the good sense to round her up and bring her back to the palace.

"Let's talk about money," Polycrates said. They were in.

We talked about money.

I was unbelievably generous. I said they could have half the royal revenues from the gold panning to share between them. Why only half, Polycrates objected, and then I told him what a half-share amounted to, in an average year, and he went all quiet. Some people believe in God, others in the big score; same thing, really. Polycrates had just had one of those road-to-Gemmagene experiences we were talking about earlier. We all instinctively lowered our voices, so as not to spoil the moment for him.

We were still discussing terms – some people have real difficulty in taking yes for an answer – when Captain Datis came in. He had a bruise on his cheek and a fat lip, and two of Gombryas' boys had hold of his arms. Something else I'd neglected to tell them about.

"Sorry about that," I told Datis, in Euxine. "I should've

told you they were coming, only I didn't think they would. They're with me."

He gave me a long look. It said: I thought you were here to throw out the foreigners and give Sirupat back to the Sirupatis, and now here you are with these *pirates*— "That's fine, then," he said. "We could certainly use the manpower."

"Try and get along with them. They're scruffy and undisciplined, but they've been on a lot of battlefields."

"What's he saying?" Olybrius called out.

"We're discussing chains of command," I replied. I didn't mention that Datis knew Robur.

"Have we got to do what he says?"

"No," I replied. "But try not to get under his feet."

Later, Datis and I had a private conversation. We need these people, I told him, but we shouldn't trust them, not with all that money at stake. We all need to remember, I said, which side we're on.

He nodded, as though I'd just said something very profound. "Understood," he said. "So I still take my orders from you."

"And me only, yes. And so do they."

"Got it." He looked happier. "How many—?"

"Five hundred," I said, "give or take. Also, they've brought heavy equipment for a thousand more."

His eyes lit up. "That's handy."

"And enough bows and arrows for anyone who wants them."

I had his attention. You can't turn a farmer into a soldier by putting him in armour, but bows and arrows are different. "You know the people of this island," I said.

He thought for a moment. "They're not fighters," he said.

"Glad to hear it."

"But we've got a lot of them cooped up in the city now,

with nothing to do. And archery's a popular sport. We could offer prizes."

I grinned. "Why not? But all I want is a dead zone, a hundred and fifty yards from the wall, where nothing can survive. You don't need sharpshooters for that, just lots of arrows in the air at the same time."

He nodded slowly. "That won't stop the bastards digging."

"The city's built on rock," I said. "No, of course it won't stop anyone undermining the walls, if they're really dead set on it, but it means it'll take time, not to mention a great deal of hard work. Why bother? If you're in for the long haul, why not just sit tight and starve us out?"

"Well, yes," he said. "Why not, exactly?"

"I have a feeling something will have turned up by then," I said.

The people of Sirupat, according to Datis, weren't fighters. Possibly the nicest thing you could ever say about anyone.

Look, about this business of war. And it is my business, I readily confess. I don't start wars, I don't fight them, I just clear up the mess, but even so I'm implicated. Abolish war and I'd starve, and so would the honest, hard-working, harmless men who depend on me. So I know where I stand as regards this war business. I'm for it. Give war a chance, I say.

Now you know that when I say that, I'm being glib and amusing, and of course I don't really mean it, because I'm the hero of this story and if you thought for one moment that I approve of war and think it's a good thing, especially if I think that because it puts money in my pocket, you'd lose all sympathy for me in an instant, and there'd be one more second-hand copy of this book on a market stall somewhere, along with all the other no-hopers that only the parchment-scrapers are ever going to buy. Of course.

So, no, I don't mean it, not for one split second. I've seen more war than anybody, except possibly Chusro Asvogel, so I know what I'm talking about. It's the worst thing there is. I've also seen plagues and earthquakes and famines and slave camps and they're all very bad, but war is the worst thing of all. War isn't just men who have no quarrel with each other hacking each other to death. War is a large number of men packed into a small, enclosed space, cold, hunger, dysentery – the smell of war isn't blood, it's shit, that godawful stench that hangs over every locale where five thousand soldiers are crowded together and three thousand of them are sick as dogs with the runs. War is waste. It's the waste it leaves behind, from uncovered open latrines to fourteen thousand pairs of winter boots at two hundred and sixty trachy a pair dumped in the desert because of a snafu at supply. It's perfectly good crops trampled and burned, perfectly good houses smashed to rubble, perfectly good horses littered dead along ninety miles of road, perfectly good rivers fouled with shit and corpses, perfectly good men swelling and going purple in the sun. War is waste: all that money, screwed out of poor farmers who can't afford it, to pay interest on loans from the Sisters to buy winter boots for soldiers being sent to the desert; all those young men rounded up by the recruiting sergeants, so there's nobody to cut and thrash the wheat or mend the fences or plough up the fallow where the thistles are self-seeding, not until the young men come back, and then they don't. War is five thousand acres of briars and withies and docks and nettles that used to be poor men's farms, and the village is deserted and falling down, and rooks and deer live there now. War is taxes going up because half the country is deserted and can't pay tax, so the soldiers have to go round the places where people still live and take the cattle and the ploughs and the seed corn in lieu, which means nobody can live there any more, leading to reduced revenue, leading to increased taxes. War is everything that's wrong with a species that allows itself to be led and ordered about by leaders and governments, and the natural, inevitable result of leaders and governments is war. So, a moment ago I lied to you. I'm not in favour of war. I'm against it.

But there: just because I don't like it doesn't mean it's bad for business, and war is very good for business. War is shipyards working five shifts day and night, sawmills and lumberyards crying out for experienced hands to work two inches away from the whirring blades. War is row upon row of long sheds full of men hammering blooms of iron straight from the smelter into thin sheets of plate, and the noise makes the ground shake under your feet. War is a hundred thousand bales of cotton FOB at Beloisa on their way to twenty thousand looms to make shirts that, in due course, Chusro Asvogel and I will strip off dead men and patch up and turn an honest trachy on. War is a massive boost to certain sectors of the economy, such as shipping, manufacturing, road haulage and the whole carrion-eating industry, of which the crows and I are a grateful part. It's fatuous and naive to claim that war never achieves anything and nothing good ever comes out of it. War is great for reforestation and wildlife; it means cheap (patched) shirts and cheap nearly-new boots for the poorly paid munitions factory worker, and a living wage in the mills for all those widows and orphans whose men didn't come back from the last big push. War is practically the universal panacea, and if you can't make money during a war you can't really be trying.

So, three cheers for the widowmaker; even so, I wasn't entirely sure I was doing the right thing bringing it to Sirupat. All very well saying it was bound to come anyway. Might as well say you're a mortal, therefore you're going to die sooner or later, so you don't mind if I cut your throat. There are strata of culpability, like the layers of an onion, and the more you peel them back, the more you want to cry.

The people of Sirupat weren't fighters, according to reliable official sources. It had been a long time since anybody had come round and scooped them up to go and wage diplomacy by other means. Which is not to say they were soft and chick-enshit; quite the reverse. They worked every hour of daylight, back-bending, arm-swinging work that first gets you fit and then cripples you, and on the rare occasions when the sun shone and they weren't working, they enjoyed themselves by going up into the hills and killing wild animals, because you need a bit of meat when your diet is mostly pulses and cereals. Not, therefore, a case of couldn't. The men of Sirupat weren't fighters because they didn't want to be, and in my book there's no higher praise than that – and that's the main reason, when you come to think of it, why women are so infinitely superior to men. But for God's sake don't tell them I said so.

The men of Sirupat didn't want to be fighters. My task, therefore, was to change their minds. I get all the rotten jobs.

I could never do what Ekkehard does, stand up in front of a thousand strangers and talk to them. More than ten people at one time and my mind goes blank and my tongue gets too big for my mouth and I'm an imbecile. That's why I have depart-ment heads in my business: I talk to them; they talk to their people; things get done. I reckon the root of the problem is that

I can't conceive of the possibility that people listening to me don't think I'm an idiot. Ten people I can just about imagine myself deceiving, if I pull out all the intellectual stops. More than that and, by the law of averages, someone's going to be immune to my particular brand of flannel and I'll be found out and exposed as the halfwit I truly am.

Just as well I had a trained specialist on hand to do the job for me.

"No," he said.

"Oh, come on," I said. "It's an acting job. You're a professional. If you want paying, I'm offering thirty staurata."

"Fuck you," he said. "I'm not going to stand up in front of a crowd of dirty peasants and urge them to rebel against the Knights. It's more than my life's worth."

Put like that I was forced to agree. Ekkehard's life isn't worth very much, even to him. "It's hardly rebellion, is it?" I said. "The Knights don't own this island."

"Tell them that."

"Curiously enough, that's the object of the exercise. Ninety staurata."

"You can stuff your money up your arse. I've gone out on a limb for you already. Now you're handing me a saw. No thank you."

"Listen," I said. It's a weird thing, but when I say *listen* in that tone of voice, they generally do, even people who know me. And people who know me ought to know by now that when I say *listen* it means I've run out of arguments and I'm trying to get my own way through sheer bluster. "I need you to do this. We need to get those farmers down there out on the walls, looking like soldiers. If we can do that, the real soldiers on the other side of the wall will count them and reach the conclusion that the city's too well defended to storm, and then there won't be any fighting and we'll still be alive by the time today's milk goes sour. If we don't, your precious Knights or her precious Sisters, whoever gets here first, are going to kick down the gate and kill everything that moves, you included. Do you understand?"

He breathed out slowly through his nose. "Why is it," he said, "that I keep saving your worthless arse, time and time again? You'd think I'd know better by now, but it looks like I don't."

"Thanks, Ekkehard. You're a pal."

"Go fuck yourself sideways with a ten-foot spike."

While he was doing his big speech (and credit where it's due, he did it very well), I tried to find out where Stauracia had got to. I had absolutely no luck at all, which tended to suggest that she had resources on the island I didn't know about. That bothered me a lot.

Ekkehard came back from addressing the people, which he'd done in the market square. He looked happy. "You shit," he said.

"Well?"

He sat down and reached for the booze. "They bought it," he said. "I think. I gave them that spiel you wrote, and I could tell they were unconvinced, so I did the big speech from *Whore's Tragedy*, you know, gentlemen in Scona now abed will think themselves accursed they were not here. Went down a treat. I guess it's pretty heady stuff if you've never heard it before."

Dear God, I thought. "They liked that?"

"What's not to like? Grown men used to cry when Einhard did it at the Gallery."

"Yes, but it's a—" I stopped and took a deep breath. "It went down well."

"Oh, yes. Cheering and stamping and death before slavery, the whole nine yards. Where you always go wrong is trying to persuade people with facts and arguments. It's why you can only write comedy. What gets people going is stuff that doesn't mean shit but sounds great. Blood, toil, tears and sweat. I have a dream. Drain the swamp. Yes, we can. It's the sound of the words and the cadences. You never managed to get that right."

The men of Sirupat aren't fighters, and I'm not a politician. "Nobody's perfect," I said.

"You're not, that's for sure," he said. "So I told them, form an orderly queue, they'll be out with the armour and the weapons shortly. You'd better see to that, by the way, before they get impatient."

As simple as that. Maybe where I go wrong is thinking people are more complicated than they really are. I told Gombryas and Olybrius to see to distributing the armour and weapons. They weren't happy about giving away our stock for free, so I wrote a bill of sale and sealed it with the great seal; the fake one, not the genuine article.

8

The Sirupati navy consists of twelve vessels, purpose-built warships, a birthday present for the king from the government of Mezentia. With these incredibly fine state-of-the-art fighting machines, the Mezentine ambassador said, you'll be able to defend your charming little island from pirates and make predatory neighbours think twice about messing with your fishing fleets. I'm guessing the king dictated a polite thank-you note, appointed the first idiot he saw as admiral and forgot all about them. The admiral clearly took his new duties seriously, because he was on board the flagship for its maiden voyage, twice round the bay, in the course of which it hit a rock. The ship was saved and later patched up good as new by Mezentine military advisers, but the admiral fell in the sea and turned out not to know how to swim. The job passed to his nephew, who appointed twelve elderly fishermen as captains of the fleet and told them to sail round the coast from time to time, just to show willing. The captains crewed the ships from their extended families and sent them out to fish for tuna, which is plentiful off the north coast of the island.

I sent for the admiral. "Out of interest," I said, "have you ever been on a boat?"

"No, Majesty."

"Very wise. The bloody things sway about. Where's the fleet right now?"

One thing I liked about the admiral, whose name was Phraates: he was honest as the day was long. "I don't know, Majesty."

"That's all right," I said. He was about twenty-eight, skinny, receding hairline, Adam's apple like he'd just swallowed a whole turnip. "Do you think you could find them for me?"

"Yes, Majesty."

"Splendid. When you find them, I want you to choose a nice secluded bay or inlet somewhere. Ask a smuggler: he'll suggest one."

"I don't know any smugglers, Majesty."

"Find one and ask him. Pay him lots of money. You do have lots of money, don't you?"

"Oh, yes, Majesty."

"Find a secluded bay or inlet, hide the ships and have them standing by. Tell the captains they take orders from you and me and nobody else. Do you think you can do that?"

"I'll have a stab at it, Majesty."

"And whatever you do, don't let anybody know where the ships are hidden. *Anybody*. Have you got that?"

"Majesty."

I sent him on his way, and I bet you anything you like the first thing he did was change out of his sumptuous purple-with-gold-braid admiral's uniform and back into the comfy old clothes he wore to go ferretting with his mates. That's the way holders of high public office ought to be, in my opinion.

Still no sign of bloody Stauracia. I summoned the priests. They'd been very quiet since my sort-of-coup, and that bothered me.

"Good news," I told them. "The king is much better."

(Which was true. He wasn't being poisoned any more, and Doc Papinian had purged him till there was nothing left in there to come out, then put him on a diet of lentils and cabbage; death would have been preferable, I'm sure, but he couldn't be allowed to die, not if I could help it. "Actually," the doc told me, "he's not bad for a man of his age. The poison's made a mess of his liver and kidneys, and if he was a dog you were fond of you'd drown him, but he can be kept going for a while."

"How long?"

Shrug. "Don't ask me. I'm not God. I'd be comfortable telling you a year. Longer than that—"

"A year will be fine," I said. "Thank you."

"Go to hell.")

"Wonderful news, Highness. Our prayers have been answered."

With a resounding no, I didn't say. "Mine, too," I said. "But in the meantime, until the king is well enough to resume his duties, we have a problem on our hands and I need you to tell me what I ought to do. You don't need me to remind you, basically I'm a stranger here. I wasn't even brought up to be a believer. I was raised by infidels. I've tried my best to learn the fundamentals of the faith, but I'm painfully aware of my own shortcomings in that regard."

They looked at me like I was a pig who'd come to them with

a great new recipe for sausages. "Anything we can do to help, Highness," one of them said. "Our sole function in life is to serve you, and in service, we're truly blessed."

Delighted to hear that, I told them, especially in light of the unpleasant treachery of their late predecessors. "No doubt," I said, "they sincerely thought they were acting for the best in betraying their people to foreign unbelievers. I can't see it myself, but the enemy can be very convincing. But I know the Knights and the Sisters, even if I don't know much about my own religion, and I know that both of them – they're just as bad as each other, trust me on this – the first thing they're going to want to do is get rid of the faith, once and for all. The Sisters are religious zealots, and the Knights know that the main thing holding our people together is their faith; break that and they can tame us and make us their slaves. This isn't just a fight for our liberty; it's a fight for our very souls."

It was as though they'd asked for wine and been given brandy; the right stuff, maybe a trifle stronger than they'd have liked. "One must be pragmatic," someone said, a bit nervously. "It may not be possible to avoid some sort of rapprochement with these people—"

"To the Eternal, all things are possible," I said solemnly, and a couple of them shared embarrassed looks, the way priests do when people start quoting scripture. "We prayed, and He gave us back our king. Now we're going to pray again, and He'll give us back our country."

I was making them nervous. Is he serious? He can't be. But he sounds serious. "We have to consider," one of them said, "the sins that our predecessors committed in our name. We can't expect the Eternal to let them go unpunished. Some sort of understanding with the foreigners—"

"It may have to come to that," I said. "But it's our duty to do what we can, which is why I sent for some friends of mine. They aren't believers, but they're prepared to fight and, if necessary, die to defend this island. With them on our side, I believe we stand a chance. And while there's still a realistic hope, it would be a betrayal of the faith not to fight. I know you agree."

Oh, God, they were thinking, he means it. "Sometimes," one of them said cautiously, "true victory lies in submission to His will, rather than a favourable result on a battlefield. If we genuinely listen to what He is telling us—"

"He's telling us to fight," I said. "That's why He sent us five hundred men and fifteen hundred suits of armour. I know it's difficult in times like these, but we have to be strong. So I'm asking you, as leaders of His ministry. What should I do?"

Later, I felt sorry for them. It's quite possible that, at some point in their lives, at least some of them may have believed in the Eternal Flame, to some extent. But you know what they say: the surest way to make yourself into an atheist is to read the scriptures, and daily contact with religion and those who practise it does tend to put an intolerable strain on even the most deeply held beliefs. For years they'd been patiently waiting for their superiors to die so they could take over their sinecures; suddenly, in a thunderclap, they'd got what they wanted, but accompanied by a frothy-mouthed zealot hell-bent on fighting a holy war against the entire civilised world. What would any sane man do under those conditions? I hoped I'd guessed correctly, and moved on.

Still no sign of Stauracia. I had fifty men from Olybrius' department out looking in barns and attics, under cover of requisitioning supplies for the siege. They came back and said they hadn't found any trace of her; also, the countryside was now pretty much deserted. The country people had either moved into the city or were holed up in caves in the mountains (yes, they'd looked: she wasn't there either) with their sheep and a year's supply of grain in jars. Talking of which, if the enemy were looking to live off the land once they got here, they were in for a sad time. All the barns had been emptied, and there wasn't so much as a stray chicken running about in a farmyard. The Sirupatis had been methodical and thorough in taking their food with them, all the harvests were already in and the livestock was up in the mountain pastures. If anyone wanted to lay siege to the city, he'd need to have control of the sea. Unless he could bring in supplies from outside, he'd starve to death long before we did.

I thanked them, then told them to load up some carts with bows and arrows and take them up to the caves. No obligation, I told them to say; if any foreign bastards come up here looking to steal your sheep and you feel like shooting at them, please do. If not, not. Up to you entirely.

I located Stauracia in the end. She turned up on a beach on the far western end of the island, just in time to welcome two thousand of the Sisters' marines ashore.

I wasn't there to hear what was said, naturally, but from what I gather she wasn't happy. She asked when the rest of the army was arriving. Sorry, they told her, this is it. There was supposed to be another thousand, but they got blown off course and ran into the Knights' main fleet. There was a bit of a scrap and now they're at the bottom of the sea, along with fourteen hundred of the Knights' men and twelve of their ships. Soon as we found out we sent back for reinforcements but we haven't heard anything yet. Until then, we're it.

Most of my life I've wished I was somebody else, but someone I'm really glad I'm not is the colonel of those marines. I imagine he got an earful of monumental proportions, followed by a solemn vow to see him court-martialled and hanged. Whether he got a word in edgeways I don't know; if he did, I imagine it was taken down in writing to be used in evidence against him. One of the things you've got to admire about Stauracia is her integrity. If she threatens you, she means it.

Well, now at least we had an enemy. I think I said earlier about the enormous relief of tension you feel when the thing you've been dreading actually happens. For one thing, instead of bottling up all your fury and anguish inside yourself, you've got someone to take it out on. I sent for Captain Datis.

"You've heard, then," he said.

"Yes, and not from you, but let's not worry about that now. They've landed. Now, what are you going to do to make it hot for them?"

One good thing I'd achieved: I'd broken him of the habit of calling me Majesty all the damn time. "I wasn't aware we were going to do anything," he said. "Let them come to us, surely."

I shook my head. "Absolutely not," I said. "Confront them in a pitched battle, of course not. Make their lives miserable, absolutely yes." I reached for my map. It was the only accurate one on the island; all the others ranged from inaccurate to dangerously misleading. The worst of the latter category was the one I'd left lying about on my desk while Stauracia was in the room. It disappeared when she did. Every little helps. "Now then," I said. "The shortest route from where they are to the city is this road here."

"Road is a bit of an overstatement," Datis said. "It's a sheep drove. Fine in midsummer, but this time of year it's a mess. Here, look, and here, it goes right through the marshes. The Chains, we call them. Nobody with half a brain goes anywhere near them till after the hay's been cut."

Sometimes it's hard to be an atheist. "Perfect," I said. "What's this big blue thing here?"

"That?" He squinted. "Oh, that. It's the Duke's drain."

"Excuse me?"

He explained. Two hundred years ago, an absentee landlord from the mainland tried to drain the Chains. He had drains and rines dug, to draw off all the water into a big artificial lake. It didn't work, needless to say, and the landlord sold up and moved on, but the lake and some of the rines are still there. "So if someone were to dig a hole in the embankment—"

"No need. Just open the sluices."

I beamed at him. "Make sure you time it just right," I said. "Timing is everything."

He did a good job. I think he must have asked one of the local farmers, because he judged it very nicely. The entire contents of the artificial lake came roaring down the rines just as Stauracia and her army were crossing the lowest point of the marshes. They had time to scramble up onto higher ground before the whole valley flooded, but they had to leave all their carts and pack mules behind: food, tents, blankets, arrows, all buried under thousands of tons of stinking black mud.

"Which means," I told Datis, "that if your boys hold off a hundred yards or so and shoot at them, they won't be able to shoot back. And they won't be able to come chasing after you, because of getting stuck in the mud. You won't kill many of them, but you'll make them very unhappy."

A sort of glow on his face told me he was starting to get the hang of it. "And that'll slow them down," he said.

"Timing."

"Timing," he said. "Got you."

The point being – I don't know if Datis grasped it fully, but he was no fool – that we didn't want to kill many of them, at least not yet. We wanted hungry mouths, to use up the few supplies they'd managed to save from the mud; and we wanted an army in being, for when the Knights arrived; and we wanted it out in the sticks, not under the walls, for the same reason. I told Datis the parable of the scales, the need to keep all three pans balanced, and I think he got it. He looked at me.

"We could win this," he said.

"No," I told him. "So we aren't going to try. But if we're lucky we might not lose it. If we aim for that, we may still be in with a chance."

He looked at me. "You didn't want to come here, did you?"

"No," I said. "It was the last thing I wanted, and this is my worst possible scenario. But I'm here now and I'm going to do the best job I can. Did I ever tell you about that time I was in prison?"

He looked at me. "No," he said, "you never mentioned that."

"The condemned cell, no less," I said, preening myself slightly. "Actually, it wasn't so bad. They're quite nice to you when they think you're going to have your neck stretched in the morning. The jailer's wife baked me a cake."

"Don't tell me. There was a file in it."

"Not likely. That would imply that I had friends on the

outside, and at that time I had no friends anywhere, none whatsoever. No, it was the priest who saved me."

"He pleaded for you?"

I shook my head. "Actually, he told me I was evil and I was going to burn in hell because of what I'd done. That's when I hit him. And the jailer rushed in to break up the fight, and I managed to snatch the dagger off his belt and stab him with it, and it just so happened that it was when they changed the watch, so there was nobody in the corridor or on the stairs. Timing, you see. They had thirty-six jailers in that prison and only one door, but at the precise moment that mattered, none of the thirty-six was where he was needed to be."

"You murdered the jailer."

I rolled my eyes. "It's not the mouse's fault if the swooping falcon hits a tree. I don't approve of predators."

"Define predator."

"That's easy," I said. "Someone who's out to get me."

At roughly the same time Stauracia was getting her boots sucked off by the mud in the south-west of the island, the Knights landed in the north-east. They'd been held up by a scrimmage with eight of the Sisters' ships, which was why they didn't manage to get there first, but they weren't too fussed about that. They had eight thousand men, adequate supplies and a siege train, and they knew from prior reconnaissance that there was a straight, dry road from the bay where they'd landed to the city.

I made a point of taking the news calmly, because people were watching, but when I heard the numbers, something failed inside me. Numbers can do that to a person. You can't spin, flannel or browbeat numbers: they are what they are. Eight thousand.

I wanted to be alone after that, but Ekkehard came in, and I'd neglected to tell the guards not to let him. "That's that, then," he said.

"What's what?"

He sat down beside me with his sympathetic face on. "You've lost, is what," he said. "You heard the man: eight thousand. Five you might just've been able to handle, but eight, you're screwed. It's all there in the war books. You can look it up if you don't believe me."

"I don't know what you're so damned cheerful about," I said. "The first thing they're going to do when they get here is hang you."

He frowned. "Why, exactly?"

"Because you were last seen making rabble-rousing speeches about imitating the action of the tiger. I suggest that your employers may take a dim view of that."

He shook his head. "No," he said, "because they'll give me full credit for persuading you to give in without a fight. Which you're going to do, obviously. I mean, those cutthroats out there on the wall are your friends. You don't want to see them die."

"I have no friends," I said. "There's just me."

"You don't mean that."

I sighed. "Think," I said. "Before I got here, there was a crisis but at least everything balanced, just about. The king's still alive, the council was tied between supporting the Sisters and the Knights, so nothing could happen. Then I got here, and suddenly the scale had a third pan. I frantically start shovelling everything I can lay my hands on into it, hoping to restore the balance. What do I achieve? The balance is upset. The Knights and the Sisters have both had their hands forced:

they've got to act to try and sieze the island before the other one does, even though they know it'll mean the most appalling war in history. But the war's coming, and unless they win it, they'll lose it, and they can't let that happen. I honestly thought I could strike a balance. I thought, if we can make it so neither of them can grab the city, just possibly we may be able to sort something out, something *sensible*, like sharing the gold equally or throwing it in the sea."

"But it's all gone to fuck," Ekkehard said kindly. "The Knights sent more men than you thought they would. You got it wrong. So what? Everybody makes mistakes. But it's all right, because you've got me. I can fix it so you get out of this alive. Isn't that all that matters?"

I breathed out slowly. "You don't get it," I said. "All my life, this has been coming, because I was born who I am. I've known ever since I was a little kid that one day I'd be there at the epicentre of the worst war in human history. Which is pretty much the same as saying, it'll all be my fault. Running away didn't help. I tried that but it didn't work. I couldn't even get myself killed, though God knows I tried hard enough sometimes. But, no, I had to end up here, here and now. So I thought, timing: let's see if we can finesse this one, just like we finessed all the others. Just balance the three pans and it might just work. And it nearly did."

Ekkehard gave me a look that fairly drooled compassion. "Nearly's very noble," he said, "but you know what? Nearly doesn't cut it, not in the long run. They've nailed your arse to a tree, old friend. It's over. Now, do you want to stay alive or not?"

Good question.

*

With all that on my mind, the last thing I wanted was to be badgered by stupid priests. Go away, I told them. I'm busy. Whatever it is, it can wait. No, they said, it can't.

They led me to the chapter house, a rather fine building I hadn't been in before. As you may have gathered, there's very little in the way of buildings of genuine architectural merit on Sirupat, but the chapter house is an exception. I have no idea who built it, or when; it seems to be an isolated example of genuinely home-grown Sirupati culture, not a pale imitation of this or a cheap knock-off of that, so I had nothing to date it by or compare it to. It's underground, and as far as I could tell it was cut out of solid rock. It's your basic dome shape, but with no visible pillars or vaulting, and light streams in through a single rose window at the apex of the dome. The rock is yellow sandstone (weird, because the sand on Sirupat is brown) and the walls are decorated with abstract and floral motifs rather beautifully done in fresco, mostly greens, yellows and a few keynotes in red. You really wouldn't think people like the Sirupatis were capable of such a thing, but apparently at one time they were.

"Things are very bad," the chief priest told me. They had a chief priest now, though when that had happened I don't know. "The unbelievers are coming. We won't be able to keep them out."

I managed not to yawn. "We'll see about that," I said. "I have five hundred brave soldiers. A thousand citizens have answered the call to arms. If the Knights think they can just barge in here—"

I was wasting my breath. They looked at me and I looked back. "It's bad," I said.

The priest nodded gratefully; thank you, the nod said,

for not bullshitting. "We knew this would happen," he said, "sooner or later. We've had time to prepare. We may lose the island and the city, but we can save what matters. If you agree."

I had no idea what he was talking about. "You think it's come to that."

"We hoped it wouldn't," the priest said, and his friends all nodded sadly. "We thought we might be able to come to some sort of arrangement. We thought, we could give them the island if they let us keep the city."

I was actually shocked. "You've been talking to them behind my back?"

He couldn't look me in the eyes, bless him. "As soon as they landed, we sent negotiators. But they wouldn't listen. Their orders are to take the city, and they believe they can do it. They said they have no authority to make deals on their own initiative. I think they're afraid that if they don't take the city, the Sisters will get it." He winced. "We were stupid: we thought we could get out of this by bargaining and trickery—"

"Finessing," I said.

"I suppose so, yes. But now it looks like our arrogance has brought the roof down on us, so we need to save what we can, while we can. You do see that, don't you?"

"Absolutely," I said. "What did you have in mind?"

He was about to reply, but another priest spoke over him. "The book," he said. "It's here."

What book, for crying out loud? "Really?"

He nodded. "Where it's always been," he said.

"But I thought—" I cut myself off short, since I didn't have a clue what I thought. The priest smiled sadly.

"That's what we wanted them to think," he said. "But what they captured was only a copy, with key passages falsified, so they wouldn't be able to profane them. They thought they were defiling the real thing, but it was just a worthless deception. That's the secret we've been keeping so long. And that's why we've got to act, now."

"That's amazing," I said.

"We didn't know whether we could trust you," a third priest chipped in. "We thought you were just some adventurer, and that as soon as you had the chance you'd sell us to the unbelievers."

"We tried to trick you," said a fourth one, whose face I couldn't see because he was behind someone's shoulder. "We tried to make it look like we were ready to do deals with the enemy. We thought you'd agree, and then we'd know you weren't to be trusted."

"We couldn't even agree among ourselves, " the chief priest said, with a dirty look down the line at someone or other. "But then you brought your own men here, and weapons and armour. We knew you were more of a patriot than we are. Some of us, anyway."

"But we can't let you fight," the fourth one said. "We can't see our people slaughtered in a war they can't win. It's better to hide the book away where they'll never find it than shed all that blood and for them to get it anyway."

That seemed to be the telling argument, the one that beat all the others, so I paused for a moment before speaking. "Are you sure they'll be looking for it?" I said.

The second priest nodded grimly. "We believe the Knights know of its existence," he said. "We believe Vonones told them. He was prepared to let them have it, so they could use it to bargain with the Sashan."

This sounded interesting, so I risked an I-don't-understand.

"If the Knights had the book," the chief priest said, "they could offer to give it to the Sashan in return for their help in the great war that's coming. With the Sashan on their side—"

"They'd do that?" I couldn't help asking. "The Sashan, I mean. They'd risk getting tangled up in the biggest war the West's ever seen, just to get hold of—"

Grim faces all round. "Yes," one of them said. "It's perfectly simple. If the Right Hand get hold of the book and defile it, it'll mean they've won. And they will have. The Revelation, the Redemption, it'll all have been for nothing. There can be no second coming. You can see why it's so desperately important."

So you people really do believe after all, I didn't say. "I hadn't thought of it in those terms," I said. "But you're right, of course. What can we do?"

"*Hide the book.*" I don't suppose he meant to shout, but he was pretty worked up. "Your uncle the king wouldn't hear of it," he went on. "He said that would be worse than letting the Right Hand take it, that it showed we didn't have true faith, that we didn't trust the Eternal to save us. We tried to persuade him but he wouldn't listen, and then he was too sick to speak, and without his consent—"

"Vonones was poisoning him," I said. Well, quite possibly he was. Somebody was.

"We thought so, but what could we do?" said the fourth priest. "But now you're here. If you agree, we can hide the book here, where it can't be found. It may be a hundred years or even a thousand, but the time will come. When the time is right, the Eternal will reveal its hiding place and the world will be healed. That's what all this is *about*," he added, raising his voice, "it must be, or why is He letting it happen. It's a test. He's testing us, and we've got to do the right thing."

Silence, which I took for consensus. "Agreed," I said. "We hide the book. As soon as possible."

Apparently I'd said the right thing. The third priest slowly got up, and I noticed he'd been sitting on a wooden box. He opened its lid and took out another wooden box. He stood there holding it.

"That's it?" I said.

He nodded. The moment was too deep for words. My left foot had gone to sleep and I was getting the most terrible pins and needles. "Let's do it," I said. "Right now."

He walked to the wall, where there was a rather fine painting of a rose climbing over some sort of stylised trellis. He pressed the centre of the rose and a hole appeared in the wall. You hear about stuff like that; I'd always assumed it was bullshit. "If you're sure," he said.

"I'm sure," I said. It was getting late and I wanted my dinner.

He put the box in the hole and pressed the rose again. The hole vanished. Nothing to it, really.

"We must all swear," I said, "never to breathe a word about this."

General murmur. "Of course," the high priest said.

"Out loud," I insisted, "so we can all hear each other."

So that's what we did. We swore by the book. It was a very solemn moment. By the time we'd finished swearing my foot was much better, and I was able to leave the room with dignity.

"What was all that about?" Ekkehard demanded.

"God stuff," I said, "routine. They needed me to bless the crops or something. I wasn't paying attention, to be honest."

"Well? Have you thought about it?"

"Still thinking."

"Don't take too long. They're less than a day from the city."
Oh, I thought. "Can you show me on a map?"

"Doesn't matter," he said, jabbing at a place on the map with his forefinger. "You can't win. I need time to make a deal. You've got to make your mind up now."

I considered the map. It wasn't the accurate one. If he was right about how far the Knights had gone, they were two and a bit days from the city. So was Stauracia. A lot depended, therefore, on whether she knew the Knights had landed. No reason to suppose that she didn't. Or that she did.

"I do have an option," I told him. "I can hold out till Stauracia gets here, then open the gate and let her in."

He really wasn't expecting me to say that. "Are you mad? Do a deal with the *Sisters?*"

"Three thousand five hundred against eight thousand," I said. "That would be stalemate. Do the math."

"You'd never do that."

"Did you know, one of the boss Sisters is my aunt?"

He stared at me. All the years we've known each other, and I still had the ability to surprise him. "You're bluffing."

"Am I, though?" I sat down and bit into an apple. "Stalemate," I repeated. "It means nobody can do anything, for fear of the consequences. When you think about it, it's the perfect state of human affairs. Nothing gets done. Nobody wins; nobody loses; nobody gets to lynch the enemy. And then perhaps we could all get round a table and start talking like sensible human beings—"

"You're insane," he said. "Go fuck yourself."

"Ekkehard," I said.

"What?"

"Have you noticed," I said, "that every time we have a

conversation, it ends with you swearing at me? It's not that I mind, but it does suggest you have a lamentably limited vocabulary."

That stung, I could see. "Sorry," he said. "I shouldn't have told you to go fuck yourself."

"Thank you."

"I should have said you're insane. You think you can twist and scheme your way out of everything, because you honestly believe you're smarter and better than anyone else in the entire world, and your ridiculous arrogance is going to get me and a whole lot of other people killed. You've reached a point where it's all some sort of game you're playing with yourself and we're just a way of keeping score, and it doesn't matter because, regardless of what happens, you're going to win. You're so full of it, it's coming out of your ears, and if I regret one thing in my life it's saving your worthless hide from the bounty hunters, because if they'd only killed you back then, none of this horrible mess would ever have happened."

I looked at him. "Apology accepted," I said.

It's a curious thing, but often when time is running out you find yourself with time on your hands. The Knights were marching on the city, best speed; the Sisters had a shorter distance to go, but were squelching rather than marching. Until they got here, I didn't have much to do, having done what little I could already. Everyone assumes that in the run-up to a big battle the commander-in-chief is rushed off his feet and working like a lunatic, but I know for a fact that often isn't the case, as witness the number of occasions on which the Great Man has found time to see me to haggle over salvage terms. I'm always at the bottom of his list of priorities, so it follows that if he's got time for me, he's got time to kill.

Now, by some disastrous perversion of circumstance, I was the Great Man, and I was twiddling my thumbs. A proper soldier would've gone round the ramparts, giving big smiles and words of encouragement to his terrified men, but I couldn't be bothered. The men on the ramparts weren't soldiers either. We understood each other perfectly, as you'd expect after working together so long. At the first sign of an actual assault, they would run via prearranged routes to the small sally port in the north wall, then make their way as quickly as possible under cover of the steep banks of a watercourse to the agreed rendezvous point in the caves in the mountains, where we'd already stashed enough jars of gold dust to make this gig modestly profitable. It won't come to that, I assured them. There won't be an assault; there'll be a siege followed by an auction, and we're going to come out of it filthy stinking rich, but just in case it does all go to hell, it'll be fine and nobody will be hurt or out of pocket. On those terms, and no others, they were prepared to stand on the ramparts and look like warriors. Like I said, we understood each other. But you can see why rousing speeches and a-little-touch-of-Saevus-in-the-night weren't called for. Which left me nothing to do but sit quietly and read a book.

Books plural: books about books. Of which there were plenty – commentaries on the scriptures, concordances, homilies and meditations and scholarly editions – but none of them were prepared to come out with it and actually tell me what it was that we'd sealed in a box in a hole in the wall down in the chapter house. Hints, yes. It could be the text of the divine revelation given to the prophet Curdas on the Mount of Wild

Roses, or it could equally well be the Master's last instructions to his disciples on the night before the Immolation, or quite possibly the Seventy-One Precepts handed down by the Great Saint on the eve of his execution by the loathsome myrmidons of the Right Hand. Anybody's guess. Not that it mattered worth a damn, but you can't help being curious.

Also, it doesn't hurt to be discovered reading the scriptures when the priests pay a visit. According to the scouts, they told me, Stauracia was making up lost time and was probably on track to get here a couple of hours before the Knights. She was clear of the marshes and her men were now able to march in a proper column, so the locals had stopped shooting at her and running away. Her forces had made no attempt to forage for food, so by now they must be hungry as well as tired, but if anything they were picking up speed the closer they got to their objective. The Knights, by contrast, were making steady rather than spectacular progress, and our scouts had observed their scouts watching the Sisters' men and hurrying back to make their reports. I told them I reckoned that meant that the Knights wanted the Sisters to arrive first; that way they could dispose of them in a pitched battle before settling down for a siege. I gave them the impression that I'd anticipated that from the outset and probably arranged for it to happen. That seemed to cheer them up and they went away.

Olybrius and Gombryas dropped by. "Haven't you got work to do?" I asked them.

"Done it," Gombryas said. "We just thought you might like some company."

Sweet, and showed how little they knew me. "In that case have a drink," I said. "The small bottle's the good stuff."

Gombryas will drink anything, up to and including lamp

oil, but Olybrius reckons he's a connoisseur. "It tastes like rats' piss," he said. "Are we staying in this godforsaken country?"

"That's not on my agenda," I said.

"Probably just as well." He poured himself another. "Though it'd make a handy base of operations. I don't suppose we'll be going back to the monastery any time soon."

"Don't be too sure about that," I said. "When this is all over, nobody's going to want me for anything any more, so I can't see any reason why we shouldn't go back. Did you manage to find out what happened to the monks, by the way?"

Gombryas shrugged. "Heard tell they'd been turned loose in Choris Seautou, but I don't know if it's true or not. I hope we can go back there. Here, what about all that money? You know, what we stashed down the—"

I shushed him. He took the hint. Not a word about the money. What money? "If things go to plan," I said, "we may be able to come back here eventually, if we really want to. But I'd rather not. It's a dump."

"True," Olybrius said. "So are most places, when you come to think of it. Are we still on for meeting up in the mountains, if everything goes to cock?"

"I said so, didn't I? And it won't. Everything's ticking along nicely like a Mezentine clock."

"They got one of those in the big hall downstairs," Gombryas pointed out. "Reckon anybody'd miss it?"

"Yes," I said. "Me. How are the lads holding up? Jitters?"

"Nah." Olybrius tilted the bottle. It was nearly empty. He tried the other bottle instead. "They know it's all bullshit. But some of the local yokels up there with them are making silly noises. You know, bet you I can shoot me a dozen steelnecks before they reach that rock there. I think some of the lads are worried they might start a real fight, and we might get sucked in."

I shook my head. "Won't happen," I said.

"The lads aren't so sure," Olybrius said. "They reckon some of the yokels are pretty stoked up."

Big smile. "Polycrates is in charge of distributing arrows," I said. "Every archer on the battlements has been issued with six arrows, and when they run out Polycrates' lads will come round with some more. But they won't. You can't start much of a shooting war with only six arrows."

That made Gombryas laugh. Anything to do with arrows amuses him. "That's smart," Olybrius said – high praise, coming from him. "I'll tell the boys not to worry."

"No," I said, "don't do that. I don't want the locals finding out, or there could be real trouble. Just tell the lads it's okay and I'm on it, all right?"

"Sure. This other stuff isn't too bad."

"Take the bottle," I said.

"Thanks. If the worst comes to the worst, we could pour it on the enemy."

I shook my head. "I think there's treaties about doing things like that."

Stauracia got there first. As soon as I was told she'd arrived, I went up a tower to get a good look.

Nothing but the very best for the Poor Sisters. It's hard to tell from a distance, but I have a fairly good eye for such things, and I reckon they were Caepians, which made them the best muscle money can buy. It's a miserable life up in the Caepa Mountains, and people are prepared to do pretty much anything to get away from there. Caepians are short, stocky, depressingly well disciplined and practically unkillable, and status in Caepian society is determined by the number of enemy toes you wear round your neck. I wouldn't have thought they'd have been thrilled about taking orders from a woman, but since they believe all foreigners are the spirits of the evil dead, I don't suppose it mattered all that much.

They lined up in front of the city gate. It was an impressive sight, but it's flat and open around Foregate, and the empty, level space only served to demonstrate how few of them there actually were. She'd have done better to stay further back, where she could've looked more menacing.

"They want to talk to you," Datis said.

I shook my head. "Tell her I'll be delighted to talk, but only when she's moved her sheep out of my orchard."

He gave me a sort of a look. "You told Ekkehard you were going to do a deal with them."

"Did I?" I smiled at him. "Oh, I say all sorts of things. I was probably trying to annoy him."

He didn't say anything for a moment. I realised he hated me. It was a disappointment but not really a surprise. "I'm not about to do a deal with the Sisters," I told him. "Not going to happen."

"You say all sorts of things. Are you trying to annoy me?"

I laughed, but it didn't make anything better. "It's one of the things about living on borrowed time," I told him. "After a while, you lose track of interest rates. Listen, if the Sisters get their hands on me after what I've done they'll rip me into little pieces. Also, I'm trying to prevent a war, not start one. Let's not fall out, not now. We need each other."

He turned and walked away. I decided I didn't like him much either.

*

Ekkehard was looking for me. I told him I'd meet him in the anteroom outside the Chapel Royal. Then I went and hid at the other end of the palace.

The room I hid in was halfway up the guard tower on the south wall. I had a splendid view of the Foregate from there. I studied the enemy for a bit, but I saw nothing I didn't know already. Then I went to see the king.

I found him lying flat in his bed. He looked awful, but better than the last time. Doc Papinian was there, mixing something in a bowl. "Go away," he said.

"How's he doing?"

"Very weak. The damage is worse than I thought. I don't think he's going to make it."

"How long?"

Papinian thought before answering. "I've stabilised his condition, but if he was going to improve he'd have done so by now, and he hasn't. I've got the last of the poison out of his system, but it's too late to do him any good. I'd say anywhere between a week and a month."

"Can I talk to him? Will he hear me?"

Papinian shook his head. "He can hear but he can't talk. If you pester him you'll just make him worse. To be honest, the best thing would be to let him go."

"Can't do that. Keep him going as long as you can."

"You don't give a damn about people, do you? Just about money. When they told me you'd murdered your brother, I didn't believe it. But now I've had time to think about it—"

"Stick at it," I said. "You're doing a fine job."

He didn't tell me to drop dead. When you know someone really well, words aren't necessary.

*

Polycrates met me in the corridor. "I've been looking for you," he said. "Did you know she's here? That bitch?"

I nodded. "Small world," I said. "Mind you, I think it's because human beings are basically honourable and decent, so there's only a very limited number of really nasty people in the world. Therefore, when there's nasty stuff to be done, is it surprising that you keep running into the same old faces?"

"It was you," he said. "It was you she was after all along."

"Don't think so, or she'd have nailed me back in Erysichthon's country. I think she got given the gig because she'd got history with me, not that it matters all that much. We made a complete and utter fool of her before; we can do it again."

He'd have grabbed hold of me, only he knew what would happen if he tried. "What are you playing at?" he said. "Did you fetch us out here to set us up?"

"*What?*"

Anger came whistling out of him, like steam from under the lid of a pot. "I don't trust you, Saevus or Florian or whatever the fuck your name is. I've never trusted you worth spit, and, guess what, I was right. We get here and what's the first thing that happens? She shows up, with an army. And it turns out you're a fucking king, *and* a duke, and you murdered your own brother. Oh, and the savages think you're God."

"They're not savages," I said quietly. "Other than that, though, basically yes."

"You think you're God."

"*They* think I'm God: there's a difference."

He swung at me. I was expecting it, so I moved back and left, but he evidently knew me quite well and anticipated me. I felt my brain shake and the flagstones hit my arse. "Answer me," he was roaring, overhead somewhere. "What are you up to?"

No teeth loosened, at any rate. "Help me up," I said, "there's a pal."

He took a step back. He was more scared of me on my knees at his feet than standing up eye to eye with him. Polycrates is smart. "What have you done?" he said. "Tell me the truth."

"Sure," I said. "The truth is, I've got us all so deep in the shit that only I can get us out again. You want the truth? You were idiots to come here in the first place, but now you're here the only way you'll ever get out again is to do what I say and trust me. If you do that, you'll be safe and there'll probably be money. If you don't, you're not going to make it, sorry. There, is that truthful enough for you?"

"How could you do a thing like that? Murder your own brother?"

"It was an accident."

"I don't believe you."

"How could you possibly know? You weren't there."

He was looking at me the way a man studies the pavement where he's just dropped a coin; he's looking for something that really ought to be there but inexplicably isn't. In Polycrates' case, I think he was looking for a human being. "We all thought we knew you," he said. "We thought you were one of us."

I thought of half a dozen replies, short, very witty and true. But they wouldn't have been helpful, so I saved them for another occasion. "I've said I'm sorry," I told him. "If I can get us out of this, I will. You're the only friends I've got in the world and I've treated you really badly, but this is deadly serious and I couldn't think of anything else to do. It's not easy being my friend. I'd have thought you'd have grasped that by now."

He didn't even swear at me. He just left.

*

"You've been fighting," she said.

I sighed. "No, I haven't."

"Looks like you lost."

I'd forgotten how much I liked her. She's evil and treacherous and as sharp as a rusty nail in a plank of wood, but she's fun. She makes me try. "Look who's talking," I said. "You do know the Knights are on their way. Eight thousand heavy infantry and a siege train."

Two thousand soldiers were studying the back of her head. A slightly smaller number were looking at mine. They could all see us, but nobody could hear what we were saying. "Also," I said, "I've got archers covering you from that tower directly behind me. I give a prearranged signal and you're a pincushion. Your men are two hundred yards away. Now I ask you, is that sensible?"

She peered over my shoulder. I was lying, but I think she believed me. "You're not going to hurt me," she said. "You need me, to save your skin."

"Interesting. Do go on."

"Very simple," she said. "My men plus your men plus anyone you can rely on in the city. The Knights count heads and realise the numbers don't work. We all sit around and wait, and then my employers send a relief army, fifteen thousand absolute minimum."

I nodded. "Then you get paid and go away and I'm stuck here in the eye of the biggest war in history. No thanks."

"No," she said. "If there's got to be a war, there's got to be a war. In which case, no need for any more pretending. We won't need a puppet king. We'll make this a province and have a proper military governor. You can go."

"Anywhere I like?"

"Anywhere you like. With all the money you can carry. Same goes for your merry band of cutthroats and anyone else you want to save."

"And in return I give you my full cooperation."

She smiled. "I do believe you've got it. Yes."

"You'd be the proper military governor?"

"That hasn't been decided yet, but probably, yes. What's that got to do with you?"

My jaw was hurting where Polycrates had hit me. "They put you in command of the expeditionary force," I said. "That's good. They can recognise innate talent when they see it, regardless of what you have or haven't got between your legs. That's very enlightened."

"One of the better things about working for the Sisters," she said. "And, yes, I can be as good a soldier as any man, thank you very much, and they know I won't sell out to the Knights. And don't say nice things about me. It makes my skin crawl."

"Fair enough," I said. "I have a suggestion, if you'd care to hear it."

"What?"

"Down there a mile or so is a harbour full of ships. Put your men on them and go home. They're only mercenaries, but a human life's a human life. Go back to preaching at fairs. It's safer."

I'd disappointed her. She'd given me credit for some degree of sense. "That's it," she said. "You're going to give the island to the Knights."

"No. Absolutely not."

"Bullshit."

I gave her my best grin. "You have absolutely no idea what I'm going to do."

"No," she said. "And neither have you."

The last word, you see. But she does it so well.

And then the Knights arrived.

I guess I have an atypical and probably misleading perspective on soldiers, because usually when I see them they're dead. The sight of eight thousand heavy infantry is no big deal, all in a day's work, but eight thousand men all standing up, not flat on their backs and faces with crows picking bits off them: I don't know. I won't say it doesn't seem right, because logically the existence of corpses presupposes a time when they were all still alive. If something's wrong with this picture, therefore, it's me being there to see it. Be that as it may, dead soldiers I know all about; living ones aren't really my department. Even so, I can tell quality when I see it. The Knights clearly had money to spend and they'd spent it wisely.

Unlike the Sisters, who'd gone for bloodymindedness and muscle, the Knights had put their money into skill and technique: Siccambres, from southern Blemya. You probably know the story. About two hundred years ago, a bunch of adventurers from all over the place showed up in Blemya, a hundred miles or so south of the Fourth Cataract, and took the place over by dint of sheer skill and ruthlessness. They ran the place very much as a business, and they stayed there because nobody could get them out. Eventually, about fifteen years back, the Blemyan king launched a full-scale crusade. The Siccambres put up one hell of a fight and killed a ridiculous number of the king's soldiers but eventually they realised they were dealing with unreasonable people who weren't going to give up, so they built a fleet of ships and sailed away. The Sashan gave them a peninsula, murderously hot in summer, freezing cold in winter, and they set up shop in the swords-for-hire business. After two centuries of constant warfare against overwhelming odds they're pretty good at what they do, and the only reason you don't see them everywhere is that they're prohibitively expensive. Typically they're hired for short, efficient campaigns to achieve a specific objective. They reckon war is a science, and if you do it properly the outcome is inevitable. Over the years I've cleaned up after them maybe half a dozen times, in the course of which I've burned very few dead Siccambres. They don't get killed if they can possibly help it, and they almost always win.

Siccambres against Caepians. Somewhere else, I could've made a fortune selling tickets.

"If it was the other way round," Olybrius said, "I'd put my money on the tall bastards."

We were watching from the tower as the Siccambres advanced on the Caepians in a classic head-and-horns formation. I could see what he meant. Two thousand Siccambres against eight thousand Caepians would be a foregone conclusion: the Siccambres, in about forty minutes, because they're unbeatable on the defensive against superior numbers. But they genuinely don't like attacking, and when Caepians are involved you never really know what'll happen. Two pans swaying. I hate that.

"Ten staurata on the tall bastards," I said.

"Done. What did you to do Polybius, by the way? He's really mad at you."

"He's always mad at me."

Head-and-horns is the oldest trick in the book and any fool can see it coming a mile off, but if you've got the numbers, it doesn't matter. Your enemy has the choice between charging your massively strong centre, in which case you outflank and envelop him with your equally strong horns, or trying to move the fulcrum of the action out onto the wings, in which case your centre ploughs through him like a battering ram and splits him in two for easy annihilation at your convenience. The only effective counter is to run away and fight another battle next week. Stauracia, it soon became obvious, wasn't planning on doing that. She'd positioned her forces directly between the Knights and the city wall, giving her nowhere to run.

"She reckons you'll open the gate and let her in," Carrhasio said, his mouth full of pistachio nuts. "You going to do that?"

"Not on your life," I told him.

"Good. I'll enjoy watching her die."

Charming fellow. "I wouldn't write her off quite yet," I said. "She wouldn't be doing something so colossally stupid if she didn't have something up her sleeve."

"Oh, I don't know," Gombryas said. "I think she's just dumb."

Siccambres don't charge. It uses up too much energy and there's a risk you might trip over and fall and disorganise the line. Instead they advance at a brisk walk, shields locked, spears forward in a layered hedge five spearheads deep, dense enough to stop arrows. They keep in step so precisely it makes masonry shake; we could feel it through the soles of our feet. As soon as they began their advance, the Caepians began an orderly withdrawal, clearly planned beforehand. They backed up until they reached the wall, where they had to stop.

"Smart," Olybrius conceded. "Means they're only fighting on one-eighty degrees instead of three-sixty."

Very smart. Even the Siccambres couldn't push over a wall; and their advantage in numbers wasn't much use to them.

Most of their men would be standing about with nothing to do, while those who were actually able to engage the enemy stood a serious risk of getting killed. Obviously they could have the victory if they were prepared to pay the price, but would it be too expensive?

"Not just a pretty face," Olybrius said. Praise indeed.

"She'd never have done it if she didn't have Caepians," Carrhasio said. "Nobody else'd let themselves get put in that position. They'd run like hares."

"Caepians are stupid," Gombryas said. "They don't give a damn."

"It ain't over yet," Olybrius said. "This should be good."

I moved away from the wall. "Let me know what happens," I said.

"You aren't going to watch?"

"Not really my cup of tea," I said. "See you later."

I left them and hurried down the stairs, nearly losing my footing because my knees had gone weak. When I put my hands against the walls to steady myself, I could feel the battle coming through the stonework. Now, I couldn't help thinking, would be a really good time to run away, while everybody else was watching the show. A pity I was on an island and didn't like boats. Even so.

"You let it happen, then," Ekkehard said.

He'd been waiting for me at the foot of the stairs. "Not my fault," I said.

"Going somewhere?"

"If I was, would you stop me?"

Ekkehard is a big man and one hell of a stage fencer, but unscripted violence scares the life out of him. "Yes," he said.

"I'm going to get a drink," I said. "Do your worst."

"You really don't want to start hitting the bottle at a time like this," he said. "You need a clear head."

"One drink," I said. "You can pour it if you like."

He poured himself one, too. "You ought to be up on the wall where people can see you," he said. "That's leadership."

"So?"

"So if you want these people to believe in you, you've got to act the part."

"What makes you think I want that?"

"The fact you didn't smash my face in and make a run for it, while you had the chance."

I nibbled a corner off my drink. They make a sort of brandy on Sirupat. It's horrible. "I imagine that's what you'd do, if you were in my shoes. Seriously, how far do you think I'd get?"

He put the whole question of my motivation into the Too Difficult basket, where it belonged. "What made that crazy woman do a stupid thing like that?"

"She thought I'd open the gate and let her and her soldiers inside the city." I took another sip of brandy. I could feel it stripping layers off me all the way down. "Or she sincerely believed she could beat the Knights in a pitched battle. Or she's not actually in command, and their general had orders: keep the Knights out at any cost. Does it matter?"

"You like her."

"I like lots of people."

"You like her a lot and now she's going to die. I'm sorry. I really can't see it myself, but you really liked her." He poured himself another, a large one. He soaks the stuff up like a desert, and it has no effect whatsoever. "Well, she's had it this time. There's no way out of that."

I think he meant it, the stupid bastard. I took a half-sheet of parchment, folded small, from the cuff of my sleeve. "I wouldn't write her off just yet," I said. "I got this from the scouts, just before the Knights reached the city. My scouts, not Datis' people or the priests."

He frowned and unfolded the little document. "I can't read it; it's in foreign. What does it say?"

I took it back. "Confirms what I'd assumed would happen, as soon as I heard where the Sisters had landed. Like any sensible tactician running a campaign in a place like this, they divided their forces. Two armies, two landing sites. The other part of the army landed last night and ought to be here any minute now."

He gazed at me. He couldn't speak.

"I like her because she's clever," I said. "Even with the reinforcements she's outnumbered three to one. So she's set up the perfect tactical solution. The other part of her army is seven hundred heavy cavalry. In the textbooks it's called the anvil and the hammer."

He was having trouble speaking, but he managed to repeat the word *cavalry*.

"Yup," I said. "Mostly useless on Sirupat because of the mountains, but exactly what you need if you've set up a classic anvil for your first act curtain." I paused. The mixed metaphors were making my head swim. "That's why I can't be bothered to watch," I said. "I know how it ends."

By dint of deep breathing he'd got his voice back. "When did you—?"

"Know for certain? When I got this. Know on the balance of probabilities? When I looked on the map and saw where the Sisters had landed. You forget, I'm in the trade. You can't hang around battlefields as long as I have and not get a nose for this stuff."

A roar in the distance. If I hadn't known it was men shouting, I don't think I'd have associated it with anything human. "They're here," I said. "If you want to see a battle that'll probably end up on the Academy syllabus, now's your chance."

He gave me that look. He wasn't acting. "You arsehole," he said. "For God's sake. Why didn't you warn me?"

I sighed. "Oh, come on," I said. "You're the enemy."

In the event it was closer than I'd anticipated. Seven hundred Aelian armoured lancers duly appeared out of nowhere and crashed into the rear of the Siccambres, slaughtering them like chickens trapped in a run, but they didn't quite have the impetus to break through and join up with Stauracia's Caepians, which was what needed to happen for a storybook victory. Once the Siccambres had got over their natural horror at taking heavy casualties – about five minutes, a long time – they pushed back against the stalled cavalry charge and the Aelians had to pull out before they were swamped. Their withdrawal almost gave the Siccambres enough time to turn and form a coherent front; but the Caepians made a supreme effort and broke through, getting in among them as they were turning and making a real mess, though it cost them heavily. The Aelians charged again and this time they made it through. According to the rules in the book, that should have been enough to make the Siccambres break and run, but I guess they'd skipped that chapter. They pushed back, and in spite of their losses they still had the numbers.

Everything was, in fact, perfectly set up for a practically obligatory intervention. Carrhasio certainly thought so. He came bustling in, drenched in sweat, which made the thin ring of hair round his bald patch droop in spikes, like a wilted crown of thorns. "Now's our chance," he said. "We can do it. But we've got to go *now*."

"Excuse me?" I said.

"It's in the fucking balance," he said, astounded that I could be so stupid. "If we go out right now, look like we're about to make a charge, the buggers'll run like hares. We won't have to fight a stroke, they'll be off and we'll have won—"

"Which buggers are we talking about?"

He shrugged. "I don't care, do I? Either of them. Look, it's *classic*. Either side, an extra five hundred men at this point decides it. And *we'd* have won it. Don't you see?"

"Have a drink," I said.

"Fuck you and your drinks. I thought you'd set all this up."

I shook my head. "Sorry," I said.

"For crying out loud." He could feel the opportunity draining away into the sand.

"All right," I said. "Tell me which side to pick and I'll do it." He stared at me. "You what?"

"Tell me who the good guys are and we'll go and help them."

"Don't you know?"

"No. Tell me."

He made a sort of moaning noise. "You prick," he said, and tottered away.

Strictly speaking, it was a draw. Looked at another way it was a famous victory for the Sisters, because they turned back a massively superior enemy from the objective; looked at a third way, it was a brilliant recovery by the Knights after a coup that should have given the city to the enemy. What actually happened was that both sides fought to a standstill, then withdrew to prepared positions, and the city now had the unusual honour of being besieged by two enemies at the same time.

"You maniac," Ekkehard roared at me. "How could you let this happen?"

I turned away from him and looked at Datis. "You agree with him, don't you?" I said.

"I think we missed an opportunity," he replied, not looking at me. "We were ready. I think we'd have been up to the task. We could have put an end to it, here and now. But instead—"

I waited, but he had no intention of finishing the sentence. "You're mad, both of you," I said. "You don't seriously think I had any intention of fighting anybody, do you?"

They stared at me. Total breakdown of communications.

Not that I cared particularly much. I didn't need either of them to do anything for me, and they'd already told me everything I wanted to know. I took the afternoon off and went for a private unconducted tour of the royal cellars, hoping to find a treasury crammed with small items of great value. There wasn't one. Oh well.

Everything now depended on a letter, written in an obscure language I barely understood and committed to the care of an unreliable courier. The proposition it made was based on a questionable premise and offered at most a modest return on a very substantial investment. A sensible man like me would put it straight on the back of the fire, but I'm not a gambler. I go in for small gains, small losses, balanced scales. I never bet more than ten trachy unless I'm cheating.

I dropped in on Gombryas and the lads for a bite to eat before turning in. Carrhasio and Polycrates weren't talking to me, and the others weren't inclined to open their hearts and minds much beyond this stuff tastes like armpits and pass the mustard. There were two guards instead of three outside my bedroom door when I got there, but they were both men I knew well. One of them looked like he wanted to say something but his mate gave him the bad eye.

"Well?" I asked him.

"Are they going to attack?" he said. "Is there going to be any fighting?"

"I shouldn't think so. I hope not."

He nodded. I hadn't put his mind at rest. I left him to it, went inside, lay down and went to sleep.

9

I woke up. There was light in the room, but not coming in through the window. I was looking up at a man I didn't know. He was wearing clean, expensive armour and he definitely wasn't a Sirupati.

"Up," he said.

There were six more just like him behind him. He was too tall for a Caepian. "Who the hell are you?" I asked.

He didn't answer. Long experience told me I was about five seconds away from getting hit with something. "Fine," I said. "Is it all right if I put my shoes on?"

"Up."

"If you've hurt my guards, I shall be seriously annoyed."

It's hard to hit a man when he's lying down. The angles are all wrong. He managed it. "Up," he said. I got up.

I didn't have far to go on my bare feet. The well-dressed man threw open the door of what had been my throne room the last time I saw it. I guessed it probably wasn't that any more. Inside I saw Datis and Ekkehard, standing behind a short,

white-haired man in a fashionable red velvet gown. He was
sitting in my chair, but stood up when I came into the room.
"Majesty," he said, and did a little bow; just enough to signify
respect without risking a crick in the neck.

The soldiers were right behind me, and the door was behind
them. "Who are you?" I asked.

"My name is Erescigal, Majesty, thank you for asking. I
am your new military adviser and chief of staff. Do please
sit down."

"Thank you," I said, a bit awkwardly because my lip was
starting to swell. He didn't seem to have noticed. I sat down in
my chair. I never liked it anyway.

"As you've probably gathered I represent the Knights of
Equity." He smiled. "You know us, obviously."

"Ever so well. What are they doing here? Are they
prisoners?"

"These gentlemen? Good heavens, no. They've been associated with our organisation for quite some time." He turned
his head and beamed briefly at them. They carried on looking at the floor. "Apparently each of them only very recently
became aware that the other was also working for us, which is
rather amusing, but compartmentalisation is the curse of our
business. They opened the main gate about half an hour ago
and let us in."

Some smart-arse once wrote: the worst words a general can
ever utter are, I wasn't expecting that. "They did that."

He nodded, very matter-of-fact. "It was your friend
Ekkehard's suggestion," he said, "but Captain Datis was only
too pleased to help him carry it out."

"I see," I said, lying as usual. "I'm sorry, what did you say
your name was?"

"Erescigal, Majesty."

"You're Siccambrean."

My perceptiveness earned me a slight head-dip of approval. "I'm the coordinator of your new national improvement and development initiative, and commander-in-chief of your military advisers. Working together, I feel sure we can deliver a bright new future for the Sirupati people."

"I'd like that," I said. "What about my men?"

The ghost of a smile. "It appears they had their own escape plan worked out well in advance. We didn't interfere. I've given orders that the gold dust they've got hidden in the cave in the mountains isn't to be disturbed, and their ships are to be permitted to leave the harbour. Properly speaking the gold dust is the property of the Crown, but I imagine you don't begrudge it to them."

"Thanks," I said. "They're my friends."

He couldn't resist. He flicked a glance over his shoulder and said, "Are you sure about that?"

"No."

A little light gleamed in his pale, businesslike eyes. "We're your friends," he said. "You can be absolutely sure about that. The Knights will be the best friends you ever had. We'll protect you, come what may. We'll always be there for you when you need us." He paused. He didn't actually count under his breath: one, two, three. "You've had a very hard life," he went on, softening his voice by a few carefully modulated semitones. "Your own family turned against you because of a tragic accident that wasn't your fault. Because of an obscure vagary of birth, you're now the unwilling king of a faraway country of which you know little, in the eye of a perfect storm. It's been a desperate struggle for as long as you can remember, and you've got to the point where you can't be expected to tell good from bad or right from wrong. I can understand that. You're only human. You've never been able to trust anybody, not even your closest friends, like this man here. Sooner or later everyone's a threat, and that's made you do things you'd never have considered doing if you'd been a free agent. Like your friend Posidonius."

He paused, waiting for a reaction. "That was bad," I said. "Probably the worst thing I've ever done."

"No," he said, gently but firmly, "not by a long way. We understand. Being human can be very painful sometimes. We truly believe we have to do dreadful things, because we have no choice. It's so much worse for a man on his own, isolated by his past and his own lies and deceptions. But that's all over now. We know everything about you, so there are no more secrets to defend. We know you," (smile) "intimately. We accept you for who you are. We're here to help you, if you'll let us."

I wanted to ask who wrote his stuff for him. "What do you want?" I asked.

"We want you to be king of Sirupat."

"They've already got a—"

"His Majesty died earlier this evening."

Oh, I thought. "I'm sorry to hear that," I said. "I think he was my only living relative who didn't hate me. Of course, he couldn't speak, so I could be wrong about that."

I got a thin smile for that. "The king is dead," he said. "Long live the king. Sirupat needs a king, now more than ever. You need a safe place, where nobody will ever hurt you again."

I nodded in what I hoped was the right direction. "What about them?"

"You mean the Poor Sisters? Don't worry about them. Even

after today's mess, the odds are still two to one, and now we're in possession. Even if they concentrated all their military resources on this one front, they wouldn't be able to shift us. Especially since you were generous enough to stock the city for a prolonged siege."

I did do that, didn't I? "Come along now," I said, "you know as well as I do, if you hold Sirupat there'll be one hell of a war."

Sad smile. "Inevitably, yes. In a way, it's better that it should happen now rather than later. It's a war that we and our allies can win, provided we hold this island and its resources. It's not just the fact that we have all the money; it's also the fact that our enemies have none. There will be a war, yes, but I don't suppose it'll last very long. A fire can't burn without fuel."

"That's what I've always run from," I said. "The thought of a war, a really big one. I've seen so many of them. I don't think I could bear it."

He looked at me (three, four, five, six). "You know," he said, "when we dread something, sometimes it's better for it to happen and be over and done with. Let the worst happen. I think Saloninus put it rather well: he that is down need fear no fall. When the worst happens—"

"Actually, I think it's 'needs'," I said. "Maybe you're right. I can't say I've ever thought of it that way. I don't suppose it matters. You're not offering me a choice, are you?"

"No."

"Fine." I shrugged. "As Saloninus also said, I do it on compulsion."

He smiled. "You know the *Ballads*."

"Best thing he ever wrote if you ask me."

"Coming from a distinguished playwright, praise indeed.

And the priest in the ballad was happy with his fate, if you remember. He'd been waiting all his life for the excuse."

I smiled. "Now you're talking," I said.

"It hurts to kick against the goad," he said solemnly. "If an excuse is all you need, we'd be happy to oblige. An excuse, coercion, absolution, whatever you feel you need. After everything you've been through, I'd say you deserve it."

"Perhaps you do understand me after all."

"I ought to," he said. "I've been studying you day and night for the last three months."

That deserved a moment's silence. "What are you going to do about the other army?" I said. "Are you going to fight them again?"

He frowned. I'd disappointed him. "Why on earth should I? They're doing me no harm where they are. And if I don't fight battles, I can't lose them. You know that woman, don't you?"

"I thought I did."

"What do you think she'll do next? If I do nothing."

"Send home for orders," I said. "She'll do as she's told."

"You think so."

"Oh, yes." I reinforced that with a dip of the head. "She hasn't exactly covered herself in glory on this mission, but it wasn't really her fault either. No promotion, but she won't be executed and she'll probably get paid. And the way she nearly had you for breakfast out there won't be lost on her superiors."

"Your aunt."

"Hard but fair."

"Personally I think she's a heartless monster without a shred of humanity in her. Mind you, I've only met her twice." He smiled. "Would you care to stay in your present accommodations or would you rather move into the royal chambers, now that they're vacant? Obviously we'll have the place cleaned up and change all the bedclothes. Or would you prefer it if we built you a brand-new palace? You can afford it, heaven knows."

"I'm fine where I am," I said. "Thanks all the same."

"That's perfectly all right. If you change you mind, just let me know."

"I will," I said. "There is one thing you could do for me, if it's no bother."

"What would that be?"

"I'd like his head on a spear in the front courtyard," I said, pointing over his shoulder. He didn't need to turn and look. "Soon would be nice, but I can wait till this afternoon if that's better for you."

This time there was something almost genuine about the smile. "Sorry," he said, "not my department. It's either diplomatic immunity or benefit of clergy; in either case I'd have to fill out a lot of forms, and the reply would still be no."

I nodded. "Fine," I said. "How about Captain Datis?"

The smile grew into something resembling a sunrise. "That wouldn't be a problem," he said.

"I don't want him," I said. "Ekkehard or nothing. But never mind. It's only me."

"Yes, Your Majesty."

He was a rank amateur. I've been wound up by experts, so I should know.

Where he'd gone wrong, I reflected, as the same soldiers marched me back, was not putting enough truth into his mix. He'd told me it wasn't my fault, that I was a victim of circumstances. *We truly believe we have to do dreadful things, because we have no choice*; that was where he'd lost me, because there's always a choice. A good man would have reached the point where he stopped running, held his hands up and offered his throat to the knife. He must have known that as well as I do, so from then on he was clearly talking honey-drenched bullshit. What he should have done was be honest with me. I still wouldn't have listened, but it would have been more professional. And he'd have had the nerve to pretend he was prepared to kill Ekkehard when I asked him to, and made me show weakness by cancelling the request. That's what I'd have done, in his shoes.

One thing I like about the Left Hand – you don't get it in the Right – is the notion that we're all sinners, and the difference between us is simply one of extent. Nobody, nobody at all, could ever possibly kneel before the Eternal Flame and say he's been good, all his life, and never hurt or screwed anybody. The important thing, the Left Hand says, is to acknowledge the truth and feel genuine remorse, and thereafter try not to do more bad stuff than you can help. Of course they mess it all up by the practice of extreme unction, whereby you confess to a priest with your last breath and you're forgiven; obviously you run the risk of being hit by a falling tree when there's no priest handy, but most people die in their beds, so it's a great way of having your cake (and someone else's cake as well) and eating it. I'm not a believer, worse luck, so I can't comfort myself with the thought of a final apology making everything right, but I'm slowly coming round to the view that if, at the very least, you're honest about what you've done and what you've allowed yourself to become, there may be some hope for you after all. For instance, I could have written this book in such a way that you'd like me and approve of all my choices, simply by twisting a few facts here and there and making people say things they didn't, and you'd never know the difference. It's what I do when I'm not writing books, after all, and it's kept me above ground and breathing for many years, often in trying circumstances. But what the hell. You probably haven't believed a word of this stuff anyway.

At the door I stopped. "Quick question," I said. "Are you still allowed to hit me if I give you any lip?"

"Yes."

"Fine. Just so I know."

The door closed. I heard a bolt. There hadn't been one on the outside the last time I'd looked. I went across to the window. My view over the city wall down to the harbour had been supplemented with a pair of shoulder blades in shiny Type Four armour. I pulled a book off the shelf and lay down on the bed. It wasn't a very interesting book, but it was better than thinking.

Some indeterminate time later, the door opened. In came Ekkehard. "Hello," I said.

The door closed behind him. Bolt noises. "This wasn't my idea," he said.

I sighed. "I could break both your arms," I said, "but what would that achieve?"

"You wanted Erescigal to have me killed. That wasn't very nice."

"I was just making a point," I said. "I knew he wouldn't have the authority. Sit down, for crying out loud. I'm not going to hurt you."

"You'd better not. I'm quite an important man around here now."

He sat. I smiled. "Is that so?"

"Yes, as a matter of fact. Originally I was supposed to have that job, military governor or what-have-you. Then he turned up with a bit of paper: someone at Area Command's changed his mind, so now I'm chief administrative adviser and political officer."

"Congratulations."

"Yeah, well. It's not like they expect me to do anything. I'm not even sure if I'm getting paid."

"I'll pay you if you like. I can do that. I'm the king."

"To do what?"

"Go away and leave me in peace. Why is it, every time I open a book, people for miles around interpret it as a desperate plea for conversation?"

He scowled at me. "I only came to tell you, Gombryas and the others got their gold from the cave and now they're on their way to the harbour. Erescigal sent a couple of men to tell them they've got safe passage. He means it. They'll be fine."

"Good," I said.

"I thought you'd be pleased. It was my idea to let them go."

"Thank you."

"Erescigal wanted to kill them or sell them down the river but I said no, that'd really put his back up. But I said—"

"If I watch them leave without lifting a finger to help me, I'll realise just what good friends they really are. Thank you for that. No, I mean it," I added, as he started giving me filthy looks. "It's always been a sort of unspoken thing with us. If one of us gets in trouble, leave him. Don't put yourself in harm's way out of stupid sentiment. They only came here because I tricked them."

"She's moving out, too."

My turn to frown. "That's interesting," I said. "Are you cleared to tell me more?"

He ignored that, reasonably enough. "She's struck camp and set off back the way she came. We don't know if she's got ships waiting."

"I wouldn't have thought so," I said. "She wouldn't have been anticipating defeat. More likely, she's trying to lure your friend out into the open for a pitched battle. It's the only way left that she could win, and all that horrible moorland and bog offers a lot of scope to an imaginative tactician. He won't do it, though. He's got nothing to gain by wiping her out."

"No," he agreed.

"So what she'll probably do is use her cavalry to raid the gold-panning stations. Now that would force your friend's hand, and he'd have to do something about it. That girl's a hell of a lot smarter than I gave her credit for. I think her problem's always been, she's tried to make a go of it in the wrong spheres of activity. She's only so-so at sneaking about and backstabbing, but she's got a real flair for legitimate strategy and tactics." I yawned. "Maybe that's what all this is about. Her chance to showcase her generalship abilities for the Sisters back home. I wouldn't put it past her."

He grinned. "You do like her."

"She reminds me of me."

"Told you."

"That's why I can't stand her."

He sighed. "Funny man," he said. "You know what, I've been thinking."

"Go on."

He leaned forward in his chair, elbows on knees. "Right," he said. "You're stuck here, for the foreseeable future. Nobody's going to come and get you out, and you can't escape."

"You know, I'd forgotten about that. Thanks ever so for reminding me."

He sighed. "You've got time on your hands, is what I'm saying. Now, when were you happiest? In your entire life?"

"Now that's a good question. You tell me. When was I happiest?"

"When you were writing plays for the theatres, back in the City. Go on, admit it. You loved it: you were in your element. Well, then."

"Well then what?"

He rolled his eyes. "They've got paper here, for crying out loud. And pens and ink. What more do you need? Let Erescigal run the stupid country and fight the stupid war. You just crack on and do what you really like doing. Fuck the lot of them. Do what *you* want."

I gazed at him. "You're mad," I said.

"No, I'm not. Stay here. Cooperate. It doesn't matter, because it's not your fault. Look, for some reason I couldn't begin to understand, you've been given a genuine gift. That's who you *are*. You're not a duke or a king or a general or a murderer or a businessman or the fucking Redeemer. You're someone who can turn out rhyming couplets that actually rhyme and set up a really good first act curtain. There's only about a dozen people in the world who can do that."

For a moment I remembered him as he used to be. People change, but not all the way through. There's almost always something left, deep down somewhere. "And you'd produce them in the City and act in them and take all the money. I thought you were going to be my administrative adviser."

"I can't hack this shit," he said. "I'm no good at it and it's dangerous. What I want to do is put together enough money to buy the Gallery of Illustration and have enough left over to put on a really smart show, something that'll have them queuing out into Cornmarket. People are crying out for good solid burlesque, and all they're getting is either vaude-ville or the arty-farty stuff that nobody can understand. It's exactly the right time, if only someone had the capital, and the vision—"

"You're not serious." I looked at him. "You're serious."

"So what if I fucking am?" He was furious. "I know who I am. I know what I want."

I beamed at him. "Money," I said. "Lots and lots of money."

"Piss off." Really angry now. "You think I want a big country estate and servants and a hundred gardeners mowing a thousand acres of lawn? Fuck that. I'd die of boredom inside of a week. What I want is for things to be how they used to be, before you came into my life and fucked it all up. Only I think I deserve a little bit more, like enough money to buy the Gallery. My life how it was, only a lot better, to compensate for all the shit I've been through on account of you. I want to be a manager, big-time, with everybody looking up to me and glad to see me when I walk into a room. People I know. People I like. Is that too much to ask, for crying out loud?"

I nodded. "And you want me to write plays for you, because the time is right for my kind of shit. Timing," I added. "It's everything." I breathed in slowly, and out again. "It's touching, in a way. You sell me to the Knights, and you still want me to do things for you."

"Arsehole."

"I take it as a compliment. You really think I'd do something to help you, in spite of everything. It shows you reckon I'm basically a good person. That's sweet."

He stood up. "I don't know why I bother with you," he said. "You try and help someone and he pisses in your face."

Meals on a tray, with wine. I asked the guard for a couple of books, but he just looked at me. He emptied the chamber pot for me by tipping it out of the window. Any situation where you don't have to do that for yourself probably constitutes luxury, but I can't pretend I was properly grateful.

Erescigal came to see me, with two guards who stayed in the room with us. "Your friends have sailed away," he told me. "Would you like me to arrange an escort for them, in case they run into pirates?"

I shook my head. "You'd be more likely to draw down the Sisters on them," I said. "Any ships flying your colours are going to catch it hot from now on."

"Up to you," he said. "I can guarantee there'll be no reprisals taken against them."

"As long as I behave myself?"

He didn't comment on that. "You should know that the Sisters' cavalry tried to attack a gold-panning station early this morning. I'm pleased to be able to report that they were beaten off, with heavy losses."

"I doubt that, somehow."

"I can bring you the dead men's heads, if you'd care to see them."

"No, thank you."

He looked at me as though I was a hair in wet paint: annoying but not worth the trouble of putting right. "There are a number of documents for you to sign," he said. "Shall I have them brought in for you?"

"If you like. Of course, they're not valid without the great seal."

He smiled. "Which is missing."

"Is it? Careless of someone."

"But that's all right," he said. "We're having a new one cut. It'll be perfectly valid once you pass an order in council authorising it."

Ah well, I thought, you do your best. "Of course," I said. "Silly of me not to have thought of it. I don't suppose you could get me a copy of Teudel's *Masques*, could you? Presumably there isn't one on the island, but maybe you could send away for it. Assuming your ships can still get through."

"As it happens, I've got one myself. I'll have it copied for you."

I looked at him. "You like Teudel?"

"On balance I prefer Burnand, but Teudel makes a pleasant change sometimes. And if there's anything else you'd like, just ask. Our ships are getting through with no trouble at all."

He'd made his various points but he was still there. "Was there something?" I asked.

He hesitated. "Actually, yes," he said. "I just wanted to tell you how much I liked *Dearer Than Life*."

"You what?"

"As it happens, it's one of my favourite plays. I saw it at the Curtain, with Andronica as the mother-in-law."

I wasn't expecting that. The worst thing a general can possibly say. "Oh. Right."

"I have a copy of it with me," he said. "You wouldn't consider signing it for me?"

To get a sample of my signature, so they could forge it? No need. "All right. If you like."

"Thank you," he said, and left me.

From time to time they brought me news. Stauracia's cavalry kept on trying to harass the gold workers, but every time they were slaughtered like sheep. Meanwhile, two thousand reinforcements had arrived from the Knights on the mainland, and three thousand Sirupatis had joined the newly formed militia, under the command of General Datis. Supply ships were landing daily, and there were no indications of hostile movements by governments friendly to the Poor Sisters. They didn't add that the reinforcements had been flown in on the backs of flying pigs, presumably because they reckoned there were limits to my credulity.

Ekkehard hadn't been to see me since that first visit, though I kept asking if he could spare me a minute. I asked Erescigal if he was still on the island. Why shouldn't he be, he said, and changed the subject.

The priests came to see me. They looked like they hadn't slept for a week. Things, they told me, were better than they'd expected. Services had been allowed to continue with very little interference, but they'd lost all representation on the royal council and nobody would give them a straight answer when they tried to find out what was happening. There hadn't been any violence. Everyone was too scared of the Siccambres to do anything, and the country people had been sent home. Yes, more soldiers had arrived. Erescigal had made sure they'd seen new faces guarding gates and street corners, and ships had definitely arrived at the harbour. Everybody had enough to eat. Some gold workers had been killed, but it was hard to know for sure how many or where, and the Siccambres made sure they were replaced immediately. As far as they knew, nobody had been inside the chapter house apart from themselves, and nobody had been asked any questions about it.

"The king's funeral is tomorrow," they told me. "We've asked for you to be allowed to preside."

"Will they allow it?"

"It's under consideration" was all they could tell me, so I asked Erescigal. He looked at me.

"Do you want to?" he said. "I wouldn't have thought you'd be interested in any of that sort of thing."

"You don't think it would be good for morale."

He shrugged. "I hadn't given it much thought, to be honest with you. What the Sirupatis think about anything doesn't matter terribly much. They're under control and there's nothing they can do. On balance I think it'd be better if things went off quietly, without any fuss. We want to take the focus off the traditional way of doing things. It helps people adjust to the new realities."

"What a good idea," I said. "Let's do that."

Timing; time; the way one moment transitions into another. A curious process, to say the least. It can be an active, vital process – every second counts, we say, which can be interpreted as, every second has value and meaning. Or it can be a process of passive accumulation, probably best expressed by the image of falling leaves. Moments die, fall, bury the dead moments that came before; time rots into history, history nourishes the roots of the future but in a thoroughly inefficient way, a million old leaves providing materials for one new one. You can't really talk about one process being better than the other. They're both right, in their place. One's terrifying, the other's very boring. One you can occasionally control, the other invariably controls you. It'll all be the same a hundred years from now, as my father used to say.

Most of what my father said was bullshit and that's no exception. The passage of time changes things; things happen, usually for the worse. Me, I like to keep busy. That sometimes means I incur fault and blame, mostly undeserved but by no means always. Small price to pay, maybe. I always tell people that if you don't take responsibility, responsibility takes you. I'm not sure that actually means anything, but if it does, it's quite profound.

Meanwhile the worst hadn't happened yet but it was happening: the war, the end of the world, my fault because I was trapped in it, like a horse in a burning barn. I still had faith, in uninvolved strangers far away, but with every identical day it was getting harder to keep my grip on it. Quite possibly I was depressed because I couldn't do anything and I couldn't run away. When things stop moving they're generally dead, unless convincingly proved otherwise. I'd probably have been more cheerful if I'd had something nice to read, but the promised copy of Teudel hadn't shown up yet and I was beginning to suspect that when it did I'd have to pay for it: more signatures, grants of land and mineral rights, charters to impress forced labour, things like that. At any rate the new great seal was an improvement on the old one. It was a portrait of me, full-face, unsmiling, very regal but somehow quite true to life. I'd never had my portrait done before, for obvious reasons.

One thing I did find while hunting for non-existent treasure was a Doubles board; presumably an unwanted diplomatic gift, shoved under a wodge of faded altar cloths in a chest in a dark corner of the cellars. I don't suppose anybody plays Doubles any more. It's a slow game, requiring thought, but you can make a lot out of it if you want to. When I was a kid, my brother Scynthius and I used to play, though we never got beyond one-mirror and he always won. My father, of course, played the two-mirror game, and he was reckoned to be not far below grand master status, though the whole point of two-mirror is that you play against yourself. He used to tell my brother that it was the only game worth playing, because the only opponent worth beating was yourself. He said a lot of things like that. He never offered to teach me to play, so I used to sneak into his study at night with a candle and use the board that was always set up on the small table under the window. I like the game because every square you land on automatically becomes hostile territory, so the more you move about, the more you box yourself in, until you're constrained to take only one path. Only when you have no choice in the matter whatsoever can you win, or lose, depending on how clever you've been. In the active game the object is to win, which is how my father always played it, but I have a soft spot for the passive game. It's taught me to understand defeat, and how defeat can in itself be a victory.

I was deeply into a game of two-mirrors when a guard came in with my evening meal: duck in a poncy sauce garnished with tiny slivers of lemon peel, which I loathe. He put the tray down and looked at me.

"That's Doubles," he said.

I looked up at him. "That's right."

"My dad and I used to play."

"My father was always too busy," I said. "But my brother and I played a lot at one time."

"The brother you killed?"

"That's the one."

He frowned at me. "How could you do something like that?"

"It was an accident."

He was between me and the light so I couldn't see the board. "Can't be any fun playing on your own."

"It passes the time."

"Aren't you supposed to be the king?"

I looked up at him and grinned. "I keep asking myself that."

He went to the door, then stopped. "About this war," he said.

My dinner was going cold, but it was horrible, so I didn't care. "What about it?"

He paused again. "I don't see how we can win."

"Really?"

He shook his head. A young man, maybe eighteen. "Not with all those countries coming in against us," he said. "No way we can fight all of them."

"That's not settled yet."

Serious look. "They tell you that but I don't believe them. The Aelians and the Mezentines and the Vesani. No way in hell we can hold them off, even if the Blemyans come in on our side. And that's not settled, not according to our sergeant, and he knows Blemyans; he was there once."

"I hadn't heard about the Vesani," I said.

"Old news," the soldier said. "Sarge says they're sending forty ships."

"Last I heard they had two hundred and fifteen," I told him. "That's hardly a big commitment. And think about who else we've got on our side."

He glared at me. "Oh, sure," he said, "we got Perimadeia and the Blueskins. Only what they don't tell you is, they're only sending a couple of divisions. And all these savages they reckon are coming down from the north: Hus and Aram Chantat. That's fine, except you really think they'll stick around when the money runs out? I don't think so."

"But the money won't run out."

"Yeah, so they say." He was sneering at my naivety. "But even if it's true and the mountains here are all made of pure gold, so fucking what? If they can't get it off the island because there's a blockade—"

"But there isn't a blockade."

"Not yet. But if the Vesani come in with those women, there will be, sure as eggs."

Women: the worst thing he could think of to call them, in context. Silly boy. "Listen." I raised my hand. "You're young. You don't know about this stuff. Now I've been everywhere and seen everything, and I *know*. You're worrying yourself over nothing. How do I know that? I'll tell you."

"Go on."

"As things are," I said, "it's all just a big pissing contest. The time to start worrying is when they start bringing in workers from outside to dig out the gold, instead of having the locals pan for it. That's the sign you should be looking for, because it means they're in a real hurry and they don't care about losing half the deposits if they can get a whole lot of the stuff out right now, when they need it. Until then—"

I stopped. He was looking at me. "Hadn't you heard?" he said.

Oh, I thought.

I'd read a memo about it. I wasn't supposed to see it, but it was in Erescigal's portfolio along with a bunch of stuff for me to sign, and I can read upside down. I only saw a few lines before he shifted the papers and covered it up, but that was enough.

What I'd seen was some technical report about the feasibility of digging the gold out rather than waiting for the rain to wash it down into the rivers. Basically, the engineer was against the idea. If you do that, he said, you risk losing up to half of what's there, because if you cut into the mountain the whole lot could come tumbling down. That would divert the streams that wash out the gold, and the collapse would probably bury the most productive seams under so much rock that it wouldn't be cost-effective to get it out.

Why would anyone want to do a thing like that? Answer: to get as much gold out as quickly as possible; to see to it that once he's done that, the remaining gold won't be available to an enemy. It'd be a calculated risk, needing an informed assessment of how the war was likely to go once it began and how long the island could be held against superior forces. If you did decide to take the risk, you'd need extra manpower from outside, and not just grunts with shovels: proper miners who know how to cut and shore up tunnels. The Knights, I remembered, operated a small but productive gold mine up in the north-east somewhere, while the Sisters were part-owners of the Peleset goldfields, almost entirely cleaned out but kept viable by the expertise of the men who'd worked it for generations. No shortage of skilled labour, if only they could be brought here safely.

One helpful thing the soldier had told me. At first he'd said the Vesani were in; then he'd said, if the Vesani come in with those women. Getting information that way is, I suppose, a bit like panning for gold: you get a plateful of garbage, included in which is a little bit of the right stuff. In other words, it was happening but it hadn't yet happened. Put it another way, it hadn't happened yet, but it was only a matter of time before it did, and then—

I'd always promised myself I wouldn't be there to see it. Preferably I'd be separated from the action by as much geography as I could get, but if the worst came to the worst, there's another way of not being there, not being anywhere. No big deal. To be honest, I haven't enjoyed my life very much, not this far at least. There's been some good bits, but I never really managed to enjoy them for what they were, because over everything there's always been this thick layer of worry and anxiety, like gravy on the vegetables in Mezentine cuisine. When everything tastes of fear and dread, even the nice things, it's hard to be enthusiastic about anything. You hang on, hoping it'll get better but knowing it's unlikely to. You can always say to yourself, if it stays this bad I'll cut my throat tomorrow, and you keep saying that and it keeps you going. Note the emphasis on keeping going, which can also be translated as running away. But I have a soft spot for the passive game. I'd toyed with it on the ship, heading for Sirupat, but things hadn't worked out and, besides, it hadn't really started to happen at that point. Now, though, I took stock of the possibilities and the open squares and I could only see one path. That's victory in the passive game, even though it leads to the very last square of all.

Fine sentiments, however, butter no parsnips. All very well to say to Life, screw you, I'll walk home from here. Not so good when they won't let you near sharp instruments or anything that can be plaited into a rope. The coverlets on my bed were things of beauty, imported specially for my use. They were quilted silk, embroidered with flowers and acanthus scrolls. Try making a rope out of one of those and see how far you get.

*

Someone came to see me. "Allow me to introduce myself," he said, with a big smile. "My name's Becco. It's an honour to meet you at last."

He wasn't Siccambrean. "I doubt that," I said. "Who are you?"

He sat down, unasked. He was a big, broad man, bald, with a little tufty beard, somewhere between forty-five and fifty. "I'm your new chief minister," he said. "I'm really looking forward to working closely with you. This is a very exciting time."

"Where's Erescigal?"

"Ah, yes." The smile turned bittersweet. "A good man in many ways. But things are different now." He paused and looked round. "It's a bit frowsty in here," he said. "Damp, too. You'll like the new quarters a lot more."

"Plenty of fresh air?"

"Decent ventilation," he said. "You could grow mushrooms in here. It's a disgrace."

You get first-class ventilation in a turret room at the top of a tower. "I quite like it here," I said. "I enjoy the view."

"Much better view from the new quarters."

Right. "When do I move?"

"Soon," he said. "Just waiting for the paint to dry. Too much damp in the air, this close to the sea. We've gone with mostly pale fawns and terracottas, but if you'd rather have something else, just say the word."

"I hate fawn."

"Me too. I don't think you can beat primrose yellow, personally, but it could be argued the light's just that bit too hard this far north to get away with it."

"And curved walls."

"Excuse me?"

"It's a round tower, isn't it? I find curved walls always darken the colour a semitone or so."

He smiled. I think he wanted me to know just how many big teeth he had. "Maybe a pale jade," he said. "Later, after you've had a chance to settle in. Nothing worse than having to camp out while people are decorating all round you."

"I don't mind staying here till it's done."

He showed me a sad face. "That wouldn't be advisable," he said. "To be honest with you, we're a bit concerned about security. Nothing for you to worry about, I give you my word, but it'll be so much easier keeping you safe in the new apartments."

I nodded. "Better fawn than dead. I quite understand."

I was getting on his nerves. Good. "Did Erescigal say anything before he left?" I asked.

"No. Should he have done?"

"I just wondered. No message for me?"

"The arrangements were all a bit last-minute. I'm sure he'd have liked to say goodbye in person, but you know how it is."

"Any chance you could pass on a message from me?"

"That might be awkward." He stopped, realising he was on the wrong track. If there really was a message and I wasn't just being annoying, he needed to know what it was. "I'll certainly do my best. What is it?"

"I'll need to write it down. You wouldn't happen to have a bit of paper and a pen?"

"Just tell me," he said. "I've got a very good memory."

"Fine," I said. "*Tis t'ar sphoe theon eridi sune'eke makhesthai? Letous kai dios hwios.* Got that?"

He blinked. "Good heavens," he said.

"You don't know Gordouli, I take it."

"Sorry, no." From the sleeve of his pseudo-monk's habit he

produced a small ivory box. From it he took a tiny ivory pen, a minute silver ink bottle and a scrap of transparent parchment the size of a privet leaf. "You'll have to spell it out for me."

I did that, slowly and patiently. For what it's worth, it's the sixth line of the messenger's speech in *The Anger of Lysimachus*, only the most famous play ever written, and the language is of course Old Aelian. Bet you he'd have been on it like a snake if I'd translated it for him. "Question mark after mak-whatsit?"

"That's right," I said. "It doesn't matter particularly, but I promised Erescigal I'd tell him. He was a nice man. I liked him."

"Me too." He sprinkled sand from the world's smallest sand sprinkler and blew it away with a sharp puff. "I'll see what I can do."

"Thank you. I'm sure you will."

Away went the pen, the ink bottle and the sand sprinkler, exactly right or the lid wouldn't shut. "Anything else I can do for you in the message line?"

"I don't think so, not at the moment. How's the war going?"

"Splendidly," he said. "Only the other day we sank four of their ships off Aechmalota. It'll all be over by Ascension at this rate, and then we can settle down and get on with our lives."

"What about the Vesani?"

He laughed. "Typical," he said. "Like the old joke."

"Remind me."

"How can you tell a Vesani by his trousers? Creosote stains, from sitting on fences."

"Oh," I said, "that one. Actually, I don't think it's terribly funny."

"Me neither. I think it's great that you and I get on so well together. We'll be seeing ever such a lot of each other from now on, so it's just as well."

After he'd gone, I felt sick, though I managed to keep it down. This mortality business: we all know we're going to die one day and we deal with it pretty well, because there're no fixed dates or assurances, so we can cheerfully pretend it'll never happen. A single drop of certainty can spoil all that. He'd as good as told me that as soon as the war was over I'd be dead. True, the war wasn't going marvellously well, especially at sea, but the Vesani hadn't properly committed themselves and a shock defeat might make them give up and pull out. Everything still to play for and too close to call; anyway, once it was over, win or lose, no more me. I'd probably killed Erescigal, too, all for the sake of clawing back a little time and playing a merry prank on a man I didn't like very much, but I wasn't too fussed about that. Or about myself, for that matter. Still, knowing for sure is different from dreading or expecting, or even vaguely hoping. The feeling of nausea passed eventually, and when it was gone it left behind an unpleasant and inconvenient kind of clarity. I didn't want to die after all, not one tiny bit, and all that stoical acceptance had just been self-deluding bullshit. A bad thing to find out just before they move you to a maximum security cell a hundred feet up in the air.

What brought about the change of heart I couldn't tell you, though probably I'd been lying to myself all along. Hope isn't a favourite with me. Hope is what makes the alcoholic pour himself another drink. It's just one of nature's scams, like love. Love puts you through the mincer just to ensure the propagation of the species, and hope keeps you hanging around when you're hurting, just in case you might come in useful for something, like the carefully saved balls of string in a mad old woman's attic. There's an old Echmen story about a man who was walking down the road and saw a woman rubbing a crowbar against a rock. What in God's name are you doing, he asks. Sewing on a button, says the old woman. Really? Oh yes, she says. But first I need a needle, but I haven't got a needle, only this old crowbar. So I'm grinding it down till it's small enough to sew with.

Actually, I think the story is supposed to illustrate the virtue of perseverance, but to me it's just all of life, neatly sewn up in a bag. How I interpret it depends on how I'm feeling and what's happened to me lately. Some days I'm the woman. Other days I'm the crowbar.

10

The tower room was nice. It had a high ceiling – too high to reach, let alone attach a rope to – and tall, thin windows – just right for shooting arrows out of, but too narrow to climb through unless you happened to be a weasel – so it was light and airy, and more of a light mustard than a fawn. The extreme thickness of the walls meant it didn't get too hot or too cold. No fireplace, of course, so in winter it would probably be a bit chilly; but I'd be dead by then, so nothing to worry about on that score. Above all, no risk of irritating visitors just dropping by for a chat. None whatsoever.

For some reason the Doubles board hadn't made it across the quadrangle and up the stairs, so I had to lie on my back and play the game in my head, with my eyes closed. I can do that, if I concentrate really hard. The move had happened right when I was in the middle of a really difficult, protracted game, a real classic; if I'd had something to write with I'd have noted it all down, it was that good. When I needed a break, I got up and went to the window, the one facing east, with a view out over the bay and the sea. I couldn't see very much from there, just an impression of a lot of ships coming and going: big ships, capable of carrying a lot of men or a substantial bulk of cargo. I stared at them for a while, hating them to death, then lay back on the bed and carried on deciding my game destiny, eliminating options by treading on them, the way I used to do back when I was free.

I remember it came on to rain. It didn't bother me. Whoever designed those windows knew his job, because hardly a drop of water got through, even though in theory one of them was always facing directly into the prevailing wind. There were shutters, but I couldn't be bothered to close them even when it poured. I liked the sound and the smell. They helped me concentrate on the closing stages of the game, which was drawing towards a remarkably close and tense climax.

I was tentatively feeling my way towards a gambit that might just close off my last potential avenue of escape and win me the game when I heard the bolt being drawn outside. I opened my eyes to find that the sun had gone down and it was as dark as a bag.

Not so much the fact that the bolt as being drawn as the way it was being done. Whoever was doing it was trying to do it quietly, and not making a wonderful job of it. As any fool knows, if you want to keep the noise down you need lubrication: a drop of oil, a hawk of spit does as well as anything, pissing on the bolt works a treat if you can reach. This idiot was waggling the bolt gently from side to side, then easing it back a quarter of an inch at a time. In some of the places I've lived and worked, the neighbours would've had the watch on him for disturbing the peace.

Not a happy sound, as far as I was concerned. Why would

someone want to get into my room without being heard? No witnesses equals deniability, but at the top of a tower? In which case, was I about to be murdered by the other side? It occurred to me that only an idiot would be bothering his pretty head with irrelevancies when his assassin was at the door. What I ought to be thinking about was staying alive, given that I had no weapons of any kind, followed by the possibilities that might ensue from a dead or stunned assassin and an unlocked door –

A faint screech, then dead quiet. He'd got the bolt drawn and was waiting – count to twenty – to see if the coast was clear. The next thing he'd do would be to come in. The door opened inwards, to my left. Chances were he'd have his knife or sword drawn in his right hand. A door makes a pretty good shield, as well as a powerful but circumscribed bludgeon. He'd know that, of course, even if he'd never actually done any of this stuff before and had learned it all from a book.

There was one chair, but it was a massive oak thing, too heavy to lift and swing. There was a pillow. It wouldn't stop a well-aimed thrust but it was probably up to muffling a vague slash. If he had a lantern I needed to be behind the door, but if he didn't I'd be better off on the other side, nicely placed to smother his right arm with the pillow while smashing his teeth in with my right fist. I genuinely thought all that in the second and a bit after the bolt stopped squealing. Amazing how fast you can think in a crisis, and how stupid you can be in such a short space of time.

A second and a bit meant I'd left it far too late (see above, timing). I was only halfway to the door when it opened. I froze, not because of any valid tactical consideration but because I hadn't a clue what to do.

I heard the door close; then a grinding noise, such as is made by those patent mechanical tinderboxes you can buy for forty trachy under the arches in Auxentia City. They're very cheap but they don't work. He tried, then he tried again. You know how it is when you just want to snatch it out of the other guy's hand and do it yourself. Third time lucky. A little local red glow, and then he lit his lamp.

"Ekkehard?" I said.

"Shut up, you fuckwit," he yelled, "do you want to wake the whole fucking palace?"

Yes, Ekkehard. Absolutely no doubt at all. I lowered my voice. "What are you doing—?"

"What do you think?"

No knife in his hand, but a sword stuck through his belt. Make that two swords. "You're crazy," I said.

"That's nice," he growled. "You always were an ungrateful little shit. Here." He pulled a sword from his belt and shoved it at me, hilt first. "Come on, we haven't got all night."

For some reason I didn't want to touch the sword, as though it was dead or slimy or something. "Hold on," I said. "This is a *rescue?*"

He was so angry he made a little groaning noise. "Don't do it," he said, "not now. Be funny later, when we've got time."

"I'm not being funny." I took a few steps back and sat down on the bed. "What are you playing at?"

"You *moron.*" It was as though his insides were swelling like a sail, and his skeleton couldn't hold back the pressure. "I knocked out two guards on the stairs. They're going to wake up any minute, and then we're *dead.* We've got to go, now."

"Just a tick," I said, not moving. "You betrayed me to the enemy and now you're rescuing me."

"Yes, for fucking crying out loud, that's *exactly right.* But we've got to go *now.* Before the guards *wake up.*"

"Why would you do that?"

A little of the pressure must've hissed out of his ears. He dropped from a rolling boil to a simmer. "Because they're going to kill you. I found out. I've been to the mainland and heard it from regional command. Soon as the war starts in earnest, they're going to stick a crown on your head and a knife in your ear, in that order. Now can we go? Please?"

"And that bothers you?"

"Fuck off," he said. "They promised me you'd be all right. We made a deal. We'll make him a fucking king, they said, he'll be happy as a pig in shit."

Maybe it was the way he said it, but I suddenly knew. "They aren't going to pay you," I said.

"You what?"

"They promised you a lot of money and now they've gone back on their word."

"That, too. But I made them promise. Not a hair of his fucking head, they told me—"

"You thought you'd be the governor of Sirupat, but they tricked you."

"So fucking what? Are you coming or aren't you? We've got to go *now*."

I laughed out loud. "And then," I said, "you remembered the stuff from the monastery. A hundred thousand in gold, but you don't know where we stashed it. And the Knights don't know either. Just me and the lads. So we need to get there *now*, before the lads do."

"They're going to kill you."

"Yes," I said, standing up, "I'd figured that out for myself. What the hell am I supposed to do with this?"

"We may need to fight our way out."

The way he said it: Ekkehard the action hero. What do they call it, the method school? Where you think your way deep into the part and pretend you're really who you claim to be? "Absolutely," I said. "Come the three corners of the world in arms and we shall shock them. Mind you don't cut yourself."

"Funny man." It was the worst thing he could think of, on the spur of the moment. He had a point.

Turned out he'd been telling the truth: he'd knocked out both the guards on the stairs. Like so many nervous beginners he'd hit them too hard, but I didn't tell him that. "I've got a boat waiting for us down at the harbour," he hissed, loud enough to wake the dead, as we crossed the stable yard. "We can get out through the sally port in the back wall—"

"The one you opened to let the Knights in?"

"—and sneak round the outside of the walls, and there's a sort of goat track thing that goes down to the beach. It's a piece of piss, I promise you."

Under normal circumstances, I wouldn't trust Ekkehard to organise a bunch of flowers for the leading lady, but it all went without a hitch. There were soldiers everywhere, hauling and unloading supplies by lamplight, digging trenches, piling up embankments and setting out fascines. All we had to do was walk around as though we owned the place and nobody took any notice. As we crossed a narrow plank over a deep ditch filled with water I pulled the sword out of his belt and dropped it. He stopped dead, nearly upsetting the plank, and swung round at me. "Just in case," I said. "Keep going."

"Lunatic."

The "sort of goat track" was an absolute nightmare. We'd ditched the lamp a long time ago, so we found ourselves scrambling down a very steep, narrow path in the pitch darkness.

Doing it quietly was impossible, but there didn't seem to be anybody around to hear. At one point he froze solid and refused to go any further. I'd seen him like that once or twice before, too scared to move, huddled and whimpering. "Come on," I said. "Give me your hand."

"Piss off. You don't know the way any more than I do. You'll get us killed."

"It's all right," I told him. "Trust me."

"What did you want to go throwing my sword away for? I'm risking my life for you and you're an arsehole."

"It's going to be fine. Just think about all that money."

"Piss off and die."

His hand was damp and clammy, like a child's. I was laughing so much inside, I hardly noticed the last hundred yards of the descent. Then suddenly the ground was level, and I could see a faint glow of moonlight reflected in the sea. "I think we're here," I said.

"Keep your voice down," he roared. "We've got to find the boat."

"You do know where it is."

"Course I do. It's here somewhere."

I found a boat. The yard was lowered and the sail neatly furled. "No," he said, shaking his head. "That's not the one."

For crying out loud. "It'll do," I said. "Get in."

We got in. He sat down. He knows as much about sailing as I do. "For God's sake be careful," he snarled at me. "You'll have us over."

I sat down, and the boat stopped swaying about. "This is useless," I said.

"It can't be all that difficult." I couldn't see his face, so I couldn't see the fear. "You just pull on a rope and that raises the mast."

"Sail."

"I meant sail. You know what I mean. This isn't a good time for fucking point scoring. And you untie those bits of string and the sail comes loose and off we go."

It was one of those still, calm nights. I could've lit a candle and it wouldn't have blown out. "Come on," I said.

"Sit down. Where are you going?"

I sighed. "It's hopeless," I said. "Even if we could get this stupid thing out of the harbour into the open sea without running it onto a submerged rock or a shoal, we don't even know where the mainland is, let alone how to make the boat go there. It's ridiculous. Why do I listen to you?"

"Sit *down*. We'll manage. We can't go back; they'll catch us."

"You clown," I said. "There's ships – *proper* ships with *proper* sailors – in and out of this harbour all day long, I've been watching them. Either they'll run us down or scoop us up and take us back. It isn't going to work. I'm going back to my nice warm, dry tower. You can do what the hell you like."

"*Arsehole*," he shrieked. "You can't do that."

"And if you've got half a brain," I said, "you'll find somewhere to hide until you can stow away on a freighter. Listen. The gold's packed in oilskin sacks down the bottom of the well in the abbot's cistern. You'll need trained divers and a heavy-duty winch."

"Screw you. I don't give a stuff about the gold." He tried to stand up. The boat rocked wildly. He sat down again. "What cistern?"

"Go through the abbot's lodgings into a little courtyard, you'll find a big stone slab with an iron ring set in it. You'll need a crane to shift it. That's all right, you're welcome. It won't do me any good, after all."

"Drop dead. We've got to leave. Now."

He was messing around with something, but I couldn't see what he was doing. The boat swayed horribly and I had that guts-scooped-out feeling I know so well. "Pack it in," I told him, but he ignored me. He'd got hold of something. I saw a shape move in the darkness, and then something hard hit me on the head.

"Sorry," he said. "Accident."

My head hurt so much I couldn't think. The fool had got hold of an oar or something. He was prodding about in the water with it, trying to pole us away from the harbour wall. "That's no good," I snapped at him, "we're still tied up. All you'll do is capsize the boat."

"Shut up."

I felt around for the rope, the one we were tied up with. It wasn't down my end. Oh God, I thought, he's untied it. "All right," I said. "We'll go back and hide in the hills, and they'll think we've stolen a boat and escaped so they won't be looking for us. Then we can find some other way off the island and—"

A terrifying lurch, and the boat swung wildly through a hundred and eighty degrees. I lost my footing and dropped like a tree, landing with my earlobe trapped against the rail. You have no idea how much that hurts. I heard two splashes. The idiot had found the other oar, and he was trying to row. I was so scared I drew my sword, but the boat did a huge wobble; it shook out of my hand and went plop in the water. "It's fine," I heard him say, "I'm really getting the hang of it now, there's nothing to it." Then the boat lurched again, something wooden and solid hit me very hard and I went to sleep.

*

I woke up. The sky was huge and blue and all around me. I was lying on my back. I was moving.

"Told you," said the voice I hated most in all the world. "Absolutely nothing to it."

I moved my head a bit. It hurt. I was looking at a sail, billowing out from a mast with a belly full of wind. "You slipped and nutted yourself on the sticky-out thing," he continued cheerfully, "and once you'd stopped badgering me I figured it all out from first principles and here we are."

I sat up. My head felt like there were tree roots growing down from my scalp into my brain. "You idiot," I said. "We're in the middle of the sea."

"I know what I'm doing," he said smugly. "The sun rose over there." He waved his arm in a perfect semicircle, "so that's west. Therefore we need to go this way. You pull on this bit of string here and it works the rudder."

"You idiot," I said. "The sun rises in the east."

His face went blank. "No, it doesn't."

"Yes, it *does*."

Silence for a count of four. "Yes, well, maybe it does. It's no big deal either way. Just means we'll make landfall on Cossiris instead of Ildra. Which is good," he added quickly, "because that way we're far less likely to run into any Knights' ships, and when we land we won't be knee-deep in hostile soldiers. Actually, I was a bit concerned about that, but this way we won't have that problem, so it's all turned out pretty well."

I looked up at the sail. "You managed that all by yourself."

"Don't sound so surprised," he said. "I have been on ships, you know. I watch people, see what they're doing. It's called taking an interest."

Nothing to be seen anywhere in any direction except sea and sky. "You realise there's nothing to drink on this boat."

"Don't be such a girl. You rig up a trap and catch the dew."

"What in?"

"And you trail a line to catch fish. Everybody knows that. Besides, we'll be there before you know it."

We were miles out to sea in an open boat built for darting round the coast, always in sight of land. "It's not that I mind dying," I said. "I'd just rather not have to die with you along, that's all. Death is significant and you'll trivialise it."

"If all you're going to do is whine, I'm not listening."

Fair enough. I wasn't exactly helping. I closed my eyes and tried to picture a map. Cossiris, the island he'd drivelled about landing on, was a little speck of rock in the middle of a ridiculous quantity of sea, so our chances of bumping into it were practically nil. Beyond Cossiris, eventually, you came to the Erdasc peninsula, a place I'd never been to and knew nothing about. "We need to turn round," I said.

"Can't. Got to go where the wind takes us."

"When you were watching and learning, you didn't see how to tack into the wind."

"No. I mean, it doesn't make sense. I can't see how you can make a sailing ship go a different direction to how the wind's blowing."

I had no idea how you tack a boat. "Fine," I said. "Let's go to Cossiris. Wake me when we get there."

I woke up out of a horrible dream and found it wasn't a dream at all. Ekkehard was sitting there smiling at me, as though he'd found me in the street and I was worth money. "Well," he said, "I did it again. Saved your life."

I could push him over the side and nobody would ever know. "I suppose you did," I said. "Thank you."

"God knows why," he said. "You've always been horrible to me. But there it is."

I stopped myself saying anything else, because I knew exactly how it would go. He'd be annoying and I'd be witty and sarcastic, and he'd end up swearing at me. So I told myself we'd had our chat, it had ended how it always did, and now we were sulking at each other. That gave me time to reflect. Yes, now I came to think of it, he had saved my life – by recklessly endangering it, admittedly, but it's the thought that counts. My life: that valuable commodity; that cause of endless pain and suffering to so many. I wish he'd been there on Stauracia's ship, on the way to Sirupat. He could have tried to save me then, and then I'd have had no trouble at all getting killed.

"Thanks," I repeated. "It was brave and generous, and you're a brave, generous man. I owe you one."

He frowned at me, as though I'd just grown an extra ear.

"You're all right," he said, with a bit of an effort. "God knows you're a difficult bastard, and you never say anything nice about anyone if you can possibly help it. And you're so self-centred I could use you to drill holes. But you write good plays, sometimes."

"Thank you."

He sighed, and looked past me at the sea. "And I'll say this for you," he went on. "You put yourself in harm's way to try and stop the big war, though if you ask me it was too little, too late. But I don't suppose there's many people would've done that."

"Bullshit," I said.

He shrugged. "You say that," he said. "But I reckon most

people in your shoes would've been too scared. Or else they might have wanted to do it but reckoned they couldn't, because they didn't have what it takes."

"Absolutely. Let's talk about something else."

"I think," he went on, "that there's some things – like stopping a war, for instance – that it takes a certain sort of person to do. Now that sort of person may not be pleasant to know or easy to get on with, and maybe he can be a bit full of it and not give a stuff about the people around him, in fact he can be a real shit sometimes, but it's those qualities, those strengths, that make it possible for him to do something big and important, even if he's not a nice person. I think that's the price he pays for the potential to do the one big good thing."

I actually thought about that for maybe a quarter of a second, before I saw the flaw in his argument. "No," I said. "Bet you anything you like, this notional heroic shit of yours had some other motive for doing the one big good thing, and I bet you that motive was entirely shitty. And if you do a good thing for a shitty reason, you're still a shit. The good is just a by-product, the excrement of evil."

He gazed at me for a moment. "There, you see," he said. "Excrement of evil, that's a good line. Like I said, you may be a real piece of work sometimes, but you do have a way with words."

Ekkehard's sunny mood lasted most of the first day, until the wind dropped. At first he kept saying things like *won't be long now* and *just a brief lull*. Then he went quiet, which was a relief. Then he got the oars out. "We'll just have to row," he said. "Come on."

"The hell with that," I said.

"Don't be so stupid."

I was so thirsty I couldn't think about anything else. "Listen," I said. "If we row, we sweat. If we sweat, we dry out quicker. We're going to die anyway, but let's not make it easy for the bastard."

He rowed for about an hour, then gave up. It was nearly dark. "Wind'll get up soon; we'll be fine," he said loudly, and didn't speak again for a long time. Then he started to snore. Marvellous.

He'd been snoring for quite some time when the wind started to get up. I prodded him with my toe and he sat bolt upright, making the boat lurch horribly. "Told you," he said. He sounded petrified.

I don't remember much about what happened after that. It was terrifying, and I was clinging to the side of the boat with both hands, and I kept promising myself, it'll all be over very soon, any second now – a splash, a lungful of water, won't take long, no big deal – but it wasn't, it just kept on, one hideous lurch after another. I thought the mast would break, but it didn't. The boat was half full of water, I couldn't understand why it didn't sink, and the wind drove us like an arrowhead through flesh. I knew we were going fast, very fast, too fast. I knew it couldn't go on much longer, but it did. At some point I heard a yell and I remember thinking, that's that, then, goodbye Ekkehard, and that's all I thought or felt; me next, I thought, and waited like a man who can see the headsman's shadow moving on the block in front of his face. I waited, and saltwater filled my mouth and nose, and I coughed and spat it out again, and breathed in and waited some more. That's more or less all I remember. Not much use as a witness, I'm afraid. I've always hated boats. I never seem to have much luck with them.

That's what I like about writing, even prose narrative, which is very much a blunt instrument compared with dramatic dialogue. You can stop, count to five, take a deep breath and start again six or twelve or eighteen (I have no idea how long) hours later; the sheer misery of that night is simply overleapt, like a knight on a chessboard. You land upright, perfectly balanced on the balls of your feet, ready to carry on with the story you want your reader to hear, which isn't necessarily exactly what happened.

Hop, skip and a jump, therefore, and there I am – there we were; he hadn't fallen overboard after all – on a boat, still floating and finally still, with the chickenshit sun peering nervously out from behind a cloud to see if the big nasty storm's really gone away.

We had no sail, and the boat was about a third full of water, and we had nothing to bale with except our cupped hands. I looked at Ekkehard, and he looked at me. My throat was too dry for talking and I guess his was the same. I took off my shirt and squeezed a sleeve, but the drop of water that fell on my tongue was salt. I couldn't spit, so I wiped it off with my fingertip.

We weren't going anywhere. We had nothing better to do, so we scooped up tiny handfuls of water and threw them over the side. He gave up after an hour or so but I kept going, even though my back was killing me, until it got too dark to see. I suppose I fell asleep at some point, because I know I woke up while it was still dark. We were moving again; mostly up and down, it seemed to me, but a bit sideways as well. I distinctly remember thinking, I don't feel sick at all, presumably this is what they mean by getting your sea legs. Then it started to rain.

Proper rain, great big fat drops and lots of them. My cupped hands filled in about twelve seconds, and you can't possibly imagine what that rain tasted like. After maybe half a dozen handfuls I kicked him awake. We spent something like an hour just drinking, completely oblivious to the boat dancing up and down and trying to smash our skulls with its rails and ribs. Dawn rose and we could see what we were doing. The boat needed baling again, so we did that. The rain stopped but the wind and the heaving continued for a long time, and then that stopped, too. The sun came out, properly this time. I lifted my head to talk to him, but he was staring at something. I turned to see what it was. It was a ship.

They were fishermen. I have no idea what language they spoke, but it didn't matter. They gave us blankets and water and stale bread and a sort of cold fish stew in small wooden bowls. We sat under the mainmast while they got on with their work. "Bet you anything you like," Ekkehard said to me, "they're going to take us back to Sirupat. I just know it, that's all."

The first thing he'd said in two days, or was it three? "They aren't Sirupatis," I said.

"Doesn't matter. That's where we're going. This soup tastes like piss."

"I like it."

"You would. Why does everything turn to shit when you're involved?"

It was a good question, one I knew I'd have to think about before I could give a valid answer. I told him I'd have to get back to him on that one, and went to sleep.

When I woke up it was starting to get dark, and the

fishermen were nearly home. The shape on the skyline was definitely land. I tried asking them what it was called. They seemed to understand the question and gave me an answer, but I couldn't tell the place-name from the verbs and conjunctions. Nothing sounded remotely familiar, so I thanked them. They were towing our boat on a long rope. I managed to get across to them that they could keep it. They were thrilled, and every one of them had to shake my hand.

Ekkehard woke up. "What's going on?"

"Land," I said. "Oh, and I gave them the boat."

"What the fuck did you do that for?" he said, and a fisherman grabbed his hand and nearly broke his wrist shaking it.

The fishermen took us ashore in their beautiful new boat. Miraculously it still had both oars. They thanked us some more once we'd landed, then walked away and left us to it.

"This isn't Sirupat," I told him.

"You don't know that. You haven't been round every inch of the coastline."

"True," I said.

"This is fucking useless. Where are we?"

"Alive," I said.

"That's not a place, you moron."

"It'll do me."

He sighed and started walking. His boots and my shoes were long gone and the beach was shingle. I didn't mind. He did. It was dark, but there was a half-moon, enough to see more or less where we were going. We walked up the beach to a low sea wall, and were arrested for vagrancy.

The watch sergeant spoke Robur. "This is Ildra," he said. "Where did you say you were from?"

I beamed at him. "Sirupat," I said.

"You don't look Sirupati."

"We're not," I said. "Is this really Ildra?"

The sergeant didn't like that. "You trying to be funny?"

Ekkehard gave me his shut-the-fuck-up look. "We were shipwrecked," he said. "There was a terrible storm off Sirupat. We've been adrift in an open boat for days. Some fishermen rescued us or we'd be dead by now. Do you know a man called Segimerus?"

I think the sergeant was as surprised as I was. "Sure," he said. "Everyone knows him."

"He'll vouch for us."

The difference a proper noun can make. "Who the hell," I hissed, as the sergeant got up to go, "is Segimerus?"

"Shut the fuck up," he hissed back. "Everything's fine. Just leave it to me."

"Who's Segimerus?"

"He keeps a bar. Now shut your face or you'll spoil everything."

That made me grin. "I owe you an apology," I said. "You got us to Ildra after all."

"Said I would, didn't I? Now will you be quiet or do I have to smash your face in?"

I sighed and leaned back in my chair. The watch house was two rooms; we were in the one that wasn't a cell, though there were two men with spears standing on either side of the door. I realised I hadn't been in a room without spearmen for as long as I could remember. I'd come to think of them as a normal part of the decor, like lampstands. My clothes were caked with salt. I'd stopped noticing that, too. I'd never have imagined the sheer fact of being alive could be so important that it blotted out all other considerations, but it did. It was all I could think about. I could remember being so stupidly blasé about the prospect of dying, back on Sirupat. The memory made me shudder. I didn't ever want to go back there.

The sergeant came back with a perfect stranger. You know these people? he asked. Sure I do, the perfect stranger said. They're all yours, the sergeant said.

"You boys look like you could use a drink," our new friend said, a little bit out of breath. He led us up a steep, narrow street with what looked like warehouses on either side, though it was too dark to tell for sure. The street was cobbled and my feet hurt, though I didn't really mind. I think Ekkehard had his teeth gritted. He was taking long strides, to get it over with. "This your first time on Ildra?" the barman asked me. I told him it was. "Not far now," he said. I thanked him. At the back of my mind I was doing the usual making-sense-of-it-all routines; this man must be the local contact for the Knights, so presumably that's how he knows Ekkehard, but of course he doesn't know Ekkehard's gone rogue, so he'll help us and everything will be fine, assuming we can get a big enough winch. Talking of which: fifty thousand, my share of the money. Rather more than I had the last time I restarted my life. Could we possibly kid this Segimerus into putting us on a ship all the way to Ogyge? Probably not, but I wouldn't be at all surprised if he couldn't get us to Beloisa, which was a much better place for sourcing heavy equipment. I nearly laughed out loud. A storm and a bit of rain; if I'd been indoors I'd probably have slept through it and never found out the truth, that life is worth it after all and not something to be kicked off like a pair of too-tight shoes.

Segimerus' bar was a substantial building, square like a box, with two gilded lanterns outside. One big room with long tables; about a third of the seats on the benches occupied. Nobody seemed interested in us. "Come on through to the back," he said. "I''ll let them know you're here."

The back was a storeroom: mostly barrels. There was an oil-lamp and four candles. "You might have told me," I said.

Ekkehard looked at me. "Didn't want to get your hopes up," he said.

"Thank you."

"Fuck that." He looked away. "You were right. I only did it for the money."

"Fifty-fifty?"

"What?"

"We share the money fifty-fifty," I said. "Half for you and half for—"

"Yes, I know what it means, thank you. Fifty thousand staurata, right?"

I smiled. "You earned it. You could've had it all, you realise."

"What are you talking about?"

"Before we left," I reminded him. "I told you where to look for it, in the cistern. You could've left me. But you didn't."

"I couldn't do that," he said. "We're friends, remember?"

"Vaguely," I said. "Will fifty thousand be enough, to buy the Gallery of Illustration?"

"God, yes. But I changed my mind. I'm through with all that now."

"Really?"

"It's like they say. You can't go back."

"I wouldn't know," I said. "I've never wanted to."

He looked at me. "Did you really murder your brother?"

"It was an accident," I told him. "We were fencing. He made a mistake."

"I'm sorry."

"Don't be," I said. "The only reason I didn't murder him was, I was too scared of what'd happen to me. If I'd known how to distil foxgloves, I'd have done him just like that."

He nodded, as though what I'd said made some sort of sense. "It doesn't matter any more," he said.

"I guess not."

The door opened. In came a large number of men. They didn't look at Ekkehard, only at me.

"This him?" one of them said.

"Yes."

I saw the fist coming. It filled my vision and bounced my head off the back of the chair.

They were men of few words, so it took me a while to get confirmation, not that I really needed it. They were bounty hunters, working for my father. Ekkehard's share would be two hundred thousand staurata. No, I couldn't see him, he'd already left.

"I'm warning you," I said, as they tied me to the rail, "I'm a lousy sailor. I throw up all the time."

"Feel free," they told me. "Not our ship."

Fair enough. I couldn't find it in my heart to hate them. Apart from the one really solid punch they hadn't done anything bad. They were just agents, and I couldn't blame them, any more than I could blame the sea. They didn't want to talk to me, and I didn't want to talk.

I overheard two of them chatting about the war. They weren't particularly interested in it, but it made a change from the weather. It'll all be over by spring, said one of them. Hell as like, said another, it's going to get really bad now that the Vesani are in. That's all bullshit, said a third, nobody knows which way they're going to jump. It'll be different once the fighting really starts.

Mostly, though, it was just being on a ship. Time passes differently. You feel it could go on for ever, even though you know it's running out fast.

"What's this?" I asked.

"Bean soup," the man told me. "Don't you like it?"

"Not much."

"It's what we're having."

"Thanks," I said. "I think I'll pass."

He scowled at me. "You can forget about starving yourself to death," he said. "We'll prise open your throat with a stick if we have to."

"It's not that," I said, "really. It's bean soup. I can't be doing with it."

"There's bread."

"Bread will be just fine."

It was stale barley bread; you had to chew till your jaws ached, and it took all the skin off your throat going down. Inconceivable as it may sound, given the number and commitment of the competition, but maybe I am my own worst enemy after all.

I know nothing at all about ships and sailing, but even I know that if you want to get from the north coast of the Friendly Sea down to the south-east corner of the Middle Sea at that time of year, you have to follow the coast anticlockwise. If you try and go the direct route, across the middle, you run the risk of getting smashed to pieces in precisely the sort of storm that

Ekkehard and I had run into; if by some miracle you survive it, you'll find yourself back in the north-east, where you started from, because that's where the wind wants to take you. That was how we'd ended up on Ildra. They call it the Home of the Wind – they call it a lot of other things, too – because between the rising of the Seven Sisters and the setting of the Dog-star, or is it the other way round, all the winds in the Friendly Sea want to go there. All you can do if your heart is set on being somewhere other than Ildra is creep along from bay to inlet, tacking like crazy and hiding in sheltered water every time there's enough breeze to sway a wind chime. Great big oar-driven warships can just about smash their way through, but only the Sashan empire can afford to build and crew monsters on that scale, and any warship that big and heavy is (under normal conditions) easy prey to lighter, lower, nimbler, faster, cheaper sloops and brigantines, such as we favour in the West, which is why we don't all speak Sashan and serve the Great King. All that weather stuff is one of the reasons why I've never for one instant been tempted to try my hand at piracy. Your earning season is woefully short, and there's too much competition.

So, even if everything went as well as possible, it was going to be a long haul. It didn't take me long to satisfy myself that the bounty hunters' crew were very good indeed; a bit over-cautious perhaps, but you only get one shot at staying alive, so fair enough. Their employers were equally professional, and I could see why. Tied to the rail of their ship was the ultimate big score, the shining pinnacle of achievement in the circumscribed universe of their vocation (me). An opportunity like me had never come up before and most likely never would again. On me depended all their hopes and dreams – money, security, a life of respected ease, the validation of all the years they'd committed to the trade and all the hardships they'd endured for its sake. It was one hell of a responsibility, though I'm ashamed to say I didn't feel it quite as keenly as I should have. From their perspective, getting me from Ildra to Port Seccone was the single most important event in their lives, the defining moment; nothing could ever matter more than getting it exactly right.

Which meant, among other things, that I didn't stand a chance. I spent days trying to figure out a way of escaping, which kept me entertained but achieved nothing else. I was chained to the rail, so there were no knots to unpick or ropes to fray against projecting edges. Even if I managed it some-how, the only way I could go was over the side; all the crew and most of the bounty hunters were far better swimmers than me. I knew that because I'd watched them. There was a circle chalked on the deck – no weapons beyond this point, in case I somehow managed to grab one. I was chained up in such a way that I could shit over the side without needing to be unlocked, and my food was shovelled into my mouth with a long wooden spoon. I'm guessing they'd decided on how they were going to do it way in advance, probably hammering out the details round a table somewhere far into the night. I'm not easily impressed but I couldn't fault them on anything. They were that good.

So there was nothing for me to do except pass the time, and there's an interesting thing, if such things interest you. Time: timing; the nature of the process by which a unit of future becomes a unit of past through the agency of the present. If there's anything in this story of mine apart from a few rather sloppy adventures in which nobody can be said to have distin-guished themselves particularly, it's a study in the operation of time. You'll have noticed my ambivalent position with regard to it. For some of the story I'm the active manager and producer of time – spinning it out, cutting it short, using time as a lever to make the strong weak and the weak strong, manipulating the gearing ratio between time and distance until getting things in the right place at the right time came very close to upsetting all the natural balance in the world – between the Knights and the Sisters, the factions on Sirupat, the third, fourth and fifth pans; as soon as they looked like their true weight was about to reassert itself, I'd sprinkle a few grains of time over a pan and set the balances swaying wildly again, like that fucking boat in the middle of the stormy sea.

All very admirable, you'll say, and enough to justify my arbitrary assumption of the role of hero; but then consider me through the rest of the story, passive, the object and the prisoner of time, time's cargo, the livestock it propels unwillingly to market. Nothing in the least heroic about that, though I'm guessing you can empathise much more with the passive, bound-hand-and-foot me, because that's what life is like, especially when you aren't the one writing the play. But if I'd learned anything along the way, and particularly in the steward's quarters on Sirupat and chained to the rail of the bounty hunters' ship, it was the merit inherent in letting time pass – I'm not entirely sure what I mean by that. Simply accepting, not resisting, what the Left Hand means when it talks about turning the other cheek: bugger that for a game of soldiers. That's just cowardice, not jumping out the window and running away because you're afraid of cutting your finger on the broken glass. The nearest I can get to making it mean anything at all is the closing stages of the passive game, in which you direct yourself into the inevitable path of defeat not through misfortune or failure but by an act of will – no, I thought not. Meaningless after all. Forget I mentioned it.

Nine days, I think, give or take a day. As far as I could make out, we were more or less exactly on course and schedule. I'd done the calculations, hindered by a certain deficiency of information (such as how fast we were going, where exactly we were and how far we had to go) and I reckoned that we still had somewhere between fifteen and nineteen days to go before we reached Port Seccone. If you're wondering where the hell that is, by the way, don't feel ashamed of your ignorance. It's not on most maps. Port Seccone is a small harbour which my father inherited from his great-uncle the archduke, who got it as part of his son's dowry. It's small and rundown and it badly needs dredging, but my father's always insisted on using it for all our maritime business because it's ours, inhouse, so to speak. He's absurdly proud of it because (in his words) it makes up the set – one of everything. A gentleman should have at least one of everything, he maintains, so as not to have to depend on strangers for anything: his own estate, his own forest, his own mountain, his own river, his own lake, his own coal mine, his own iron foundry, his own mill, his own ship, his own harbour, his own army and so on. I pointed out to him once, only joking, that he hadn't really got the set because he didn't have his own sea. He got quite upset and sent me to my room.

And the morning and the evening were the ninth incredibly boring day, and it was dark, and I fell asleep. I was woken by yelling and heat. I opened my eyes and saw red plumes fifteen feet high. The ship was on fire.

One of the bounty hunters was crouching over me. He had a hammer and a cold chisel. It occurred to me that I was comprehensively chained to a substantial oak rail. It was bright as daylight because of the fire. He pushed me back to give himself room to work.

I've had a lot of experience with cutting rivets, so I could've told him. You need something firm to rest on, like a tree stump or an anvil. Trying to cut a rivet with the work balanced on your or someone else's knee is an accident waiting to happen. It didn't wait very long. He bashed the chisel with the hammer, the blade skidded off the rivet and sank into my thigh. I yelled. He dropped the chisel. He scrabbled for it on the deck, got hold of it, dropped it again. It bounced and went skittering over the side into the deep blue sea.

He let out a wail of rage, terror and frustration, all three packaged up together like a tin miner's dinner. Clearly he hadn't got another chisel, or at least not where he could get at it. We were only fifty-odd yards from the shore, but the ship was going to burn up or sink with me still firmly secured to it: the one and only, the big score, all his troubles over for ever and ever and never having to work again. I can't say I was thrilled about it either, but he was out of his mind with anger and loss.

He jumped up. "Don't leave me," I screamed at him, but he went away, not far; he came back with a saw and an axe. The fire was close enough to be uncomfortable. I could hear splashes in the water, men jumping overboard. He was sawing the rail. The saw clented, about halfway through. He roared abuse at it, left it stuck in the rail and picked up the axe. It was an oak rail. There wasn't time.

I was howling at him: don't leave me, get on with it, hurry, I'm going to *die*. Whether it helped or hindered I don't know; I don't suppose he was paying me any attention. I could feel the fire cooking the skin on my face. He gave the rail an almighty kick; it splintered where he'd chopped a wedge out of it, but it didn't break through.

Someone else was yelling at him. I looked round. Another man, I couldn't see his face, was laying into the other side of the rail with a sledgehammer. It broke. The first man had another go at the splintered rail. He gave it an almighty hack, which did the job. The effort made him stagger back. He tripped and fell backwards into the fire. His clothes and hair caught; he tried to get up but all his strength had turned instantly into steam, and all he could do was scream. The other man had hold of the length of rail I was still chained to. If I went in the water, the weight of it, and the chains, would drag me straight down to the bottom. All that effort for nothing. The big score. My life.

Something flashed, down in the water. He saw it the same moment I did. Something brass or gold, and a voice yelling at us, jump, jump. He hesitated, and I realised the source of the voices was a boat. The hell with it, I thought. I leaned backwards until I toppled, and a moment later the water hit me. I remember how it stung on my burned skin, and then I was being dragged. My head caught a hard lump of wood, presumably the side of the boat, and I was aboard, alive, coughing up seawater.

There was a splash. The man from the ship had jumped in and was thrashing about in the water next to the boat. Someone leaned across me, holding something long. It proved to be a spear. He stuck it into the man in the water, and he went down and vanished.

The brass thing I'd seen proved to be a Peguilhan siphon. My back was to it as we rowed back to land.

The ship went down in a tall column of steam as they ran

the boat up the beach and lifted me out on my section of rail, like game brought home from the hunt. They'd rowed out to save us, in a boat fitted with a Peguilhan siphon. They'd saved me and speared the bounty hunter. Life is full of surprises.

They had a driftwood fire going, about halfway up the beach. I noticed they were wearing monks' habits. Monks do a lot of things to bring in much-needed cash money; they make mead and cider, they spin yarn and weave cloth, they copy out books, but an order of wreckers? New one on me.

"Where is he?" said a voice I recognised, and I thought, oh.

11

"God, you're a mess," she said.

I should have figured it out the moment I saw the Peguilhan siphon, but terror has a way of addling your wits. The monks, men dressed as monks, were her crew, the League of Mercy or whatever they call themselves; last I saw of them, we were turning them loose in the desert to walk to the coast after we ambushed them and took back all the stuff they'd robbed from us. It seemed a lifetime ago and a different state of existence, but from the way they scowled at me I concluded that they remembered and bore grudges. Screw them.

I looked up at her. She was immaculately dressed in a riding outfit of red silk brocade with hambone sleeves, nicely set off by a simple pearl necklace. "What's going on?" I asked. I thought it was a reasonable question, but she sighed.

"I just saved your stupid life," she said.

"Ah."

She nodded, and someone brought her a stool. She sat down behind me. Someone was dabbing at the gash in my leg with something liquid in a bowl that stung like hell. "Those men were going to take you to your father. You knew that, didn't you?"

"Yes."

"So he could kill you."

"Yes."

"Well, then." In the firelight she looked like an angel. "Just as well I came along, isn't it?"

I didn't feel strong enough for a fight, or even our usual exchange of pleasantries. Even so, one must make the effort. "That depends," I said.

"Why do you have to be a jerk about everything? You were going to die. I rescued you. Couldn't you be just a tiny bit grateful?"

I wouldn't have minded listening but I really didn't want to talk. "The siphon thing." At that moment I couldn't remember the name Peguilhan. "You set fire to the ship."

"Only way," she said briskly. "It didn't occur to me they'd chain you to the side like that. You were lucky."

My head was splitting and my throat was still raw from coughing up seawater. "What are you going to do with me?"

She rolled her eyes. "Typical," she said. "Everything's always got to be about you, hasn't it?"

Yes, apparently. I really wish it wasn't. "I'm sorry," I said. "I'd like to know, that's all."

"The hell with what you want," she said. I'd offended her, apparently. "Get him on the cart; it's time we moved on," she told someone or other. "I want to be in Opona by sunrise."

On the cart they sawed up the section of rail and hacksawed through the chain, leaving me with a couple of steel charm bracelets I could've done without but otherwise free as a bird.

They had the sense not to try and cut rivets on a cart in the dark, for which I was truly grateful.

"You arsehole," one of the monks said to me. "You make me sick."

I didn't answer.

"Six days we were out in the fucking desert," he said. "One mouthful of water each to last a whole day. We could've died. And now, here were are, risking our lives to rescue you. Fuck that. You call it right, because I don't."

"What's she going to do with me, do you know?"

He didn't answer. Fair enough.

Day broke and we were still on the road. We stopped. Someone lit a fire and boiled a big pot of water. I looked round for her and saw her talking to people, too far away to hear what she was saying. Someone came and offered me a drink from an enamel canteen. "Though you don't deserve it," he added. "After what you put us through back in the desert."

"I know. I'm sorry."

"No, you're not." He sat down beside me while I drank. "That was one hell of a show," he said.

"Excuse me?"

"Last night." He was considerably younger than the other monks I'd spoken to. He sounded like he was having fun. "That siphon thing. Marvellous piece of kit."

"Worth a lot of money," I said.

"I hope we keep it." He took the canteen from me and swallowed four greedy mouthfuls. "Come in bloody useful, something like that. A couple of pumps on the handle and whoosh!" He illustrated joyfully with both hands. "One sweep and the whole side of the ship was burning."

"Amazing," I said.

"You bet. And the great thing is, that stuff carries on burning even if you pour water on it." He lowered his voice. "She told the Sisters it got lost along with the galley, so nobody knows we've got it. Don't see why you couldn't use it on land as well as on a boat. Brilliant thing to have by you in case anything ever goes wrong."

It took me a while, but I gradually got the story out of him. After the Knights arrived in force, she was told to pull out in good order and wait on the mainland for further instructions. Someone, I don't know who, mentioned to her in confidence that her handling of events on Sirupat hadn't won her any friends back at head office – which was unfair, if you ask me; she did as good a job as anyone could've done, under trying circumstances, but that's the Sisters for you. So she wrote to her crew and told them to meet her, taking a leaf out of my book, I flatter myself; she liberated a few bits and pieces from the expeditionary force before she slipped away, the siphon, some supplies, a trifle of money, and then set off overland with a view to getting as far away from the coming war as she possibly could. She'd gone as far as Choris Seautou when she happened to bump into Dariau Asvogel, who mentioned in conversation that someone or other he didn't know had just made the biggest score of all time: half a million staurata, the bounty on Florian met'Oc. You know, he added, your friend and mine Saevus Corax. A pity, Dariau added, because opportunities like that don't come up every day and if only he'd known in time who I really was—

She thought quickly. She had no idea where I was or what sort of ship I'd be on, but she figured it out from first principles – roughly when I'd left Sirupat, when and where Dariau had heard the rumour; combine that with what every sailor knows about sailing down the coast in the off season and she had a fair idea of where we'd have to pass by. Once she'd established that, she rode like hell across country to get there before the ship did—

"Why?" I asked him.

"You what?"

"Why did she go to all that trouble, just to get hold of me?"

He laughed. "She doesn't tell us stuff like that," he said, "and we don't ask."

"Sensible."

We shared a look. "You know her, then."

"Oh, yes."

Grave nod. "So your guess is as good as mine, really. Though I wouldn't be surprised if that half million isn't something to do with it."

"You reckon."

"Sure. I mean, your old man isn't going to care who hands you over so long as he gets you, right? Or there's that other one, the Elector."

"My brother-in-law."

"I heard he's upped his offer to five hundred fifty thousand. Sort of like an auction." He frowned. "Lovely relatives you've got."

"You should meet my aunt."

He looked blank, then went on: "What a load of bastards. No offence," he added.

"None taken."

"They sound really horrible. Can't say I'd be happy in your shoes."

"I haven't got any shoes."

Another blank look, then he glanced down at my feet.

"Shit," he said kindly. "Here." He dived into a duffle bag he had next to him and produced a pair of boots. They were grey with mildew. "Try those."

"You sure?"

He waved away my uncertainty. "Get on," he said. "They're not my size and they're not worth anything."

They weren't my size either, but I put them on anyway. "Thanks," I said. "Now I can die with my boots on."

He laughed like that was the funniest thing he'd heard in all his life.

We didn't make Opona by dawn as she'd hoped. The road was bad after some recent rain, and the driver of the cart in front of mine somehow contrived to get stuck in a stone-built gateway. Everybody jumped off to help break it down apart from my new friend the young monk, who stayed to guard me. He was watching the demolition efforts, and the hilt of his knife was sticking out of his belt. I didn't owe him anything, apart from a pair of worthless boots.

It occurred to me: my life or his. I could almost see the sunlight flashing on the swaying pans. Two human beings, which one is worth more: to society at large, his friends and family, to himself? Which of us – think before you decide – would you have chosen?

Me too. I stayed where I was.

It was my second visit to Opona. Most people never go there. Those who go there once and somehow contrive to leave rarely come back if they can help it. It's the roadhead for the vast linen plantations of the Ops valley, and every year the workforce is topped up with expendable people: prisoners of war, indentured criminals, debtors working off their time. It's the damp that gets them, Chusro Asvogel told me once. He makes a lot of money in Opona, though he doesn't go there himself.

It hadn't changed much since I was there last. In fact, the two visits were remarkably similar in several ways. Both times I arrived unwillingly, under guard, wearing steel bracelets, on a cart. The first time, I was there because I'd miscalculated the dimensions of a window: I thought it was big enough to get through. I didn't take to Opona. It's what you might call an unsalubrious neighbourhood. Give you an example: the night I left, a guard broke his neck and a horse went missing. It's that sort of place.

"Been here before?" I asked the monk.

He nodded. "Gives me the creeps."

"It's not so bad," I told him. "I've been in worse places than this, believe me."

"Yeah? Such as where?"

"Sirupat."

He considered that. "Never been there."

"Don't bother," I told him. "It's a dump."

"That's where the war is, right?"

"Excellent reason for not going there."

He shrugged. "War's all right," he said. "I'm going to be a soldier one day."

Opona – the last square in the passive game. In the theology of the Left Hand, the Redeemer somehow contrives to cancel out all the sins of the world by allowing himself to be strung up on a gibbet. I can't see it myself. What use to anybody is a god who loses? Surely you'd want your god to be the biggest, strongest, meanest sonofabitch in the whole of Heaven. But I guess it follows, because the Left Hand has traditionally been the sect of losers – the poor, the downtrodden, the victimised, the inept; the sort of people who know they'll never win, no matter how many gods they have on their side. So, in order to make sense of the universe, they make a virtue of losing. Losing, they say, is good. Loss is victory, and victory is loss. All the things that normal people regard as virtues are vices to them – courage, strength, wealth, success, power, the ability to dominate others and bend them to your will. You can see why, when I first learned that I was destined to be the Redeemer, I laughed like a drain. That's just cheating, I said. You cheat and you still don't get to win.

I don't think anybody's ever told them about the Left Hand in Opona, though I imagine it would go down big if anyone ever did. There's a big square in the middle of town where dealers bring workers they've bought on spec and auction them off. It's a place where a man can truly discover his own value; is he worth anything to anybody or not? Many are brought but few are purchased; the linen farmers don't like buying on the spot market and only go to the auctions to make up unexpected losses mid-season, when every pair of hands is valuable. I've never had the privilege of going up on the block in that market, which is probably just as well. I know my own worth without needing to be told. If I was me, I wouldn't buy me, not even if you threw in the boots.

Just off the big square is an inn, the Shining Path. It's the only place in Opona with proper stabling for draught horses, so that's where we went. From the stable window you can look out over the sea and see the ships rounding the little cape. My pal the young monk tied me to a beam. "She's afraid you'll skip out," he said, as though he thought she was being totally unreasonable. I sat and watched the ships for a while, and then she came to see me.

"You dickhead," she said. "You really know how to make trouble for people."

I thought about that. "I'm good at it," I said. "I get a lot of help, mind."

She wasn't in the mood. "Have you any idea how much all of this has cost me?"

"About two hundred staurata," I replied, though I was just guessing. "You stole the siphon, so I'm not counting that."

"Fuck you," she said. "It means I can't go back to the Sisters: they'll be wanting my head on a pike. I'll never be able to do business with the Knights ever again. Quite likely they'll be after my blood, too. Everybody's going to hate me for ever and ever. I might as well be you."

"Don't say that. It's too horrible."

"Will you stop making stupid jokes? It's not funny. The Sisters and the Knights. I must've been out of my mind."

"I wouldn't worry too much about them," I said, "either of them. I have an idea they aren't going to matter quite so much before very long."

"Bullshit," she said. "They're going to come out of this stupid war you started stronger than ever. They're going to rule the fucking world. And they're both going to want to hang me, because of you."

I sighed. "Just as well you're about to come into a lot of money," I said.

"You what?"

"Half a million staurata. Or half a million plus fifty grand, if you go with my brother-in-law."

She looked at me. "Half a million staurata. For you."

"I'm worth it," I told her. "To them."

"You aren't worth twenty trachy."

"Intrinsically, no. But it's what people are prepared to pay."

She looked at me some more. I got the impression she was very angry. "You're full of it, you know that? Because you're a duke's son, you think you *matter*. All your life you've had people crawling over you because of who you are. Not what you are, but who. I think that's disgusting."

"So do I," I said. "though I have to say, it hasn't done me much good, all things considered."

"You clown. Who cares what you think?"

I felt like I was missing the point somehow. Time to change the subject. "So," I said, "which of them is it going to be?"

"What?"

"My father or my brother-in-law. The Elector's offering fifty thousand more, but my father's closer, and you know what they say, many a slip and all that. This may be one of those cases where it's wiser to go with the lower offer."

She hit me. Anyone who says girls can't hit worth a damn doesn't know what he's talking about. She trapped my lower lip against my teeth, and that hurts.

She was sucking her knuckles. "You didn't answer my question," I said, as best I could with a thick lip.

"Neither."

"Excuse me?"

"Not your horrible father and not your disgusting brother-in-law. Not anyone." She fumbled in her sleeve and produced a knife, a folder with an ivory handle. Come to think of it, it used to belong to me. She opened the blade and I heard it click.

Well, I thought. So this is the end of the line: last square of the passive game. I was surprised to find that I wasn't bothered after all. My throat cut in a barn, tied to a post like a bullock. There are worse ways to go, I guess. "Really," I said. "I didn't know you hated me so much. Not half a million staurata's worth."

"Oh, shut up," she said, and cut the ropes.

The worst thing a general can say: I wasn't expecting that. Mind you, I'm not a general.

I felt there was a point that needed to be clarified. "You're not going to kill me."

"No."

"In spite of everything I've done."

She gave me an oh-for-pity's-sake look. "You need to get over yourself," she said. "Yes, you can be a real piece of work sometimes. But if you're trying to make yourself out as some kind of unspeakable monster that needs to be put down for the sake of humanity, you've got delusions of grandeur. Sorry to break it to you, but there's at least seven people nastier than you that I can think of just like that. Well," she couldn't help adding, "six."

"Are you on the list?"

"Oh, definitely."

We looked at each other and the inconceivable penny dropped. Maybe I should've seen it coming, or at least entertained it as a possibility; no, scrub that. I like her a lot, but it wasn't an idea I could ever have had. Me or half a million, cash? Oh, come on.

"What I had in mind," she said, rather quickly, not looking at me, "was a partnership. You've got the men and the facilities, I've got the contacts for the really big undertakings. Together we could really give the Asvogels a run for their money. You don't get the fat contracts because nobody likes you. You piss them off cracking stupid jokes. I know how to talk to people in authority. Well?"

I looked at her. "Five hundred thousand staurata," I said.

"Blood money. I don't do that. I have principles."

"Like hell you do."

"Look," she said. "Do you want to join forces or not? Because now everybody knows who you are, you're going to have a hell of a job just showing your face out of doors, let alone fixing up deals with major governments. Obviously I need to expand but I haven't got the capital to go up against an outfit like the Asvogels, so really it boils down to a question of infrastructure – are you listening to me?"

I was staring out of the window. "You might want to have a look at this," I said.

She leaned over me. What she saw was a fleet of ships.

That's hopelessly inadequate. All you could see was ships: long, high-sided war galleys, two hundred oars each side in banks of three. It was a sight that nobody had ever seen before, certainly not in our part of the world, and which I sincerely hope nobody will ever see again. I bet you a squirrel could've crossed from the harbour to the cape, jumping from mast to mast. It was the most beautiful sight I'd ever seen in my entire life, and you know how I usually feel about ships.

"My God," she said. "What is it?"

"Oh, that," I said, trying to sound flippant, but my voice cracked up. "That's the Imperial Sashan navy. My guess is, they're on their way to annex Sirupat."

She gazed at me. "What have you done?"

I couldn't speak for a moment. I had to breathe in and out deeply a couple of times. "I wrote a letter," I said. "I used your

galley to send it, as a matter of fact. I really didn't know if it
was going to work or not, not till I saw *that*. It's like a dream
come true."

"You *maniac*. What did you—?"

"I wrote to the Sashan emperor," I said. "In my official
capacity as king of Sirupat and defender of the faith or whatever you call it, sealed with the great seal and everything.
Basically, I gave him Sirupat."

"You can't just give away countries."

"Oh, yes you can," I said. "My family does it all the time:
dowries and stuff. I also pointed out that the Poor Sisters, a
religious group of great power, were hell-bent on obtaining the
revenues of Sirupat to finance a crusade against the true faith."

"That's bullshit."

"Obviously the emperor didn't think so," I said. "I told him
in my letter that I knew for a fact that the Sisters' sole object
was to spread the cult of the Invincible Sun, by force if necessary, all across the East, through Sashan and right down into
Echmen and beyond. I said I couldn't stand by and let that
happen, so I was officially calling on him to intervene, in the
name of the Redeemer—"

"But they're all Right Hand in Sashan."

"Who isn't," I told her, "me. I formally denied the Left
Hand heresy, in writing. By accepting the surrender of Sirupat,
I told him, not only would he frustrate the infidel crusaders,
he'd have a once-in-a-lifetime chance to unite the true faith
and put an end to a thousand years of schism and sectarian
violence. Probably that's what swung it, but I guess we'll
never know."

She gazed at me. "You did that."

"Yup," I said. "It means there isn't going to be a war."

That took a moment to sink in. "I suppose not," she said.

I couldn't take my eyes off all those beautiful ships. "You bet your life not," I said. "Look at them. In midsummer, maybe, when the winds are in the right direction and speed and manoeuvrability count for more than sheer bulk; right now, though, even if all the governments in the West were to get together and send out every ship they've got, they wouldn't stand a chance against that lot. There must be eighty thousand men on those ships, and total command of the sea. There won't even be a siege. The garrison will just fold up and go quietly, and the Sashan will take over. No bloodshed," I said. "Not even raised voices." I turned away and looked at her. "And I did that," I said. "Just me and some paper and ink. Though I say it myself, that's smart."

"Yes," she said quietly. "I suppose it is."

"Thank you. Your opinion matters to me. Anyway, you can see what I mean about the Sisters and the Knights not mattering very much. With the Sashan holding Sirupat and the gold supply cut off, the governments they lent all that money to will go broke and have no choice but to default on their loans. That'll be the end of both banks. They'll have far too much on their minds to bother about you."

"Or you."

"With Sirupat gone, I'm nobody. This is just as good as if there'd been a monster earthquake and the whole island sank under the sea." I paused for a moment to listen to what I'd just said. Not my fault. I didn't start it. "I did hear a rumour a while back about my brother-in-law the Elector being into the Knights for something around two million, but I don't suppose it's true. You can't have everything."

*

It was a bit awkward after that. I wanted to find some reason for what she'd done, other than the one which seemed to present itself, but I couldn't. Like the old joke about the drunk under the lamp. You know that one? Bet you do. It goes like this.

An officer of the watch is patrolling one night and he comes across a drunk, scrabbling about on the ground under a lamp. He's a kind-hearted watchman (this is fiction, remember) so he asks, what are you looking for? Dropped my key, says the drunk. So the watchman gets down on his hands and knees and helps look for it. Long search, no key. Finally the watchman says, you sure you dropped it here? No, says the drunk, over there, by my house. Then what the hell are you looking over here for? There's more light here, says the drunk.

Told you you'd heard it. The point being, I didn't want to look for my key where it was, presumably for fear of finding it. So I had it occur to me that her real motivation was the hundred thousand staurata, hidden on Ogyge. Bet you anything you like, I told myself, that Ekkehard told her about it in an unguarded moment, and now she wants it. The big score, after all: everybody wants the big score; what else is there to want? She knew (here I had to flatter myself outrageously, but I can do that if I really set my mind to it) that she'd never get me as far as Port Saccone, not with the deadheads she had for muscle; hadn't I had a golden opportunity to leg it when the cart got stuck in the gate, so she was perfectly justified in thinking that way. No: a hundred thousand in the hand is worth half a million that eludes you at the last moment in the prickliest part of the bush. It's still more money than the mind can comfortably conceive of, more than you'd ever spend in a lifetime unless you like to while away your afternoons building palaces and then burning them down. That would account for all the known facts, I told myself. Smart girl, that, and a realist into the bargain.

Fine, I thought. "We need to go to Ogyge," I said.

We'd spent the morning watching the Sashan fleet, trying to count it, giving up. Once they were clear of the bottleneck around the cape, they'd have a clear run to Sirupat across the open sea, which would be easy as pie at this time of year, going in that direction. Somewhere between eight hundred and a thousand ships. I'd been hoping the Great King would send a fair-sized fleet. It never occurred to me that he might send them all.

"Really?"

"Yes," I said. "Straight away. I've got a large sum of money stashed away there. It could be our working capital. For the partnership."

"Where's Ogyge?"

"It's an island off the north coast, about three miles off Mesembrotia."

She thought for a moment. "We'll have to go overland," she said, "at this time of year, so that means due west till we hit the Northern Mail, up that as far as the Lakes; is there a road going north from the Lakes? I don't know that area."

I looked at her. Smart and well-informed, and maybe she'd already been thinking about how you get from Opona to Ogyge. "Best thing would be to follow the river valleys," I said. "It's a bit of a dog-leg, but quicker in the long run."

"Whatever," she said. "I'll tell them to get ready to leave."

It's never a barrel of laughs on the Northern Mail at the best of times. It's a good road, arrow-straight, magnificently built on an embankment, rubble under a layer of crushed rock under a layer of gravel and pebbles overlaid with inch-thick slabs on a bed of sand, with all the trees and bushes cut down for a hundred yards' width on either side so there's nowhere you can be jumped out on from. But it runs across flat, open country and the wind howls round you all the time, cutting you to the bone and making it impossible to hear what anybody says to you. That was probably just as well. She didn't seem to want to talk to me, the way my sister used to be when I'd forgotten her birthday, and I didn't mind that at all.

So I filled in the time thinking about what had just happened. I was still alive. There wasn't going to be a war. The banks were about to be in desperate trouble, and even if they recovered from it, they no longer had any reason to hassle me. I'd even contrived to square myself with the Right Hand, which meant I'd be able to set foot on Sashan soil without risking instant death. I'd managed to bring all this about without shedding gallons and gallons of blood, which was nice. Apart from my family and maybe a few surviving Left Handers, nobody was after me any more. And my father couldn't live for ever, and if the Elector lost all his money in the bank crash—

A man might have been forgiven for thinking that he'd reached the last square of the active game, but it didn't feel that way. More of a beginning than an ending, I had this nasty feeling, and not the beginning of anything good. I wasn't sure about the prospect of life as newly unmasked Florian met'Oc. I'd been him once, but all he did was get me in trouble (like Ekkehard and all my friends, not to mention my relations) and I never wanted to see him again, especially in a mirror. As far as I was concerned, he was never me. Instead I made myself Saevus Corax, lovingly crafted out of the very finest sustainable lies by an artist who really cared about his work. He was fun while he lasted, but I had an unpleasant feeling I wasn't going to be allowed to keep him.

"What's the matter with you?" she asked me, as we sat under the cart, sheltering from one of those sudden storms you get in the hills at that time of year.

"I don't know," I said. "What's the matter with you?"

"Don't change the subject. You've hardly said a word for three days." She scowled at me. "I ought to tell you, sulking's not an attractive trait."

"I'm not sulking."

She was staring out at the gap between the bottom of the cart and the ground. Nothing to see but rain in the distance and water dripping off the boards close up. "You got away with it, then."

By coincidence, just what I'd been thinking. "I guess so," I said. "I'm still alive. That's score one to me in the great game of Being."

We were both wet through, with no change of clothes left; everything we owned was soaked through. The water dribbling down my face was the closest I ever get to tears. I can't cry myself, so God has to do it for me. "Don't be like that," she said. "You did good. You stopped the war."

I faked a yawn. "I got out of there in one piece," I told her. "Stopping the war was the only way I could think of to manage it. I'd have sneaked out and run like a hare if we hadn't been on an island."

"Balls," she said. "You stopped the war. You were willing to die, remember? On the ship?"

"Can we talk about something else, please?"

"You did everything you possibly could to make sure there wouldn't be a war."

I think she knows me quite well. Otherwise, why did she choose the one thing that made me most uncomfortable to rub my nose in? "Fine," I snapped, "I stopped the war, which would never have started except for me. In order to do that, I played chess with people's lives and fucked up the economy of the known world to the point where it'll take decades to recover. People are going to starve to death this winter because of what I just did. I'd do it all over again in a flash if I had to, but it's still not a happy thought for me, so could we please change the subject?"

She grinned. "You don't like it when someone says something nice about you."

"Quite," I said. "I don't trust liars."

All she did was smile at me. "That's rather good," she said. "You say the cutest things sometimes."

It was still raining when we reached the Lakes, and kept on raining all the way round the edge, and halfway up the Eastern Military, which we'd decided on as the quickest route to the north coast. The tents got so sodden they split, so we slept sitting back to back under the wagons with the rain hammering on the floorboards over our heads and dripping down through the cracks between them. No way to get a fire started when everything's soaking wet, so we ate stale soggy bread and drank the water puddled in the crowns of our hats. It's a glamorous life on the road, and you can see why I prefer it to perfumed luxury. By the time we reached the coast we stank of wet wool and mildew and none of us could stop shivering. We paused in Nishrada to buy a second-hand winch from a copper mine, which took most of our ready cash. What do you want it for, they asked me. I can't remember what I told them.

It hammered down all the way across Mesembrotia. We were on country roads now, and the carts kept getting stuck. Unsticking them meant shovelling mud, laying down mud-soaked sacking under the wheels, pushing and shoving up to our knees in mud, sliding and falling down in mud, skinned knuckles and gashed hands and faces, bits of sopping wet muddy rag wrapped round the cuts to stop the bleeding, eyes full of rain, tempers raw, words spoken in haste and festering afterwards like blackthorn tips just under your skin. She had the sense to keep out of the way but I had to muscle in and take charge, because it always infuriates me when I watch people doing things wrong. Suffice to say I didn't make many friends among the monks, though they learned quickly enough to do as I told them. By the time we reached the coast we were barely human, more like a pack of snarling, hungry dogs. I left the rest of them huddled in a barn on the edge of town and went looking for a boat.

No boats. Only a lunatic would put out to sea in those conditions. How long? Hard to tell. When the storms set in from the east, it could be weeks before you'd even think of getting on a boat. Ogyge? Hadn't I ever heard of rip tides? Not a chance. The only way you're going to get to Ogyge this side of the equinox is if you go up the coast twenty miles to Calumno and come in on a slant, but then you'll be stuck there for a month because there'll be no way back, and nobody's going to want to take you there, not for any money.

So we went to Calumno. No boats at Calumno, and just asking got me growled at. Why? Because about a month ago, some lunatic turned up wanting to go to Ogyge, just like I did, and he talked poor old So-and-so into taking him there, with some big heavy thing in a crate and five or six goons. They were there a day or so and then the man and the goons came back with a load of heavy parcels wrapped in oilskin. Poor old So-and-so said, are you mad, that much weight, in this weather, but the lunatic wouldn't listen and the goons cut up rough, so they sailed anyway, got as far as the Six Goblins and the boat hit a rock and went all to pieces. Old So-and-so and one of the goons made it ashore, but the goon died the next day, on account of all his insides being smashed up when the waves ground him against the rock. And that was before the weather really got nasty, so no boat, not till equinox—

"That's all right," I said. "I changed my mind. Thanks anyway."

So much for the big score. Come to think of it, I never heard of anyone who actually made it. Substantial profits, yes, accumulated over time; but the once and future bonanza, all your troubles over in one lucky strike, no. Unless you define all your troubles being over as the last square in the active game, where you win all along the line and screw it up at the very last moment. That seems to happen a lot, in my experience.

"What are you doing?" she asked me.

"Crying," I said. "Go away."

For Ekkehard, of all people. When they told me about him in Calumno I felt a moment of shock, like I'd just walked into a door with my eyes shut, but I didn't burst out blubbering all over the place. That came later, just when I thought I'd put him out of my mind for good. Ekkehard, who repeatedly sold me down the river and died trying to steal my money. I felt like

I'd murdered him, by putting the temptation in his way. But it was really just an accident, like the last time.

Finally it stopped raining. We put up lines and hung out our clothes to dry in the biting cold wind. The monks were profoundly unhappy – all that travel and misery and nothing to show for it. I wasn't at my best and brightest, and she was keeping herself to herself. We were more or less out of money, two of the horses died and one of the carts was a write-off. I kept telling myself: yes, but you're not on Sirupat. It should have made up for everything. Maybe I wasn't doing it right.

She found a bit of wood and some pebbles and made a Doubles board. I have no idea what put it into her mind to do that. "Teach me to play," she said.

I don't kid that easily. She'd played before. In fact, she was better at the game than I was, as I discovered shortly after we started playing for money. Notional money, of course, since we didn't have any of the real stuff and no prospect of getting any. But it passed the time.

"It's a funny thing," she said. "We seem to get on like a house on fire when we're on opposite sides of something. Your move."

She'd only left me one. I made it. Down she came on me like a ton of bricks. "Game," she said. "Right, how much do you owe me?"

"Just a second," I said. "I'll work it out."

"I make it five hundred and fifty thousand, one hundred and seven staurata."

I made it a hundred and seven, but I could see her point. "IOU?"

"Forget it," she said. "I'm feeling generous. Go again?"

"Why not?"

She was setting out the pieces when two horsemen rode up. They had big floppy hats, to keep the rain off, so I didn't see their faces. "'Scuse me," said one of them. "Do you know a place round here called Calumno?"

"Polycrates?"

He nearly fell off his horse. Gombryas (under the other hat) let out a whoop of joy, jumped down and gave me a hug that nearly broke my ribs. He trod on the Doubles board, I couldn't help noticing. "We heard you were dead," he told me, tears running down his stupid face. "We heard bounty hunters got you."

"They did."

"What's she doing here?" Polycrates said.

"She's who rescued me from the bounty hunters." Two stunned faces, so I couldn't resist adding, "We're going into business together, so meet your new boss."

"You fucking what?" Polycrates roared.

I put a finger to my lips and shushed gently. "If you don't like it, you know what you can do," I told him. "You, too, Gombryas."

Gombryas took three deep breaths, one after another. "Well, you're still alive," he said. "That's good, anyway."

"While I think of it," I said, "don't bother going to Calumno, because there's no money. Ekkehard got here before we did, but he drowned. The money's at the bottom of the sea."

Polycrates curled up in a little ball and started sobbing in swear words. Gombryas looked at me, then at her, then rolled his eyes. "Glad you're all right," he said. "We'd better tell the others."

They got back on their horses and rode away. I could hear Polycrates cursing in the distance for quite some time. She'd picked up the Doubles board and was holding the two halves together along the break.

"Linen backing and a bit of glue," I told her. "No problem."

"Can't be bothered," she said, and dropped them.

Nuts, I thought. Still, might as well have a stab at it. "Listen," I said.

She stood up. "I'm not in the mood for talking right now."

She walked away. I got up and trotted after her, feeling like an idiot. "Will you please listen? Thank you. It's like this."

"Well?"

Come on, you can do this. Imagine it's a scene in a play. That didn't help one bit. "Nobody ever let me go before," I said. "I always had to beat up a guard or jump out of a window."

She just looked tired. "So?"

"And I've spent my whole life with people after my blood," I said. "Everybody I meet, I'm asking myself, does he know who I really am? I'm sorry. I can't help it. That's what that kind of a life does to you."

"I know who you really are," she said. "But what the hell. You're nothing special, once you get to know you."

It occurred to me that that was the kindest thing anyone had ever said to me. "No," I said, "I'm not. I used to be, but with any luck that's all over now."

She nodded. I'd parsed the compliment correctly; clever me. "It's all right," she said. "I'm patient. I can wait. And while I'm waiting something better might come along, you never know." She started walking again. "Your friend hates me."

"Polycrates hates everybody."

"The other one didn't seem exactly thrilled, either."

"Gombryas hates you, too," I said. "And I don't think you've met Carrhasio yet. Don't worry about them. It's no big deal."

"Really?"

"Absolutely," I said. "It seems like only yesterday I hated you to bits. And now I owe you half a million staurata. People change."

"No," she said, "they don't. You can shed your skin but underneath you're still the same snake. Well, aren't you?"

"I don't know," I said. "I've never really been me before."

She stopped again. "I bet you half a million staurata you'll never change," she said. "And I bought a pig in a fucking poke. Silly me, never mind." Then she walked away, and this time I let her go.

The debt is very much on my mind. Half a million is an awful lot of money.

She dissolved the partnership the next day, much to the relief of both crews. I'm ashamed to admit it, but I felt like I'd just been let out of the condemned cell. I still tell myself from time to time that I misread her completely, and if she'd known what was passing through my mind she'd have wet herself laughing. I don't think so, but what do I know? I borrowed seventy staurata from Olybrius – his life savings, just about, and I have no idea when he'll get it back – so she'd have enough to buy bread and lentils and steerage on a ship home. So much for the big score. I'm starting to think that maybe there's no such thing.

Polycrates called a heads-of-department meeting. "You've made a real fuck-up of everything," he told me. "We've got no money, all our stock's gone, we haven't got a place to go to any more and now there isn't going to be a war, so we don't have any work." He gave me one of those looks that comes straight from the heart. "Could it get any worse? Don't think so."

"I agree," I said. "So what do you want to do? Should we give it up and go our separate ways?"

Nobody spoke. "Come on," I said, "let's deal with this. I think Polycrates is right. Everything's gone wrong for this company and I'm to blame. Do you want to carry on but without me, is that it? Somebody say something, for crying out loud. This is no time to be polite. I want to know what you think."

Still nobody spoke. "Fine," I said. "Your last chance. Anybody who thinks he can run this show better than I can, stick your hand in the air and we'll vote on it. Polycrates? Come on, I'll vote for you."

He was flushed and very angry. "I never said that," he said. "I never said I was smarter than you. Just that you'd made a lot of stupid mistakes, that's all. And now you've admitted it, and that's fine. Meeting over, as far as I'm concerned."

"It wasn't your fault," Gombryas said. "Not really."

Various heads nodded. "Just promise me one thing," Carrhasio called out. "That bitch. She's not coming back, right? Because if she is, I'm leaving."

But it's all right. This story has a happy ending. A week later, civil war broke out in Blemya and we got the contract. It wasn't long before we were all back where we belonged, pulling boots off dead feet and stacking up dead men like bricks in a clamp. I was nervous as hell in case bounty hunters came after me, but we had no trouble at all in that direction, and when we sold the stuff at Auxentia Fair, Ormus Asvogel told me the heat was off, for the time being. The Elector had had to default on his bank loans and was broke, and my father had been hit for massively increased taxes because of the economic collapse back home. The money simply wasn't there, so I was safe, for now.

"Fancy you being a fucking duke," Ormus said, pouring me a drink.

"Duke's *son*," I corrected him.

"You, of all people." He grinned. "I always thought you were just another chancer. Did you do it? Really murder your own brother?"

"Yes," I said.

"Fuck me sideways," he said, with something like admiration. "You think you know someone. You want to try some of these shrimps. They're not bad at all."

Truth is ephemeral. It endures no longer than the lifespan of the last credible witness, and then you're free and clear. Also, I've found that the best course is to talk a lot and say as little as possible, and always listen carefully, just in case I learn something I didn't know.

I've spent the last fifteen minutes trying to decide which of the tangled shambles of metaphors I've been using to end with. The game, maybe; the last square of the active game, because I chickened out, or cheated. Or something about time and timing, because that's relevant, too, or perhaps I'd be better off going with scales and balances – time in one pan, truth in the other, me in the third pan squirming like a landed fish.

The hell with it. A better man than me once said that the story is never over, and it never ever ends with a wedding. This has been something of a new departure for me, telling the truth: how it actually happened instead of how it should have happened. I'm not sure I'll ever do it again. I can't really see what's to be gained by it.

Anyway, that's more than enough about me. What have you been up to lately?

The story continues in . . .

Saevus Corax Captures the Castle

Keep reading for a sneak peek!

extras

orbit

meet the author

K. J. Parker is a pseudonym for Tom Holt. He was born in London in 1961. At Oxford he studied bar billiards, ancient Greek agriculture and the care and feeding of small, temperamental Japanese motorcycle engines. These interests led him, perhaps inevitably, to qualify as a solicitor and immigrate to Somerset, where he specialised in death and taxes for seven years before going straight in 1995. He lives in Chard, Somerset, with his wife and daughter.

Find out more about K. J. Parker and other Orbit authors by registering for the free monthly newsletter at orbitbooks.net.

if you enjoyed
SAEVUS CORAX DEALS
WITH THE DEAD

look out for

SAEVUS CORAX
CAPTURES THE CASTLE

by

K. J. Parker

Look out for Book Two of the Corax Trilogy.

1

The other day, for want of anything better to do, I tried to figure out how many people I've killed over the course of my life so far. I came up with a total of eighty-six. That surprised me.

A note on methodology. I'm talking here about people I've killed with my own hands, not the rather large number for whose deaths I could arguably be held morally responsible. Also excluded are those – twenty-seven, give or take – whose deaths I've ordered at the hands of others. If you count them in as well, we get a bottom line of one hundred and thirteen. Either way, that's a lot.

Bear in mind that I'm not and never have been a professional soldier. In my defence, I think I can honestly say I've never killed anyone out of malice, spite, idealism, revenge, for financial gain or just for the sheer hell of it. All those homicides were, as far as I'm concerned, justified; it was them or me. Either directly, because they were coming at me with a weapon, or indirectly, because they were trying to catch me or prevent me from escaping, or they knew something about me I daren't let anyone else find out; not my fault, because I didn't start it. I've never started anything in my entire life (well, hardly ever) and all I ask is to be left in peace.

A number like eighty-six begs a serious question. Has my life – to date – been worth eighty-six lives of my fellow human beings? To which I reluctantly but without hesitation answer: no, no way. Worth a single one of them? By any meaningful criteria: no.

Define meaningful criteria. For example, some philosophers

claim that in a fight or any form of serious conflict the better man always wins, because winning is the definition of being better. If I'm just that split second quicker with my block, parry and riposte, I'm a better fighter, therefore a superior animal, therefore I deserve to win; by the same token, if I'm a tad slower than you are or your feint high left suckers me into walking straight into your low right jab, God or natural selection has spoken and I've got nothing to moan about as my lifeblood soaks away into the sand.

Actually, I'd happily accept that, if it wasn't for the inconvenient fact that the first man I ever killed – my brother, as it happens – was incontrovertibly the better man; not just morally, ethically, intellectually, so on and so forth, he was also a brilliant swordsman who'd have been remembered as probably the leading fencer of his generation if he hadn't died at age fifteen, on the point of my sword, during a practice bout I'd tried my best to avoid taking part in. Who was worth more, him or me? I'm not even going to bother answering that. I only mention it to prove that the best man doesn't always win, and therefore the proposition is flawed. A shame, but there it is. You can't argue with the facts, though I've spent my life trying.

Meaningful criteria: what, for crying out loud? Making the world a better place – no, I reject that. Making the world a better place isn't my job, I never signed up for it and it's not my responsibility. I would argue that the world is probably just fine as it is and people are about as good as they're capable of being. I've seen a lot of change and a lot of idealists. The change has invariably been disastrous and nineteen times out of twenty an idealist was to blame. Not making the world a worse place; well, on occasion I've tried, even put myself to a certain degree of inconvenience – as witness the ghastly mess on the island of Sirupat a few years back, which (four parts miracle, one part me) didn't end up as the biggest, most destructive war in human history. The objection to that is that, for all I know, I've done loads of things that have led to really bad stuff not happening and never even knew it, let alone intended the consequence. I may have failed to save a child swept away by a river, and that child would've grown up to be a second Odovacar or Felix the Conqueror, who'd have slaughtered millions in pursuit of some crazed messianic dream. By the same token the sixpence I tossed in a beggar's hat yesterday morning may have made the difference between starvation and life for the same kid. Or maybe it was you who tossed that coin. I wouldn't put it past you.

The hell with it. Eighty-six is definitely not something I'm proud of, but neither am I cripplingly ashamed. Definitely, the next time someone comes at me with a knife or a warder tries to stop me escaping from the condemned cell, the thought of the eighty-six martyrs isn't going to stop me or even slow me down. I am who I am, I do what I must, I didn't start it, it's not my fault. Now read on.

The worst thing about my line of work is when we're called in late. We need time – to get there, to plan out the job, decide how many carts and barrels and sacks and wicker baskets we're going to need, how we're going to do the clearing up and then shift the stuff to where we need it to be. Most of all, we need to get on site before the bodies start swelling up and the flies get into them.

It's probably very wrong of me, but I don't much care for flies. Crows I can take or leave alone – they have so much in common with me, after all – and dogs and foxes run away before you come close; even slugs don't get to me the way flies do. It's an irrational reaction. Flies don't do nearly as much repulsive physical damage as birds or mammals. They don't chew off extremities or peck out eyes. And what's a fly, compared to a human being? They're so small, they really shouldn't register, let alone matter. Logically, therefore, Brother Fly and Sister Bluebottle shouldn't bother me to the extent they do. Logically, it should be quite the reverse. Crows and foxes and rats come to gorge, stuff their beaks and muzzles with everything they can get for free; flies are *constructive*. They firmly believe in the future; a better future, for their larvae and their larvae's larvae. To them, taking account of scale, a dead body is a promised land, given to them by Providence as a place where they settle down, lay eggs, raise families, improve themselves, develop an orderly egalitarian society under the rule of law, quite possibly evolve in due course into a race of perfect beings, like the gods only rather less self-centred.

Even so, I dislike them. Their buzzing gets to me, and the way they move in swarms, one shape made up of thousands of restless, fast-moving components. Maybe it's because they aren't scared of me, the way crows and rats and foxes are. Maybe it's because they have no real cause to be scared of me, because I'm too slow and predictable to be a threat. I like being a threat. It means I get left in peace.

In my line of work, we aren't nearly as constructive or positive as the flies. We get called in when there's been a battle, to clear up the godawful mess. In return for gathering up and burning or burying the bodies, the dead horses and the smashed-up hardware, we get to keep the armour, weapons, clothes, shoes and personal effects, which we patch up and sell. For this privilege we pay good money, cash in advance; and, since there are always two sides to a quarrel, we have to pay double, to the ultimate winner and the ultimate loser, because beforehand there's no way of knowing which will be which. Factor in the overheads – I employ five hundred men; the bigger outfits, such as the Asvogels or the Resurrection Crew, field squads four times that – and make provision for the occasional disaster, like a whole train of fully-laden carts getting washed away in a flooded river or ambushed by bandits, and you'll be forced to agree with me that we earn our profits, such as they are. Vultures and parasites we may be, but we put in a lot of hard, dirty work for our disgusting and inhuman gains. Morally, that makes no difference whatsoever, but a lot of people can be fooled into thinking it does, and I sincerely hope you're one of them.

Imagine my joy, therefore, when Count Sinderic, instead of fighting a pitched battle with the Avenging Knife on a flat, level plain half a mile from a major seaport, decided to send his cavalry to intercept the enemy as they crossed the Table-top, a plateau eight hundred feet above sea level, only accessible through a narrow pass through the foothills of the Spearhead Mountains.

I was tempted to wash my hands of the whole thing and go home, but I couldn't. I'd borrowed money at silly interest to buy the rights to this war, which I normally wouldn't have touched with a ten-foot pole, but it was the only war in town, so to speak, and we hadn't worked for a while. An unfortunate consequence of my noble and heroic acts on Sirupat (see above) had been an abnormally long spell of peace, and such action as there had been recently had been snapped up by the Asvogels, who paid stupid money for the rights with a view to starving out the smaller operators like myself and thereby achieving a monopoly. Thanks to them, I'd had to bid well over the odds for this idiotic scrap between Sinderic and his latest crop of rebels. My margins were already as thin as a butterfly's wing, and now I had to go zooming off into the mountains or risk defaulting on my loans, which would spell death for my business and a deplorable number of broken bones for me personally.

We got there in the end. Sinderic had sent his cavalry because he needed to cover a lot of ground quickly; we therefore had to do the same, but we had carts loaded with empty barrels and hampers, which tended to bounce off and scatter all over the ground every time a wheel ran over a rut or a stone. There comes a point, travelling in that manner, that the faster you try and go the less progress you make. We settled down into a grim, earnest trudge. We tried travelling by night as well as by day, but that was hopeless because we wore out the horses; quite a few of them went lame, and that slowed us down even more. "The hell with it," I told Gombryas when he nagged me about how slowly we were going. "We'll just have to take our time and get there *properly.*"

It's all about perspective. I was muddy and bruised after helping fix a cracked axle, he'd been sitting on the box of a wagon all day, with nothing to do except experience the passage of time. "At this rate," he said, "by the time we get there, everything'll be maggots. You hate maggots. You've told me that enough times, God knows."

"Absolutely true," I told him. "But if we rush, we'll break more axles and take longer getting there, and then there'll be even more fucking maggots. Nice and steady does it. That's being sensible."

Gombryas is my friend. Define friend. I see him every day. I talk to him without having to think carefully about what I say. If I broke my leg, he'd do what it took to see me all right, provided he didn't have a very good reason not to; and vice versa. I know a lot about him, and he knows a certain amount about me. Some things he does amuse me, and his more disgusting habits don't offend me, because his value to me outweighs the revulsion. He works for me (at a flat rate plus a share of the profits) and he's very good at his job, which is an important one. If

I tell him to do something, it generally gets done, so on balance he makes my life easier. If he died tomorrow, I'd be sorry and upset. If he died tomorrow and someone equally good at his job stepped immediately into his shoes, I'd still be sorry and upset. We choose to overlook each other's faults. He's familiar, like inherited furniture. Just occasionally, he says something that hadn't already occurred to me, and there are some things he thinks about so I don't have to. He knows me very well (which isn't the same thing as knowing a lot about me). We trust each other, up to a clearly defined point. He's my friend.

"Fuck you," said my friend. "Why don't you and me and Polycrates go on ahead on the riding horses, and then we can make a start before everything's gone completely shit, and the wagons can catch us up?"

I hadn't thought of that; and I'm supposed to be smart, and he's supposed to be thick as a brick. I spent a frantic moment trying to think of a reason why not, but failed. "That's not a bad idea," I said. "See to it, would you?"

Immediately he started whining. I was supposed to be in charge; why did he have to do every single bloody thing? I explained that it was because he was so smart, and thought of things I was too dim to envisage. He didn't know what envisage meant. He called me some names and stopped the cart, so he could get down and run around organising things. He likes doing that, though he always moans about it.

There are lots of little valleys and combes all around the edge of the Tabletop, and you could have a quite substantial battle in one of them and nobody would ever know, because you'd be completely hidden from sight. But we had no trouble finding the right place, thanks to the crows, and the stink.

And the starlings. Starlings aren't big carrion eaters, but they like flies, grubs and maggots. A huge flock of them whirred up off the ground, so loud we could hear them as soon as we broke the skyline. They lifted before the crows did. Starlings getting up are a cloud, whereas crows are like snow falling in a blizzard, only in the other direction. It always makes me feel guilty when I disturb so many thousands of my fellow creatures. They're getting along just fine, minding their own business in these hard times in the carrion trade, and then I come along and spoil everything. Foxes and badgers and other mammals always act like criminals caught in the act. They lift their heads, give you a horrified stare and run for it, like they know they're doing something wrong. But crows yell abuse at you, and threaten you with lawsuits for restraint of trade.

"Told you," Gombryas said. "God, what a stink."

But after a while you stop noticing it. For a while I lived next to a tannery, and people passing by in the street would stop dead, cover their faces and retch; as far as I was concerned, it was just ordinary breathing air. You can get used to all sorts of things. "It's not so bad," I said. Gombryas threw up. Maybe it was that bad after all.

The first thing you do when you find a battlefield, after making absolutely sure there's no active soldiers on site and, if you're Gombryas, wiping the last dribble of sick off your chin, is make a thorough skirmish of the field. It's amazing how often you think you've done it all and finished, and then you come across a dell or a dip or a little fold of dead ground, and guess where the heaviest action was, the heroic counterattack, the desperate last stand of the Imperial guard. By that point you're already behind schedule, in grave danger of being caught out by the spring floods or missing the ships you've booked all that expensive cargo space on; furthermore, you've calculated precisely how much food and water you need to supply five hundred men for the return journey, not to mention oats and hay for the horses…So Gombryas and Olybrius and Carrhasio and I trudged through the swollen, purple bodies, figuring out what had happened. If you know what happened, you know where to look. Simple as that.

On this occasion, to begin with, it didn't make sense. Then I realised why.

"Stone me," I said. "The Knife won."

"Don't talk stupid," Carrhasio said. He was a soldier most of his life, so he reckons he knows about strategy and tactics. "They never stood a chance."

Not long after that we found a sunken river. The bulk of Count Sinderic's army, running for their lives, had slithered down one side, then found the opposite bank was too steep and slippery to climb. The Knife, meanwhile, had crossed the river further up, which meant they could station their archers on top of both banks and shoot up Sinderic's men, floundering in the deep, fast-running river below. There was no cover, the current made it hard to stand up, let alone shoot back with any accuracy or effect; escape upstream was out of the question, so a fair number of the poor bastards tried to go downstream, and were caught at a sharp bend, where the water suddenly got deep; the Knife's archers on the bank enfiladed them as they tried to swim back against the current, and the few who weren't shot drowned.

"Piss and fuck," Polycrates observed, gazing down at the tangle of sodden bodies. "That's no bloody good."

I could see his line of reasoning. A significant percentage of our profit comes from clothing – shirts, trousers, tunics, coats, boots, hats. Nearly a week of being buffeted about in fast-running water does even the sturdiest fabrics no good at all. There was no point stripping the bodies, all their clothes and footwear were irreparably spoiled. Basically, all we'd be able to salvage from this site would be metalwork; and iron, especially chain mail, isn't exactly improved by being soaking wet. It goes without saying, the principal form of defensive armour issued to Sinderic's men was a knee-length long-sleeved mail shirt. By the time we got them back to somewhere we could work on them, they'd be solid blocks of rust.

"Some people," Eudo observed solemnly, "have no consideration for others."

Absolutely. We wouldn't be able to burn the bodies in their sodden clothes, which meant either stripping them and dumping the clothes, an exercise which I felt might prove distasteful, or else digging a very big deep hole (in thin, stony soil) and burying them. Leaving them in the water to let nature take its course was out of the question, since the river feeds the aqueduct that supplies fresh water to Audoria, a substantial market town and our next destination if we wanted to get to the coast in time to catch our ships.

Mercifully, half a mile downstream from the main killing point was a dense reed bed. It had acted as a filter, keeping the bodies from being carried any further. I gave Eudo a hundred men and left him to it. Gombryas and a hundred more went back up the hill to deal with the rest of the battle, where at least the salvage would be dry, the bodies would burn and we might even pick up some stuff somebody might eventually want to buy. The rest of the crew stayed with me, and we tackled the worst of it. There's a considerable degree of inherent technical interest in what we do, and you'd probably find a detailed account of how we solved our various problems both informative and useful, but I'm afraid you're out of luck. I can't face reliving all that again just to satisfy your morbid curiosity. We got the job done, that's all I'm saying.

By the time we'd finished we were all miserable, except for

Gombryas. He collects body parts from famous people (he rents a converted smithy in Boc Bohec, where he's got them all on display, desiccated and nailed up on boards or carefully pickled in bottles), and to his great joy he found Count Sinderic, dry and reasonably well preserved apart from a hole in his skull, which ruined it as a collectible. After a certain amount of careful thought, he decided to keep an eye and six fingers for himself, and the other eye and fingers, nose, toes, ears, dick and scalp to use as swapsies with other collectors. The residue, after much soul-searching, he chucked on the bonfire along with those of the common people who were dry enough to burn. On balance, he told me later, there was more to be gained from scarcity value than selling or trading additional pieces, not to mention the aggravation involved in getting any of the larger bits home.

"Gombryas," I asked him, as he meticulously smeared the inside of the scalp with saltpetre, "will you keep a bit of me when I'm gone?"

He looked at me. He doesn't like it when I get morbid.

if you enjoyed
SAEVUS CORAX DEALS WITH THE DEAD

look out for

THE LOST WAR
The Eidyn Saga: Book One

by

Justin Lee Anderson

This sensational epic fantasy follows an emissary for the king as he gathers a group of strangers and embarks on a dangerous quest across a war-torn land.

The war is over, but peace can be hell.

Demons continue to burn farmlands, violent mercenaries roam the wilds, and a plague is spreading. The country of Eidyn is on its knees.

extras

In a society that fears and shuns him, Aranok is the first mage to be named king's envoy. And his latest task is to restore an exiled foreign queen to her throne.

The band of allies he assembles each have their own unique skills. But they are strangers to one another, and at every step across the ravaged land, a new threat emerges, lies are revealed, and distrust could destroy everything they are working for. Somehow, Aranok must bring his companions together and uncover the conspiracy that threatens the kingdom—before war returns to the realms again.

Chapter 1

Fuck.

The boy was going to get himself killed.

"Back off!"

Aranok put down his drink, leaned back and rubbed his dusty, mottled brown hands across his face and behind his neck. He was tired and sore. He wanted to sit here with Allandria, drink beer, take a hot bath, collapse into a soft, clean bed and feel her skin against his. The last thing he wanted was a fight. Not here.

They'd made it back to Haven. This was their territory, the new capital of Eidyn, the safest place in the kingdom—for what that was worth. He'd done enough fighting, enough killing. His shoulders ached and his back was stiff. He looked up at the darkening sky, spectacularly lit with pinks and oranges.

The wooden balcony of the Chain Pier Tavern jutted out over

the main door along the front length of the building. Aranok had thought it an optimistic idea by the landlord, considering Eidyn's usual weather, but there were about thirty patrons overlooking the main square with their beers, wines and whiskies.

Allandria looked at him from across the table, chin resting on her hand. He met her deep brown eyes, pleading with her to give him another option. She looked down at the boy arguing with the two thugs in front of the blacksmith's forge, then back at him. She shrugged, resigned, and tied back her hair.

Bollocks.

Aranok knocked back the last of his beer and clunked the empty tankard back on the table. As Allandria reached for her bow, he signalled to the serving girl.

"Two more." He gestured to their drinks. "I'll be back in a minute."

The girl furrowed her brow, confused.

He stood abruptly to overcome the stiffness of his muscles. The chair clattered against the wooden deck, drawing some attention. Aranok was used to being eyed with suspicion, but it still rankled. If they knew what they owed him—owed both of them...

He leaned on the rail, feeling the splintered, weather-beaten wood under his palms; breathing in the smoky, sweaty smell of the bar. Funny how welcome those odours were; he'd been away for so long. With a sigh, Aranok twisted and turned his hands, making the necessary gestures, vaulted over the banister and said, "*Gaoth.*" Air burst from his palms, kicking up a cloud of dirt and cushioning his landing. Drinkers who had spilled out the front of the inn coughed, spluttered and raised hands in defence. A chorus of gasps and grumbles, but nobody dared complain. Instead, they watched.

Anticipating.

Fearing.

Aranok breathed deeply, stretching his arms, steeling himself as he passed the newly constructed stone well—one of many, he assumed, since the population had probably doubled recently. A lot of eyes were on him now. Maybe that was a good thing. Maybe they needed to see this.

As he approached the forge, Aranok sized up his task. One of the men was big, carrying a large, well-used sword. A club hung from his belt, but he looked slow and cumbersome, more a butcher than a soldier. The other was sleek, though—wiry. There was something ratlike about him. He stood well-balanced on the balls of his feet, dagger twitching eagerly. A thief most likely. Released from prison and pressed into the king's service? Surely not. Hells. Were they really this short of men? Was this what they'd bought with their blood?

"You've got the count of three to drop your weapons and move," the fat one wheezed. "King's orders."

"Go to Hell!" The boy's voice cracked. He backed a few steps toward the door. He couldn't be more than fifteen, defending his father's business with a pair of swords he'd probably made himself. His stance was clumsy, but he knew how to hold them. He'd had some training, if not any actual experience. Enough to make him think he could fight, not enough to win.

The rat rocked on his feet, the fingertips of his right hand frantically rubbing together. Any town guard could resolve this without blood. If it was just the fat one, he might manage it. But this man was dangerous.

Now or never.

"Can I help?" Aranok asked loudly enough for the whole square to hear.

All three swung to look at him. The thief's eyes ran him up and down. Aranok watched him instinctively look for pockets, coin purses, weapons—assess how quickly Aranok would move. He trusted the rat would underestimate him.

"Back away, *draoidh*!" snarled the butcher. The runes inscribed in Aranok's leather armour made it clear to anyone with even a passing awareness of magic what he was. *Draoidh* was generally spat as an insult, rarely welcoming. He understood the fear. People weren't comfortable with someone who could do things they couldn't. He only wore the armour when he knew it might be necessary. He couldn't remember the last day he'd gone without it.

"This is king's business. We've got a warrant," grunted the big man.

"May I see it?" Aranok asked calmly.

"I said piss off." He was getting tetchy now. Aranok began to wonder if he might have made things worse. It wouldn't be the first time.

He took a gentle step toward the man, palms open in a gesture of peace.

The rat smiled a confident grin, showing him the curved blade as if it were a jewel for sale. Aranok smiled pleasantly back at him and gestured to the balcony. The thief's face confirmed he was looking at the point of Allandria's arrow.

"Shit," the rat hissed. "Cargill. Cargill!"

"What?" Cargill barked grumpily back at him. The thief mimicked Aranok's gesture and the fat man also looked up. He spun around to face Aranok, raising his sword—half in threat, half in defence. Nobody likes an arrow trained on them. The boy took another step back—probably unsure who was on his side, if anyone.

"You'll swing for this," Cargill growled. "We've got orders from the king. Confiscate the stock of any business that can't pay taxes. The boy owes!"

"Surely his father owes?" Aranok asked.

"No, sir," the boy said quietly. "Father's dead. The war."

Aranok felt the words in his chest. "Your mother?"

The boy shook his head. His lips trembled until he pressed them together.

Damn it.

Aranok had seen a lot of death. He'd held friends as they bled out, watching their eyes turn dark; he'd stumbled over their mangled bodies, fighting for his life. Sometimes they cried out, or whimpered as he passed—clinging desperately to the notion they could still see tomorrow.

Bile rose in his gullet. He turned back to Cargill. Now it was a fight.

"If you close his business, how do you propose he pays his taxes?" Aranok struggled to maintain an even tone.

"I don't know," the thug answered. "Ask the king."

Aranok looked up the rocky crag toward Greytoun Castle. Rising out of the middle of Haven, it cast a shadow over half the town. "I will."

There was a hiss of air and a thud to Aranok's right. He turned to see an arrow embedded in the ground at the thief's feet. He must have crept a little closer than Allandria liked. The rat was lucky she'd given him a warning shot. Many didn't know she was there until they were dead. Eyes wide, he sidled back under the small canopy at the front of the forge.

Cargill fired into life, brandishing his sword high. "I'll cut your fucking head off right now if you don't walk away!" His bravado was fragile, though. He didn't know what Aranok could do—what his *draoidh* skill was. Aranok enjoyed the thought that, if he did, he'd only be more scared.

"Allandria!" he called over his shoulder.

"Aranok?"

"This gentleman says he's going to cut my head off."

"Already?" She laughed. "We just got here."

All eyes were on them now. The tavern was silent, the crowd an audience. People were flooding out into the square, drinks still in hand. Others stood in shop doors, careful not to stray too far from safety. Windows filled with shadows.

Cargill's bravado disappeared in the half-light. "You... you're... we're on the same side!"

"Can't say I'm on the side of stealing from orphans." Aranok stared hard into his eyes. Fear had taken the man.

"We've got a warrant." Cargill pulled a crumpled mess from his belt and waved it like a flag of surrender. Now he was keen to do the paperwork.

Perhaps they'd get out of this without a fight after all. Unusually, he was grateful for the embellishments of legend. He'd once heard a story about himself, in a Leet tavern, in which he killed three demons on his own. The downside was that every braggart and mercenary in the kingdom fancied a shot at him, which was why he tended to travel quietly—and anonymously. But now and again...

"How much does he owe?" Aranok asked.

"Eight crowns." Cargill proffered the warrant in evidence. Aranok took it, glancing up to see where the rat had got to. He was too near the wall for Aranok's liking. The boy was vulnerable.

"Out here," Aranok ordered. "Now."

"With that crazy bitch shooting at me?" he whined.

"Thül!" Cargill snapped.

Thül slunk back out into the open, watching the balcony. Sensible boy. Though if this went on much longer, Allandria might struggle to see clearly across the square. He needed to wrap it up.

The warrant was clear. The business owed eight crowns in

unpaid taxes and was to be closed unless payment was made in full. Eight bloody crowns. Hardly a king's ransom—except it was.

Aranok looked up at the boy. "What can you pay?"

"I've got three..." he answered.

"You've got three or you can pay three?"

"I've got three, sir."

"And food?"

The boy shrugged.

"A bit."

"Why do you care?" Thül sneered. "Is he yours?"

Aranok closed the ground between them in two steps, grabbed the thief by the throat and squeezed—enough to hurt, not enough to suffocate him. He pulled the angular, dirty face toward his own. Rank breath escaping yellow teeth made Aranok recoil momentarily.

"Why do I care?" he growled.

The thief trembled. He'd definitely underestimated Aranok's speed.

"I care because I've spent a year fighting to protect him. I care because I've watched others die to protect him." He stabbed a finger toward the young blacksmith. "And his parents died protecting you, you piece of shit!"

There were smatterings of applause from somewhere. He released the rat, who dropped to his knees, dramatically gasping for air. Digging some coins out of his purse, Aranok turned to the boy.

"Here. Ten crowns as a deposit against future work for me. Deal?"

The boy looked at the gold coins, up at Aranok's face and back down again. "Really?"

"You any good?"

"Yes, sir." The boy nodded. "Did a lot of Father's work. Ran the business since he went away."

"How is business?"

"Slow," the boy answered quietly.

Aranok nodded. "So do we have a deal?" He thrust his hand toward the blacksmith again.

Nervously, the boy put down one sword and took the coins from Aranok's hand, tentatively, as though they might burn. He put the other sword down to take two coins from the pile in his left hand, looking to Aranok for reassurance. He clearly didn't like being defenceless. Aranok nodded. The boy turned to Cargill and slowly offered the hand with the bulk of the coins. Pleasingly, the thug looked to Aranok for approval. He nodded permission gravely. Cargill took the coins and gestured to Thül. They walked quickly back toward the castle, the thief looking up at Allandria as they passed underneath. She smiled and waved him off like an old friend.

Aranok clapped the boy on the shoulder and walked back toward the tavern, now very aware of being watched. It had cost him ten crowns to avoid a fight...and probably a lecture from the king. It was worth it. He really was tired. The crowd returned to life—most likely chattering in hushed tones about what they'd just seen. One man even offered a hand to shake as Aranok walked past; quite a gesture—to a *draoidh*. Aranok smiled and nodded politely but didn't take the hand. He shouldn't have to perform a grand, charitable act before people engaged with him.

The man looked surprised, smiled nervously and ran his hand through his hair, as if that had always been his intention.

Aranok felt a hand on his elbow. He turned to find the boy looking up at him, eyes glistening. "Thank you," he said. "I... thank you."

"What's your name?" Aranok asked. He tried to look comforting, but he could feel the heavy dark bags under his eyes.

"Vastin," the boy answered.

Aranok shook his hand.

"Congratulations, Vastin. You're the official blacksmith to the king's envoy."

***

Aranok righted his chair and dramatically slumped down opposite Allandria. The idiot was playing up the grumpy misanthrope because every eye on the top floor was watching him. He looked uncomfortable. Secretly, she was certain he enjoyed it.

Allandria raised an eyebrow. "Was that our drinking money, by any chance?"

"Some of it..." he answered, more wearily than necessary.

Despite his reluctance, Allandria knew part of him had enjoyed the confrontation—especially since it had ended bloodless. The man loved a good argument, if not a good fight—particularly one where he outsmarted his opponent. Not that she'd had any desire to kill the two thugs, but she would have, to save the boy. It was better that Aranok had been able to talk them down and pay them off.

"You could have brought my arrow back," she teased.

He looked down to where the arrow still stood, proudly embedded in the dirt. It was a powerful little memento of what had happened. Interesting that the boy had left it there too... maybe to remind people he had a new patron.

"Sorry." He smiled. "Forgot."

She returned the smile. "No, you didn't."

"You missed, by the way."

Allandria stuck out her tongue. "I couldn't decide who

I wanted to shoot more, the greasy little one or the big head in the fancy armour." The infuriating bugger had an answer to everything. But for all his arrogance, she loved him. He'd looked better, certainly. The war had been kind to no one. His unkempt brown hair was flecked with grey now—even more so the straggly beard he'd grown in the wild. Leathery skin hid under a layer of road dust; green eyes were hooded and dark. But they still glinted with devilment when the two sparred.

"Excuse me..." The serving girl arrived with their drinks. She was a slight, blonde thing, hardly in her teens if Allandria guessed right. Were there any adults left? Aranok reached for his coin purse.

"No, sir." The girl stopped him, nervously putting the drinks on the table. "Pa says your money's no good here."

Aranok looked up at Allandria, incredulous. When they'd come in, he wasn't even certain they'd be served. *Draoidhs* sometimes weren't. Innkeepers worried they would put off other customers. She'd seen it more than once.

Aranok tossed down two coppers on the table. "Thank you, but tell your pa he'll get no special treatment from the king on my say-so, or anyone else's."

It was harsh to assume they were trying to curry favour with the king now they knew who he was. Allandria hoped that wasn't it. She still had faith in people, in human kindness. She'd seen enough of it in the last year. Still, she understood his bitterness.

"No, sir," the girl said. "Vastin's my friend. His folks were good people. We need more people like you. Pa says so."

"Doesn't seem many places want people like me..."

"Hey..." Allandria frowned at him. He was punishing the girl for other people's sins now. He looked back at her, his eyes tired, resentful. But he knew he was wrong.

"Way I see it"—the girl shifted from foot to foot, holding one elbow protectively in her other hand—"you've no need of a blacksmith. A fletcher, maybe"—she glanced at Allandria—"but not a blacksmith. So I want more people like you."

Good for you, girl.

Allandria smiled at her. Aranok finally succumbed too.

"Thank you." He picked up the coins and held them out to her. "What's your name?"

"Amollari," she said quietly.

"Take them for yourself, Amollari, if not for your pa. Take them as an apology from a grumpy old man."

Grumpy was fair; *old* was harsh. He was barely forty—two years younger than Allandria.

Amollari lowered her head. "Pa'll be angry."

"I won't tell him if you don't," said Aranok.

Tentatively, the girl took the coins, slipping them into an apron pocket. She gave a rough little curtsy with a low "thank you" and turned to clear the empty mugs from a table back inside the tavern.

The girl was right. Aranok carried no weapons and his armour was well beyond the abilities of any common blacksmith to replicate or repair. He probably had no idea what he'd use the boy for.

Allandria raised the mug to her lips and felt beer wash over her tongue. It tasted of home and comfort, of warm fires and restful sleep. It really was good to be here.

"Balls." A crack resonated from Aranok's neck as he tilted his head first one way, then the other.

"What?" Allandria leaned back in her chair.

"I really wanted a night off."

"Isn't that what we're having?" She brandished her drink as evidence. "With our free beer?" She hoped the smile would cheer him. He was being pointlessly miserable.

390

Aranok rubbed his neck. "We have to see the king. He's being an arsehole."

A few ears pricked up at the nearest tables, but he hadn't said it loudly.

"It can't wait until tomorrow?" Allandria might have phrased it as a question, but she knew he'd be up all night thinking about it if they waited. "Of course it can't," she answered when he didn't. "Shall we go, then?"

"Let's finish these first," Aranok said, lifting his own mug.

"Well, rude not to, really."

Her warm bed seemed a lot further away than it had a few minutes ago.

orbit

Follow us:

/orbitbooksUS

/orbitbooks

/orbitbooks

Join our mailing list
to receive alerts on our
latest releases and deals.

orbitbooks.net

Enter our monthly
giveaway for the chance
to win some epic prizes.

orbitloot.com